important legal battle pending in the U.S. Supreme Court and is a good read for those of us intrigued by the earliest Americans."
                                                              —Tony Hillerman,
                                              New York Times bestselling author

"*People of the Raven* draws you into a magnificent, sweeping world—America, circa 7300 B.C.—that is so real you can almost breathe in the air of it. It tells a bighearted story of war and peace, love and violence, with a cast of richly drawn characters. This is a novel that will stay with you for years—I guarantee it."
                                              —Douglas Preston, *New York Times*
                                      bestselling author of *Tyrannosaur Canyon*

By Kathleen O'Neal Gear and W. Michael Gear
from Tom Doherty Associates

People
of the
Black Sun

A PEOPLE OF
THE LONGHOUSE NOVEL

Kathleen O'Neal Gear and
W. Michael Gear

TOR®

A TOM DOHERTY ASSOCIATES BOOK
NEW YORK

This is a work of fiction. All of the characters, organizations, and events portrayed in this novel are either products of the authors' imaginations or are used fictitiously.

PEOPLE OF THE BLACK SUN

Copyright © 2012 by Kathleen O'Neal Gear and W. Michael Gear

Maps and illustrations by Ellisa Mitchell

A Tor Book
Published by Tom Doherty Associates, LLC
175 Fifth Avenue
New York, NY 10010

www.tor-forge.com

Tor® is a registered trademark of Tom Doherty Associates, LLC

ISBN 978-0-7653-6560-6

Tor books may be purchased for educational, business, or promotional use. For information on bulk purchases, please contact Macmillan Corporate and Premium Sales Department at 1-800-221-7945, extension 5442, or write specialmarkets@macmillan.com.

First Edition: October 2012
First Mass Market Edition: September 2013

Printed in the United States of America

0 9 8 7 6 5 4 3 2 1

To Jake and Shannon,
our faithful muses for Gitchi

Acknowledgments

There is a magical word in the Seneca language, usually stated at the beginning of the story, and by which a story may be told as a serial: *ensegaha'a*.

It has taken us around a half million words, and four books, to convey a semblance of the richness and complexity of the Peacemaker tale. In this uncertain age when publishing is changing dramatically, and no one is certain what shape the "book" will take in the future, it was not an easy decision for our publisher to approve such a long series. We would like to thank Tom Doherty and Linda Quinton for allowing us to tell this story with the proper respect.

We'd also like to thank our excellent editor, Susan Chang, for making sure we told it to the best of our abilities.

B.C.

13,000	10,000	6,000	3,000	1,500

PEOPLE *of the* WOLF
Alaska & Canadian
Northwest

PEOPLE *of the* EARTH
Northern Plains & Basins

PEOPLE *of the* NIGHTLAND
Ontario & New York &
Pennsylvania

PEOPLE *of*
the OWL

Lower
Mississippi
Valley

PEOPLE *of the* SEA
Pacific Coast & Arizona

PEOPLE *of the* RAVEN
Pacific Northwest &
British Columbia

PEOPLE *of the* LIGHTNING
Florida

PEOPLE *of the* FIRE
Central Rockies &
Great Plains

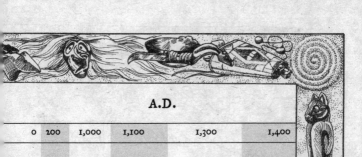

A.D.

| 0 | 200 | 1,000 | 1,100 | 1,300 | 1,400 |

PEOPLE *of the* **LAKES**
East-Central Woodlands
& Great Lakes

PEOPLE *of the*
WEEPING EYE

Mississippi Valley
& Tennessee

PEOPLE *of the* **MASKS**
Ontario & Upstate New York

PEOPLE *of the*
THUNDER

Alabama & Mississippi

PEOPLE *of the* **RIVER**
Mississippi Valley

PEOPLE *of the*
LONGHOUSE

New York
& New England

PEOPLE *of the* **SILENCE**
Southwest Anasazi

The
**DAWN
COUNTRY**

PEOPLE *of the* **MOON**
Northwest New Mexico
& Southwest Colorado

The
**BROKEN
LAND**

PEOPLE
of the
**BLACK
SUN**

PEOPLE *of the* **MIST**
Chesapeake Bay

Skanodario Lake

Coldspring Village
Hilltop Village

Wyango Village Canassatego Village

Hansera Village
Tyor Village
Agweron Village
Wenisa Village
Shookas Village
Decanasora Village
Riverbank Village
Sedge Marsh Village
Tehana Village

IROQUOIA
The Lands of the
People of the
Longhouse

Atotarho Village
Turtleback Village
Bur Oak Village
Yellowtail Village
Cornplanter Village
White Dog Village
Cornstalk Village

Forks River

Singleleaf
Village

Monster Rock
Village

Wild River
Village

Rapid River

The Lands of the People of the Dawnland

Forks River

Rapid River

Quill River

Hawk Moth Village

Singleleaf Village

Wild River Village

Bog Willow Village

Pine Hill Village

IROQUOIS

Rapid River

Quill River

Nonfiction Introduction

The term "bury the hatchet" dates to around four hundred years ago, just after European colonists arrived in northeastern North America and became acquainted with the traditions of the native peoples, but the practice of ending violence by burying weapons has a much older history.

Archaeologists debate the origins of the tradition, but one thing is probably certain: the elite members of Cahokian society practiced this rite. Cahokia, a World Heritage Site just outside of St. Louis, Illinois, is truly one of the world's magnificent archaeological sites. Cahokia was a part of the Mississippian moundbuilder tradition. We wrote about this culture in *People of the River* in 1992. In twenty years, we have learned so much more about their astounding empire, which flourished from around A.D. 700–1550. Peoples who belonged to this cultural tradition covered the eastern half of the United States with mound cities and were master architects, builders, astronomers, surgeons, as well as shell, stone, copper, and fabric artisans. Cahokian traders plied their wares across the North American continent. And they, like Iroquoian peoples five hundred years later, also "buried the hatchet."

At a unique hilltop site in the American Bottoms region of Illinois, the Grossman Site, archaeologists discovered a large collection of buried weapons (Pauketat, 2009). The site contains more than one hundred houses, and was occupied by the Cahokian elite. Near one of the council houses, archaeologists excavated a cache of seventy buried ax heads. The largest, which had been deliberately placed on top of the cache, weighed around twenty pounds, and was twenty inches long. Interestingly, the ax heads had been laid into the pit in discrete sets, as though each clan, or family, had taken turns. Usually they were placed in the pit in pairs, but one set contained twelve ax heads.

From an archaeological perspective, this is clearly a symbolic act. In our modern culture it would be like finding a collection of buried swords with Excalibur on top. Lest you've forgotten, Excalibur was King Arthur's legendary sword.

We can only speculate about what Cahokians might have believed, but we know that Iroquoian peoples thought that burying weapons would submerge them in the river of Great Grandmother Earth's blood that ran beneath the surface of the earth. Her blood purified the weapons, cleansing them of the hatred and despair associated with warfare.

The earliest reference to Iroquoian peoples burying weapons is found in the rich oral history of the Peacemaker tale.

We say "oral" history, because it's generally believed that North American's native cultures had no written languages. Many archaeologists have suspected for a long time that such an assumption is false, but it's been very hard to prove that the symbols we find in the archaeological record represent a written language. Wampum (more correctly called "otekoa") may be the exception. At least a "proto-language," a precursor, it may have been much more.

The problem arises because of definitions of what constitutes "writing." Wampum consists of a set of blackish-purple and white symbols, recorded most often with shell beads. However, the Iroquois believe that before shell wampum existed, wampum was created with black and white painted pieces of wood. The Mohawk say that the first wampum was made using different colors of eagle quills (Tehanetorens, 1999, p. 12). Wampum could be "read" by anyone who'd been trained.

The earliest European historical records corroborate that each bead, row, or character had a definite meaning, and further state that both sides of the belt were read. Lengthy documents, for example the minutes of meetings, and the details of treaties, the Constitution of the League of the Iroquois, and much more, were recorded on belts so completely that they could still be read centuries later. In the 1700s, Moravian missionary John Heckewelder reported that wampum readers had the ability "to point out the exact place on a belt which is to answer each particular sentence, the same as we can point out a passage in a book" (Heckewelder, p. 108), and added that a great deal depended on the "*turning* of the belt," saying that "it may be as well known by it how far the speaker has advanced in his speech, as with us on taking a glance at the pages of a book or pamphlet while reading."

Knotting wampum, tying the shells in place, was considered to be a spiritual activity in which writers "talked" their messages into the shells, which sounds very much like they were recording words or phrases. And this was apparently an ancient tradition. Archaeologists have found wampum beads that date back more than two thousand years to the Adena Culture in Ohio (Slotkin and Schmitt, pp. 223–225). We wrote about Adena and Hopewell cultures in *People of the Lakes.*

The term "wampum belt" is slightly misleading. In our culture a belt is something that encircles the waist. Depending upon how much information was being recorded, Iroquoian belts could be four or five feet long and just as wide. Prehistorically, they may have been even larger.

Because wampum belts faithfully recorded the details of treaties, they presented both the original thirteen colonies, and later the United States government, with a problem. Wampum belts were evidentiary—they had a legal status in courts. It is perhaps no surprise that Indian Agents, traders, state authorities, and anyone else who had access to purchasing wampum belts were hired by the government to acquire these belts so that they could be destroyed. The resulting loss of information can be likened to the destruction of the Mayan codices by Bishop Diego de Landa in A.D. 1562, or the destruction of the Library of Alexandria by Patriarch Theophilus around A.D. 391. The destruction of a people's history is always the first step of conquerors.

Keep in mind, human beings are storytellers. Our cultures are founded upon stories, interpreted through them, and survive because of them. Destroying a civilization doesn't require warfare or plague or starvation. Cultural midnight is always only a generation away. History has demonstrated many times that causing the death of a culture is a relatively easy process: First, destroy a people's written records. Second, destroy their language. When there's no one left who can recite the stories of the people, and no documents to tell the young about them, assimilation into the dominant culture is virtually inevitable. Why?

Because when a people's words are lost, they must re-story their world from the traditions of alien nations.

Imagine, for a moment, what it must have been like for Henan Scrogg and Solon Skye, the last two people in the twentieth century able to read the original wampum of the Code of Handsome Lake, knotted by the Prophet himself in the early 1800s (Johansen and Mann, 2000, p. 328). Now imagine what it would be like today to lose the last two people who could read the Declaration of Independence and the Bill of Rights. Certainly Faithkeepers would keep both documents alive as long as possible through oral history, but the truth is that oral traditions are mutable. They change with the failing memories of the elders struggling to preserve them—especially if the young no longer care about such "fables."

The People of the Longhouse, the Haudenosaunee, managed to save some of the most critical wampum belts. They can be seen today in excellent repositories like the Iroquois Indian Museum in Howes Cave, New York (www.iroquois museum.org), which was established by the state of New York in 1891.

We encourage you to take a trip to see these fragile beautiful pieces of American history. Each is a story worth seeing.

Ensegaha'a . . .

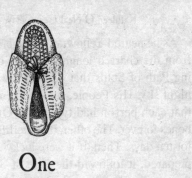

One

As Sonon strode through the evening forest, his black cape parted the sea of frigid air, leaving ice crystals swirling behind him. Every twig on the maples and giant sycamores was sheathed in white. Far out in the trees, owls watched him with their feathers fluffed out for warmth, their eyes shining.

Deep cold was a quiet monster. It slithered into clothing, stiffened leather, and afflicted bones with agony. Its unnaturally silent voice made ears crave even the slightest sound. The sheer vastness of the frozen land pressed down upon him tonight.

What is my offering? What can I give him to help him?

When he crested the hill and gazed out across the valley where hundreds of campfires glittered, he took a few moments to contemplate the next few days. He suspected they would be some of the most difficult of his existence.

He inhaled a deep breath, and started down the hill toward the warriors who had waged the battle. Frozen flowers hid amid the shriveled leaves on the sides of the trail, dead, folded in upon themselves.

As he neared Yellowtail Village, smoke flowed upward from the charred longhouses and obliterated the glittering Path of Souls that painted a white swath across the night sky. His People, the People of the Hills, believed that each person had two souls. One remained with the bones forever. The other, the afterlife soul, stayed on earth for ten days. Then, if it were lucky enough to be properly prepared, it followed the Path of Souls to a long bridge that spanned a dark abyss. On this side of the bridge were all the animals a person had ever known in his life. The animals who had loved him helped him across. Those that he had mistreated chased him, trying to force him to fall off the bridge into eternal darkness. If his animal helpers were strong enough and he made it to the other side, he would be greeted by his ancestors in the Land of the Dead.

Some people, however, had trouble finding the Path of Souls. Especially those who died violently.

His eyes narrowed. On the battlefield below, dead bodies lay contorting as they froze. There must be thousands of glistening soul lights, lost souls, out there bobbing and swaying in confusion, searching for loved ones to take care of them. If Sonon closed his eyes, he could hear their spectral cries rising.

He folded his arms beneath his cape, trying to stay warm while he continued thinking.

Yes, maybe . . .

Perhaps the single greatest truth of life was that the dead were not dead. Their shadows lived. They wandered the forests, slept in crackling fires and ancient sycamores, they huddled in grass that wept and stones that whimpered. They were the painted prayersticks that Great Grandmother

Earth used to dance life in and out of this world. If humans could only learn to watch shadows pass like a mountain did, they would understand that death was just a whisper.

"Is that my offering?"

War songs lilted through the sparkling air, mixing eerily with the sobs and moans coming from the destroyed villages.

"Yes," he said softly, deciding. "A glimpse from inside the mountain."

Two

As Grandmother Moon edged above the rocky valley rim, her gleam flecked the bare tips of the trees, and the cold night took on a blazing opalescence.

Where she stood on the catwalk of Bur Oak Village, Matron Jigonsaseh spread her feet and tucked short gray-streaked black hair behind her ear. An unusually tall woman, she had seen thirty-nine summers pass. She had large black eyes, a small nose, and full lips. Her belted cape, woven from twisted strips of foxhide, hung to her knees. The only weapon she carried was her war club, CorpseEye, shoved into her belt. Only a few days ago, she had been called War Chief Koracoo. When she had accepted the position of village matron, she had undergone the Requickening ritual. Her dead mother's soul had been raised up and placed in her body, along with her name: Jigonsaseh. Koracoo hadn't grown accustomed to either the position or the name yet. When people called her Matron Jigonsaseh, she often didn't realize for an instant that they were speaking to her.

She gazed out across the battlefield. The bulk of her

army had been destroyed in that gently rolling part of the bowl-shaped valley to the west, just beyond Reed Marsh. In the silvered gleam, she could see the dead. Bodies froze at different rates. Those still warm created black spots upon the frosty grass. Thousands of black spots. How many? She tried to estimate. Perhaps four thousand out there, and another eight or nine hundred in the meadow to the east of the villages?

She braced her forearms on the palisade, and squinted.

Evening carried the pungent scents of smoldering long-houses and old blood.

She concentrated on the war songs that filled the winter night. She longed to be out there in the camps with the men and women who'd waged the battle today. She missed that companionship . . . and the solace of friends who understood what the fight had cost her.

She bowed her head for a long moment, staring at the tangle of bodies encircling the palisade, enemy warriors who'd tried to assail the walls and failed. Here and there, the ladders they'd thrust against the forty-hand-tall palisade lay like disorganized lattices, the rungs frosted and shining.

All night long, her souls had kept repeating the battle, forcing her to live through it over and over . . . *six thousand enemy warriors flow swiftly, steadily, across the rolling valley swathed in mist, their clan flags fluttering. They come on like waves, dying all the while, flooding forward to engage my two thousand archers stationed in the maples . . . volleys of arrows piercing the fog, rising above it, and arcing down in iridescent streams . . .*

Only a warrior could understand the unspeakable beauty. The battle had writhed and roared, shimmered with a thousand crystal eyes. Magnificent. Terrifying beyond words.

As though to remind her of her duties, sobs of grief and the delirious cries of the wounded rang out in the plaza below. One man in the Wolf Clan longhouse kept coughing wetly, gasping. Lung wound. She had tended many such wounds. If he and his family were very lucky, it would be over soon.

She licked her chapped lips and tasted bitterness. A fine deep-gray powder of ash continued to rise from the smoldering walls. She had ash in her hair and eyes, ash in her throat. For the rest of her life, she would remember the gritty flavor that pervaded this cold night . . . and the miracle that had ended the attack . . . *my son lifts his hands and a monstrous storm swells above the eastern horizon and crashes down upon the battlefield in shrieking, whirling blackness . . . warriors scatter like brittle old leaves.*

She laced her fingers and squeezed them together in a stranglehold, desperate to keep her emotions at bay. When the next few days had passed, and she'd done the things that needed to be done, then she would grant herself time to make sense of it.

She still had things to do. *I must see Cord.* She owed the Chief of the People of the Flint more than she could ever thank him for. Without his help today, the Standing Stone nation would have been wiped from the face of Great Grandmother Earth. Cord's help, and the support of the three Hills People villages that had turned on Chief Atotarho and fought on her side, had made the difference between life and stark oblivion. She had already gone to the Hills matrons and chiefs. She'd left Cord for the last because seeing him was the most difficult.

. . . on the river twelve summers ago . . . staring at me with such longing . . . the black roach of hair bristling down the middle of his skull shining with new-fallen snow . . . his deep voice like velvet . . . "If things were different . . . if our nations were not at war . . ."

She studied her village, Yellowtail Village, thirty paces away. It was the smaller sister village of Bur Oak Village. Numerous charred holes gaped in the three concentric rings of palisades that encircled the village. All three longhouses had sustained damage. Roofs had burned through, flaming bark walls had toppled to the ground in smoking heaps. For the night, her villagers had torn down the intact bark walls that separated their interior chambers and tried to fill the gaps in the exterior longhouse walls. Firelight streamed around the mismatched squares. The central plaza bonfire blazed, flickering over the dark shapes of dozens of people who tended the dead, laid out in rows. Oddly, the feet were all even, the toes pointing upward like short stubby posts. It would have been foolish to waste the warm space inside the crowded houses on them. Their afterlife souls were not in their bodies, but roaming around the village in the form of glistening soul lights, eating the dregs in the cooking pots, trying to speak with their loved ones. Jigonsaseh's own daughter, Tutelo, would be there tending the bodies, probably working through the night, despite the fact that her own husband had been killed yesterday afternoon, and grief must have swallowed her world.

Jigonsaseh let out a slow breath. As it condensed in the icy air, Wind Woman gently swirled it into firelit spirals.

Tomorrow, the bodies would be prepared. The strongest souls would be Requickened in living bodies, their confusion and agony ended. They would live again. Then, ten days from now, the main burial feast would be held. When completed, the souls that had not been Requickened could be on their way to the Path of Souls in the sky, and the bridge that led to the Land of the Dead beyond.

I must see Chief Cord.

She shoved away from the palisade and headed for the closest ladder, where she climbed down, and tiredly walked toward the wooden plank gates.

The guard, short and burly, swung them open. "Matron Jigonsaseh, you should not be out alone. Shall I assign you guards?"

"I appreciate your concern, but it's not necessary. Return to your duties." Her hand, however, instinctively dropped to CorpseEye where he rested in her belt.

"As you wish, Matron."

The gates swung closed behind her without another word.

She walked eastward across the battlefield, weaving through the corpses, and down the long littered slope toward the Flint People's camp. Dropped bows, water bags, weapons belts torn free by desperate hands, and severed body parts lay tumbled across the ground. All around her, people with torches wandered through the blowing smoke, searching faces, clothing, jewelry, trying to recognize bodies. Their expressions were haunted. The shock was just setting in, turning their hands shaky.

Jigonsaseh rubbed her burning eyes.

Before war cries had split the day, it had been a splendid clean morning, filled with the laughter of children dashing across the plaza, and the happy barking of dogs. It was hard to believe that their world had been obliterated in such a short time.

She marched out of the killing field and straight for the sentries who ringed Chief Cord's camp. Any other chief would have placed his camp in the middle of his warriors, where he'd be better protected, but Cord had been a war chief for most of his life. He preferred to have his back against a small moonlit pond. The water glittered and cast reflections over the faces of the five people seated on logs around his fire. On the far side of the circle, she could see him clearly. Tall and muscular, he had a long pointed nose and piercing brown eyes. He'd seen forty-one summers pass. A black roach of hair ran down the middle of his shaved head. Turtle shell carvings decorated his black cape. The snake tattoos on his cheeks seemed to coil and strike as he spoke.

"Halt!" one of the sentries shouted at her. "Identify yourself."

He boldly stepped in front of her.

Jigonsaseh tiredly braced her feet. "I am Jigonsaseh, Village Matron of Yellowtail Village, and a friend to Chief Cord. I request a meeting with him, if he is not too tired."

At the sound of her deep voice, Cord instantly rose and walked toward her, his long legs stretching out, covering the distance in mere heartbeats.

She called, "May I speak with you?"

"Of course. Let her pass, Deputy War Chief," he ordered.

The sentry leaped to obey, and Jigonsaseh walked to meet Cord. They stood eye-to-eye for what seemed like an eternity.

. . . reflections off snow dancing over his tattooed face . . . the strength in his dark eyes enough to convince me we could achieve anything . . . slim rations eaten at the same fire . . . his closeness a physical torment . . .

Cord said, "Will you join me?"

"I would, thank you."

As she neared the fire, the other warriors rose and bowed to her.

Cord said, "That will be all for tonight. We will reconvene tomorrow morning when War Chief Baji is better."

Men wandered away, muttering to one another, casting glances over their shoulders at Jigonsaseh.

"Baji is hurt?"

"Nothing dramatic. Her left arm is swollen. A glancing blow from a war club."

Jigonsaseh relaxed a little. She'd known Baji since she was a girl of barely twelve summers. The tie between them went beyond clans or nations. "Please tell her I am concerned about her."

"I will."

Cord gestured to the log where he'd been sitting. "Please, sit. May I dip you a cup of tea?"

"No, but I thank you for the offer."

She lowered herself to the log, pulled CorpseEye from her belt, and rested him across her lap. Unconsciously her hands smoothed the well-oiled wooden shaft. The club had been in her family for generations, passed from warrior to warrior. He had an ancient presence, like a great old war chief who has seen too much, and longs only to rest until the next battle begins. The carvings on the shaft added to his presence. The antlered wolves seemed to be trotting after the winged tortoises, who were in turn being hunted by prancing buffalo. The red quartzite cobble tied to the club's head glinted in the firelight. It had two black spots that resembled staring eyes. She had no idea how much blood the club had absorbed over the long summers, but more than she could imagine.

Cord sat beside her, four hands away, and shifted to face her. His black roach glittered with firelight.

She began, "I don't know what to say to you."

He smiled. "Then tell me what you think of this strange alliance between the Flint, Hills, and Standing Stone nations. Will it last?"

"It must," she said firmly. "For all our sakes. I plan to work very hard to assure that it does."

She looked at the superb snake tattoos in the frame of his oval face and noticed for the first time how deeply the lines cut his forehead. Others ran down his cheeks like careless chisel scratches, broken only by the prominent knife scar that slashed across his square jaw. When she lifted her gaze, his mouth tightened slightly. While she'd been studying his face, his gaze had been locked on her eyes, probably assessing the emotions he saw there.

Very softly, he asked, "Are you well? I know this was a terrible day for the Standing Stone nation. You lost so many."

She jerked a nod. "Ninety percent of our army."

"How many trained warriors do you have left?"

"We will count tomorrow, but my guess is around three hundred. Plus another forty-one warriors from Atotarho's army that joined our side this afternoon, including War Chief Sindak."

His face slackened. "Three hundred out of how many?"

"When the morning began, we had over three thousand."

He seemed to be holding his breath, then he slowly exhaled the words: "What will you do?"

"One thing is certain: Atotarho will be back. High Matron Kittle is still in council with the other elders. It's an informal meeting. Tomorrow, the Ruling Council will officially meet to decide our course of action."

He hesitated, opened his mouth as if to speak, then closed it for several moments, before he finally said, "May I be so bold as to offer you advice?"

"I have always greatly valued your advice."

He dipped his head respectfully and shifted to stare at the flames dancing around the logs in the fire. As always, the attraction between them was like lightning about to strike, almost unbearable.

"I would like to suggest that the Standing Stone nation abandon these last two villages and come with us to the Flint nation. We will adopt every member of your clans. We are stronger as one nation, than as two."

Stunned, she didn't respond.

More softly, he added, "Last summer, when your son thought he would wed Baji, he allowed himself to be adopted into the Flint People. We Requickened in him the soul of one of our greatest ancestors, Dekanawida. Is it so hard to imagine being adopted by us?"

She gave him a faint smile. "Well, Cord, I think maybe my son, whom we still call Sky Messenger, belongs to all clans and all peoples. My nation, however, that is something else."

"Believe me, I know the import of my suggestion, but if you do not accept, I greatly fear—"

"Cord . . ." She gripped his hand where it rested on the log between them. "You are very generous to offer, but I can't recommend that to the Ruling Council. You're talking about the death of the Standing Stone nation."

He flipped his hand over, twined his fingers with hers, and matched her grip. "Listen to me. You have three hundred trained warriors left, plus another forty-one that you don't know if you can trust, and you do not know that Chief Atotarho is gone."

"No, but it seems—"

"Yes, he and his faction of the Hills People fled the battlefield in the monster storm today, but by now they are regrouping, assessing damage, and making decisions that may wipe the Standing Stone nation from the earth anyway. Please"—he lowered his voice—"consider fleeing to join another nation. It doesn't have to be the Flint People. If you'd prefer, I suspect the People of the Landing would take you. They've been hit hard by the Mountain People in recent moons. They would probably be glad to renew the spiritual strength of the clans by adopting—"

"I can't," she repeated, and the lines at the corners of his brown eyes deepened. "We're desperate, old friend, but not that desperate. Not yet."

With trepidation, he disentangled his hand from hers before gently stroking her hair and anxiously studying her face. "When the time comes . . . if the time comes . . . remember my offer."

She had the overwhelming urge to hold him. But that would complicate both of their lives. "Thank you. I . . ." Her voice dwindled when she noted how attentively his warriors were watching them. She scanned the closest fires. Warriors either stared blatantly, or pretended to be looking into their supper bowls and water cups, while casting furtive glances their way. An awkward silence had descended. "My visit seems to have caused a disruption."

"Well, frankly, it isn't every day that a member of the Ruling Council of the Standing Stone nation appears, walking alone, in the middle of a Flint war camp. You startled them."

"If so, they are exceptionally well trained. Not a single one attempted to bash my brains out before he checked with you."

"Fortunately for him." Cord smiled and removed his hand from her hair.

Conversations instantly began to return to normal, and were eventually replaced by laughter and war songs.

Jigonsaseh said, "Cord, as you well know, I'm not given to small talk. I must thank you for what you did today. I don't know how, but—"

"It's not necessary. Truly."

"It is for me. You are an old ally, but you were under no obligation to come to our aid. Our Peoples have been at war, off and on, for generations. It could not have been easy for you to convince your Ruling Council to send warriors to support us, and I have no words for the gratitude in my heart."

His handsome face showed no emotion, but his dark eyes probed hers. "I'm just sorry it took so long. If we'd arrived a few hands of time earlier, more of your people would have survived."

"Would they?" Jigonsaseh tilted her head uncertainly. "It seems to me you arrived at exactly the instant Power demanded."

"Yes," he mused, his eyes suddenly distant, seeing the

battle again. "That was odd, wasn't it? We had been in the fight for only a short time when the freak storm swept over the horizon. I've never witnessed anything like it before."

"Nor have I."

On the fabric of her souls, she saw Sky Messenger turn to face Elder Brother Sun, lift his hands, and felt the air sucked from the battlefield. A deep-throated rumble echoed to the east, then a black wall of clouds roared over the horizon. Only Sky Messenger dared to face the storm. He'd clutched his best friend's, War Chief Hiyawento's, daughter to his chest, protecting her . . . and the storm had passed over them, leaving them untouched.

Cord said, "Dekanawida has become a living legend." He gestured to something behind her. "I noticed he has spent the past hand of time walking the battlefield alone. Is he as stunned as everyone else by the rumors racing through the war camps?"

She glanced over her shoulder, and spotted her son, Sky Messenger, on the far eastern edge of the forest with his head down. He must be lonely and, she suspected, confused, trying to make sense of the day. "I suspect so."

"Has he said anything to you about the miracle?"

"What could he say, Cord? I don't think he knows yet how to interpret the storm."

Cord made an airy gesture with his hand. "I'm sure my warriors add to his difficulty. They are awestruck. They believe he called the storm, and say he is the legendary human False Face prophesied to don the cape of white clouds and ride the winds of destruction at the end of the world." He looked back at her with slightly narrowed eyes, as though it hurt to look at her. "Do you believe it?"

She hesitated. "I believe his Dream. As to the source of the storm, I fear to offer an opinion. The implications . . ."

Blood-scented wind swept over them, flapping Cord's black cape around his long legs, and jingling the turtle shell ornaments. For two old war chiefs, bloody wind was as familiar as the feel of a war club in their hands. Nonetheless, she saw his fingers clench, and she knew he was holding on to life, cherishing the breath moving in his lungs.

Unwisely, she reached out to place a hand upon his shoulder. Something about the softness of his expression built a warmth in her heart. She longed to stay, to sip a cup of tea and talk of old times with him, but feared where it would lead. "I have duties to attend to. I must go, Cord. I thank you for your kindness."

As she rose to her feet, she tucked CorpseEye back into her belt.

His jaw clamped, as though making some decision.

"Wait. Please?" he said.

He stood up and swiftly pulled her into his embrace. For a time, she let herself drown in the sensation of being held. It had been a long time since she'd allowed a man to hold her. She was aware of the softness of his worn cape and the rhythmic pulse of his breath against her throat.

She slipped her arms around his waist and pulled him hard against her. They stood like that, clutching each other for long enough that CorpseEye's quartzite cobble head felt like it might break her ribs. The camp went silent again.

Finally, she pushed away, and said, "Very dangerous, Chief Cord. There are those among your own People who would consider this consorting with the enemy."

"I've faced danger before. I'll risk it."

As they gazed at each other, a connection grew between them. Like a rope being stretched tight, the fibers strained, about to fray and break loose. As his smile faded, conflicting emotions danced across his handsome face.

"Cord, I'm sorry that we can't—"

"It's *not* impossible." He clenched his fists at his sides, as though struggling against his own impotence. "Join my people. Please present the possibility to your Ruling Council. Let them decide. That way no one could ever accuse you of suggesting it as a way to further your personal interests." He paused. "That is, providing you think it would be in your personal interest to share your life with me."

She lowered her eyes and watched the brassy splashes of light cast over the hearthstones by the flames. They fell irregularly, like leaf-shaped puzzle pieces cut from a golden sunset.

Smiling ironically, she said, "Actually, it would be far more in my interest if you moved to my village. That is the tradition of our peoples. When men marry they move to the wife's village. That would suit me even better."

His brows lifted. "I hardly think that's a good idea. Your village may well be doomed."

She laughed. Warriors' humor. Bizarre, given the circumstances.

She touched him one last time, squeezing his hand. "Sleep well, my friend."

She turned and headed back across the freezing battlefield.

Three

Just a shred of sound, an exhale from a human throat.

Twenty paces ahead, a small sparkling cloud of frosted breath formed in the darkness.

The most feared witch in the land, Ohsinoh, watched it drift through the maple trunks. He'd finally located his enemy, the man they called Sky Messenger. Ohsinoh continued easing his leg through the frozen ferns, his movements barely hissing through the winter forest.

Just beyond the maples, Sky Messenger aimlessly wandered among the dead. A tall man, and muscular, Sky Messenger had a round face and slender nose. Straight black hair brushed his shoulders. Following behind Sky Messenger was his pet wolf, Gitchi.

Ohsinoh frowned. That could complicate matters. The bond between Sky Messenger and the old gray-faced wolf smacked of the supernatural. The wolf would die protecting him. Which meant Ohsinoh would have to kill the wolf first.

In the distance, the half-burned villages of Bur Oak and Yellowtail nestled together. The three rings of palisades that surrounded each village—constructed of upright logs—had been burned through in so many places they resembled mouths of rotted teeth. Smoke continued to rise from the charred areas. Even at this late hour, firelight gleamed through the gaps. Though men and women still stood on the rickety catwalks, keeping watch should the enemy return, they looked exhausted. Many heads nodded, trying to stay awake.

Ohsinoh silently inhaled and let his breath out slowly. Somewhere in the trees behind him, a Flint warrior paralleled his course. A hired murderer. A traitor to Chief Cord. To enlist his skills tonight, Ohsinoh had been forced to pay the man enough to ransom a small village.

Sky Messenger leaned over to peer into the eyes of a dead woman warrior. His lips moved, speaking to her, saying something soft that Ohsinoh couldn't hear. How convenient that he was completely alone, except for Gitchi. Where, Ohsinoh wondered, was Sky Messenger's avowed friend and protector War Chief Hiyawento?

Ohsinoh's gaze shifted to the south where Hiyawento's camp nestled on the hilltop.

Dark figures moved around the fire. Hiyawento was probably there, still grieving over the murder of his two baby daughters. Was he remembering their smiling faces? It must grow harder every day to teeter around the edges of the emptiness that had grown inside him. By now, Hiyawento's souls must be dark open chasms that dropped away forever, as though all the light in the world had been obliterated in a single stroke when his little girls died.

Ohsinoh barely stifled a delighted chuckle. That had been too easy. Not even a challenge for his witchery.

Sky Messenger lifted his face and seemed to be

studying the campfires of the dead that sprinkled the night sky, perhaps speaking with the Blessed Ancestors who lived along the Path of Souls that led to the Land of the Dead.

As Ohsinoh watched him, his sense of triumph dwindled, returning to a hatred so potent it left him feeling slightly ill. He'd first met Odion—Sky Messenger's boyhood name—when he'd seen eleven summers. Odion had been a pathetic, whimpering little fool, terrified of everything. Ohsinoh had hated him for it.

As he pursued his prey, Ohsinoh clutched the evil-looking charm he carried in his right hand—a tortoise-shell covered with animal fur. Two white eyes, carved of shell, stared out from the center of the fur. It was unnerving, even to him. The charm reminded him of the old stories of half-human beasts that had wandered the land just after Tarachiawagon, the Good-Minded Twin, created the world. He'd found the charm among his mother's things, cached beneath a dead red cedar tree in the far-away country of the People of the Dawnland. His mother, Gannajero, had been dead for twelve summers—but her death still devastated him. The violent manner of her murder had doomed her afterlife soul to wander the earth forever. At the age of thirteen summers, he'd been lost, starving, without hope . . . until her soul had stalked from the darkness and crouched before his fire. *"You young idiot. Get up! I've come to share all my secrets with you. If you've the sense to obey me, you are about to be rich and powerful."*

Her fierce words had given him back his purpose in life. He'd changed his name from Hehaka to Ohsinoh. She'd told him every place she'd cached rare Trade goods, and witch's charms. Since that night, he'd often caught glimpses of her wandering soul light as it slipped through the shadowy forest.

His gaze returned to his enemy. Sky Messenger and his filthy friends had killed her.

Ohsinoh had been struggling for summers to avenge her. All of his life, he had worked and scraped to find every bit of knowledge he could about Power . . . and he had. His abilities had become the stuff of legend. People said that if anyone dared kill him, he would rise from the dead and torment his murderer for eternity. He'd become the most-feared man in the world . . . until today's freak storm had turned Sky Messenger into an ethereal figure of awe, no longer quite human. Ohsinoh had heard warriors muttering that Sky Messenger was the long-awaited prophet, the reborn Spirit of Tarachiawagon. Sky Messenger's newfound fame ate at Ohsinoh's vitals like a fanged beast.

Tonight, old enemy, I will avenge my mother and show these fools that you are mere flesh and blood . . .

He inhaled a soothing breath, and the scent of the marsh penetrated the battlefield stench.

His eyes slowly panned to the west. Like a crescent moon, Reed Marsh curved around the charred villages, protecting them on the north and west sides. Its wet fragrance mixed oddly with the stenches of blood and smoke, turning it poignant and velvet. Birds perched on the tallest cattails, their eyes glowing.

A gust of wind fluttered his bluebird-feather cape. Ohsinoh pulled his hood forward to shield his face from the bitter cold.

Sky Messenger continued on his way, stopping often,

apparently to gaze down into the eyes of the dead, now frozen in their skulls and sheathed in frost. As the dead bodies stiffened, they thumped and gurgled, teeth gnashed, and gasses hissed.

The old gray-faced wolf never left Sky Messenger. Gitchi kept scanning the tree line, his eyes shining in the brilliant light cast by the campfires of the dead. Tonight, the sky was a conflagration. The wolf stared directly at Ohsinoh and went rigid. He lifted his muzzle to sniff the air. Assessing the danger.

Ohsinoh went stone still.

Sky Messenger suddenly noticed his wolf's gaze and stared out at where Ohsinoh stood.

Ohsinoh called, "It's Odion, the boy who was always afraid."

Sky Messenger responded with Ohsinoh's boyhood name. "I'm still afraid, Hehaka."

"But why? You are the great man now. Elder Brother Sun obeys Sky Messenger's commands." He vented a low mocking laugh. "Isn't it enough?"

Sky Messenger appeared to be thinking about the question. After what seemed a long time, he answered, "I know where it is."

Confused, Ohsinoh tilted his head. "Where what is?"

"Her pot."

Ohsinoh took a quick step toward Sky Messenger, breathless, unable to believe his ears. A gust of wind flapped his feathered hood around his face. He had to be sure. "Which pot?"

"You know the pot I mean. Her soul pot."

As though Ohsinoh was suddenly back in that terrible

meadow, he could hear his own pathetic voice whisper, *"She sucked out my soul. . . . she sucked it out with that eagle-bone sucking tube and blew it into the little pot that she carries in her pack. . . . She told me that when she kills me, my afterlife soul will never be able to find its way home. I'll be chased through the forests forever by enemy ghosts."*

Gannajero had been the greatest witch who had ever lived. She'd stolen hundreds of souls—including his.

Losing your afterlife soul caused insanity. Before Ohsinoh realized it, tears leaked from the corners of his eyes, blurring his vision. Finding that pot and releasing his soul so that it could return and take its place in his body again had been one of his lifelong goals.

Suspiciously, he asked, "Why do you tell me this?"

"You've been searching for it for a long time, haven't you? If I'd known, I would have told you sooner. Do you remember our last camp on the river where she ambushed us?"

"I do."

"Walk due northeast about one thousand paces, and you will see a small oval clearing on a hillside surrounded by maples. There are three rocks in the middle of the clearing. That's where she died. Just before Mother found us, Zateri took the soul pot from the old woman's pack and buried it between the rocks." Sky Messenger stared hard at Ohsinoh. "Do you want me to go with you?"

Ohsinoh didn't answer for a time. He was thinking about the old woman's death. He hadn't been there, but the story had moved up and down the trails for many summers afterward. He'd heard it so often it was engraved on his soul. Baji, Odion, Zateri, and some other children he didn't know, had killed Gannajero, axed and stabbed her to death like small rabid animals.

"No," he said, and backed away, moving deeper into the trees. Even though he'd been searching for that pot for more than half his life, he would accept no help from this man.

Sky Messenger must have assumed he was gone, for he petted Gitchi's head and slowly made his way to a high point overlooking the Flint People's camp. He gazed longingly at the warriors wrapped in blankets and hides. Beyond the camp, forested hills rolled endlessly to the northern horizon.

Ohsinoh eased through the trees, continuing to watch Sky Messenger. Why had the man offered to help him find the precious pot? They had never been friends.

Sky Messenger bowed his head, heaved a sigh, and seemed to be staring at the ground.

Was he thinking about Baji? Only a few moons ago, she and Sky Messenger had been lovers. Everyone had expected them to marry. For reasons Ohsinoh didn't understand, it hadn't happened. Sky Messenger was now betrothed to a fourteen-summers-old woman named Taya. An arranged marriage. Nothing more. Sky Messenger's sense of honor had to be vying with his need for a woman he'd loved since childhood. Perhaps he was trying to dream a new future—one that could never be.

Ohsinoh silently laughed, his heart returning to the task at hand.

Sky Messenger turned away from the Flint camp and headed back for the firelit stillness of Bur Oak Village, probably seeking shelter from the icy darkness and the soul-rending sounds of the battlefield. Perhaps from his memories of Baji.

If Ohsinoh didn't hurry, he would miss his chance.

A foot crunched the frost, too close to believe. Finally, the Flint warrior . . .

"You're a fool, Ohsinoh."

Hiyawento's voice came from his right, less than ten paces away. Panic seared Ohsinoh's veins. He gripped his evil charm, spread his arms, and slowly turned.

War Chief Hiyawento carried a war club, but had no guards. He stood alone, unmoving, as though a block of sculpted darkness. He was tall, with a narrow beaked face and burning eyes. Black hair blew around his shoulders. Dressed in a worn, knee-length, buckskin cape, he might have been any ordinary warrior, were it not for his stunning presence. It was like a tingling heaviness in the air— the sense a man gets before a cougar leaps upon him from a ledge above. No one who had ever stood before Hiyawento had doubted either his will or his abilities to crush his enemy.

"I'm going to kill you, Hehaka."

Ohsinoh's laugh was a little too high pitched. "Have you become a miracle worker, too? Like your demented friend Sky Messenger?"

"He just showed you kindness, and you call him demented?"

"He's just feeling magnanimous. After all, everyone is whispering his name with reverence. He has become a Spirit creature."

Hiyawento boldly walked to stand less than three paces from Ohsinoh.

Hiyawento towered over him.

"You gave my daughters the poisoned cornhusk doll, didn't you?"

Ohsinoh's chest vibrated with a soundless chuckle. "It wasn't my idea, you know."

"Dear gods! They had only seen three and five summers. You coward! Why didn't you kill me?"

"Were it a personal matter, I would have, Wrass. Unfortunately, it was just a hired task. My instructions were to kill your heart, to take the fire from your words. I did."

"Was it your father's idea?" Hiyawento's grief filled his taut voice.

"Of course. Chief Atotarho fears you. I don't know why. You're a pathetic excuse for a war chief. Always sniveling, always voting for peace. Do you know your own warriors despise you?"

Hiyawento's feet crunched frost as he took another step toward Ohsinoh. "After I kill you, I'm going to kill your father."

Ohsinoh laughed out loud. "But he has thousands of warriors to protect him, and he's coming back, you know. You don't really believe he ran away today, do you?"

"He and his entire army ran off like scared rabbits. I saw him being carried away on a litter."

Ohsinoh casually propped his fists on his hips. The shell eyes of the charm flashed in the moonlight. "Well, I'm sure Father needed to regroup, to take stock of how many of his forces had survived the battle and to plan his next move. You and your friends are overwhelmingly outnumbered. By the way, how many warriors did you leave at Coldspring Village?"

Hiyawento seemed to freeze.

"My guess is that you left only perhaps one hundred

men and women to defend the walls. After all, you had little to fear. At the time, you and your wife, Zateri, were fighting on my father's side. He's going to punish you, you know. Treason—"

"We'll be home soon."

"*Not* soon enough."

Hiyawento shifted his weight to his other foot. "Why would you care?"

Ohsinoh's teeth flashed. He shook the tortoiseshell charm. As it uttered its menacing snakelike rattle, he glimpsed a shadow emerge from behind a broad sycamore trunk, only three paces from Hiyawento. The soft sound of a skillfully placed moccasin carried.

Hiyawento's shoulder muscles suddenly tensed. But he did not turn.

A contemptuous laugh escaped Ohsinoh's lips. "You should have killed me when you had the chance, Wrass. Now, it's too . . ."

Hiyawento leaped and swung. His war club cut the air like lightning, crushing Ohsinoh's ribcage. Before Ohsinoh had even fallen to the ground, Hiyawento spun on his toes and lunged for the Flint warrior behind him. The rapidity of Hiyawento's response had momentarily shocked the tall gangly man. He had his war club up, but he was off-balance, in the process of stepping forward. Hiyawento's club slammed into his enemy's, knocking him backward a step, leaving an opening. Hiyawento sprang forward, broke the man's neck, and danced away. When he was sure it had been a killing blow, he took a deep breath, searched the forest for other foes, and again turned to look at Ohsinoh. His eyes gleamed.

Pain like lightning blasted through Ohsinoh's chest. He

lay curled on his side in the frost-sheathed ferns, his arms wrapped around his crushed chest, groaning. Frothy blood leaked from the corner of his mouth. Gannajero's hideous charm lay at his side, within reach, but he hadn't the strength to reach for it. Shock possessed his senses. He could only cough in agony and stare. With each breath, his broken ribs grated against one another.

Hiyawento walked to stand over Ohsinoh like a dark avenging Earth Spirit.

As Hiyawento lifted his war club to finish the job, Ohsinoh gasped, "Sky Messenger's vision . . . is false . . . the storm was . . . a coincidence."

Hiyawento's face betrayed no emotion. He regripped his war club, tightening his hands; it hung in the darkness, stationary, the polished wood gleaming with an edge of moonlit fire.

Ohsinoh chuckled. "You know it . . . don't you?"

After what seemed forever, Hiyawento's deep voice punctured the quiet. "This is for my daughters, witch."

Hiyawento brought his club down with all the strength in his muscular arms.

Ohsinoh's skull cracked open like a ripe melon dashed upon a rock. Hiyawento hit him again, and again, until the soulless witch's face was unrecognizable. When he finally stumbled back, his fists ached so badly that he had to pry the fingers of his right hand loose from the club's shaft.

He slipped the club into his weapon's belt and rubbed his mouth with the back of his hand. His gaze immediately sought Sky Messenger's position. His friend had made it unharmed across the battlefield and stood talking with the guards at the gates of Bur Oak Village. The firelight seeping from the village reflected from his round face, giving it a sunlike glow.

Hiyawento nodded in relief.

After the ferocious events of the day, he'd feared someone would wish to kill Sky Messenger. Especially given the whisperings that he was no longer human, but an immortal Spirit. Such claims tempted small men with delusions of grandeur.

It would have never occurred to him that he'd be fortunate enough to find Ohsinoh, his daughters' murderer, dogging Sky Messenger's path. The Faces of the Forest must have heard his prayers.

Hiyawento waited until Sky Messenger disappeared inside the Bur Oak gates, then he turned.

On the far southern hilltop, campfires gleamed. His wife, Zateri, the Matron of Coldspring Village, would still be awake, worried, wondering where he was. She'd be holding their last daughter, eight-summers-old Kahn-Tineta, in her arms, grieving, as he was, for all they had lost in the past few days—and no doubt terrified of what the future would bring.

Hiyawento bent down, used the dead witch's feathered cape to wipe the blood off his war club, and took one last hard look at the body. How strange that he had to reassure himself the man was, indeed, dead.

The white eyes in the middle of the tortoiseshell charm glinted in the grass beside the witch. They seemed to be filled with deadly promise and staring right at Hiyawento.

A chill went through him. He shook it off, and glared at the charm. "Before this night is through, I will have cut your master's body to pieces and scattered them far and wide. None of his followers will ever be able to recognize him and Requicken his soul in another body."

Hiyawento lifted his club, and paused, studying the gigantic sycamores that dotted the forest. Each was a lost warrior. They would be watching him now, judging his worthiness.

He bashed the charm to splinters. Chunks of tortoiseshell cartwheeled away, clacking as they struck frozen rocks.

When he straightened up, somewhere out on the battlefield a foot began to tap. Rhythmic. Haunting. A percussion backdrop to the eerie symphony created by the other stiffening bodies.

He listened.

Though the night was filled with sound, a silence too great to be born lived inside him. His daughters were gone. The spaces their voices had carved in his souls boomed like finely crafted drums, hollow, empty, filled with faint circling echoes.

Grief and rage were twins, forever linked, both born in a wounded heart. Where one ended and the other began, he no longer knew.

He was certain of only one thing. Destroying Ohsinoh had not even dimmed his need to kill.

Ohsinoh had just been a hired murderer. The real culprit was the evil cannibal-sorcerer, Chief Atotarho.

Hiyawento unlaced and removed a chert knife from his belt pouch, then bent down, and began cutting Hehaka's body apart, condemning his afterlife soul to wander the earth alone forever. He would not even dignify the corpse by thinking of its witch's name.

Four

Chief Atotarho drew his black cape more tightly around him and scowled out at the old leaves gusting by. Wind Woman's breath scoured the highlands, sucking away any warmth his fire radiated, and leaving his twisted body in agony. Every joint in his body ached, and each time he shifted position, sharp pains lanced down his arms and legs. They made a powerful accompaniment to the sheer rage that ate at him.

My forces ran away today!

He glowered out across the land. They'd made camp on a high rocky ridge three hands run to the north of Bur Oak Village. Slabs of rock made stair-step patterns around them, descending into valleys on either side of the ridge. From this height, Atotarho could see all the way across the rolling hills of the Standing Stone nation and to lands of the People of the Hills, his home.

He shoved another branch in his fire, and waited for the leader of his personal guards, Negano, to return from speaking with the other deputy war chiefs who stood talking twenty paces away in a grove of wind-whipped pines.

"I asked a simple question. What's taking so long?"

Could it be that without War Chief Sindak, none of his deputy war chiefs knew how to lead? Or maybe Sindak's treachery had caused irreparable rifts among his warriors? The dominance struggles, warriors seeking opportunities to climb in the ranks, had already begun. He'd had to put down three fights tonight.

Given the day's events, he wondered what was happening back in his village? Was High Matron Kelek adjusting to her new position? He prayed the runner he'd sent, the fastest man in the Hills nation, would reach her tomorrow afternoon.

Gods! His own daughter, the matron of Coldspring Village, had turned against him today. Worse, she'd taken two other Hills People matrons with her. He tried to imagine how it had happened. Had Zateri spent days or weeks convincing matrons Kwahseti and Gwinodje to betray him? Their disloyalty might have even gone on for moons without his knowledge.

She had ruined his plans.

He had intended to destroy the Standing Stone nation, and immediately proceed westward with his army to wipe out the Landing People. He'd even hoped that the weather would hold out long enough for him to attack the starving villages of the People of the Mountain.

Now, none of that will happen . . .

He roughly massaged the fingers of his left hand. Like knobby sticks, he could no longer fully straighten them. They remained slightly clenched in hawklike talons.

One man, he couldn't identify the voice, shouted, "I saw it, Negano! He called the storm. Don't tell me what I did or did not see today!"

It irked him that this same discussion must be going on all over his camp. His warriors must be whispering about the events of the day with awe in their voices, even longing.

The ten deputy war chiefs quieted. He glared at them. Were they casting their voices to decide who would be the new war chief? Well, they could do all the voice counts they wished. When out on the war trail, it was his decision to make.

Another powerful gust blasted the ridge top, and his fire sputtered wildly. One instant he was smothered in warm smoke and the next submerged in icy air.

Finally, Negano broke away from the gathering and walked toward Atotarho through the firelit darkness. A tall man who'd seen thirty-two summers pass, Negano had long black hair. He'd tied it back with a cord, but it still whipped around his oval face. He had his brown eyes squinted against the onslaught.

When he stood on the opposite side of the fire, he bowed deeply. "My Chief, we are divided in our assessments as to the best route to track down our enemies. It will be difficult, given that we must carry litters filled with the wounded and dead from today's battle, and we cannot take the main trails. That's the point of contention. Most of our warriors wish to go home first to care for their relatives before we engage in any other attacks."

"Did you cast your voices for a new war chief?"

Negano seemed slightly confused by the change of topic. "No, we decided that our warriors need the night to calm down and be able to consider their choice."

"Since we are on the war trail, it is within my rights as Chief to appoint that position, is it not?"

"Of course." Negano nodded. "Your warriors may not be happy about that, but—"

"I could care less what makes them happy. They are warriors. It's their duty to obey me. How many wounded and dead do we have to slow us down?"

Negano braced his hands on his hips and seemed to be thinking about it. "We don't have an exact number yet, but I would say around two hundred wounded, and we're carrying around one hundred dead. At your order, we left the rest of our dead relatives on the battlefield to become homeless ghosts."

The resentment in Negano's voice was clear. Atotarho ignored it and tucked his hands beneath his cape to keep them warm. "What is your personal opinion of the trail we should take to hunt down our enemies?"

Negano blinked, hesitated. "Most of us agree that if we must do this, we should follow the trail that runs on the north side of the Forks River."

"Why the north side?"

"Because, my Chief, our enemies are smart enough to correctly fear that you have already dispatched thousands of warriors to destroy their home villages in punishment for their actions today. They will try to get home as quickly as they can—that means running the trail on the south side of the Forks River."

Negano crouched down and extended his hands to the flames. Wind flipped his long hair around his face. "For part of the way—at least for tomorrow—the trail runs just below the northern river bluff, which means they won't be able to see us as we get into position to ambush them."

"Where will we cross back to the south side?"

"The Seagull Shallows. The river narrows there, and

Traders from a variety of nations cache canoes at the narrows. The last time I was there more than fifty canoes were hidden in the brush, but I have seen as many as one hundred there."

"Let us assume there will be fifty canoes. If we can average six warriors in each canoe, that's three hundred warriors crossing each trip—"

"Not exactly," Negano interrupted, and looked as though he instantly regretted it—which he should have. Interrupting a chief was a killing offense. Nervously, he licked his lips. "Forgive me, my Chief, I only wished to say that the canoes are of different sizes. I think we can average six in each canoe, but two will need to row back to pick up more warriors. That means really only four crossing at a time."

"Then that's two hundred crossing at once. That means it will take ten trips to cross our army of two thousand. Three hands of time at most."

"Yes, but . . ." Negano shifted, pulling his cape closed beneath his chin. "We must also transport the litters filled with wounded and dead, and they are—"

"How long will that take?"

Negano gestured uncertainly. "It's hard to guess. They are unwieldy. Perhaps another one hand of time."

"Four hands of time total."

Behind Negano, the deputy war chiefs moved around their fire, trying to keep their backs to the icy gusts. Their low voices carried a dark hostile timbre.

Atotarho tipped his chin to the deputies. "What are they most worried about?"

"Hmm?" Negano turned to look and heaved a sigh. "Almost everyone lost a friend or loved one today. As I said, while they, too, wish to punish those who fought against us, they wish to go home first, to lick their wounds, and care for their injured or dead relatives. If we engage in another battle before returning home, they fear the cost will—"

Atotarho broke in, "I don't wish to hear any more on the subject."

Softly, Negano responded, "Yes, my Chief."

"We are currently on the south side of the Forks River. That means we will have to cross it twice, once to get to the north side and once to get back. Eight hands of time. Is that your assessment, as well?"

"Yes, my Chief."

"Very well. That means we do not have the luxury of resting tonight. Roust our warriors from their blankets and get them on the trail as soon as possible." Atotarho reached for his walking stick, and grunted as he shoved to his feet.

Negano's eyes went wide. "But, my Chief, our warriors are exhausted. They must rest or they will never be able to fight—"

"Do it now, *War Chief*."

Almost too stunned to speak, Negano stammered, "W-War Chief? You are appointing me? My chief, I do not think I am the right person—"

Atotarho turned and careened down the ridge toward where his own personal guards waited by his litter.

He did not see Negano rise, but when he looked back over his shoulder, his new War Chief was tramping through the darkness toward the assembled deputies.

A short time later, cries of indignation rose . . . but quickly died down, followed by the rapid steps of men and women scurrying to ready their forces to move.

Five

As dawn approached, windblown veils of snow wavered across the pale blue valley. From her position on the Bur Oak Village palisade, Jigonsaseh could see the warriors beginning to stir. Campfires winked as hundreds of men and women passed before them.

Up and down the Bur Oak catwalks, her forces stood with bows nocked, waiting for the return of Atotarho's army. She'd dispatched scouts to track him, but none had returned—which meant they were probably dead. Atotarho could attack them again at any time. Villagers rushed around the plaza, trying to get the walls repaired before the attack came. The dank scent of fear hung like a pall in the frigid air.

She leaned against the frosty palisade and tiredly studied Yellowtail Village; it sat like a rotted husk. At her order, the entire exterior palisade had been torn down and stockpiled to repair the Bur Oak palisades, but the two inner palisades remained. Through the charred holes in them, she saw that the most badly burned of the three longhouses had, during the night, been stripped bare of bark, the pole frames dismantled, and everything usable piled in enormous heaps around the plaza. Between the palisades, where the makeshift refugee housing had been, piles of debris smoldered and probably would for a long time. In the next two days, everything would have been carried to Bur Oak Village to fortify it. They didn't have enough warriors left to guard two villages.

The rest of Yellowtail Village needed to be completely dismantled, and soon. She didn't wish to leave it for the use of attackers who could capture it and attack Bur Oak Village from within her own walls. She'd discuss it with High Matron Kittle as soon as the exhausted High Matron rose from her bedding hides.

Jigonsaseh looked behind her. Every possible space in Bur Oak Village, including the narrow lanes between the palisades and the rear of the longhouses, now contained makeshift housing for refugees. In the plaza below, construction continued. They had piled some of the building supplies around the circumference of the Council House and, as workers came and went, carrying wood or bark, or heavy coils of rope to lash poles together, clatters sounded. Large stew pots hung on tripods at the edges of the central bonfire, available for workers to fill bowls when they had a spare moment. Though each person was allowed only one bowlful, there were no guards on the pots. Every warrior was needed for other duties. People crowded the plaza. Some laughed and talked. Others sobbed for lost loved ones. Still others uttered dire speculations of what tomorrow would bring—and ate far more than their allotted share. She'd witnessed one man go back four times and come away with a heaping bowl.

The worst part for her was the lilting strain of

triumphant joy that twined through the groans and cries of the wounded. Many fools believed they had won yesterday's battle.

She knew better.

Her gaze searched the plaza. On the western side, near the Hawk Clan Longhouse, forty-one Hills warriors, men and women who had defected to her side yesterday afternoon, stood in a tight knot, their uneasy eyes scanning their new compatriots. Atotarho's former War Chief, Sindak, stood among them, speaking in a low voice. His warriors' heads nodded and, as though satisfied that they understood what he wanted, Sindak turned away. His attention lifted to the palisades, surveying the Standing Stone warriors on the catwalks. When he caught Jigonsaseh's gaze, he stopped and stared.

Her eyes narrowed.

Once, a long time ago, he had been a trusted friend, one of the men who had valiantly fought to help her rescue her captive children. After that, however, he'd returned to Atotarho Village where he'd gradually risen through the ranks to War Chief. Despite the fact that she understood a warrior's overwhelming desire to protect his own people, she did not understand Sindak's willingness to serve a mad chief, a man he knew to be a monster. It was a failing she found hard to forgive. Not only that, as War Chief, he had slaughtered Standing Stone villages filled with innocent people, and that was impossible to forgive.

What was he doing here? She hadn't had time to assess his motives yet. At a critical instant during the next attack, was he supposed to rally his warriors and start killing people inside the palisade?

Sindak excused himself from the knot of warriors, and

stalked through the bustling crowd to the closest ladder that led to the catwalks. A small commotion broke out as he shouldered past the Standing Stone guards and made his way toward her, crossing the bridges that connected the palisade rings. The guards had orders to treat the Hills warriors as friends, within reason. After all, they'd risked their lives when they'd turned against Chief Atotarho.

Sindak gave her a tight smile as he approached. He had seen thirty-one summers pass, and had a lean face with deeply sunken brown eyes. Short black hair clung to his cheeks. His tan cape swayed, flashing the white geometric designs that decorated the bottom.

As he leaned against the palisade beside her, he bluntly said, "You've forgotten that I know that look. You think we're spies, don't you?"

"The possibility has occurred to me."

Wind fanned the central bonfire and a fog of blue wood smoke blew around them. Sindak waited for it to pass, before he said, "We're not."

"That's good to hear. However, your word is just not good enough, War Chief. You and your people worry me."

His lips pressed into a hard line. "Until yesterday, I had never led an attack against Yellowtail Village. No matter how hard I had to argue in war councils, or what I had to do to bribe warriors to side with me, I did it. The last thing in the world that I wanted was to—"

"'Until yesterday,' those are the important words. Just a few hands of time ago you led warriors in an attempt to destroy the Standing Stone nation." Jigonsaseh extended her palm to the dead bodies stacked along the base of the palisade, then moved it across the decimated villages. The predawn shadows devoured the horrors, but he understood.

Sindak expelled a breath. "I was overruled in council and given specific orders from High Matron Tila herself. If your Ruling Council had ordered an attack upon my village, Atotarho Village, would you have followed those orders?"

"I would. Without an instant's hesitation."

Sindak's muscular shoulders relaxed a little, though his face retained its taut expression. "We are warriors. We all do our duty, Matron."

She watched him flip up his hood against the falling snow, and tried to fathom what he must be thinking. If their positions had been reversed, she'd be desperately worried whether or not she'd made the right decision. "Statements about duty sound curious coming from a War Chief who abandoned his army and fled to the enemy."

Sindak seemed to freeze for a heartbeat, then he turned and gave her a level stare. "Our duties changed when our nation split in two and three Hills villages joined your side. We had to choose where our allegiance lay. We did."

Jigonsaseh grunted softly and let her gaze roam the snowy hillside to the west. Dark forms slinked across the white background—wolves feasting upon her relatives. Snarls and growls carried as they competed for corpses.

"Tomorrow, if you allow it," Sindak said, "my warriors and I will help gather the dead bodies of your people, and Sing them to the afterlife. Perhaps that will forge some trust."

"Trust is not so easily purchased, Sindak. Hundreds of the refugees in the plaza below are from your most recent attack on White Dog Village. They hate you, War Chief."

"I understand that. I only pray they give us a chance to prove . . ."

His voice faded when he noticed Jigonsaseh's grip tighten on the shaft of her belted war club. CorpseEye was cold tonight. Stone cold. As though the Spirit of the club had sailed far away, to another place and time.

Anxiety widened Sindak's dark eyes. "What's he telling you?" He pointed to CorpseEye.

"Nothing. We're safe. For now."

In relief, Sindak sagged against the palisade and exhaled hard. "Don't do that to me. If my good friend Towa had been here, he would have run screaming."

A half-smile turned her lips. "I'd forgotten you once held CorpseEye." *The night you saved my life by throwing me my club. The night you and your best friend fought on my side with great bravery.* "How is Towa?"

"He is well. He married eight summers ago and moved to Riverbank Village. He's spent most of the past twelve summers off on some wild Trading expedition. In fact, a Flint Trader came through Atotarho Village two moons ago, and said he'd seen Towa carrying a pack of buffalo horn sheaths he'd gotten in the far west. He was headed to the Mountain People villages to Trade them for corn." He paused and his brows knitted. "However, about one-half moon ago, when the violence intensified, Towa returned home to Riverbank Village."

"I doubt he found much corn in the Mountain villages, but if he did, he's a wealthy man now. Most villages have already eaten their seed corn, which means they have nothing to plant next spring."

Desperation and despair seemed everywhere. She briefly closed her tired eyes and rubbed them. When she opened her eyes, she found Sindak looking at her solemnly.

"We are not spies, Matron," he repeated. "I give you my oath."

"Will you and your warriors swear an oath of loyalty to the Standing Stone nation?"

He glanced down at his people. Many of them were staring at him, talking in low voices. "That, Matron, would be treason. Of course not."

"Your warriors do not consider themselves traitors already? I'm fairly certain the Hills Ruling Council does."

"Which Hills Ruling Council?" he countered.

She tilted her head. "Ah. I see."

"Do you? Let me explain so that I'm certain we understand each other. We did not turn against our nation. We turned against Atotarho. So far as we are concerned, we follow the rightful leader of the People of the Hills, his daughter, High Matron Zateri."

Down in the plaza five people started a round dance, their arms around each other's waists. As though nothing was wrong in the world, their voices rose in song. One man kept stumbling, laughing.

The sight left her hollow. Were they still so flushed from yesterday's "victory" that they thought themselves invincible?

As though reading the tracks of her souls, Sindak said, "I'm sure you've heard the same things I have, but just in case you haven't, your villagers are saying that it doesn't matter if Atotarho attacks again, because Sky Messenger will protect the Standing Stone nation."

"I've heard that foolishness, yes."

"Is it foolishness?" Sindak propped an elbow on the palisade and searched her face.

"You can't believe that. He's just one man."

"True, but I was there when he called the storm. I saw it crash down over the hill, sweeping my army from the battlefield—"

"And every other army," she added.

Curiosity lit Sindak's eyes. "You don't believe he called the storm?"

"What I believe is that he is right about this Peace Alliance. That is enough for me."

A confused smile creased his lean face. "I wouldn't let that get around, if I were you. If his own mother does not believe—"

"I believe in peace, Sindak," she replied in a firm voice.

The breeze tousled his hood around his face. "I remember the loathsome tone in your former husband's voice when he used to call you a Peacemaker. It still turns my blood cold."

"Well, Gonda has changed."

"Haven't we all?" Sindak frowned at the dancers. As the firelight fluttered in the wind, it cast the shadow of his beaked nose across his cheek. "If we were traitors why would we have volunteered to stay and help protect your villages? That doesn't make any sense."

"It does if Atotarho specifically instructed you to turn against us during the next battle."

"Oh," he breathed, "now I understand. We are to commit suicide for our chief while killing as many of you as we can?"

She lifted a shoulder. "Maybe. It would help if you told me what you expect to get out of this arrangement, Sindak. Why are you here?" To leaven the tension a little, she asked, "You're not still smitten with me, are you?"

His lips quirked. "That was a long time ago, but I have never been 'smitten' with you. It was undying love. I was a silly youth."

She chuckled.

His head dropped forward until his chin rested on his chest. He had a thoughtful expression. "What do I expect to get? I haven't thought that far ahead. And I'm exhausted. Perhaps we should discuss this later in the morning, after we've both had a chance to—"

"No, now. Tell me what you hope to gain?"

He lifted his head, and his jaw went hard in annoyance. She could see his teeth grinding. "You remember that I'm a Hills warrior, correct? Maybe you should explain your perspective on the command structure here. Do you think I take orders from you?"

"You'd better."

He actually laughed, and they smiled at each other. "All right. Let me try to force my foggy souls to think." He paused for a long while, before saying, "First, I want Atotarho dead, and the People of the Hills reunited with Zateri as High Matron of all our people. Next, I want peace throughout the land, as you do. Beyond those things, I have no idea." He shoved away from the palisade. "And now, I am off to find my blanket." He strode down the catwalk.

She called, "Tell me one last thing?"

He turned. "What?"

"Where is Atotarho? Why don't we see his campfires out there? Our scouts haven't returned."

Firelight reflected in his dark eyes. "I've been wondering the same thing. My guess is that he's on the trail."

"Headed where?"

"If I knew that, Matron, my stomach would finally sink to its proper place."

"Get some sleep, Sindak."

He started to walk away, then stopped short, and turned back to give her an amused look. "With regard to your earlier question about my being 'smitten.' Just so you know, a part of me will always be in love with you. That's your penance for being such a great war chief. Silly young warriors become obsessed."

She laughed softly, and he gave her a sweeping bow, then continued toward the ladder.

Six

Elder Brother Sun had not yet crested the eastern horizon, but already the bellies of the drifting Cloud People shimmered, and a pale lavender glow lit the forest. As the leafless maple branches swayed in the morning breeze, soft rustling filled the air.

War Chief Baji of Wild River Village rose from where she'd been rolling up her blanket and stretched her aching back muscles. The battle yesterday had been fierce. As she turned left to examine the battlefield that lay between her camp and the partly burned villages of the Standing Stone People, her gaze lingered upon the dead. Strange things happened to corpses as they froze. Yesterday afternoon most of the bodies had been lying flat. This morning, misshapen arms with clawlike hands reached high into the air, as if pleading with the sky gods—or perhaps cursing them. Necks had twisted grotesquely. Mouths gaped in silent cries. Eyes, frozen in frosty pits, seemed to strain to see a familiar face, waiting for their loved ones to find them.

She glanced expectantly at the gates of Bur Oak Village.

The snow had stopped, but a dusting still frosted the shoulders of the guards who stood there.

He's coming. I know he is.

Thin streamers of smoke rose from the charred palisades. Through the gaps, she saw people gathered, engaged in a village council meeting, trying to decide what to do next. Their forces had been devastated by Chief Atotarho's attack, leaving them more vulnerable than they'd ever been. Baji and her forces could not stay to help them. She felt hollow and guilty, but she and her People had their own problems at home, not the least being that they feared Chief Atotarho would take out his vengeance on the Flint nation for supporting the Standing Stone nation against him.

Behind Baji, wooden bowls clacked against horn spoons as men and women finished their simple breakfasts of cornmeal mush, spiced with whatever variety of jerky they'd had left in their packs. Coughing and laughter carried, as well as the deep groans and fever-laced cries of the wounded. Weapons clattered as war belts were tied around waists and quivers and packs were slung over shoulders.

Baji slipped her hand beneath her buckskin cape and massaged her left arm just above the elbow where she'd sustained a blow from a war club wielded by one of the Hills People warriors. The purple lump was the size of a balled fist. Fortunately, she was right-handed. It would not impair her ability to swing her own club, though it would scream when she drew back her bow.

Her gaze returned to the gates. She tried to force her thoughts to other subjects but, as always, Dekanawida—the man others called Sky Messenger—was there.

. . . beneath me, smiling, staring upward through the

veil of my hair, his brown eyes filled with a dreamy warmth. Rocking, sweat-soaked, pine pollen cascading from the trees, sheathing our nakedness in pale yellow that resembles the glitter of sunlight.

Memories from last summer.

As the light strengthened, burial teams with litters began to trickle out from the villages and course through the corpses, identifying and loading relatives.

Her adopted father, Chief Cord, also dispatched two teams for the same purpose. As he led the teams onto the battlefield, Baji watched him. His black cape decorated with turtle shell carvings, symbols of his clan, waffled around his long legs.

As though he sensed her gaze, Cord turned to look at her. He had a long pointed nose and a square jaw. The black roach of hair down the middle of his head gleamed.

To avoid his eyes, she picked up her rolled blanket, woven from twisted strips of rabbithide, and tied it around her waist, over her cape, then knotted her weapons' belt just above it. The bone stilettos clacked against the chert knives. She was tall and muscular, with a small nose and large dark eyes. Her long black hair hung to her hips when it wasn't braided. She'd heard men call her beautiful. Were it not for the ugly knife scar that cut across her chin, she might have been.

She looked back at Bur Oak Village again. The gates were still closed.

. . . his deep voice singing lullabies to me in the middle of the night, holding me as though I am the only thing that stands between him and oblivion. Enough love in his eyes to sustain me for the rest of my life.

Cord frowned, broke away from the burial teams and

walked toward her. When he got to within two paces, he said, "After yesterday's miracle, he must be overwhelmed with requests for audiences. Why don't you go to him?"

Baji jerked the laces of her cape tight beneath her chin, and reached down to pick up her war club. As she tucked it into her belt, she added, "Father, he is betrothed to another. Do you really think it's appropriate for me to march into his future wife's longhouse and ask for a private meeting with my former lover?"

Sympathy tightened his mouth, and she couldn't stand it. She turned away. "Camp is almost packed up," she said sternly. "How much longer will it take the burial teams? We should be going soon."

"We have some time. Time enough, I think."

Baji knew that he meant, *Time enough to wait for Dekanawida.*

"That's foolish, Father. The longer we are gone, the more likely it is that Wild River Village will be attacked. I think we should—"

The gates of Bur Oak Village swung open and Dekanawida stepped out into the sunlight. Just the sight of him made her clamp her jaw to contain the welling emotion. She couldn't seem to get a deep breath into her lungs.

Cord didn't even turn to look. He could tell from the expression on her face. "I'll take care of making sure the war party is ready. Take as long as you need."

Father walked past her, leaving her standing alone, gazing across the expanse of frozen bodies to the only man she had ever trusted. He was very tall and broad-shouldered. He'd tucked his jet hair behind his ears. As he marched toward her, it swayed just above the shoulders of his black cape. Determination set his jaw. His slender nose flared with deep breaths. Gitchi, his old gray-faced wolf, walked at his side.

Baji strode to meet Dekanawida halfway. She suspected they both knew how things must be, though neither of them wished to admit it.

Gitchi's ears went up when he recognized her, and he loped forward to greet her with his tail wagging. Baji knelt down and put her arms around his thickly furred neck. "I miss you so much, Gitchi. How are your paws?"

She reached down to stroke his leg. His stiff joints hurt all the time, but he was still a great war dog. He'd saved her life many times. Gitchi whimpered and licked her face.

Dekanawida caught up and waited until Baji rose.

She gazed up into his eyes, and the world seemed to die around them. The voices of the war party ceased, the wind hushed. She heard only the pounding of blood in her ears.

Baji asked, "How is Tutelo? I heard her husband was killed yesterday."

As though he knew she was deliberately avoiding the only subject between them, he softly replied, "My sister is grieving, trying to be brave for her young daughters."

When they'd been slaves together as children, Tutelo had been the youngest, just eight summers, but she'd rarely cried. Love for her filled Baji. "Tutelo is the bravest person I know. I was so hoping to see her this morning, but we'll be leaving soon."

"How soon?"

"As soon as we've finished collecting our dead from the battlefield."

Their gazes held and the unbearable longing in his eyes left her feeling as empty as a shattered pot.

"I'm leaving soon, too, though I haven't told anyone yet."

Baji straightened. "Where are you going? The new alliance needs your guidance."

"Perhaps, but we need allies far more desperately. We can't be the only ones who believe that the war must end. There are others. I must find them and convince them to make peace with us."

"Father plans on doing the same thing among the People of the Mountain this winter. If everything works out, by Spring, our new alliance may have tripled in size."

He swallowed hard and lowered his gaze. He seemed to be trying to decide how to tell her something. "Baji, please thank Cord for me. He—"

"He's right there." She pointed. "You can thank him yourself."

"No. I—I need to speak with you."

He lifted his gaze again. The longer they stared at each other, the more her emptiness increased.

Baji hesitated, then, in a reverent voice, asked, "Will you tell those you meet about your Dream?"

Dekanawida tenderly reached out to stroke her hair, but his hand halted before he touched her. He closed his fist on air and drew it back. In a strained voice, he said, "Baji, I know you are War Chief, and you have duties, but I want you to come with me."

She blinked in confusion. "I can't."

"Just for one moon. Surely Cord will grant you that."

"My people are in danger, Dekanawida. It's impossible."

Dekanawida wrapped his arms around her shoulders and powerfully crushed her body against his. "I need you, Baji. Please come with me?"

A warm rush flooded her veins, frightening in its intensity. "You are betrothed to another."

His lips brushed her face, and he murmured against her hair, "My marriage is a political alliance. My future wife told me so herself." He tightened his embrace.

For a blessed timeless moment, she allowed herself to believe that she could go with him, and happiness filled her. She slipped her arms around his waist and hugged him so hard her injured arm shook. "I can't abandon my village now. Not when we may be attacked at any instant by Atotarho, or the Mountain People, or the People of the Landing. You know I can't. If you were still a deputy war chief, you would do the same."

. . . but he needs a bodyguard. There is no one better to protect his back than me.

Dekanawida slowly released her. A mixture of disappointment and despair shone in his brown eyes.

"I knew you'd say that. I had hoped not, but . . ." He expelled a breath. "You've always been the honorable one. I have just one last thing to say. Baji—"

"Please, don't." She knew that tone of voice. "It's useless, we can't—"

He continued as if she hadn't interrupted. "—my feelings for you have not changed. No matter what happens, I will find a way for us to be together, to marr—"

"Let it go, Dekanawida."

He frowned out at the battlefield for a long time, watching the burial teams. The Standing Stone People were piling the dead near the Bur Oak Village palisade. The mound was already three or four deep.

Finally, he softly asked, "Are you sure?"

"I have to be."

He bowed his head, and seemed to be mustering his strength. At last, he said, "If you ever need me or . . . or want me . . . send word. I'll be there as soon as I can."

The Flint burial teams had lifted the litters and were carrying them toward the war party. They were almost ready to leave. She said, "And if you are ever really in trouble, Dekanawida, you know I'll be there."

He balled his fists at his sides. "Yes."

Their gazes locked. Both desperate. Both at a loss for anything else to say.

She petted Gitchi's big head one last time, and smiled when he wagged his tail. "Please tell Tutelo I love her."

"I will."

The hardest thing Baji had ever done was to nod, turn her back on him, and stride away.

She did not glance back. It would have been a small selfish act that would have given him hope.

Seven

Sky Messenger

My heart slams against my ribs as I watch her walk away.
Dreams die with each step.

"Come, Gitchi," I whisper.

I stride back to Bur Oak Village with Gitchi trotting slightly
ahead. Hearing my Flint name, Dekanawida, and touching
her, have left me feeling wounded and dazed. Everything
inside me shouts to go after her, that if we have more time
to talk, we will find a way to be together. But my feet resolutely do not turn from their path. They carry me down the
hillside, through the dead grass, and out into the corpse-
filled meadow east of Yellowtail and Bur Oak villages. As
Elder Brother Sun edges higher into the sky, he casts shadows behind each frosty body. Like dark fingers, they im-
ploringly reach for the villages, or perhaps to their relatives
who walk the battlefield. To the west, beyond the burned
villages, snow creates a patchwork beneath the leafless
maples and sycamores that rise and fall like dove-colored
waves.

My shoulder muscles contract, bulging through my shirt.
Almost all the warriors of the Standing Stone nation lie dead

upon the grassy plain just beyond Reed Marsh. Thousands. Their frozen bodies create a rumpled blanket of small white humps. No mourners have ventured out that far to search for loved ones, but they will, soon.

I follow Gitchi, veering around two teams carrying burial litters piled high. As the morning warms, Wind Woman blows the snow across the battlefield like a low sunlit haze. It mixes with the acrid black smoke rising from the smoldering village palisades, smoke on its way to the Sky World where it will deliver knowledge of the battle to the Blessed Ancestors.

Weeping mourners flow around me like phantoms, averting their gazes. When they do accidentally meet my eyes, they quickly bow and look away. Soft reverent murmurs carry as I pass, which makes me feel hollow. They have known me since I was a child. They watched me grow up, become a deputy war chief, and transform into what I am today. Or, rather, what I became yesterday afternoon: something alien, not quite human. A man to fear. I myself have not yet come to grips with the freak storm. How can I expect them to treat me differently?

I put my head down and walk straight for Bur Oak Village. Though the exterior palisade has mostly been repaired, the inner palisades are little more than a collection of flimsy blackened logs, leaning against one another, ready to topple at any instant. Our People believe that the souls of lost warriors move into trees, and it is these trees that we cut for palisade logs, thereby surrounding our villages with standing warriors. I ache for these lost souls. They must feel as though they, too, failed in their duty to protect the People.

Reed Marsh is alive with birdsong. Snow coats the cattails. They are glistening white stalks in a sea of shallow blue water. I can make out the largest birds that perch upon the stems. Hawks. They sway in the cold breeze, hunting the marsh for breakfast.

Voices drift from inside Bur Oak Village. The council is still in session, awaiting my return. I pick up my pace. Wampa guards the gate. She has seen twenty-four summers and wears a slate gray cape decorated with brown spirals. A war club is tucked into her belt, but she also carries a bow and quiver slung over her left shoulder. She has already cut her black hair in mourning—as I will do later today. It hangs in irregular locks around her oval face, highlighting her wide mouth and narrow lips . . . which press tightly together as I approach.

I ask, "How is the council proceeding?"

A dusting of dark gray ash continues to fall, coating the snow. Gitchi trots through the gates ahead of me and into the plaza, where he stands looking back, waiting.

Unlike the mourners, Wampa stares straight at me, but there is curiosity behind her gaze, as though she's not quite sure how to respond to me. Me. A friend of more than fifteen summers. Guardedly, she says, "I haven't heard much shouting. That's a good sign."

"Generally, yes. Though this morning I think it's because no one has the strength to shout. We're all still staggering about like ducks hit in the head with rocks."

As I try to pass by, Wampa grips my sleeve to stop me, and whispers, "Sky Messenger, tell me the truth."

The warriors on the catwalk above us stop, and start to gather, seeking to listen to our conversation. Four men and two women, bows and quivers slung over their shoulders, look down at us.

"I know very little, Wampa. The council hasn't decided—"

"We lost around three thousand warriors yesterday. What are we going to do? There are barely three hundred trained warriors left in the entire Standing Stone nation. The rest are children and elders barely strong enough to draw back—"

"That is what the council is discussing, Wampa. Give them time."

With a faint tinge of panic in her voice, she says, "I've heard that Chief Atotarho still has four thousand warriors. Four thousand of the eight thousand he started with. Do you think that's true?"

The catwalk erupts with the low hiss of conversations.

Reluctantly, I nod, and Wampa swallows hard.

"That's the best estimate we have. Two thousand of his warriors were from Coldspring, Riverbank, and Canassatego villages—the villages that made peace with us. And we think another two thousand died in the battle. That leaves four thousand. Our scouts tried to count the warriors still alive as they fled through the forest yesterday, but no one knows how accurate that number is."

She releases my sleeve and slowly lowers her hand to rest on the hilt of the war club tucked into her belt. "Even if the true number is half that . . ."

She doesn't have to finish. We both know what it means.

I fold my arms across my chest and stare down at her with my brows lowered. "The great warrior woman hasn't given up, has she?"

"Of course not. We're going to survive this. I just don't have the faintest idea how. The Flint People are leaving"— she flings a hand in the direction of Baji, but I dare not look— "and I've heard that Zateri's faction of the Hills People will also be heading home to their villages. It's foolish for us to remain here. Maybe we should abandon Bur Oak and Yellowtail villages and go with them?"

I shake my head. "That notion has already been entered into the council, Wampa. Chief Yellowtail suggested it, and High Matron Kittle objected. Despite our hasty battlefield alliance with Matron Zateri's faction yesterday, Kittle does not trust the Hills People. She said our newfound alliance is too uncertain, and that if we move there and they change their minds, we will be surrounded by enemies. There are so few of us left, we can't risk it."

"Then perhaps the Flint People? Chief Cord—"

"He is a good friend, yes. But our alliance with the Flint People is just as precarious. While Cord may continue to support us, we have no way of knowing what the other Flint matrons or chiefs will do once they hear that our nation was almost exterminated yesterday. They may use it as an opportunity to finish the job."

Her eyes narrow as she gazes out across the misty battlefield. She is a tough warrior. I have seen her prowess in battle. But despair touches her words: "Then we are alone."

The warriors on the catwalk are silent.

On this dreadful day, only Wind Mother's song through the marsh hallows and heals. We all seem to be listening to it.

I straighten my shoulders and, with a confident nod, say, "Others will join us. I give you my oath. Though the gods know, befriending the Mountain People is going to take a strong stomach."

Wampa laughs. Before Atotarho came to power and changed the Hills People, the Mountain People were the most unfathomable, contrary, and brutal People in the land. It's inconceivable that the Standing Stone nation and the

Mountain People could ever be friends. Nervous chuckles eddy across the catwalk. On the war trail, when things looked hopeless, I was always able to make my warriors laugh. I laugh, too, joining them.

"That's the old Sky Messenger talking," Wampa says softly, for my ears alone. "He was one of the finest warriors in the Standing Stone nation. But I think he is gone. I heard Matron Jigonsaseh talking this morning. She says you have given up your weapons for good. So while many of us will be fighting to the death for our people . . . you will not."

Her words are not an accusation, but a subtle question. "My duty rests elsewhere, old friend. I must gather more allies for our cause—the cause of peace. If I march into the villages of the People of the Landing or the Mountain People with a war party at my back, or a war club in my hand, my message will ring hollow. They will not listen to me. I must go alone . . . and unarmed."

She glances up at the warriors gazing down upon us, judging their expressions. "You'll be killed on sight, Sky Messenger. We have, after all, been slaughtering their people, burning their villages, and stealing their families for slaves for generations."

"They may kill me. But if they don't, and I have a chance to speak honestly with their councils, I believe I can win them to our side."

Wampa utters a disbelieving grunt. "You are either deluded or a very great Dreamer."

"I'm hoping for the latter."

The catwalk erupts in laughter again.

Wampa smiles and points through the gate to the council house. "Go on. I've delayed you long enough. The council needs you."

Before I pass by, I grip her shoulder hard and stare into her dark eyes. "My Dream is true, Wampa. We must make peace with our enemies, or we are all doomed. I . . ."

My voice fades as the vision blossoms behind my eyes and consumes my world.

. . . An amorphous darkness rises from the watery depths and slithers along the horizon like the legendary Horned Serpent who almost destroyed the world at the dawn of creation. Strange black curls, like gigantic antlers, spin from the darkness and rake through the cloud-sea—

"Sky Messenger?" Wampa shakes me.

I snap from the vision and return with a gasp. The sunlight is so bright it hurts. "S-sorry. I-I'm sorry."

I close my eyes for a moment, trying to see nothing, not this world, not the world of the vision. Just nothing. Still, somewhere inside me there is brilliance . . . *and I'm falling . . . tumbling through nothingness with the flowers of the World Tree, made of pure light, fluttering down around me—*

"Are you all right?" Wampa asks. "You were there, weren't you? When the sky splits and Elder Brother Sun flees into the dark hole in the sky, leaving the world to die?"

I rub my eyes, nod.

Wampa edges closer and hisses to me, "I believe you. So do our warriors. We all believe. Just tell us how to help you make peace, and we'll do it. Even if we have to eat at the same fire as those accursed Mountain People."

I suck in a breath, and the smoke from the smoldering palisades stings the back of my throat. "You're a good friend, Wampa. When I know what to ask, I will. Thank you."

From the catwalk, a man says, "We believe you, Sky Messenger." A woman adds, "We won't let you down, Sky Messenger." More voices rise.

I look up into their blazing eyes, eyes alight with faith in me, and their hope is suddenly like a cape of iron around my shoulders. It is I who cannot let them down.

I give them a confident nod, lift a hand, and walk through each of the three gates in the palisades. When I step into the village, Gitchi falls into step beside me.

Refugees from destroyed Standing Stone villages crowd the plaza. In the entire Standing Stone nation, there are only two villages left now, Bur Oak and Yellowtail, and they almost ceased to exist yesterday. Lean-to shelters line the entire eastern wall. Children race in front of them with dogs trotting at their heels. Every child is half-starved. Their bellies are distended. Bars of ribs press against thin leather shirts and dresses. High Matron Kittle had to send food to every Standing Stone village last autumn, and even to one Hills village that requested help: Sedge Marsh Village.

In an unfathomable twist of fate, the deaths of over three thousand warriors yesterday suddenly means we have plenty of food. Ordinarily, we would survive by raiding other nations, taking food, slaves, and other necessities. After yesterday's battle, we no longer have to do that. To keep it safe, we have hundreds of caches of food buried in wooden barrels in the forest nearby. It will be enough to last until next summer. Soon, these starved faces will fill out and the children will smile and play again . . . unless we are raided and our caches discovered and stolen.

Because High Matron Kittle fears this, she'll ration food for moons.

I gaze around the plaza at the adults clustered in groups, talking. Desperation lines their faces.

I pass by without a word, heading for the council house where it squats to the left of the central plaza bonfire. The bonfire burns in the very center of the village. As I walk, I glance to my right at the Deer Clan longhouse, Kittle's longhouse, then the Hawk Clan longhouse. The houses are constructed of pole frames covered with elm bark. Their arched roofs soar forty hands high. Straight ahead, to the south, the longhouses of the Wolf and Snipe clans stand. Every roof has been burned through in several places. Many of the bark walls are blackened. Once the palisades have been fully repaired, the clans will begin repairing and rebuilding the longhouses. That is, unless the council decides we should abandon these villages and throw ourselves on the mercy of our neighbors. If we beg to be adopted into another nation, the Standing Stone People will cease to exist.

None of us can bear the thought.

I stride for the council house door. Just before I enter, I say, "Gitchi, I want you to stay here. Guard the door to the council house."

He obediently drops to his haunches, and vigilantly begins studying each person who passes by.

The leather curtain over the entry billows in the breeze, and a rush of warm air envelops me. I shiver and duck past the curtain into the house. As I do, a hush descends. After the brilliant sunlight, my eyes need time to adjust to the firelit darkness. I see only the faint curve of the house walls, hundreds of black shapes, and orange flames.

Jigonsaseh, the village matron of Yellowtail Village, and my mother, calls, "Please join us, Sky Messenger."

I blink, trying to hurry my eyes, and see the rings of benches that encircle the fire in the middle of the house. Each person and clan has a place. The Ruling Council of the nation, composed of six clan matrons and the High Matron, Kittle, sit on the innermost ring, nearest the fire.

The next ring is reserved for village chiefs, war chiefs, and visiting matrons. The outermost ring is crowded with Speakers. Each of the five villages in the Standing Stone nation has four Speakers, elected representatives who convey group decisions and ask questions on the group's behalf. The Speakers for the Warriors cluster on the north side of the outer bench. The Speakers for the Women are on the east bench. The Speakers for the Men sit to the west. The Speakers for the Shamans fill the south bench. The rest of the house is open. Anyone from any village who wishes to listen to the council's deliberations may attend these meetings. Today, people line the walls, packed shoulder-to-shoulder. As my eyes grow accustomed to the firelight, I see that every head is turned in my direction.

Mother and High Matron Kittle stand together before the Ruling Council. Both watch me as I weave through the benches to reach them.

The sacred False Face masks, representing the Faces of the Forest who control sickness, perch high upon the walls. Their empty eye sockets capture the firelight and seem to glow. Carved by expert hands, they are made of wood, feathers, human hair, cedar bark, shell, and fur. They have bent noses and crooked mouths. Each is alive—watching and listening to the puny affairs of men. Their Powers come from the Spirit creatures who live in the forests, the air, and under water.

My gaze clings to the Doorkeeper Mask. It represents the Spirits who dwell at the rim of Great Grandmother Earth. Long black hair drapes over the red forehead and black chin, making the bent nose protrude from between the silken strands. The whistling mouth sucks sickness from wounded bodies and blows it into the Sky World where Elder Brother

Sun burns it to ashes that are then used to purify the sick or scare away evil Spirits.

"Are the Flint People headed home?" Mother asks. She has seen thirty-nine summers and is very tall, as tall as I am, twelve hands. Short black hair, streaked with silver, frames her oval face. She has a narrow nose and full lips. Through the fine doehide leather of her white cape—painted with black bear paws—muscles bulge. She was once a great war chief. She still practices with her bow and club every day. Despite the fact that she is now a village matron, yesterday she led the Yellowtail warriors into the fight.

"They are," I answer, and move to stand at her side before the flickering fire.

"I pray their journey is safe and they arrive home to find all is well." Mother turns to the matrons on the second ring of benches. "When will the Hills People be leaving?"

Matron Zateri rises, and I spot Hiyawento, who sits on the bench next to her, his arm around his eight-summers-old daughter, Kahn-Tineta. Just seeing Hiyawento and Zateri, knowing they are here, soothes me. Because of the horrors we endured together as children, we are inextricably linked. They live inside me as much as my own souls do.

Zateri smoothes her hands on her buckskin cape. She is just twenty-two summers old, short and girlish. From the back, she is often mistaken for a child. Her two front teeth stick out slightly. To those who do not know her, she appears frail and weak. Slowly, with precision, she says, "I have discussed the issue with Matron Kwahseti of Riverbank Village and Matron Gwinodje of Canassatego Village. We will be leaving as soon as we have identified and collected the bodies of our warriors from the battlefield. Hopefully, we'll be gone by midday."

Matron Kwahseti stands up beside Zateri. She is thirty-five with gray hair. "Please understand, we do not wish to leave you. We know how many warriors you lost yesterday before we entered the fight on your side, but we fear our own home villages will be Atotarho's next targets. We must make certain our relatives are safe."

High Matron Kittle turns, and firelight sheaths her beautiful face, reflecting from her large dark eyes and perfect nose. Even at forty-four summers, she is renowned as the most beautiful woman in the Standing Stone nation. She does not wear a cape, just a smoked elkhide dress, painted around the collar with yellow hawk wings, that molds to every curve. "We understand, but could you possibly leave a few hundred of your warriors with us, as a symbol of the new alliance between our two nations?"

"As you know, Sindak and his forty warriors asked to remain to help you," Zateri answers. "We approved their request."

"Yes, but we need more, High Matron."

Kwahseti, Gwinodje, and Zateri whisper together.

I search the gathering. Where is my betrothed, Taya? She must be here. Because she is only fourteen, a woman of no position, she cannot sit on the reserved benches. But somewhere out in the crowd, she must be watching me. While I do not see Taya, I do see my sister, Tutelo. She stands with her arms crossed over her chest, her gaze fixed upon me. Mourning hair drapes irregularly around her pretty face. Where are her young daughters? Perhaps they remained in the Bear Clan longhouse, speaking to their dead father, saying good-bye.

Zateri turns away from the other Hills matrons to gaze at

me. "Sky Messenger, have you Dreamed anything about the next few days?"

I spread my arms. "You know my Dream, Zateri. Whether it will come true tomorrow or next summer, I cannot say."

"But you haven't Dreamed anything specific about any of our villages?"

"No."

"Then we must assume the worst." Kwahseti exhales hard.

Murmuring passes along the walls as speculations fill the council house.

Kittle holds up a hand, and the voices die down. "Please, continue, High Matron Zateri."

Zateri hesitates before she says, "We have a great deal to do when we get home. We have decided that we must combine our villages so that we may protect each other. Coldspring Village and Riverbank Village will be moving to join Canassatego Village, since it is the farthest away from Atotarho Village. We dispatched messengers last night, instructing our villages to pack up and move as soon as possible. But our children and elders will make it slow-going. Once they arrive, they will still be very vulnerable. And they must pack and transport every kernel of corn they have."

Kwahseti adds, "You know how many warriors Chief Atotarho still has. After yesterday's battle, between our three villages, we possess only around two thousand warriors. One thousand five hundred are here. In addition, we left a total of around five hundred at home to protect our three villages. They will have to hold off any attacks upon Canassatego Village until we arrive. Atotarho will destroy our families if he can."

Zateri says, "We're sorry, High Matron Kittle. We've already discussed this possibility. We would leave a contingent here if we could, but we honestly can't spare a single person at this point in time. However, when we have secured our new village, we give you our oaths that we will send you warriors. We don't guarantee that there will be many, but we will send as many as we can."

Kittle clamps her jaw. "How long will that be?"

"Perhaps ten days. Fifteen at most."

Kittle boldly looks around the council house, meeting each person's gaze, as though silently assuring them that they can survive until then. She projects a confidence that, at terrible times such as these, seems to calm the world. When her gaze returns to Zateri, she says, "We are deeply grateful for what you did yesterday. Without your help, the entire Standing Stone nation would have been wiped from the face of Great Grandmother Earth. We are in your debt. As you journey, we pray Sodowegowah does not see your faces."

Sodowegowah is the harbinger of death. Once he sees your face, you cannot escape.

"Thank you, High Matron," Zateri responds with a nod and asks, "May we ask, High Matron, what you plan to do? Will you move, or stay to fight? You know, of course, that my father is already planning to attack you again."

Kittle turns to gaze into Matron Jigonsaseh's eyes. Mother gives her a stony look. I know that look. They must have argued about this issue. Mother did not agree with the decision, but she will back Kittle no matter what.

Kittle runs a hand through her black hair, and replies, "We will stay and fight."

Dire whispers move through the people standing along

the walls. They shift like a herd of deer, shying at a strange sound, preparing to flee.

I say, "High Matron, may I address the council?"

Kittle's head dips. "Of course."

My gaze locks with Hiyawento's. He is War Chief of Coldspring Village in the Hills nation, and my oldest and dearest friend. The first time he saved my life, I'd only seen eleven summers. He has chopped his black hair short in mourning for his two murdered daughters. His eagle-like face, with its beaked nose, shines in the firelight. When the end comes, he will be there. I have seen it. He is with me when the Great Face shakes the World Tree and Elder Brother Sun flies away into a black hole in the sky. I lift my chin and in a loud voice, announce, "I will be leaving, as well. I—"

"*What?*" Matron Kittle shouts. "Are you insane? I forbid it! We need every warrior now!"

Mother's gaze is upon me, stern, unblinking. "Please, let him finish, Kittle."

Kittle glares at Mother, then flicks a hand at me. "Finish."

The crowd rustles as people shove to get closer, to hear me better. My gaze remains locked with Hiyawento's. Despite his grief, Power lives in his eyes. He is the strongest man I've ever known. He nods to me, as though encouraging me to continue. He knows the Dream, and knows the end is swiftly rushing toward us.

As I draw breath, something catches my attention in the rear of the house. Gitchi noses aside the door curtain. As the wolf's lean body slides into the council house, a dark form follows him. The figure's black cape flares around his legs. The old, tarnished copper beads that ring his collar flash azure in the firelight. He has his hood pulled up, but when he turns to look at me, the blood drains from my body, leaving me light-headed. Inside, where his face should be, it is empty. Just a black oval, darker than his black hood. It is as though I'm staring straight into a bottomless obsidian abyss. Gitchi remains by the entry, but Black Cape slips through the crowd. As he moves, he doesn't seem to be tethered to the ground, but floating above it.

I force myself to look away, knowing he will find me soon enough.

I say, "Chief Atotarho has refused to make peace, but there are other potential allies out there. I wish to go to the People of the Landing to ask them to join our peace alliance. I will not leave until they agree. Then I will proceed to the People of the Mountain, and perhaps even venture into the Islander's Confederacy north of Skanodario Lake."

The silence is so powerful it has an ominous presence. Only the crackling fire disturbs the council house.

Kittle breaks the spell. "Are you so anxious to throw away your life? We need you here! If nothing else, you can wander among the People repeating your vision to give them hope. As High Matron of this nation, I refuse to—"

Mother reaches out and touches Kittle's hand, urging her not to continue this tirade. "As part of the Ruling Council, I will cast my voice to allow Sky Messenger to walk among the other nations, seeking peace. If he fails, we are no worse off than we are today. But if he succeeds—"

"He won't succeed!" Old Matron Daga, from the destroyed White Dog Village, blurts as she rises on spindly legs. Toothless, with snowy hair, she has a fierce expression. "The Landing People despise us as much as we do them. If Sky Messenger goes to them begging for peace, they will see it as a sign of weakness and attack us faster than lightning! I agree with High Matron Kittle. I will not approve this peace mission." The way she says "peace" makes it sound like a curse. She sits back down and glowers at me.

On the third ring of benches, to the west, a man stands up. I can't see his face, but I know the way he moves. My father, Gonda, says, "May I be recognized, High Matron?"

Kittle nods.

Gonda hesitates for a moment, before he says, "I have spoken long and hard with my son. I may not agree with his method, but I understand his goal. Sky Messenger is no longer a deputy war chief. Instead, he has become a peace chief. One man, more or less, will make no difference to our survival here. I beseech the council to approve his mission."

Conversations erupt across the house, forcing High Matron Kittle to lift her hands and shout, "Silence! This council is in session. Is there anyone else who wishes to address this matter?"

"I do." Hiyawento rises. His gray cape, still blood-soaked from yesterday's battle, sways around his tall body. His lean face is haggard. He turns all the way around, letting the crowd see him, and know him. He was born in Yellowtail Village. When he left to marry the Hills woman, Zateri, he was declared Outcast and a traitor. Yesterday, when Hiyawento and Zateri turned their forces against Atotarho's army, they became the stuff of legend, heroes whose names will forever be spoken with reverence throughout the Standing Stone nation.

Hiyawento calls, "I have already discussed what I am about to tell you with Matrons Zateri, Kwahseti, and Gwinodje, and they have approved my request. As War Chief, I must lead my People home and make sure they are safe, but if this council approves Sky Messenger's mission, I will finish my duties at Coldspring Village, and meet him on the trail to the east of Shookas Village. I—"

A mixture of clapping and cheers rumbles through the house.

High Matron Kittle lifts both hands and holds them in the warm firelit air until the disturbance dies down. Her beautiful face has gone somber. Firelight makes the yellow hawk wings around her collar appear to flutter. She says, "I assume that the assembled Hills matrons believe in Sky Messenger's mission?"

Zateri answers, "We do, High Matron."

Gonda calls, "If you please, High Matron, may I say that I think it will make an impression on the Landing People when representatives from both the Standing Stone nation and the Hills nation approach them about peace."

Nods go through the chiefs and matrons, and spread to the crowd.

I dip my head to Hiyawento, thanking him. He gives me a small smile. We both know the Dream. We must face it together. I only wish Baji was going with us. If we had a Flint War Chief along, our peace delegation would be even more impressive.

Just the thought of her leaves my heart beating a dull staccato in my chest.

Blessed Ancestors, I need her. She is my strength.

Father continues, "I would ask one other thing, if I may?"

"What is it?" Kittle says coldly. She appears anxious, eager to end this council meeting so that village repairs can continue. She must be terrified every instant that we're already being surrounded.

"I would ask that when Sky Messenger and Hiyawento decide to head for the country of the Mountain People—"

"If they make it that far," Kittle says ominously.

"Yes, if they do, I wish to be allowed to go and meet them there. Other than Atotarho, I believe the Mountain People will be the greatest obstacle to our alliance, and I may be able to help win them to the side of peace."

Mother's face tenses. She takes a step toward Father before she catches herself. They have been divorced for twelve summers, and Father's new wife, Pawen, is standing in the crowd behind him. Mother says, "Gonda, you know as well as I do that Yenda has been made Chief of Wenisa Village. Surely you do not expect to—"

"I do, in fact." Father smiles broadly. "I'm looking forward to sitting across the fire from my old enemy—the man who destroyed Yellowtail Village twelve summers ago—and discussing peace."

"He will laugh in your face," Mother warns.

"Perhaps. Nonetheless, I understand him. I've fought against him often enough that I believe I know how he thinks, and therefore, I may be of use."

Kittle massages her forehead. This must seem bizarre to her. She is desperately worried that the Standing Stone nation is on the brink of destruction, and she has three fools who, instead of planning to defend their decimated villages, wish to trot out, preaching peace to neighboring nations.

Kittle says, "There are two requests before the council. How do you cast your voices?"

Matron Daga immediately says, "No."

Mother votes, "Yes."

One by one, every other matron votes yes, including High Matron Kittle.

Kittle returns to Matron Daga. While the vote was being taken, Chief Yellowtail has been speaking with her in a low calm voice, perhaps explaining the benefits. Her elderly face has gone from fierce to resigned. She lifts her hand and calls, "High Matron, if you please."

"Yes, Matron Daga?"

"As Chief Yellowtail has pointed out to me, we should all be united on this issue. If Sky Messenger, Hiyawento, and Gonda can go to the others nations and say that we all agree peace is the way, it will, perhaps, lend more weight to their message. I would, therefore, like to change my vote to yes."

Every person standing along the walls quiets. "Is there any further discussion of this issue?"

No one speaks.

"Very well. We have achieved One Mind of Consensus. Your requests have been approved by the High Council of the Standing Stone nation. Sky Messenger, you may leave any time you wish. Gonda, you will wait until Sky Messenger sends word for you to meet him at Wenisa Village, then you may leave."

Gonda nods his thanks.

"As for the rest of us . . ." Kittle pauses. "We must begin preparing for war."

Kittle gazes out at the crowd. "You all know your assignments. We do not have enough warriors to effectively defend two villages. So, temporarily, the people from Yellowtail Village will be moving into Bur Oak Village. The Snipe Clan and Wolf Clan will get the Bur Oak Village palisades rebuilt as soon as possible, while the Deer Clan fills Bur Oak with water and food. The Hawk Clan will be responsible for making good arrows that fly true, and stockpiling them beneath the catwalks of the three rings of palisades. While the repairs are coming along, the Bear and Turtle clans will be responsible for protecting the villages. Any questions?"

There are none.

"Very well, I fear we haven't much time. This council is dismissed. Let us get to work."

A soft din rises as people begin filing out of the council house.

Kittle stalks past me with barely a glance.

People rise from the benches and filter around me. Over Mother's shoulder, I see Father making his way through the crowd, heading for the exit. Atotarho's former war chief, Sindak, walks at his side. They glance at each other uneasily. It is a strange sight. Less than one-half moon ago, Sindak led the war party that destroyed Father's village, White Dog Village.

Black Cape, whom I call The Voice, since frequently that is all I know of him, is slowly circling the walls of the house, waiting for me. The hair at the nape of my neck prickles. *What does he want? It must be urgent for him to brave the crowds of the council house.*

Tutelo stands alone on the southern wall, beside Gitchi. But she seems to be watching The Voice. A long time ago she named him Shago-niyoh. None of us know his true name.

Mother says, "Are you still committed to this foolishness of going alone into the heart of enemy territory?"

"I am."

"You know, of course, that as soon as Atotarho hears of your mission he will dispatch warriors to murder you."

"Oh, I'm sure of it," I casually reply.

Mother scowls at me. "And you still refuse to carry weapons?"

"When Hiyawento arrives, he will guard me."

"That may be many days."

"I'll be all right."

She shakes her head. "This is a bad decision, my son. I pray the Forest Spirits take pity upon you."

As Mother walks away, following the crowd outside, the black form closes in, and I smell his distinctive scent, as though the odor of ancient destruction clings to his cape.

When only Tutelo, Gitchi, and I stand alone in the council house, The Voice walks straight to me, leans close, and whispers, *"Sodowegowah has seen her face."*

"Who? Whose face?"

As if blown by a wind I cannot feel, his cape billows. He backs away, and gracefully walks out the door.

When he is gone, it takes me a moment before I can manage to get a deep breath into my lungs.

My sister walks forward with Gitchi at her side. Her eyes are tired, tortured. She loved her husband very much. "What did he say?"

"That Sodowegowah has seen her face."

"Did you understand?"

"No." I reach down to stroke Gitchi's gray muzzle. He affectionately licks my hand.

As we walk outside into the morning sunshine, I slip my arm around her shoulders. "How are my nieces?"

"Still sleeping, I hope. It was a hard night for us."

"Baji said to tell you she loves you. She says you're the bravest person she's ever known."

Tutelo looks up. "I wanted so to see her this morning. Is she gone?"

"Yes."

"And when are you leaving, brother?"

"As soon as I've filled my pack, and said good-bye to Taya."

"I didn't see her at the council meeting."

"She wasn't feeling well this morning."

Tutelo slips her arm around my waist and holds me close as we cross the crowded plaza to the Deer Clan longhouse.

Eight

Though afternoon sunlight painted the rolling hills with swaths and streaks of gold, indigo shadows encircled the patches of snow that lingered in the most thickly wooded areas, mostly on the north slopes. War Chief Baji kept searching them, identifying the slightest movement, or shift of colors. Fortunately, the only things she'd seen all day were animals and birds. The rich scents of damp earth and old autumn leaves filled the air.

When the trail curved through a rocky defile, Baji's pace slowed to a walk. Breathing hard, she looked around. Massive gray boulders the size of longhouses piled atop one another here, and extended for perhaps four hundred paces. She turned, saw her deputy, and called, "Dzadi, take four men and scout the top of the rocks."

Deputy Dzadi, a big man who'd seen forty-six summers, lifted a hand, selected his scouts, and trotted away. She watched two men climb up and scamper across the rocks that lined the northern side of the trail. Dzadi and two other warriors took the southern side. Dzadi was out front, searching the boulders for hidden warriors. He was known far and wide for the puckered burn scars that dis-colored his face and muscular arms. He'd been captured by the enemy three times during his life, and escaped each time. He was one of the bravest men she knew, though age was beginning to slow him down. The village warriors had at first voted Dzadi as War Chief, but he had refused the honor, saying he was too old. Instead, he'd thrown his support behind Baji. Afterward, the warriors had over-whelmingly cast their voices to make Baji the new War Chief of Wild River Village.

Baji took the time to untie her belt pouch and pull out a strip of venison jerky. She ripped off a chunk and chewed it slowly. Five hundred warriors slowed behind her, and conversations broke out. She heaved a sigh. As she did, Cord came up beside her and scanned the way ahead. In the distance, the trail ascended a steep hill, rising up out of the valley like a dark serpent.

"What do you think?" she asked her adopted father.

Cord's eyes narrowed. "We're probably safe. The footing on top of the rocks is treacherous, too many gaps and cracks to negotiate, but I'm glad you are vigilant." The black roach of hair that thrust up from the middle of his shaved head had just a touch of silver, and lines etched the flesh across his tanned forehead. Otherwise, he did not look his forty-one summers. The snake tattoos on his cheeks still appeared crisp and detailed, not shriveled with wrinkles. The thick knife scar that slashed his square jaw shone whitely in the winter glare.

Cord said, "How are the wounded faring?"

"Better than I would have thought. Those who can run are managing to keep up. Those who can't have crawled upon the litters, joining the dead, and are being carried.

Tomorrow we'll be able to move a little faster. The litters will be lighter."

As her lean body cooled down, her sweat-soaked war shirt clung to her body, chilling her. She shivered and bit off another chunk of jerky. The meat had been smoked over a hickory fire. The rich tang tasted wonderful. She finished it slowly, then retied her belt pouch.

At the far end of the rocks, she saw Dzadi wave to her, indicting the defile was safe. She nodded to Cord and they broke into a trot again, running side-by-side through the deep shadows. Behind them, the low drone of hundreds of feet beat the air.

As they plunged down the trail between the boulders, Cord said, "Did you come to an agreement?"

"With whom?"

He gave her a disgruntled look—his silent way of asking if she thought him stupid.

Baji sighed. At least he'd waited to ask until afternoon when it didn't hurt so much. "He asked me to go away with him."

"He's leaving?"

"Yes."

"Where is he going?"

"In search of allies. He says we are not alone. There are others out there who agree that the war must end. Others who may wish to join us."

Cord frowned and the snakes tattooed on his cheeks seemed to coil tighter. "He's right. The alliance needs more warriors. As it stands, we have barely half the forces of our enemy."

"And the war has been long and difficult. Every nation south of Skanodario Lake is ripe for harvest. Atotarho knows it. He will not wait for us to move. His own faction of the People of the Hills is starving."

"Every nation is starving, except ours."

Baji looked at him askance. "That's the problem. We have food. You can be certain they'll be coming for it."

They trotted out of the rocks and over the crest of the hill where she gazed down upon the thickly forested valley below. It was all second-growth, dense stands of stubby trees that had invaded after a lightning-caused fire. Blackened stumps and trees still dotted the landscape. Stripped from their branches by the fierce winter winds, leaves had piled knee-deep in the middle of the trail. Her war party would be forced to slog through them.

A finger of breeze tugged hair loose from Baji's long braid and left it hanging in black curls around her sweating face. She brushed it aside. "I don't like the looks of that trail."

"I don't either. Even after we clear the leaves, we'll have to pass through that section where the trees grow so densely they resemble black walls on either side of the path."

Even worse than the trees along the trail, the small valley was rocky and steep-sided. If they were attacked here, there was no place to run. Carefully, she searched the high points for evidence of treachery, but saw only windblown leafless trees.

Baji gestured with her bow. "I'm going to dispatch a party to clear the leaves. That will make it easier going, and give us a warning if someone is hiding in the shadows."

"Good idea. Our warriors will appreciate having time to catch their breaths," Cord said. "You've been pushing them hard."

"I want to get home."

"And, I suspect," he said in a knowing voice, "as far from Dekanawida as you can. But I will miss him. He is a great warrior and a—"

"Was," she corrected. "He *was* a great warrior. He's abandoned his weapons for good."

"Well, that is the way of many Dreamers, though I've never thought it wise."

Baji picked up her pace, pounding down the incline toward the leaf-choked trail where they would temporarily stop. Cord trotted beside her. "I'm worried about him, Father. If he is attacked—and you and I both know he's made himself a target—he has no way to defend himself. He needs a guard, someone to protect him."

Cord laughed softly. "Perhaps you've forgotten the storm yesterday?"

"I haven't." The images had been seared into her souls. "Father, do you really believe he called the storm? Or was it coincidence?" She felt like a traitorous dog asking the question. If she, who loved him more than life, didn't fully believe, did anyone?

"He called the storm, my daughter. I saw it."

She shook her head, not in denial, just uncertainty. "Faith is a hard thing. How do you do it?"

He smiled at her. "Simple. Believing is the doorway to believing."

As they neared the leaves, he slowed to a walk, and the warriors behind them sighed in relief. Laughter broke out, followed by happy voices. Cord said, "Not only that, I believe Dekanawida has Powerful allies in the Spirit World. I met one of them once."

Baji gripped his arm and dragged him to a stop in the

middle of the trail, forcing warriors to flood around her. *"When?"*

Cord tilted his head to a small clearing off the trail, a place where they would not be overheard. She followed him to the sun-splashed meadow, surrounded by maples. Snow glistened at the base of the trunks and frosted the leafless limbs.

She called, "Dzadi, please select a group to clear the leaves from the path and scout the area, then start moving the war party through."

"Yes, War Chief."

Dzadi walked through the warriors, tapping men on the shoulders. In less than twenty heartbeats thirty men had trotted out and begun using their war clubs to beat a path through the deep leaves and scout the forest.

Baji turned to study Cord with sharp black eyes, waiting for him to answer her question. His eyes took on a glazed look, as though remembering.

"Twelve summers ago, that last night when the old woman attacked us on the river. I had followed Odion's path, seen where he'd been captured by her warriors. I was tracking him. I still don't know what to make of what had happened next."

Baji waited. "What did you see?"

"At first? Just a strange ripple, as though the darkness itself was blowing in the wind, then a shine of tarnished copper beads. Finally, a black cape appeared, and a man seemed to coalesce inside it. He glided weightlessly through the trees, apparently also following Odion's steps."

Baji stopped breathing. Her eyes felt like burning coals. "Did you speak with him?"

"Oh, yes," Cord answered with a laugh. "For a long time. I spoke with him twice that night. The first thing he told me was that if I was going to help my friends, I had to hurry, because you were surrounded and outnumbered three to one—"

"Meaning us?"

"Yes, your party was down on the riverbank. When I arrived, I saw War Chief Koracoo . . . sorry. I mean Jigonsaseh . . . I saw her standing facing the evil old woman. You were all surrounded, just as Black Cape had said." He paused to study Dzadi's team. They had managed to knock about half the leaves out of the trail. She couldn't see the scouts. They were probably examining the depths of the forest. "That's when the Spirit came to me again."

"Again? Why?"

He exhaled the words, "It's a long story. I had my bow aimed at the old woman's chest, and he told me that I could not kill her. He said there were many who had claims upon her life, but I was not one of them. He said I didn't have the right. I think he meant that only you, Wrass, Odion, and Tutelo had the right to kill her for what she'd done to you."

Baji had never told anyone the grim details what had happened to her that long ago winter. She didn't want to see it in their eyes when they gazed at her. "Was he handsome? With long black hair and nose bent slightly to the right?"

Cord's eyes narrowed. "How do you know that?"

"Tutelo named him Shago-niyoh. We all saw him."

Cord held her gaze. It was powerful, like wings lifting her. He asked, "What is he? Do you know? Is he one of the Faces of the Forest, or a—"

"I think he's lost, Father. A warrior condemned to wander the earth forever. He helped us escape."

"Why have you never told me this?"

She gave him a lopsided smile. "Why have you never told me of your encounter with him?"

Cord hesitated, as though trying to decide. "I don't know, I wasn't sure anyone would believe me, and I guess I thought it was . . . personal."

Baji untied her water bag from her belt and lifted it to her lips, taking a long drink. The cool water soothed her throat as it went down. She took another greedy swallow, then she handed the bag to Cord, and looked out at the valley again. This area was known as Rocky Meadows for the gray slabs of cap rock that jutted up at odd angles across the flats and along the crests of the surrounding hills. She said, "Shago-niyoh is more than a lost soul. He's Dekanawida's personal Spirit Helper."

"Blessed gods, I knew it. Even that night, I had the feeling the creature was watching over Odion."

When the trail had been mostly cleared, Dzadi waved to the war party, and led the warriors down into the dense tree-lined portion of the trail, kicking up leaves as they went. Almost impenetrable walls of forest lined the trail ahead of them. Their colorful capes and headbands contrasted sharply with the cold shadows. A few men laughed nervously when the trail narrowed and they had to fall into single file.

As he watched their progress, Cord said, "Have you ever seen him again?"

"No." Her gaze remained on her warriors. "Have you?"

"No."

Their war party had gotten too far ahead for her comfort. "Come on. Let's catch up."

Cord's steps pounded behind her.

The leaves on the trail were still ankle-deep and slick beneath her moccasins. They caught up with the party just as it started up the far side of the valley. Hundreds of warriors were stretched out ahead of them, moving like ants up the steep incline in the distance. At the top, dark green pines stood like sentinels.

Baji's gaze lingered on the trees. Wind Woman touched the branches, causing sunlight to flash through the needles.

But there was something . . . odd.

Glitters. In the sunlit air in front of the pines.

"Oh, dear gods!" she shouted. She broke into a dead run, crying, *"Go back! Take cover. Form defensive positions! Run!"*

The shining arrows toppled the first twenty men in line, cutting them down like dry blades of grass beneath a chert scythe. The battlefield roared, its distinctive voice striking terror into her heart—a mixture of shrieks, grunts, and wails. The wounded were crawling, trying to make it to the safety of the—

"Baji!" Cord's heavy body struck her and knocked her to the ground just as arrows cut the air over her head—coming from behind her!

Laughter erupted as enemy warriors flooded from the trees with triumphant grins on their faces. Hills People warriors. She'd seen many of these faces during yesterday's battle. Atotarho's men. They let out whoops and dashed for Baji and Cord.

She glanced at Cord. Blood streamed around the arrow that had pierced his right side. "Stay down, Father!"

In one smooth movement, Baji rolled to her feet, drew an arrow from her quiver, nocked it in her bow, and let fly. Her first arrow lanced through the closest man's heart. She killed two more. The warriors behind them didn't even slow down. They leaped over the dead bodies and charged Baji.

One arrogant fool cried, "My brothers are hunting down your filthy lover right now. I wanted you to know before I crush your skull!"

As her own men tried to rush to her side, the feathered shafts of Hills People arrows streaked past. Her friends went down, some shot as many as four times.

How did my scouts miss this?

Baji tossed her bow aside and jerked her war club from her belt. Spinning low, she slammed the fool's feet out from under him, rose and crushed the second man's chest, and lunged for the third. As she swung for his head, she saw Cord stumble to his feet with his war club in his hand and wade into the onslaught. His distinctive Turtle Clan war cry rang out. Grunts and cries rent the blood-scented air.

As if he were here, fighting at her side, as he had so many times, she heard Dekanawida shout, *Baji, get down!*

And at the far corner of her vision . . . to her left . . . she saw a flash. Just a small glint, but like a rock thrown into a pond, it seemed to leave a wake in the cold air. Baji just had time to leap. . . .

Nine

Blighted as though by perpetual wind, the moonlit slope bristled with tormented shapes: pines with branches on only one side, the twisted trunks of leafless sycamores, rocks scoured as smooth as polished agate. Some of the boulders stood half-again as tall as War Chief Negano, and he was a tall man, lean and muscular, with long black hair. His plain undecorated buckskin cape flapped around his legs as he hiked up the trail through the icy wind.

Across the narrow valley, hundreds of campfires glistened. He could hear the laughter of his warriors, and the hum of conversations. They made a strange contrast to the deep bass notes of the battlefield, where low groans and sobs lilted like perverse music. They had used their clubs to silence the Flint wounded. These cries came from his own people.

Negano had just visited the field where his wounded had been carried. The grasping hands, the pleading voices of men and women who just wanted to be carried home to die so that their families could Requicken their souls in new bodies and they could live again—all of it had made him ill.

When dry leaves crunched behind Negano, he spun around with his war club lifted . . . but all he saw were the glowing white faces in the valley below. Moonlit visages of the Flint warriors they'd slaughtered that afternoon. The valley bottom had been the heart of the ambush, the killing pen. Hundreds sprawled there, a feast for the wolves whose shining eyes winked up and down the valley.

Negano sucked in a breath and let it out slowly.

He should have been ecstatic. His ambush had been perfect! Brilliantly planned and executed.

But on nights like this, he swore he was being tracked by enemy ghosts. He lowered his club, silently berated himself, and turned back to the trail, heading up to where Chief Atotarho camped just below the crest of the hill. Five men, the Chief's personal guards, stood behind the old man.

As he walked, Negano continued to hear footsteps, soft, carefully placed. It took an act of will not to whirl around again.

The Flint People were fighters. It did not surprise him that death would not stop them. Negano's cape was spattered with their gore. In the distance, to the west, he could see the bodies of those who'd made it out of the killing pen and desperately tried to flee. They'd scrambled up the wind-combed hills like terrified rabbits. Few had escaped. Negano had commanded two thousand warriors to Baji's five hundred. The enemy hadn't had a chance.

A twig snapped behind him. Negano instinctively spun on his toes to face his attacker . . . only to see nothing.

Laughter erupted from the Chief's personal guards, and Negano clamped his jaw. Were they laughing at him, or at some joke that had been told?

"You're being a fool," he growled at himself. "Stop it."

At the age of thirty-two summers, Negano had lived with death, and the dead, for so long they rarely left him, waking or sleeping. Somehow, though, tonight was worse than usual. He could feel vast solitudes pressing down upon his lungs, squeezing the air out, and he felt certain Sodowegowah was standing right there, backed by an army of ghosts, all staring him in the face.

Negano cursed himself and marched straight toward where his chief sat on a rock, clutching a long stick in his hand. Atotarho's hunched back looked like a misshapen pack hidden beneath his clothing. When the old man heard him coming, he looked up. The black pits of his eyes, staring out of a cadaverous face, made Negano's belly muscles go tight. They were alive with malice.

Negano called, "It is I, my Chief. Do not be alarmed."

The circlets of human skull that decorated Atotarho's black cape flashed as he prodded his fire with the stick, sending tornadoes of sparks swirling into the cold night air.

He didn't appear to be in good humor. Negano inhaled to prepare himself. He knew perhaps better than anyone, for Negano had been the head of the old man's personal guards until last night. Negano had never had designs on the position of War Chief . . . too much responsibility, too little reward . . . but here he was. No choice now but to try and make the best of things.

Out on the far side of the narrow valley, a group of warriors began singing the Victory Song. Deep and triumphant, their voices swelled over the winter-bare trees. Other warriors joined in, then more, until the valley of the dead echoed with exultation.

Chief Atotarho stopped tormenting his fire to listen. His wrinkled face twitched. He had seen sixty-four summers pass, and had suffered from the joint-stiffening disease for the past twenty. His bent, crooked body pained him constantly. His enemies said it was the Spirits' revenge for his witchery. Negano knew better. The old chief wasn't a witch, but he hired witches, like the frightening Ohsinoh, to do his bidding. In this way, entire villages vanished, poisoned or decimated by strange plagues. No man in the world was feared more than Chief Atotarho . . . except perhaps Sky Messenger. That must be galling the old man.

As Negano approached, he saw the freshly chewed human ribs that lay around the fire pit, cast there by the chief after his teeth had stripped the cooked flesh away. Who had the person been? A chief probably, or maybe a war chief. Possibly the great Cord himself? Atotarho refused to consume lowly warriors.

Atotarho snapped, "What took you so long? I summoned you over one-half hand of time ago."

Negano bowed. "Forgive me, my Chief, I had to check on the wounded. They—"

"In the future, you will come immediately when I call for you."

Negano straightened, confused. "But, my Chief, I am now War Chief. It is my duty to make certain the wounded are being well cared for. When we return to Atotarho Village, their families will wish to know that I did everything possible to—"

"We'll be leaving the wounded here tomorrow. We have other priorities."

Negano stiffened. The words were a slap in the face. It was inconceivable that they would not carry the wounded home to their families as quickly as possible. "I don't understand?"

"That doesn't surprise me. When I divided our forces yesterday, sending two thousand warriors back into Hills country, did you think I did it for no reason?" Atotarho glared at him. As a symbol of his dedication to war, he'd braided rattlesnake skins into his gray hair. They lay in plaits along his sunken cheeks.

"I'm sorry, my Chief," Negano apologized again, "I understood that you wished to punish the rogue Hills villages that had sided with the enemy and fought against us, but I thought that as soon as our group of two thousand had taken care of the Flint war party, we would, naturally, return home."

"In the future, you will not assume. Have you determined how many total warriors deserted after the Standing Stone battle and today's fight with the Flint People?"

"Out of the four thousand that lived and remained loyal to you, only a few hundred. Some went home, but some will certainly return. They're just out in the forest, hunting, getting their bellies full and trying to make sense of what happened. They'll be back. Yesterday, when Zateri, Gwinodje, and Kwahseti betrayed us and joined the enemy, I think many of our warriors could not bear the thought of killing their own relatives. Then when Sky Messenger called that monstrous storm . . . a few fled to join the enemy, including War Chief Sindak. Gods, while I do not agree with Sindak's actions, I understand his reasons. It was like watching one of the great heroes at the dawn of creation."

The awe in Negano's voice seemed to anger the old man. Atotarho's teeth ground beneath the thin veneer of wrinkled skin that covered his jaw. In a thin reedy voice, he asked, "Fortunately, he'll soon be dead. Providing you followed my orders and dispatched warriors to hunt him down?"

"I did so last night. If they managed to slip by Jigonsaseh's scouts, they should have arrived at Bur Oak this morning and have been watching for him."

Atotarho used one of his clawlike hands to massage his aching knee. "I want every deserter hunted down and killed, starting with Sindak."

"Of course. I thought that once we'd carried the wounded home, we would—"

"We're not going home."

Negano blinked, as though clearing his eyes would make it easier to grasp this latest lunacy. His gaze sought out the chief's personal guards, standing in a group five paces away. They'd been listening to his conversation with the chief, and now stared at Negano as though expecting him to do something about this madness. After all, he was War Chief. The wounded must be carried home. It was his duty to explain these facts to the Chief.

The new leader of the Chief's personal guards, Nesi, sharply dipped his head toward Atotarho, urging Negano to say something. Nesi was a big, square-jawed giant with a heavily scarred face. He had seen forty summers pass. A decade ago, Nesi had been the War Chief of Atotarho Village. He understood Negano's new duties better than Negano did.

Negano braced his feet. "My Chief, as you well know, our warriors have fought two hard battles in as many days. They're exhausted. Many of their friends and family members are injured. Some are dying. Our warriors expect to take them home where they can be properly cared for."

Atotarho calmly rested his stick across his lap, and sternly repeated, "I told you, we are not returning home."

"Do you plan to remain here until the wounded can travel?" It was the only reason he could think of.

"At dawn, we're going back to Bur Oak and Yellowtail villages."

When Negano cast a glance at Nesi, the giant frowned and shook his head; he was just as confused as Negano. Negano said, "Do you plan to attack those villages again?"

Wolves got into a fight over one of the bodies in the killing pen, and a snarling, growling cacophony arose. Negano could see eyes coalescing around the pair that fought, creating a jewel-like silver ring. The battle lasted barely ten heartbeats before one of the wolves yelped and whimpered away.

Atotarho waited for the commotion to die down. "I wish you to dispatch a messenger tonight to the new High Matron of our nation. Inform Kelek that we will remain in Standing Stone country for another half-moon, perhaps even a moon. That should be long enough. Also, after our war parties have destroyed the traitorous villages, she should immediately dispatch two thousand warriors back to Bur Oak Village to aid us."

"Very well."

"I also wish you to dispatch messengers under white arrows to carry the news of our great victory to other nations. Have them say that the Standing Stone nation is on the verge of extinction, and we are about to assure it." He aimed a crooked finger at Negano's heart. "I especially wish messengers to be sent to the Mountain People. Tell them that if they wish to ally with us for a few days, we will be able to exterminate the Standing Stone nation even faster."

"I doubt they'll accept, my Chief. They hate us. Even if they do accept, it will take them seven or eight days to arrive."

Atotarho just stared at him.

"I'll dispatch the messengers immediately. Now, Chief, if we may, I'd like to return to our former discussion. What will we be doing in Standing Stone country for another moon? How will we feed our warriors while camping in a winter forest?"

Negano waited for an explanation of how he planned to use their current force of one thousand seven hundred warriors, and then another two thousand.

Atotarho did not answer. He'd occupied himself tossing more branches on the fire. Sparks whirled through the air.

"Chief, three thousand seven hundred warriors is a huge force. I ask again, how will we feed them?"

"Now that you know we are not going home, you should start by stripping the Flint bodies of every shred of food they have in their packs, then ration it to our warriors. It will take days for our reinforcements to arrive. By then, I'm sure you will have thought of something to keep the army fed. After all, you are War Chief. It's your responsibility."

When Atotarho offered no further information, Nesi,

who stood where the chief couldn't see him, stabbed his war club at the Chief, insisting that Negano ask the necessary questions to finish the discussion.

Negano sighed and asked, "What is it you wish to accomplish in Standing Stone country, my Chief?"

Atotarho prodded the fire again. The burning logs crackled and spat. Orange light fluttered like huge wings through the nearby pines, and sparks gushed into the darkness. Atotarho lifted his wrinkled face to watch them climb into the Sky World. He appeared to be offering a silent prayer.

When he looked back at Negano, the old Chief murmured, "I plan to teach a lesson none of our enemies will ever forget."

Negano's eyes narrowed. "What lesson? Do you plan to take the Standing Stone villagers hostage? To make them slaves? I'm sure our villages would appreciate being able to increase their numbers, but there are thousands of survivors from the Bur Oak and Yellowtail battle. How will we feed so many on the way home?"

In a low deadly voice, the Chief replied, "We're not going to feed them."

Negano let that sink in. "Very well, but it is my duty to inform you that I believe capturing them will be harder than you perhaps realize. Despite the fact that we have one thousand seven hundred warriors left after this afternoon's battle, the Standing Stone clans will have spent all day repairing their damaged palisades—*and three rows of palisades surround each village,*" he added forcefully, and saw Nesi nod in approval. "They are not fools. We nearly destroyed their entire army yesterday. They must be expecting us to return to finish the job. By the time we arrive, they will be prepared for us. We—"

"Get to your question."

"My Chief, we have less than one-quarter the warriors we did when we attacked yesterday. If we assault their palisades, it will be a long drawn-out struggle. We will lose at least half our current forces, leaving us with perhaps eight hundred. Truly, my Chief, I do not believe it's worth the blood. Our warriors are tired, they wish to go home. Next Spring we can undertake such a campaign with the full force of our army and—"

"Are your ears filled with pine sap?"

Negano shifted. "How have I offended you?"

"We are not going to assault their palisades."

"But how will we get hostages if we do not attack?"

"Oh," he replied in a gloating voice, "they'll walk right out of their gates and into our arms. You see, we're going to starve them to death."

Negano stood perfectly still. The old chief was clenching and unclenching his grotesquely deformed hands, as though ready to twist Negano's head off.

He glanced at Nesi and the former War Chief's stern expression gave him no leeway. Negano said, "My Chief, I feel I must make you understand what's going on in our warriors' hearts. It's not just the wounded and dead that concern them. Yesterday was like a blunt beam swung to their bellies. They are stunned. It appeared to them"— *and to me*—"that Elder Brother Sun obeyed Sky Messenger's commands. He has become a walking, breathing legend. They're terrified of him. Not only that, your own War Chief defected to Sky Messenger's side yesterday."

He spread his arms. "Chief, *your own daughter* fought on Sky Messenger's side. Your daughter!" More softly, he continued, "Your warriors are reeling. They need to think about all this. If you insist that they immediately engage in another battle, they may—"

"Insolent fool!" Atotarho roared in rage. "Pray you don't find yourself staring as your guts come tumbling out of your belly in the middle of the night!"

Negano had no doubt but that his life was in danger. There was more he needed to say, and should say. Instead, he opted to protect his own hide, and bowed deeply. "Forgive me, my Chief. I realize you have not yet finished your plan. When you do, I would appreciate it if you could explain it to me in detail."

Behind the chief, he saw Nesi roll his eyes and throw up his hands. He thought Negano a coward—which is exactly how he felt.

Atotarho ordered, "Leave me. Find and dispatch the messengers as I instructed. If you're still alive, I'll call for you again in the morning."

"Yes, my Chief."

Negano turned and, with as much dignity as he could, walked down the hillside, but he could feel Nesi's stare lancing through the back of his head.

Ten

The high-pitched scream punctured the night, waking Hiyawento from a sound sleep. Instinctively, he leaped to his feet with his war club in his hand. Breathing hard, he frantically tried to identify the threat. An uproar rose as other sleeping warriors threw off their blankets and grabbed for weapons. In less than ten heartbeats dozens of people had gathered around Hiyawento's fire, murmuring, asking questions. Conversations carried on the frigid night breeze.

It took Hiyawento a few instants to hear Zateri say, "Hush, you're all right. We're safe."

He swung around to see his wife holding Kahn-Tineta against her chest. Their daughter clutched Zateri's sleeves in sheer terror, and her huge eyes darted over the darkness.

"But Mother, I saw him! He was right there!" She thrust an arm toward the dense sumacs to the north. Their leafless branches had a spiky appearance.

Their camp stretched over the hilltop like a glimmering blanket, dotted with hundreds of campfires. Though camped close together, each village had separated. Cold-spring Village occupied the southern portion of the hill-top. Riverbank was to the north, and Canassatego Village stood on the highest point to the west. In the distance, to the east, the Forks River twisted through the bottom country like a silver serpent.

Hiyawento held up a hand and called, "Forgive us, please return to your bedding hides. Everything is well."

Warriors muttered and eventually drifted back to their own camps, leaving Hiyawento and Zateri alone with their wildly sobbing daughter. All three of them had cut their hair in mourning over the deaths of little Jimer and Catta, his murdered daughters. As well, they were mourning the passing of the High Matron of the People of the Hills, Zateri's grandmother, Tila.

Virtually no one these days had hair longer than his or her shoulders.

Zateri asked, "Are you better?"

"No!" Kahn-Tineta choked out and buried her face against her mother's cape. "He's still out there."

As the panic drained from Hiyawento's muscles, his heartbeat began to slow, and the feeling of impending doom that had become his constant companion returned. He couldn't seem to shake it. It was as though he could feel Sodowegowah's icy breath upon his cheek.

As he walked toward Zateri, Kahn-Tineta shrieked, "Father! Father!"

She wriggled out of Zateri's arms, and ran to him, her arms up, her fingers working in a "take me, take me," gesture.

Hiyawento lifted her, and her legs went around his

waist. He kissed her hair, and said, "Let's sit down beside your mother."

Kahn-Tineta had her chin propped on his shoulder, and every muscle in the girl's body trembled. He stroked her hair softly. "You're all right," he whispered. "Look around you. The camps are quiet and still."

"The witch is out there, Father! I saw him!"

Hiyawento lowered himself to a cross-legged position on the hides beside Zateri and shifted Kahn-Tineta to his lap where he could look into her wild eyes. "Where did you see him? Show me."

"Right there!" she pointed again. "He sneaked from the trees and was watching me. He's going to get me!"

Zateri gave him a wrenching look. Firelight flickered over her flat face with its wide nose. Her two front teeth, which stuck out slightly, made her lips appear to protrude. She mouthed the word, "Again."

This was the second night in a row that the "witch" had come to Kahn-Tineta in her dreams.

Hiyawento stroked his daughter's back and gazed directly into her dark eyes. "I told you, my daughter, the witch is dead. I killed him. What did I do after that? Do you remember?"

"You dismembered his corpse and scattered the pieces far and wide so that no one could ever find him and Sing him to the afterlife."

"That's right. Dismemberment also immobilizes the angry Spirit of the Dead, so it can't run off seeking revenge."

She sobbed. "But he came back to life, Father! Just like the stories said he would. He can't die! He's still after me."

Zateri folded her arms over her chest, hugging herself, and lifted her face to study the moon-silvered night sky. A few Cloud People drifted across the charcoal background, their edges gleaming. It had only been seven days since they'd left Kahn-Tineta with her grandmother Tila and trotted off to war with the Standing Stone nation. How could they have known that Zateri's father, Atotarho, would hire Ohsinoh to kidnap their last daughter so that he could use the little girl as leverage against them? He was unnaturally canny. Even then Atotarho must have suspected that Coldspring, Riverbank, and Canassatego villages were secretly aligning against him.

"Well, don't worry," Hiyawento said, pandering to her fear. "If he returns, I'll shoot him through the heart and crush his skull again. He'll never get you. I'll—"

"He got me once! He stole me right out of Atotarho Village!"

He adjusted her cape, straightening it around her small body. "Well, I wasn't there to protect you, but I am—"

"Father, I—I wish Sky Messenger was here to protect me."

Hiyawento smiled sadly. "I wish he were here, too. I miss him. But if he were here, do you know what he would tell you about the witch?"

She blinked wide eyes. "What?"

"Sky Messenger would tell you that condemned souls change after death. When souls discover they can never reach the Land of the Dead, they are so overwhelmed with grief, they seek out the comfort of loved ones. Usually, they return to their home villages to move unseen among their relatives. They eat the dregs from the cooking pots—that's why we often hear them rattling for no reason at night. Lost souls take comfort from familiar surroundings. They are too distraught to even think of kidnapping little girls they barely know."

Kahn-Tineta tucked a finger in her mouth and began sucking on it . . . a thing she had not done in five summers, since she was three.

In a firm voice, Hiyawento said, "You're safe, Kahn-Tineta. I give you my oath."

His daughter slowly began to relax in his arms. Her cries became less choked, but still punctuated with occasional sobs.

"Not only that . . ." He reached down to pull the small medicine bag from her cape. It hung around her neck, suspended on a braided leather cord. "Your mother is one of the greatest Healers in the land. She makes powerful Spirit medicines." He held the bag up to his daughter's nose. "What do you smell?"

She sniffed. "Wood nettle and white oak."

"That's right. They can counteract even the most powerful witchcraft. That's why your mother told you never to take this off."

Kahn-Tineta angrily wept. "Why didn't Mother give it to me before you both left to go to war? Maybe the witch wouldn't have gotten me!"

As her fear receded, it was replaced with anger, which was a good sign, but the words seemed to tear Zateri's heart. Tears filled her eyes. She rose. When she ambled over to the fire to place two more branches on the flames, sparks swirled up around her. An orange gleam coated the tears on her cheeks.

"We were just overwhelmed and not thinking right," Hiyawento explained. "It won't happen again."

Kahn-Tineta stared hard into his eyes, as though judging the truth of his words, then her arms went around his neck in a stranglehold, and she pressed her cheek against his. "Give me your oath as a warrior of the Hills nation."

In a deep solemn voice, Hiyawento replied, "On my life, as the War Chief of Coldspring Village, I give you my oath that you will never be alone again. One of us will always be with you to protect you."

She pushed away to stare at him, judging his sincerity. "I believe you."

"I appreciate that." Hiyawento kissed her forehead. "Now, if you'll try to sleep, I'll stand guard."

"Will you? Really?"

"I'll be standing right there." He pointed to the place where Zateri stood by the fire.

Kahn-Tineta rested her head on his shoulder and sighed deeply. "Thank you, Father."

Hiyawento rocked her in his arms until she fell asleep, then he carried her back to her bed and drew the hides up around her throat. When he started to rise, her tiny hand shot out and grabbed his, clutching it. Her eyes were still closed, half-asleep, but she wouldn't let go.

Hiyawento knelt at her bedside, holding her hand until sleep loosened her grip. Only then did he tiptoe away, and walk to the fire to stand beside Zateri.

"She's asleep?"

"Yes. Finally." Unconsciously, he lifted his hand to massage his injured left arm, just below the shoulder, where Deputy War Chief Negano's war club had connected. The bruise ran deep, probably all the way to the bone. The pain was intense.

"Hiyawento, you must sleep tonight. You're hurt and exhausted. I'll find someone else—"

"If she wakes in the night, I want her to see me standing here."

When Zateri gazed up at him with tormented eyes, his own unbearable grief returned. He wrapped an arm around her narrow shoulders and hugged her. "I'll be all right."

Neither of them spoke for a time. Between them lay the indestructible bond of two people who have seen their worlds destroyed, of childhood captivity and torture, of horrific battles, and friends lost . . . and two people who have held beloved children in their arms while they convulsed and died. They had been through so much together, but never before had Hiyawento felt this gut-deep mixture of rage and despair. The emotion was unnatural, even inhuman. It covered everything like an impenetrable black cloak, blotting out the light, draining joy from the very air he breathed.

Out in the forest, branches smashed into each other as Wind Mother's violent son, *Hadui,* beat his way through the trees and dashed across the hilltop battering anything in his path. He appeared to be headed north, chasing after the flocks of moonlit Cloud People. Whirlwinds of old leaves and twigs careened in his wake. As he rushed through the camps, people cursed in surprise and sparks exploded from fire pits. They trailed through the night sky like swirling ribbons.

Zateri asked, "What do you think we're going to find when we make it to Canassatego Village?"

He wasn't sure how to answer that, though he'd been thinking of little else. "The night I killed the witch, he told me we wouldn't make it home in time."

"Gods, I pray that was just bluster." Her eyes reflected the firelight. "Do you think he meant our villages would be destroyed before they could move? If Atotarho did that, our warriors' indignation and rage will be uncontrollable." She sucked in a breath and exhaled hard. "It will mean civil war."

He tossed another branch onto the fire, expecting the night to be long and cold. "We started the civil war, my wife, the instant we ordered our warriors to fight against their own nation. Nothing can stop it now."

Zateri's delicate eyebrows drew together. Thoughtfully, she whispered, "There must be a way."

Eleven

Wind blew Matron Jigonsaseh's hair into her eyes and rattled the wooden beads around her throat. She shoved the strands away, and continued striding across the sunny Bur Oak plaza. She could tell from the sudden gusts and the change in temperature that another storm was coming. They had even less time to complete repairs than she'd thought.

Near the center of the plaza, High Matron Kittle stood observing six warriors who used ropes to pull the new logs into place in the exterior palisade. The men grunted with the effort, and their faces streamed sweat. Autumn had been very rainy, followed by several deep snows. The sodden logs were heavy and unwieldy. The workers struggled to keep them from falling back to the earth and crushing the men beneath.

Jigonsaseh stopped at Kittle's side. Four longhouses arched in a semicircle around them. Lines of men, women, and children filed in and out of each one, carrying pots of water and baskets of seeds, corn, and beans. One woman had dried squash vines around her neck. The squashes, still attached, knocked together as she walked, producing a hollow thumping sound. The villagers wore no capes, just knee-length shirts, dresses, and brightly painted leggings. A light shower of brown autumn leaves pirouetted around them as they worked.

Jigonsaseh counted the number of women carrying water pots. Not enough. She would have to tend to that. They could live far longer without food than they could without water.

Without turning, Kittle asked, "How is our defense?"

"Almost nonexistent. Deploying our warriors outside the palisade is a waste, Kittle. I know that's what the council approved, but—"

"And Wampa?"

Jigonsaseh gauged the hard lines in Kittle's face. There would be no convincing her to shift their forces now. Jigonsaseh sighed, and said, "Though she is the new War Chief of Bur Oak Village, she has no objections to subordinating herself to War Chief Deru for as long as necessary. She knows he has more experience."

"What of our scouts and lines? Is everyone in place?"

Jigonsaseh quietly took a breath and let it out. "Yes, we have scouts in the tallest trees. As for our lines, we have barely enough warriors to encircle the village. Even then, they are so widely spread out they are almost no protection at all. They will perhaps, be able to let one arrow fly before they'll have to turn tail and run for safety. It's a waste of effort. We should pull them all in to defend the village so that when the scouts signal a warning, we'll be ready."

Kittle watched the groaning laborers slowly haul the log, hand-over-hand, into place. Muscles bulged and sweat ran down their faces. When the logs were in place, warriors on the catwalk lashed them to the standing logs, securing them into the palisade. Finally, she said, "That's the last section of the exterior palisade to need repairing, isn't it?"

"Yes."

"Good. They're working fast."

"They'd better. At this rate, we won't even be able to start repairing the longhouses until tomorrow afternoon."

"I know that," Kittle said in a clipped voice.

"We must repair the inner palisades first, then we—"

"*I know.*" Kittle glared up at her, for Jigonsaseh was two heads taller, and an exhausted expression slackened her features. "There's another subject I'd like to discuss with you, and I want you to tell me the bald facts."

"Have I ever done otherwise?"

"No, but we've never been in a position like this before."

Wind tormented her cape until it whipped around her legs in snapping folds. Kittle paused until the gust passed. "If you were Atotarho would you still be in camp, tending your wounded? On your way home? Or on your way here?" A swallow went down her throat. "How much time do we have?"

Jigonsaseh spread her legs and her war club, CorpseEye, swayed where it was tied to her belt. She reached down to wrap her fingers around the smooth polished shaft. It took less than five heartbeats for a tingle of warmth to spread through her palm and up her arm. "Not long, Kittle. He knows how vulnerable we are. However, if he's decided to attack us again, his warriors will be upset, grousing about not being to carry their injured friends and loved ones home. I think he's so crazy now that he doesn't care about tradition or the souls of his dead relatives. I think he'll push this thing to the end."

Kittle's oval face with its perfect nose and large dark eyes sagged. She tucked her shoulder-length black hair behind her ears, and said simply, "I'd give anything for two hands of sleep."

No one in either village had slept well last night. The wails and groans of the wounded had wrung shudders from the very wood of the longhouses. Fortunately, the worst off had died during the night. This morning, the bodies had been carried outside to await the burial ceremony, and the last of the wounded had been moved into the Council House. Constant whimpering and cries filled the air.

Out in the forest a flock of jays burst into flight and soared away amid a riot of squawks and chirps. One of their lines had probably shifted and startled the birds.

Jigonsaseh gazed out through the open gates to her own village thirty paces distant. "How much of Yellow-tail Village has been cleaned out?"

When they'd decided to repair Bur Oak Village and abandon Yellowtail Village, there had been an outcry among Yellowtail villagers. Every chamber in Yellowtail Village was filled with the injured, or dying. Everyone knew that moving them might kill them. It had required great patience for Jigonsaseh to go to each family and convince them that if they were attacked again, it might be the only way to save their children.

"About half, last I heard."

Jigonsaseh's eyes narrowed. "If you do not object, I think I'll take over supervising the evacuation. Perhaps I can speed up the process. As you know, many of my villagers are not happy about this move."

"I would appreciate your help. And"—she exhaled the word—"when that's done, I want you to take over our entire defense."

Jigonsaseh shifted uneasily. "I will if you wish, but I'm not sure that's a good decision. War Chief Deru is perfectly competent to—"

"I know that. I want you up there leading our warriors. They trust you."

She nodded. "Very well."

Kittle's gaze lifted to the sky where Cloud People gathered over the northern hills. The trees visible through the gates had already taken on the curious sheen of stormlight. "We'll have snow by nightfall."

The refugee lean-tos propped against the innermost palisade were falling down. Currently empty, they resembled little more than piles of sticks and bark. Yesterday's miraculous storm had ripped apart every lean-to, and shredded the longhouse roofs, before rolling out into the forest where it tore whole trees from the earth and cast them about like kindling.

Kittle said, "We'll have to find a way to roof those lean-tos before snowfall. What of your villagers? We have no more room in any of our longhouses. Where will your people sleep? Do you plan to have them stay one more night in Yellowtail Village, tending the wounded, until we can—"

"I don't think that's wise. If we're attacked, it will split our meager forces in two. No, we will move the wounded here, as well as the rest of my villagers."

"Where will you move them to?"

"I've ordered the children of the Turtle Clan to collect every sleeping hide in Yellowtail Village. After that, they will gather the branches torn from the trees by yesterday's storm, and bring them here. We'll throw up branch frames and cover them with hides. It will do."

Memories of the black whirling winds yesterday made her think of Sky Messenger. If he'd been running at a good steady trot, by now he should be close to the territorial boundary of the Standing Stone nation. She prayed he was still safe.

"Worried about Sky Messenger?" Kittle said.

"How did you know?"

"Because I'm worried about Taya. After they said goodbye, Taya spent a good two hands of time lying in her hides weeping."

Jigonsaseh frowned. "They barely know each other, Kittle. I hardly think she is pining away—"

"I suspect her emotional mood may mean she carries your son's child."

Jigonsaseh straightened. Sky Messenger and Taya could not marry until she had proven her worthiness by conceiving. If it were true, they could wed as soon as he returned. Jigonsaseh did not know if that fact would please her son. Sky Messenger wanted Baji. Clan politics precluded any such marriage. Perhaps, if Taya was with child, he would finally accept his fate, marry her, and fulfill his duty to his clan.

She said, "At most, your granddaughter is one moon pregnant. Her emotional mood could be nothing more than the aftermath of the battle. Let us wait before we rejoice."

"Agreed."

The wind shifted and the odors of sweating bodies and wood smoke wafted over them. Jigonsaseh evaluated the holes in the inner palisades. At least five or six gaping charred ovals remained. If they didn't replace that burned wood before the next attack came, the enemy would only have to breach the exterior palisade in one place, and they could flood through the entire village.

"Let's talk about the inner palisades. I think we need to reorganize the work so that—"

"That's because you think like a war chief. If you'd been a village matron for summers, you'd realize that food and water will be just as essential when we are attacked. I can't afford to shift anyone now."

Three boys, five or six summers old, dashed by with dogs loping at their heels, laughing as they weaved through the lines of workers. Their faces were sheathed in afternoon gleam. One of the dogs, overeager to play, took a flying leap and knocked the lead boy down. The other two boys saw their chance and piled on top of him, squealing as they wrestled.

Jigonsaseh said, "If you don't wish to shift workers, perhaps we could organize the youngest children to fill water jars."

Kittle didn't answer. Her thoughts seemed far away.

"Did you hear me?"

Kittle blinked. "Don't you think it's odd that none of the surrounding villages have sent runners to inquire about our welfare? They must have seen the smoke from our burning villages yesterday morning. At least a few runners should have arrived by dawn today."

"Perhaps they fear Atotarho's army is still here."

"Nonsense. Any responsible matron would have sent at

least one man to sneak in, take a look, and hightail it
home with the news. Don't they care if we're alive or
dead?"

"Perhaps they are more afraid of being attacked themselves, and are keeping every warrior inside their palisade
walls."

Kittle fumbled with her shell bracelets, rearranging
them. They clicked. "But we also haven't seen that odious
little Trader, Tagosah. He's always here showing off his
latest trinkets around the first day of the moon. He's never
late."

"Rarely late. Not never. Don't exaggerate."

Jigonsaseh studied the warriors on the catwalk. Their
gazes were fixed on the scouts who stood in the tallest
trees, searching for threats. No alarm had been given. They
hadn't even signaled that a lone passerby approached.

"There's another thing I wish for you to consider, Kittle. Once everyone has cleared out of Yellowtail Village,
we should dismantle it. We need stronger logs for the interior palisades, and we must build more housing in Bur
Oak Village. More important, we don't want our enemies
to capture it."

Kittle heaved a breath. "You're right. The last thing we
need is to have Hills warriors lining the palisade of Yellowtail Village and shooting into Bur Oak Village. Very
well, I will leave it to you to tear down your own village."

A strange silence caught her attention. Her right hand
unconsciously tightened around CorpseEye while she
searched the longhouse roofs and leafless branches of the
surrounding trees. "There are no birds."

"Hmm? What?" Kittle stared at Jigonsaseh as though
her soul were loose.

Jigonsaseh's senses abruptly sharpened, focused on sound, and sound alone. She sifted out the village noise, and let her attention drift beyond the walls of the palisade. No dove calls. No finch chirps. There was no flutter of panicked wings in the air.

Because they'd already burst into flight or taken cover.

Any decent warrior knew to stop and listen when animals started warning one another. The fact that she'd barely noticed the flock of panicked jays spoke to the gravity of her morning.

The warriors on the catwalk stirred. Two men ran to the side overlooking Reed Marsh, and a clipped conversation broke out.

The scouts in the trees.

Panicked cries rose from the marsh.

Kittle looked up. "What's happening?"

As Jigonsaseh started to back away, to run for the catwalk, she said. "Get everyone inside the palisade."

"What? Why?"

"Just do it!"

Jigonsaseh ran hard for the nearest ladder. Hundreds of arrows leaned against the palisade wall behind the ladder, along with pots of water, wooden drinking cups, and bags of jerky to be used only by warriors protecting the village.

In the plaza below, Kittle shouted at two young men, "Tell everyone in Yellowtail Village to grab what they can, and get inside our palisades immediately!"

"Yes, High Matron." They dashed away.

Just as Jigonsaseh set foot upon the catwalk, cries came from the warriors in the field to the north . . . then more came from the south. A corresponding roar went up from the warriors on the catwalk, and they started charging around, scrambling for a better position.

"Matron?" War Chief Wampa called. "Our lines are falling back! War Chief Deru must have ordered them to flee!"

Jigonsaseh leaned on the palisade to survey the situation. To the north, over the top of Yellowtail Village, she caught glimpses of warriors fleeing through the trees. The northern line had broken and warriors sprinted for Bur Oak Village like terrified mice with a mountain lion bounding behind them.

Jigonsaseh strode for the knot of warriors who stood gaping, their gazes leveled on the grassy plain to the west, beyond Reed Marsh. Several gestured wildly with their arms.

"Where is the enemy? Show me."

Wampa used her bow to point. "Look at the tree line, Matron, just out of bow range. They just appeared."

Jigonsaseh scanned the weave of trunks and brush with a practiced eye. Barely visible, enemy warriors casually lined out, as though they had all the time in the world to get into position. She swung around. "War Chief Wampa, dispatch teams to gather arrows and stack them on the catwalk. After that, not a single warrior leaves his or her position without my permission. Do you understand? Keep the gates open until the Yellowtail Villagers are inside, then open it only as necessary for our retreating warriors to enter."

"Yes, Matron!"

Wampa ran. First she assigned warriors to bring up the arrows, then she trotted to the portion of the catwalk overlooking the gates, where she leaned over and shouted to the men below, "Open the gates! But I want them closed the instant our last warrior is inside. After that, open them only on my order or the order of Matron Jigonsaseh!"

"Yes, War Chief!"

Along the eastern palisade wall of Yellowtail Village, people flooded, carrying armloads of belongings. More supported litters. The wounded and dying moaned each time one of the rushing litter-bearers stumbled.

Tutelo and her young daughters trotted beside the litter carrying her dead husband, Idos. He'd been washed and dressed in his finest war shirt, the one with blue beads down the sleeves. His eyes had sunken, his lips pulled back from his gums.

"Wampa?" she shouted. "Leave the dead outside along the walls. There's no space for them inside!"

Wampa nodded and leaned over the palisade to relay the latest order.

Tutelo drew her daughters against her sides and watched as her beloved husband's body was gently lowered onto the pile of dead stacked along the eastern wall.

Blessed Ancestors, there would be no time now to perform the proper rituals to send the dead on their journey to the Land of the Dead. Thousands of afterlife souls would be wandering around the village, crying out to their relatives.

Frightened voices erupted from the plaza. Jigonsaseh turned. A group of elders surrounded High Matron Kittle and the flurry of conversation was growing louder. Matron Daga shook a fist in Kittle's face. Chief Yellowtail kept speaking to her in a tranquil voice, trying to calm her down.

Jigonsaseh's thoughts began working out the permutations, trying to decipher her enemy's strategy. Who was

Atotarho's new War Chief? Did she know him? What were his weaknesses? Not that such knowledge would give her much time. If the Hills army encircled Bur Oak Village and laid siege, eventually they would walk right through the front gates, kill all of the elders, and take the women and children hostage to serve as slaves. After that, they'd burn the villages so that anyone who escaped had nothing to return to.

Her duty was clear. She had to keep her people alive for as long as she could, and make certain that Atotarho knew the valor of the Standing Stone nation. If it took the last breath in her body, she would make sure his losses were staggering.

Jigonsaseh unslung her bow, pulled an arrow from her quiver, and nocked it. As she monitored her retreating lines, she prepared herself for the worst she could imagine.

Twelve

As twilight engulfed the valley, the falling snow resembled wavering sheets of gray silk blowing in the faint wind.

Jigonsaseh stood beside Sindak with her legs braced, staring out at the field of dead to the west. For more than two hands of time, Atotarho's warriors had been stripping corpses, and mutilating the bodies.

"What's he doing? Why hasn't he attacked?"

Sindak wiped snow from the bridge of his hooked nose. "He knows feeding the army comes first. Men with empty bellies desert and flee. As to the mutilation, he's feeding his warriors' souls. Condemning your relatives to wander the earth forever will make Atotarho's army feel better."

Clan war cries erupted, and she saw several men start dancing, holding severed heads in their fists.

Sindak said, "I've tried to get a rough count, but people have been shifting around so much, I haven't been able to. How many men, women, and children are in this village?"

"Too many," she answered, seeing no reason to lie to him. "Around two thousand four hundred. Most are elderly or children."

His gaze bored into hers. Snow had accumulated on his black hair. As though he'd just realized it, he brushed it off, and flipped up his hood. The edges of the tan leather caught the firelight and framed his narrow face with a flickering oval. "You're in serious trouble, Matron."

She laughed grimly and turned away.

Sindak asked, "Do you know why Atotarho allowed all of your warriors to return unharmed today? They were fleeing like rabbits. He could have dispatched a few hundred men to chase after them, and they would have killed many. But he didn't. He let them return to the safety of the village."

His features had set into hard unyielding lines. The lines of a War Chief's face, a man struggling to understand every possible nuance of his enemy's actions.

While she stared into his eyes, blood surged so loudly in her ears it dimmed the noise in the plaza. "Blessed gods, I've been so occupied with the council and the village's defense—"

"That you haven't had time to think like Atotarho? Of course not. Besides, I know him better than you do, and I have had the time."

Jigonsaseh massaged her brow as she cursed herself for being a fool. "Atotarho knows that no matter how much food and water we managed to pack into the village before he arrived, it will run out eventually."

"Yes, and the more mouths that need water and food, the faster it will run out. How long can we last?"

The fact that he'd said "we" interested her. Had he truly thrown his lot in with theirs? Wind flapped his hood around his face. He reached up to clasp it beneath his chin, holding it in place until the gust passed.

She answered. "If it was just food, we could last seven days with what we have stockpiled inside Bur Oak Village, and if we can get to our buried caches outside, we could last all winter. But—"

"How much water is there?" The crow's-feet at the corners of his eyes deepened. He looked at the longhouses.

"Three or four day's worth, but the marsh is ten paces away. If we're lucky, we'll be able to send out teams in the night—"

"You won't," he cut her off. As he shook his head, firelight gilded the hook of his nose with an edge of flame. "Accept that fact now. The marsh provides excellent cover. He'll have it surrounded by noon tomorrow. Maybe even tonight. Anyone who steps out of this village will be dead. The cover of darkness won't matter."

"Maybe, but the cover of darkness works both ways. The hunters can easily become the hunted."

Jigonsaseh's fingers tightened around CorpseEye until her hand ached. Of course, Atotarho had men to waste. If his warriors were killed, he had plenty more. She did not. She would have to institute drastic measures to conserve their water. Suddenly, every flake of snow drew her attention.

She lurched forward and called, "War Chief Deru?"

Deru, who stood ten paces away down the catwalk, tramped toward her with his red cape swaying around him. He was a big, muscular man with a squashed nose. His left cheek had been crushed by a war club many summers ago. As he walked passed Sindak, he gave his former enemy a slit-eyed glare. Clearly Deru didn't trust Sindak.

Sindak just stared back, expressionless.

Deru bowed. "Yes, Matron?"

"I want you to organize teams. Find every pot in the village not already full of water and empty it. We need to dispatch people to the marsh to fill them. After that, as they are emptied, I want the pots placed along the drip lines of the longhouses to catch the snow runoff."

"I'll see to both immediately."

He started to turn away, but she gripped his arm, forcing him to look back at her. They'd fought side-by-side for many summers. He'd once been her deputy war chief, yet she had no idea how he would respond to her next order. Quietly, she added, "I must discuss this with the Ruling Council before we can implement it, but I want you to begin making preparations. Mark every dying victim in the village. Consult with the Healers, Bahna and Genonsgwa. If they agree that there is no hope of the victim's recovery, we need to stop wasting food and water on them."

Deru's jaw clamped. A swallow went down his throat. He briefly looked over her shoulder, out at the campfires. "You and I must talk soon. I need to know what you know." He gave Sindak an unpleasant glance, as though blaming him for the order.

"Give me one-half hand of time, Deru, then meet me here."

"Yes, Matron." Deru strode away.

Jigonsaseh's gaze must have been like a lance. As though in defense, Sindak folded his arms beneath his cape, shielding his vulnerable chest.

"The time for pleasantries is over, *old friend*. I need to know every detail of Atotarho's army, every possible vulnerability, Atotarho's quirks, his habits, every weakness of the new War Chief, every—"

"Matron, I'm not sure who the new War Chief—"

"Speculate."

Sindak rubbed his jaw. He probably hoped that once Atotarho was dead, the Hills nation would reunite and he and his warriors could return home to take up their old lives. But if that did not happen, Sindak would become the most hated traitor in the history of his people, his name cursed forever. His actions would also cause all of his warriors to be declared Outcasts by Atotarho's faction of the People of the Hills. None of them would be able to return home again.

He seemed to be thinking about that. After what seemed a long time, he replied, "Maybe Negano. He was in charge of Atotarho's personal guards for five summers. The chief trusts him, but it could just as easily be—"

"Tell me about Negano."

Sindak tightened his folded arms. Muscles bulged through the leather of his cape.

Through a tense exhalation, he said, "His weaknesses . . . all right. First, he's inexperienced. While he carried the title of deputy war chief, he's never actually served as one. He was the leader of Atotarho's personal guards, composed of five or six warriors. He doesn't understand how an army works. As well, if he's been promoted over other more worthy people, there will be a lot of resentment. As the leader of the chief's personal guards, he's used to respect. It will be a shock for him. He's going to stumble for a while as he finds his way and earns the trust of the men and women who were passed over."

"What do you think of him personally?"

Sindak shrugged. "He's not innovative, but he's competent. Once he gets settled into the position, I think he's capable of being a good War Chief. However, you should be aware that it won't really matter who Atotarho's war chief is . . . because Atotarho gives most of the commands himself."

She listened, processing the information, trying to determine how she might be able to use it. Below, High Matron Kittle and Gonda exited the council house, carrying teacups, and wearily tramped across the plaza toward the Deer Clan Longhouse, undoubtedly praying they could finally get some sleep. Every few paces, someone stopped and demanded to speak with them. The Ruling Council had ordered Jigonsaseh to lead the fight for as long as necessary, which excused her from council meetings—at least until she was sent for. She wondered what decisions had been arrived at, and how it would affect the fight.

"Who do you think was promoted as the leader of Atotarho's personal guards?"

Sindak shrugged. "That's more difficult. I don't think the chief really liked any of his other guards, though they were all good men. Honestly, I can't even guess."

"Try."

Suspiciously, he cocked his head. "Why?"

"I need to know if he can be bribed, or convinced that his chief is insane and leading his people to destruction."

"What you're really saying is you want to know if we can convince him to kill the evil old man. Correct?"

"Yes."

Sindak unfolded his arms and, as he turned toward her, his dark, deeply sunken eyes reflected the wavering firelight. "Well, he might have opted for a young, strong warrior like Lonkol, or a seasoned veteran like Nesi, his War Chief of many summers ago." Sindak's brows plunged down over his hooked nose. "If it's Nesi, there is no chance whatsoever of swaying him in our direction. He is a man of great integrity. Loyal to a fault."

"And if it's Lonkol?"

His head waffled. "Maybe."

In the plaza, Kittle finally made it to her longhouse, said a few final words to Gonda, and ducked beneath the curtain, disappearing into the warmth. A line of people followed her inside, calling questions.

Gonda took a drink from his teacup and surveyed the village. No one had remained to question him. He was merely a refugee, the Speaker for the Warriors from White Dog Village, a village destroyed by the man standing next to her, War Chief Sindak of the People of the Hills. When Gonda saw Jigonsaseh and Sindak standing together on the catwalk, he tiredly walked toward them.

"If you were still in charge of Atotarho's army, how would your warriors be lined out?"

Sindak's gaze roamed the surrounding hills, then he knelt on the catwalk and started drawing lines in the snow. "Keep in mind, after he left here, Atotarho probably split his army down the middle. He wanted to punish the rogue villages, so I suspect he dispatched three war parties to each village—Coldspring, Riverbank, and Canassatego—with orders to burn them to the ground. He—"

"Explain why you think he would split his army. It would be sheer foolishness."

Sindak looked up at her. Snowflakes melted on his cheeks. "He's insane. The fact that his daughter Zateri led the betrayal will be eating him alive."

"If you're right, that means there are only two thousand out there."

Sindak didn't even blink. "Yes, so we're only outnumbered eight to one. Are you telling me you feel better?"

Gonda's steps crunched the snow as he came up behind Sindak and, teacup in hand, peered inquiringly over Sindak's shoulder at the sketch. His long red cape had an orange tint in the firelight.

Sindak continued, "He has two thousand trained warriors—not children carrying their childhood bows, as fill your ranks. Atotarho's forces will be bedded down on every high point around this village. They'll be concentrated here"—he sketched the position—"here and here. In addition, substantial forces will have been deployed to cut off the trails, to isolate you. Lastly, a thin line will fill in the most vulnerable gaps. Over here in this drainage, and up here where the trail cuts through the cap rock." He stared for a time at the lines he'd made in the snow, nodded, and stood up again. "At least, that's what I'd do."

As Gonda handed the warm teacup to Jigonsaseh, he said, "I thought you might be cold."

"I am. Thank you."

Gonda glanced back at the lines Sindak had sketched in the snow, and pointedly asked, "Why do we care what Atotarho's *former* War Chief would do? He's not out there. He's in here with us."

"Because he trained those warriors, you fool," Sindak defended. "Even you should grasp that. You once trained warriors when you were War Chief Koracoo's deputy—before she removed you in favor of War Chief Cord."

The lines of Gonda's round face drooped. "Not very subtle, Sindak, pointing out that we both qualify as 'former.'"

"I thought you'd appreciate that."

A small amount of her distrust had seeped away as

Sindak talked. He didn't appear to be holding anything back, or trying to deceive her. "I heard that Gonda offered to adopt you and your warriors into his clan."

Gonda nodded. "I did. He refused."

Sindak knocked off the snow that had accumulated on the shoulders of his cape. "My warriors are considering it. But you know as well as I do that they believe themselves patriots. They desperately want to go home to their families."

Bluntly, Jigonsaseh said, "Atotarho is going to kill their families, Sindak. They may already be dead. If not, their relatives need to get out now and make their way here. Perhaps you should dispatch one of your warriors with that message? I give you my oath that the Standing Stone nation will adopt any member of their families who—"

"I'll tell them."

Jigonsaseh turned to watch the enraged sobbing people in the plaza. The circle broke up and men and women sauntered away in different directions.

"Now, Matron, I want you to tell me something," Sindak said.

Gonda scowled. "That sounded like a command, not a request. You are addressing a member of the Ruling Council, you pusillanimous insect. You will keep a civil tongue—"

She cut Gonda off, "What is it, Sindak?"

Sindak gave Gonda a disgruntled look, then propped his hands on his hips. The motion caused his tan cape to flare out around his body. The white geometric designs on the bottom flashed in the firelight. "We've heard a thousand versions of Sky Messenger's vision. I want to hear it from you. I assume you memorized it to make sure you could repeat it exactly. You wouldn't want to make an error before an enemy council that Sky Messenger would later have to correct." He pointed a stern finger at her, a warning gesture. "Word for word, Matron."

She chuckled at his audacity. This was the man she remembered from twelve summers ago. Too brash for his own good.

Gonda's mouth opened to say something vituperative, but she replied, "I did memorize it."

"Good. I'm listening."

Images from the vision flared behind her eyes. Brilliant and dark, and reverence filtered through her exhaustion.

Thirteen

"Keep in mind, I don't tell it as well as he does."

"I suspect no one does," Sindak answered.

Jigonsaseh shook the snow from her hood. Clumps of white fell onto the catwalk. "It will probably help if you imagine his deep voice, not mine."

Sindak sank back against the palisade again, his intent gaze upon her, totally ignoring Gonda. Snow lilted through the air around him, the big flakes falling slowly. "I'll try."

She took a drink from the cup of spruce needle tea, and steam curled up around her face. The sweet tangy flavor didn't soothe her taut nerves, but it warmed her belly.

"When the dream begins he can't feel his body, just the air cooling as color leaches from the forest, leaving the land strangely gray and shimmering. As he watches, the blue sky goes leaden, and the rounded patches of light falling through the trees curve into bladelike crescents. That's when he first senses his skin . . . but it's a faint, not really there, sensation. He has the overwhelming urge to run, but he can't feel his legs at all. His fingers work, clenching into hard fists, unclenching. A great cloud-sea swims beneath him. He says it's a dark restless ocean, punctured by a great tree with flowers of pure light."

"The sacred World Tree? Whose roots sink through Great Grandmother Earth and plant themselves upon the back of the Great Tortoise floating in the primeval ocean below?"

As images from the Creation Story filled her, she clutched Gonda's teacup more tightly. "Yes."

Her gaze briefly fixed on Gonda's, then focused on the palisade at the opposite end of the village, behind the Snipe Clan longhouse. Through the veil of snow she saw a group of four warriors talking, their bows slung over muscular shoulders.

"As though the birds know the unthinkable is about to happen, they tuck their beaks beneath their wings and close their eyes, roosting in the middle of the day. Noisy clouds of insects that, only moments ago, twisted through the forest like tiny tornadoes, vanish. Butterflies settle to the ground at Sky Messenger's feet and secret themselves amid the clouds. An eerie silence descends."

Sindak didn't seem to be breathing. He watched her with slightly narrowed, unblinking eyes.

"Morning Star flares in the darkening sky and, as though she's caused it, fantastic shadow-bands, rapidly moving strips of light and dark, flicker across the meadow. He—"

"So . . ." Sindak interrupted, "now he's standing in a meadow. The cloud-sea is gone?"

"Let her finish," Gonda said.

"It's complicated," she added. "Spirit Dreams have a logic of their own."

"But where is the meadow? Has he ever seen it before?"

"At this point in the Dream," she replied, "it nestles in the heart of the cloud-sea."

"Ah, I understand." He sank back against the palisade.

As Jigonsaseh told the story, she could hear Sky Messenger's voice, filled with awe and foreboding. "Dimly, he becomes aware that he is not alone. Gray shades drift through the air around him, their hushed voices like the distant cries of lost souls. He knows that they are the last congregation. The dead who still walk and breathe. Then he hears Hiyawento call, 'Odion?' and he turns to see Hiyawento standing in the meadow beside him. Hiyawento points out beyond the cloud-sea. At the western edge of the world, an amorphous darkness rises from the watery depths and slithers along the horizon—"

"Horned Serpent? The Spirit beast who almost destroyed the world at the dawn of creation?"

Annoyed, she said, "Will you let me finish?"

Sindak's mouth pursed then he said, "But it's hard not to ask questions."

"Endeavor," Gonda said.

"I apologize."

Jigonsaseh sighed. "When strange black curls, like gigantic antlers, spin from the darkness and rake through the cloud-sea, Elder Brother Sun trembles in the sky. Right beside him, a black hole opens in the universe and Elder Brother Sun slowly turns his back on the world to flee. There is a final brilliant flash, and blindingly white feathers sprout from his edges. Sky Messenger is certain that he's flying. Flying away. And he knows that if Elder Brother Sun leaves us, the world will die . . . unless he does something."

She swiveled her head to peer at Sindak. He stared at her fixedly. His narrow beaked face was beaded with melted snow.

"Just as Sky Messenger realizes that it is up to him to stop the death of the world, a crack—like the sky splitting—blasts him. He looks down and sees a great pine tree pushing up through a hole in the earth, its four white roots slashing like lightning to the four directions. A snowy blanket of thistledown blows toward it like a great wave, spreading out all over the world."

Sindak stood so still, he resembled a stuffed man-skin.

"Sky Messenger staggers as his body comes alive in a raging flood. When he turns to speak to the Shades, a child cries out. The sound is muffled and wavering, seeping through the ocean of other voices. It sounds like the little boy is suffocating, his mouth covered with a hand or hide. Fear freezes the air in his lungs. As though the man has his lips pressed to Sky Messenger's ear, he orders, 'Lie down, boy. Stop crying or I'll cut your heart out.'"

Sindak moved, shifting his back to a new position against the palisade. Clearly, he longed to ask a question, but he held his tongue.

"Then the Dream bursts. For a time, there is only brilliance. Then Sky Messenger sees the flowers of the World Tree, made of pure light, fluttering down. They're all around him, fluttering down into utter darkness . . . and he's falling, tumbling through nothingness with tufts of cloud trailing behind him."

When she'd finished, she lifted the teacup, and took another drink. Each telling was like a journey to another world, a place where time ran more slowly, as though the

Creator himself were dragging his feet, afraid of what was to come.

"Who is the man?" Sindak's dark eyes had gone wide and wet.

"The man we cut apart outside Bog Willow Village."

Sindak's forehead furrowed, then his awed expression dissolved like mist in sunshine, becoming hard and filled with hatred. "What does that piece of filth have to do with the vision?"

Jigonsaseh said, "I don't really understand it, Sindak, though I was there when Old Bahna, our village holy man, explained it to Sky Messenger. He told Sky Messenger that 'A man who hates has no eyes. He is a prisoner of darkness.' Bahna said the point was forgiveness."

Sindak made a deep-throated sound of disgust. "Forgiveness? He wants Sky Messenger to forgive that piece of filth? That's a bad idea."

"I thought so, too," Gonda remarked.

Jigonsaseh said, "Bahna told Sky Messenger that all of his life he's been hiding from a memory, and that he's been afraid for so long, he doesn't know how to stop. He told Sky Messenger that he lived in a prison that he repaired every day. He added new chinking, new logs, and sealed himself in, over and over. Bahna told Sky Messenger that he had to stop it, to escape, or he'd never be able to truly see the ghosts of grief and desperation that haunt this land. That's why that foul War Chief—"

"That foul War Chief is dead, Matron," Sindak noted. "How can forgiving him accomplish anything?"

"Bahna says he's not dead. He says that just as a warrior breathes soul into every arrow he creates, a man can breathe soul into a memory. He said Sky Messenger's hatred has kept the War Chief alive."

"How is Sky Messenger supposed to accomplish this foolish task of forgiveness?"

Logs cracked in the plaza bonfire, belching gouts of black smoke and blue-green flames. People yipped and ran a short distance away, then returned, one at a time, to the stew pots. Sparks whirled upward into the falling snow.

"He already has. Sky Messenger and his betrothed, Taya, returned to Bog Willow Village and collected as many of his bones as they could find, then Sky Messenger prayed the 'piece of filth's' soul to the afterlife. He says he forgave the man."

Jigonsaseh turned and leaned her back against the palisade beside Sindak, staring out at the fire-warmed roofs of the longhouses, still mostly free of snow. Smoke escaped from the smokeholes and curled through the air in blue streamers. The workers had used rolls of bark stripped from the Yellowtail Village to repair the roofs. They were a different color, lighter brown, and created a patchwork.

"All right, let's return to my original question. In the vision"—Sindak crossed his arms—"when Elder Brother Sun flees into the black hole, where are Sky Messenger and Hiyawento standing? Where is the meadow? Does Sky Messenger think it's a real place?"

"He does. But he doesn't know where it is. Why?"

Sindak turned sideways and propped his right elbow on the palisade, facing her. "I want to be there, that's why. They're going to need loyal friends."

After all the summers of war between their peoples she found it a curious statement. Refugees from the White

Dog Village battle filled the plaza below: Gonda's village. "And are you a loyal friend, War Chief Sindak?"

He stared at her, apparently unoffended. "During the battle yesterday, both Sky Messenger and Hiyawento were right beside me. I could have killed them a hundred times. I have never, except in self-defense, lifted a weapon against either man." He paused for two heartbeats. "Everything goes back to those children, Matron. They were chosen by Power. And you and I both know it."

When she didn't respond, he gruffly shoved away from the palisade, glared at Gonda, and walked to the closest ladder, where he climbed down to the crowded plaza.

Jigonsaseh watched him until he rejoined his warriors, then she turned her attention back to the campfires on the distant hills, wavering through the veils of snow.

She propped her elbows on the palisade and finished the dregs of spruce needle tea in her cup. It had gone stone cold. "How did the Council Meeting go?"

"They're all terrified beyond the capacity for thought. No decisions were made."

She handed his cup back. When he took it, their fingers briefly overlapped, which she found comforting. Over the long summers since their marriage ended, their enmity had faded and transformed into a deep friendship that she cherished.

"Sindak says Atotarho may have sent half his warriors away to punish the three Hills villages that opposed him."

Gonda paused as though thinking it over. "Do you believe it?"

"I'm not sure it matters. He's speculating just like we are. We won't know anything until daylight tomorrow."

Fourteen

The sloping hillside in front of Zateri descended to the west, flattening out into a broad gently rolling plain. For the most part, winter-gray oaks and maples covered the plain, but here and there red veins of willows stood out, tracing the paths of creeks and rivers that flowed into Skanodario Lake. In the low places, mist created shimmering white spots.

She glanced back at Kwahseti and Gwinodje. They stood with their war chiefs, surrounded by a few warriors asking questions. They had donned their white ritual capes, and the folds of the painted leather shone in the bright light. The color of the wolf paws painted on their capes defined their lineages. Kwahseti's white cape had red paws for Yi's lineage. Gwinodje's had black paws for Inawa's lineage. Zateri's white cape had blue wolf paws. All of her life they had symbolized Tila's lineage. With the death of her grandmother, however, they now symbolized Zateri's lineage. While the other matrons endeavored to extricate themselves, Zateri gazed out across the vista.

She had ordered them to stop for one hand of time to allow the litter-bearers and the walking wounded time to rest in the warm meadow, and to give her the time to speak with matrons Gwinodje and Kwahseti. They would reach Riverbank Village tomorrow, and had no idea what they would find. If they were lucky, Kwahseti's messenger had reached the village first, and her people had packed up and moved to Canassatego Village. In that case, they would find just an empty village, a place to rest for a time before they themselves continued on to Canassatego Village. But if Kwahseti's messenger had not arrived in time . . . if Atotarho's warriors had reached Riverbank Village first, they would find it burned to the ground and the slaughtered bodies of their relatives strewn across the forest.

Zateri shivered in the cold breath of wind that swept the hilltop and rustled through the bare-branched maples. Old autumn leaves whirled around her. If Riverbank was gone, it meant her own Coldspring Village was also probably gone. And she had no doubt but that her father had told his warriors to be especially destructive. Since Atotarho knew that cannibalism horrified Zateri, she'd already begun preparing herself for a burned-out husk of a village filled with gigantic piles of half-eaten human bones.

We live in an age of madness.

She looked at Hiyawento. Two paces away, he sat cross-legged in a patch of sunlight, gently rocking their sleeping daughter in his arms. They'd cut Kahn-Tineta's long hair in mourning for her dead sisters. As Hiyawento gazed down at her pretty face, her mouth opened slightly, revealing her missing front teeth. She could tell from Hiyawento's expression that he longed to touch her, to stroke her chopped off hair, but didn't wish to wake her.

Hiyawento's gaze shifted to the beaded belt he'd been stringing just before Kahn-Tineta had crawled into his lap. After the deaths of Catta and Jimer, he'd started gathering fresh water shells, white and purple, grinding them into long cylinder-shaped beads, and stringing them on thread made from twisted elm bark. Almost finished, the belt was completely white except for two tiny human figures near the front ties. They were deep dark purple. As he studied them, silent rage twisted Hiyawento's features.

A chill went through Zateri. No matter what role Ohsinoh had played, ultimately his baby daughters had been taken from him by Atotarho. The need for vengeance was consuming his soul. So far, he had managed to contain it, accepting that they had to get their warriors to Canassatego Village. But when they'd accomplished that, when he knew Zateri and Kahn-Tineta were safe, his inner dam would burst, and he would leave his enemy's world in flames.

Kwahseti and Gwinodje separated from the group of warriors and walked toward Zateri's fire with their heads down in quiet conversation. Their war chiefs, Thona and Waswanosh, trailed a few paces behind them. The war chiefs made a strange duo. While Waswanosh was of medium height and slender, Thona was the tallest and most heavily scarred man in the Hills nation. The scars on his face and burly arms resembled tangles of white cords. He was known for his skill with the war ax. Waswanosh's skill was battle strategy. Together, along with Hiyawento's brilliance at tactics, they made formidable leaders.

As Gwinodje and Kwahseti neared her position, they both gave her worried looks.

Kwahseti apologized, "Forgive us for taking so long.

Our warriors are concerned about what we will do to-morrow."

Zateri didn't have to ask what she meant. The word *if* hung in the air like a granite boulder suspended over their heads. "As am I. That's one of the things I wish to discuss with you."

As the matrons seated themselves on woven willow mats spread around the fire, Zateri added another branch to the flames. She waited until Kwahseti had dipped two cups of tea from the pot nestled at the edge of the flames and handed one to Gwinodje. "Zateri, shall I dip one for you also?"

"No, I've had my fill, but thank you."

Zateri waited a few moments longer, giving them time to get settled, then she lifted her voice: "Come. Let us bring order to the world."

Gwinodje and Kwahseti respectfully bowed their heads, waiting for Zateri to finish the opening, as her Grandmother Tila had done for more than thirty summers. Midday sunlight streamed through the wind-blown branches. Kwahseti, Gwinodje, and Zateri sat in a perfect triangle. Their white ritual capes signified their *ohwachiras,* or maternal lineages. Since the deaths of Zateri's two aunts, she was the only female left in Tila's direct line. It was a daunting position. Their ohwachira, kinship group, could trace its descent for thousands of summers back to a common ancestor. In the case of the Wolf Clan, that descent traced back to the Creation of the World, and a great woman leader named Dancing Fox who had bravely led their clan through a dark underworld and into this world of light.

All of Zateri's life, Grandmother had trained her to

understand the role of the Wolf Clan ohwachiras. They had power because of them. Ohwachiras possessed and bestowed chieftainship titles, and held the other great names of their lineages. They bestowed those names by raising up the souls of the dead and Requickening them in the bodies of newly elected chiefs, adoptees, matrons, or others. The ohwachira also had the right to remove a soul, and take back the name from anyone who disgraced it. The nation's sisterhood of ohwachiras also decided when to go to war, and when to make peace.

Zateri finished the opening, "I pray that Great Grandmother Earth hears our voices and guides us in our decisions for the good of all things, great and small. I would speak first, if there are no objections."

The matrons shook their heads, and glanced at their war chiefs.

Three paces behind Kwahseti, her War Chief, Thona, crouched, waiting to be called upon should the council find it necessary. Three paces behind Gwinodje, her War Chief, Waswanosh, stood with his arms folded tightly across his broad chest. Hiyawento had not moved, but he'd lifted his head to listen.

Zateri smoothed her hands over her white cape and squared her narrow shoulders. "Let me speak straightly, I need to know how you think your lineages view Matron Kelek's ascension to the position of High Matron of our nation."

Usually, upon a High Matron's death, the oldest female in her direct line underwent the Requickening ceremony, received the dead High Matron's name, and—if the former High Matron had so specified—was installed not only as the new matron of the entire clan, but also as the

High Matron of the Hills nation. However, during the last meeting of the Wolf Clan ohwachiras, where Tila had presented the possibility of Zateri following her, there had been objections. Unfortunately, Tila had died without making her final successor known. Regardless of who was selected as High Matron, there should have been no question but that the High Matron would come from one of the Wolf Clan ohwachiras, which meant that Zateri, Inawa, or Yi should have ascended to the position. No one understood yet what Chief Atotarho had done to assure that the Wolf Clan would be replaced by the Bear Clan in Atotarho Village, but he'd obviously made some kind of "arrangement."

Kwahseti shoved short gray hair away from her eyes. "The leader of my lineage, Yi, must be livid. The Wolf Clan has led the nation well for more than thirty summers. To have the Bear Clan suddenly assume leadership is an outrage."

Zateri waited for her to continue. When she didn't, Zateri said, "Gwinodje?"

Gwinodje had been staring at her fingers, lacing and unlacing them in her lap. She and Zateri were both small-boned and childlike. "I think Inawa, the leader of my lineage, must be deeply troubled. She will suspect foul play on Atotarho's part. I imagine she is wondering what kind of deal was struck between Kelek and Atotarho to accomplish the task. Everyone knows the Wolf Clan is the largest and most powerful clan in the nation. By all rights, a woman from one of our lineages should have ascended to the High Matronship."

Zateri's short black hair hung at chin level, shining at the corners of her vision. "Since Yi and Inawa both live in

Atotarho Village, what sort of repercussions have there been?"

Kwahseti snorted. "Repercussions? I imagine Yi is on a rampage, organizing our lineage for a political campaign to overturn Kelek's ascension. Things must be getting ugly between the clans."

Zateri looked across the fire.

Gwinodje's thin heart-shaped face tensed. She thought about it, before quietly answering, "Zateri, you know that Inawa objected heartily to having you follow your grandmother. She knew that if your grandmother did not appoint you, her own lineage would assume the leadership of the Wolf Clan. Inawa would have become High Matron of the nation. She must be stalking about like a stiff-legged dog. In fact, I imagine her indignation enlivens every conversation in Atotarho Village."

Zateri took a moment to glance at Thona and Waswanosh, judging the war chiefs' expressions. Both appeared to be analyzing the information.

Zateri said, "As we are all aware, my appointment as High Matron of our faction of the Hills People is temporary. Once we have melded our villages with Canassatego Village, every ohwachira will have a chance to speak with its members about who they wish for High Matron. Until then I plan to—"

"But, Mother," Kahn-Tineta said with a sleepy yawn and opened her eyes. She rolled over in Hiyawento's arms to stare at the matrons' council.

Zateri turned to look at her daughter. Black tangles framed her pretty young face. "My daughter, we are in council. Perhaps your question could wait—"

"But, Mother, Great Grandmother wanted you to be

High Matron." Kahn-Tineta sat up, rubbed her eyes. "She told me."

Zateri started to dismiss the suggestion, but Kwahseti held up a hand. "Wait. I wish to hear this story. When did your great grandmother tell you this?"

Zateri sighed, and turned around to face her daughter. Hiyawento's gaze focused on Kahn-Tineta with eagle-sharpness.

Kahn-Tineta must have felt the weight of the council's attention. She tucked a finger into the corner of her mouth, and slurred, "The day she died. I was lying beside her on her shleeping bench while she shtroked my hair, and said she was going to tell me a secret that I couldn't tell anyone."

Gwinodje and Kwahseti glanced at each other.

Gwinodje calmly asked, "We need to know her exact words, Kahn-Tineta. Do you understand what that means? Her *exact* words."

Kahn-Tineta nodded. She removed her finger from her mouth to say, "Grandmother hugged me very tightly, and said, 'Can I tell you a secret?' I said, 'What is it?' and she said, 'I'm going to name your mother as Matron of the Wolf Clan when she returns, but you mustn't tell anyone.'"

Kwahseti said, "And you've been a very good girl, because you haven't, have you?"

Zateri understood Kwahseti's meaning. If the event truly had occurred, why hadn't Kahn-Tineta told them such important news?

"No, Matron Kwahseti," Kahn-Tineta answered. "Great Grandmother asked me if I could keep her words locked in my heart until it was announced." Kahn-Tineta looked around, meeting each person's eyes. "That's why I haven't said anything. I'm good at keeping secrets . . . and it hasn't been announced . . . has it?"

Kwahseti replied, "No, dear girl, because your great grandmother left for the Land of the Dead before she could tell anyone. What else did she say?"

Kahn-Tineta's eyes narrowed slightly, as though something had occurred to her but she wasn't certain she should say it. She glanced up hesitantly at Hiyawento.

He gently said, "It's all right, Kahn-Tineta. You can tell us."

Kahn-Tineta licked her lips and swallowed. "I told great grandmother that I wasn't sure Mother wished to be High Matron."

Zateri bowed her head. "What did she say to that?"

"Oh, she said, 'That's not a surprise. No one does.' Then she poked me in the chest with her finger"—Kahn Tineta rubbed the spot—"and said, 'You remember I said that. Someday you will have to make the choice of whether or not to lead your people. It is an overwhelming responsibility. But I suspect in the end you will choose to place the welfare of the Hills nation above your own. You will shoulder the burden for the nation's sake. Just as your mother will.'"

Zateri's throat suddenly ached with emotion. "Was that all she said?"

Kahn-Tineta crossed her legs in Hiyawento's lap and shook one moccasin while she frowned at the swirls of blue smoke gliding above her. "No. I told her I wasn't so sure you would because Father didn't wish to move to Atotarho Village, because he hated Grandfather Atotarho."

At the mention of Atotarho's name, Hiyawento's arm muscles tightened as though fit to burst through his shirt. He frowned down at his daughter. "Kahn-Tineta, look at me."

The girl looked up but cringed at his stern expression.

"Are you telling the truth?"

"Yes, Father!" she cried indignantly. "I wouldn't lie about this!"

He glared at her for a few moments, until he'd satisfied himself. "All right. Go on. What else did your great grandmother say?"

"She told me a story," Kahn-Tineta replied weakly, as though her father's expression made her wish she hadn't said anything at all.

"What story?"

Kahn-Tineta tucked her finger in her mouth again, sucking it for a time to soothe her fears, before saying, "She told me that my great-great-great grandmother used to have a saying. She said that for every one person hacking at the roots of hatred, there were thousands swinging in its branches, and I'd better not do that or I'd fall and break my neck. Great Grandmother told me the only way to survive in this world was to make sure I was the one with the hatchet." Around her finger, Kahn-Tineta slurred, "I liked that shtory."

Gwinodje blinked thoughtfully and turned to Zateri. "That sounds very much like something your grandmother would have said, Zateri."

"Yes," she smiled sadly. "Grandmother told me that same story when I was a child. I loved it, too."

Below them, stretched across the hillside, warriors began rising, dusting off their clothing, and preparing to leave. Sounds of weapons clattering replaced the low drone of conversation.

Thona rose to his feet to stand like a scarred giant behind Kwahseti, waiting to be recognized.

Zateri looked up at him. "Please ask your question, War Chief Thona."

Thona's eyes narrowed. He turned first to Hiyawento, then to Waswanosh, as though silently asking what they thought, before he gazed at Zateri with hard eyes. "High Matron, no child could make up such words. We all agree upon that, yes?"

Hiyawento said, "Yes."

Nods went round the fire.

Thona continued, "If your daughter speaks the truth, as we all suspect, you have been robbed of your rightful position in this nation."

Waswanosh hesitated, rubbing his chin while he considered. "I agree, High Matron."

"You must do something about this crime," Thona said.

Waswanosh nodded. "You can't just stand by and allow this to happen. Despite the fact that we have the largest and most powerful clan in the nation, it will make us look like feeble fools."

Zateri turned around to look at Hiyawento. He seemed to be glaring at the ground, but he was seeing something at a great distance, perhaps in the future, or the past. Kahn-Tineta had leaned her head against his broad chest and continued to suck her finger while she glanced around at the adults.

"Hiyawento?"

He looked up with fiery eyes, then they slowly cleared as he returned to the here and now. In a powerful voice, he said, "This only makes a difference if you've decided that our nation should be reunited. If we plan to remain as a separate nation, it should be of no concern to us whom the Old Hills People choose as their High Matron. We must define what our 'nation' is. Are we the New People of the Hills or not?"

Hisses passed around the fire, Gwinodje shaking her head at something Kwahseti whispered. Thona and Waswanosh stared at Hiyawento with pensive eyes, deep in thought. Finally, Thona nodded in agreement.

Hiyawento said, "Every action we take in the next few days depends upon that decision. If we wish to reunite we cannot, must not, attack our relatives in any of the Hills villages."

"But what if they attack us?" Waswanosh asked.

"We defend ourselves, but we do not send out warriors to attack them."

Thona shifted. As his teeth ground, the crisscrossing scars on his face moved like a tangle of white worms. "I do not wish to sit by and allow our villagers to be relentlessly attacked while we bide our time in the hopes that the new High Matron, Kelek, will see the wisdom of reuniting our peoples."

Zateri noted that he'd said "peoples" not "people." Thona had already been thinking along the same lines as Hiyawento, assuming that the separation into two nations was inevitable. A similar thing had happened generations ago among the People of the Dawnland. One faction had split off and called themselves the People Who Separated.

Zateri said, "Kwahseti, your thoughts on this?"

Kwahseti ran a hand through her gray hair, and shook her head. "I would hear Gwinodje's thoughts first."

Zateri turned to Gwinodje. As all eyes fixed on her, Gwinodje blinked and frowned at the flickering fire.

She said, "I confess that, after Atotarho is dead, I would like to see our peoples become one nation again. We all have relatives scattered throughout the other Hills villages. Frankly, I don't wish to consider them my enemy forever."

Zateri nodded, and turned back to Kwahseti. "And you?"

Kwahseti toyed with the cup in her hands. "There is another possibility. If we remain as two nations, and Sky Messenger can create a Peace Alliance between all our peoples, we will still be able to see our relatives—"

"Forgive me for interrupting, Matron," Thona said. "But that is a very big 'if.' I do not believe we should base our decisions upon that possibility. A Peace Alliance is, in my thoughts, the least likely outcome of this war."

"Yes, probably," Kwahseti exhaled the words. "But in my heart, it is what I most hope for, and what I am willing to risk almost everything for. What of you, Zateri?"

Zateri's brow lined. Her gaze went around the fire, studying the tense expressions. At last, she looked at Hiyawento. "My husband?"

Hiyawento seemed to think about it for a time, then he set Kahn-Tineta on the ground, and rose to his feet. As he straightened to his full height, his beaked face went hard. His soft words were powerful, striking at the heart like knives: "Sky Messenger's vision *will* come to pass. Elder Brother Sun will cover his face with the soot of the dying world and everything we love will die . . . unless we do something to stop it. Peace is not an option. It's a necessity for survival."

Like the pause after an indrawn breath, a curious silence held them. Wind gusted through their camp, scattered the embers in the fire, and whipped the flames into crackling fury.

When it died down, Thona said, "Peace is a comforting notion. I understand. However, at this very instant Atotarho is planning to wipe our faction of the Hills People from the face of Great Grandmother Earth. If we do not strike him first, that is exactly what's going to happen. Perhaps, peace can wait a little longer."

"No," Zateri said firmly. "I, like my husband and Sky Messenger, believe peace is our only hope."

Gwinodje and Kwahseti spoke softly again, then Gwinodje turned. "Yes, Zateri, but how do we accomplish it before our villages are annihilated?"

She sat for some time on the mat before the fire that overlooked the long slope to the west, her shell bracelets flashing in the sunlight that fell through the swaying branches. A queer rhythm pulsed her blood, not like her heartbeat, more like music trickling up from a covered pit that fell forever into a black abyss.

"We must use the clan mothers, not warriors."

Kwahseti's brows drew together as she frowned. "How?"

Gwinodje sat forward. "I think I understand! First, we must dispatch messengers to Yi and Inawa, telling them that Tila's last words were to appoint Zateri as her successor—and Zateri claims that right." Words spilled from her lips. "Then we must ask them to dispatch messengers to the other ohwachiras! We—"

"Every ohwachira except those of the Bear Clan. We should leave that decision to Yi and Inawa," Zateri said with a lifted finger. "The Bear Clan must be overjoyed at Kelek's ascension, probably celebrating their new power. Our words will be of no consequence. We are traitors in their minds."

"But if you think the Wolf Clan should take a stand

against Kelek, we should tell Yi and Inawa," Kwahseti said.

Zateri carefully considered her next words. She had the sense that they were all suspended upon a zephyr above oblivion. The slightest wrong move now . . .

"I think Yi and Inawa will know what to do without any suggestions from us, Kwahseti. We are at a great disadvantage. We must be careful. While we have declared independence, if we ever wish to reunite the nation, we must work with the established clan authorities. Yi and Inawa face Kelek every day. Kelek must be swelled with triumph right now, and lauding her victory. However, the Wolf Clan must give her a chance to defend herself before it—"

"Zateri," Kwahseti said with a touch of malice, "she ascended to her position as High Matron through underhanded negotiations with Atotarho. You know it's true. Atotarho must have assured Kelek that she would become High Matron in exchange for something. What?"

Hiyawento said, "In exchange for retaining his position as chief. He knew that as soon as Zateri became High Matron she would remove him."

Zateri nodded. "I would have."

Thona spread his feet and squared his broad shoulders. "How do we survive long enough for the clans to take action? And I think we must fight back if Kelek does not step down as High Matron."

Zateri quietly said, "I don't think so, War Chief. I agree with my husband. We must take no action against Kelek or the rest of the nation. It's not up to us. No matter what Kelek has done, punishing her must remain the prerogative of the Bear Clan. If a Wolf Clan matron had ascended to the position of High Matron through treachery, we would claim the right to deal with it ourselves, wouldn't we?"

Kwahseti nodded. "Absolutely, and if any other clan tried to depose her, regardless of her crimes, we would declare a blood oath and hunt them down."

Gwinodje turned to look at her war chief. "Waswanosh? You have not spoken in a while. Should we fight, as Thona suggests, or merely defend ourselves while we rally the support of the other ohwachiras?"

"Forgive me, Matron. I am . . . off-balance. However, I find myself more in agreement with High Matron Zateri. If we *can* use the ohwachiras to accomplish our task, we should. Thona is right, too, though. There must be a time limit. If we wait too long, we will be two nations forever."

Zateri waited for more comments.

They all stared at her.

"I fear our patience will be determined by what we find at Riverbank Village tomorrow."

"And at Canassatego Village the day after," Gwinodje said with trepidation in her voice. "If all of our villages are gone . . ." She sucked in a breath at the thought. "I will cast my voice with War Chief Thona and commit my warriors to destroying Atotarho, and anyone who sides with him, no matter the cost."

Kwahseti nodded, then Waswanosh. When Zateri turned to Hiyawento, she found him staring directly at her with slitted eyes. "My husband?"

His teeth ground for several moments, while he met each person's eyes. "That will be for the rest of you to decide. I won't be there."

Thona half-shouted, "*What?* You would leave at a moment like—"

"I would," Hiyawento interrupted in a commanding voice. He and Thona glared at each other. "I must be at Sky Messenger's side when the end comes. I *will* be at his side."

Thona leaned toward him threateningly, his hand on his belted war club. "Without you here to lead your warriors, it may come faster than you anticipate." He turned to Kwahseti. "Matron, with your permission, I will return to my duties before I cause a disturbance."

"You may go, Thona. Thank you for your counsel."

Thona bowed to the matrons, glared at Hiyawento again, then stalked away with his cape jerking around him.

Kwahseti vented a sigh. "Please excuse him. He's desperate."

"As we all are," Hiyawento countered.

Gwinodje stared at her hands, twisting them in her lap. Waswanosh stood silently behind her.

Quietly, Zateri said, "If there are no more issues to be presented, I will dismiss this council."

Fifteen

Snow fell from the night sky like weightless white feathers, drifting down around Sonon, frosting the hood and shoulders of his black cape, and softly alighting on the bowed head of the woman kneeling in the trail five paces in front of him. Leafless maples swayed gently behind her, their branches already shining with a thin white crust.

The woman was exhausted, gasping hoarse lungfuls of air. She'd unbraided her long hair, and it draped in perfect glistening waves around her beautiful face. Tiny arcs of snow crested her high cheekbones and iced the lashes that fringed her large black eyes. She'd been running all day without a break, desperately trying to reach Sky Messenger.

Unbeknownst to her, Sonon had been at her side the entire time. Sooner or later, he knew she would see him.

She collapsed in the middle of the path and curled into a fetal position. She made no sound, but when she succumbed to shivering, the dark curve of trail seemed to tighten around her, holding her tall body in a lover's grasp.

Sonon tilted his head.

There were always souls whose burden of suffering seemed so great that it became an obscenity, a thing that could not be borne by any sane person. At the age of twelve summers, her village had been burned, her parents killed, and she and her two sisters had been sold into slavery. All three of them had been brutalized. Then her sisters were sold to bad men and hauled away. Within hours they'd both been murdered—leaving her alone. Or rather, in the company of a small group of children from many nations. Among them, Wrass, who was now called Hiyawento, Tutelo, Zateri, and the man she knew as Dekanawida.

She had lost so much.

He hurt for her.

For a time, he watched the snow fall. The forest had gone silent. He could hear each flake that settled upon the branches and rocks.

The woman on the trail shoved up on one elbow. Snow-covered jet waves cascaded around her slender, muscular body. Her shoulders heaved. Was she weeping? He couldn't see her face. She'd rolled onto her hands and knees, and fought to shove to her feet, but her legs shook too violently.

Flakes whirled and spun around the woman, tousling her hair over her eyes. The woman angrily brushed it aside, sat up, and propped her elbows atop her knees as she massaged her temples. Forlorn, she murmured, "Dear gods, I can't believe I'm lost. I know this country."

Slowly, so as not to startle her, Sonon moved out of the trees and onto the path directly ahead of her. His black cape must be almost invisible in the darkness and falling snow.

But Baji was a warrior. She saw him.

Fast as lightning she lunged to her feet and pulled the war club from her belt, ready to swing it with deadly accuracy. Her legs wobbled so badly, they barely held her. "Show yourself now, you worthless worm!"

He opened his arms, revealing that he carried no weapons, and called, "I mean you no harm."

Her eyes widened, and the war club in her fists trembled. Barely above a whisper, she called, "*Shago-niyoh?* Dear gods, please tell me Dekanawida is all right?"

It didn't surprise him that her first question was not for herself, but for the only man she'd ever loved. "He is well enough."

Her shoulders sagged. The white chert nodule lashed to the club's head dipped toward the snow, blended with it. She spread her feet to brace her weak knees. "There are warriors after him, trying to kill him. Do you know that?"

"Yes, I know."

Angry, she said, "Then why are you here? You should be with him!"

He walked toward her and she stiffened. When he stood less than three paces away, he said, "I thought, perhaps, you might have questions for me."

Using the sleeve of her war shirt, she wiped the tears from her cheeks. "Get away from me. Dekanawida is the one who needs you."

Sonon cautiously took another step toward her. She did not back away, but her fingers clutched her war club so tightly that her nails went white. The scent of her fear pervaded the night air.

Softly, he asked, "How are you feeling?" and gestured to her head wound. Blood caked the area behind her right ear.

Baji ignored him while she tied the club back to her belt. A bold move, given how close he stood. "It's healing. I'll be all right."

"And what of your father, Chief Cord? Did he escape?"

Her gaze searched the white-sheathed branches of the maples, and darted over the brush. Out in the forest, a few large boulders hunched like white-caped monsters. She stared at them. "I saw him carried from the field of battle, but I . . . I can't . . ." She shook her head and dread twisted her features. "I can't remember. Gods, what's wrong with me?"

Gently, he said, "Head wounds. They knock the souls loose for a time."

Her black eyes riveted on Sonon's face, at once pleading and demanding. "Is Father all right? Do you know?"

"No, I'm sorry. I followed you when you left the battle-field. I don't know what happened after that."

Apprehensive, she asked, "Why did you follow me?"

He replied gently, "Most people have questions. About themselves. About where they are. I know these trails very well."

She sucked in a breath and turned around, bewildered, studying the forest. The white veil was growing heavier by the instant. "The only thing I want to know is how to find Dekanawida. Is he on this trail?"

He heaved a sad sigh. "Yes."

"How far ahead of me?"

"Are you sure you wish to find him? You don't have to, Baji. There are other—"

"I *must* find him!" The slightest hint of panic entered her eyes, then it turned into a glare. "I told you, he's being hunted by murderers. The last thing Atotarho's warrior—"

"And you believed him." She must have or she wouldn't be here.

She gave Sonon a withering look. She'd always had a fierce way about her. "You mean he lied to me?"

"No. There are two warriors on Sky Messenger's back-trail. It's just that your belief is what—"

"Blessed Spirits, he has no weapons!" she cried. "Don't you understand? Stop wasting my time and tell me how far ahead he is. He needs me."

She clamped her jaw and her beautiful face went as hard as granite. Her patience was wearing thin. He could tell from the killing glitter in her eyes.

"Baji, he does need you. He always has, but just this once, you must think of yourself. You—"

"Can I help him?"

The straightforward simplicity of the question touched him.

Blessed gods, she knows . . . and she doesn't care. I underestimated her.

He stood still for a long time, holding her gaze, before he nodded. "Yes, but there is a great risk. You could be a distraction, and many people get so turned around here that they never—"

She stalked by him, just brushing his shoulder with hers, and broke into a shambling dog-tired trot.

"Baji, please don't do this."

She didn't slow down, but called, "You did, didn't you?"

She disappeared into the darkness and storm.

Sonon hung his head and studied the place where she'd lain in the trail. Her body had sculpted the snow. When she'd seen twelve summers, he'd often charted her course by such impressions. Her course and those of the other captive children. What had he expected her to do? He was, after all, the ghost that inhabited the murdering place. She had always chosen life, especially life for those she loved.

Nothing could stop her from trying to save them, not even the threat of losing her own soul and being condemned to wander the earth forever.

The snowfall dwindled and through breaks in the clouds, he glimpsed the brilliant Path of Souls that led to the afterlife. The campfires of the dead sparkled and winked, as though the ancestors passed back and forth in front of them.

Such longing swelled his heart that he had to look away.

An old hermit, a Trader from the far West, had once told Sonon that those who suffered long enough for the sake of others would always be found. He said that while all lost souls would be shown the way to the Land of the Dead after the human False Face wiped the world clean of evil, even before that there was hope—because faithful friends never gave up.

He wanted to believe. For her sake.

Unbidden, a face flashed and vanished behind his eyes.

Hopocan.

He tried to block the images, but like all true horrors, they paid no attention to individual wants and needs.

She, too, had been a great warrior woman. In his sixteenth summer, Sonon and Hopocan had been trotting down the war trail, side-by-side, smiling at each other, when the attack came. An arrow pierced Hopocan's back. He'd carried her home and covered her with soft elkhides from which she never again rose. At first, she'd grown ashen and corpselike. Then her real suffering began. The evil Spirits of gangrene edged from her wound and slithered into her body. Puss leaked from her mouth and enormous worms lived in her flesh. Her muscles decayed, hanging together only by transparent sinews. Had her affliction come from a natural source, she would blessedly have died one moon earlier. But the malignant living creature had been sent by the Ancestors. Sonon had rocked her in his arms until it was over.

He lifted his eyes to the Cloud People. Grandmother Moon's light slivered their edges as they traveled south, trailing the veil of snow beneath them. Hopocan was up there somewhere, sitting before the campfires of the dead, laughing and telling stories. He prayed she had forgotten him. The possibility that she might be waiting for him was too great a burden to bear.

After her death he had spent many torturous moons trying to make sense of it, and had come to believe that her staggering sufferings were, in reality, a glimpse granted by the Ancestors of a greater truth: The "Law of Retribution" extended far beyond the world of the living. It coiled in the heart of existence itself—and existence demanded that someone pay the price of war. Hopocan had not been called; he had.

He turned to look back at the trail.

The white slash weaved through the forest, glistening as it filled up with snow, obliterating Baji's tracks. He couldn't let her get too far ahead.

When he fell into a steady, distance-eating trot, he whispered, "Yes, Baji, I did."

Sixteen

War Chief Hiyawento stood tall and straight, his nocked bow gripped in his hands, watching his warriors appear and disappear, moving through the stark trees, searching the forest for either intruders or survivors of the River-bank Village battle. The stench of carrion was everywhere. Drawn by it, wolves had come in the night, prowling for the food inevitably left in the wake of war parties. Occasionally, a man shouted at the animals, and warning growls and barks erupted in response.

Wind Woman flapped his short hair around his eagle face as he turned to examine the smoldering palisades that sent black smoke trailing across the blue midmorning sky. The village sat on the highest terrace of the Sundrop River, a small rushing stream that babbled over rocks as it cut its way across the tree-covered hills. Inside the village, Zateri, Kwahseti, and Gwinodje wandered through the destroyed longhouses. Their ominous voices carried.

The story was clear. The villagers had received Kwahseti's message to leave as soon as possible, but a small contingent of warriors had remained behind. If he'd been at Coldspring Village when such a message came, he would have done the same thing. Get most of the people out, but leave warriors—all volunteers—to guard the walls for as long as possible, delaying the enemy, giving their fleeing relatives more time to reach the safety of Canassatego Village. As best he could tell, thirty warriors had remained. Men and women who knew it was a death sentence, but stayed anyway.

War Chief Thona wandered the ruins with his jaw clamped, a handful of trusted deputies at his side. When Thona pointed, deputies bent to collect the bones of the fallen. Most were blackened. Those warriors had died in the fires, still at their posts on the walls. Others, the survivors, had been chopped apart. Their bones bore the unmistakable evidence of cannibalism. The long bones of the legs and arms had been split open with war clubs to get to the roasted marrow inside. Several showed "pot polish," the sheen associated with having been stirred in a ceramic pot for a long time.

Hiyawento's pulse beat a dull rhythm in his ears. Did Coldspring Village look like this? Or worse? Had any of the villagers managed to escape? Or had they been attacked before they could leave? His souls spun hideous images.

Curses rang out in the forest. A man shouted. A woman tried to calm him down. Dread tingled the winter-scented air. Every person feared this place and the lost souls who roamed the shadows. They were all anxious to be away, to get to Canassatego Village to find out which of their relatives had survived.

Hiyawento looked inside the destroyed village again.

Sky Messenger had told Hiyawento once, just a few days ago, that he could see them . . . the lost souls. They appeared as small yellowish lights bobbing across battlefields or through the husks of destroyed villages. Sometimes, he heard them weeping, confused because their relatives wouldn't talk to them, not understanding they were dead.

Hiyawento bowed his head and glared at the brown oak leaves tumbling across the ground in the cold gusts of wind. He felt dead inside. *Too much violence.* It gutted the world. His body echoed with emptiness, as though the deaths of his daughters, and the constant warfare, had chased his souls away, leaving behind a hollow cocoon filled with rage. Is that how these lost souls felt?

He searched for any glint of bobbing soul lights, but saw only wind-tormented branches and ash and smoke whirling through the air.

Thona stalked across the decimated village, exited the gates, and came to stand beside Hiyawento. His heavily scarred face was grim and determined. "We should be on our way."

"Matron Kwahseti has decided not to bury the remains of your relatives?"

Thona shook his head. "We'll return when we can and care for them. Right now, we must care for the living. Canassatego Village may be under attack as we speak. If so, our living relatives need our help more."

Zateri, Kwahseti, and Gwinodje walked through the smoking gates, talking softly, their faces pale and cold, as though what they'd seen had drained them of warm blood from their bodies.

Zateri's desperate gaze clung to Hiyawento's. She must be seeing the same hideous images he was: Their home burned to the ground, cannibalized dead bodies strewn across the forest . . .

Kwahseti's gray hair flipped around her squinted eyes. She stared at Hiyawento, then Thona. "Call in our warriors. We're leaving now."

"Yes, Matron," Thona answered. He cupped a hand to his mouth and yipped his distinctive lone wolf cry.

Warriors instantly began to emerge from the forest and trot toward the village, coalescing into a whispering, eddying army of exhausted men and women.

Just before Hiyawento turned toward the trail, voices went up at the outer margins of the army, but they were not warning voices. A path opened as warriors backed away, allowing a single man to trot forward.

"Who is it?" Zateri asked as she moved to stand at Hiyawento's side. "Can you tell?"

"No."

The man came forward at a sluggish trot, as though his legs felt like granite weights. He was tall, with a Trader's burly shoulders. Long black hair draped the front of his undecorated soot-coated cape. Faint recognition began to dawn on Hiyawento. The man had a straight nose. His mouth clamped into a white line. He kept squinting, as though he couldn't see very well at a distance.

"Towa!" Hiyawento broke into a run, rushing to meet him.

When Towa recognized him, a tired smile came to his lips. They embraced, pounding each other's back hard enough to leave them breathless.

"Blessed gods," Towa said. "We feared you were all dead."

"No, my friend, we—"

"Tell me quickly," Towa said as he shoved away. "Are the stories true? Did Sky Messenger lift his hands and call a gigantic storm that swept the warriors from the battlefield?"

"Yes, yes, he did. Now tell me, did everyone make it safely to Canassatego Village?"

Zateri, Kwahseti, and Gwinodje crowded around them, listening. Chief Canassatego came up behind Gwinodje, his wrinkled face somber, framed with gray braids. Thona stood behind Kwahseti like an angry giant.

Towa swallowed hard and nodded. "Yes. I led the Riverbank Villagers there. A few hands of time later, villagers from Coldspring Village rushed the palisades, crying that Atotarho's forces were right behind them." He took a deep breath and took a few moments to look at the assembled matrons. "Matron Gwinodje, Chief Canassatego, your village was so well prepared it was astonishing. They flung open the gates for the Coldspring refugees, then lowered bracing logs across them and ran to man the catwalks. Our warriors were already up there, standing shoulder-to-shoulder with yours. When Atotarho's forces hit the walls it . . . it was a grisly sight. Within the first quarter-hour we killed so many that the dead piled against the palisades three deep." He bowed his head as though unable to continue. A dread silence possessed the army. Every ear strained to hear his story. "After three hands of time, it was over. The remnant of Atotarho's army that survived fled."

Thona looked shocked. "What fool led the attack? Why didn't he back away when he saw he couldn't breach the walls?"

"A deputy war chief from Turtleback Village appeared to be in charge, but you can't blame him. He died very early in the attack. After his death, his forces seemed to have no head. They just threw themselves at the walls as though senseless rage motivated them."

"How many died?" Zateri asked in an emotionless voice, as though she'd already braced herself for the worst.

Towa stared at her with an agonized expression. "Inside Canassatego Village, we lost one-hundred-eleven. Another one hundred fifty-two were wounded. But outside . . . I'd say Atotarho attacked with maybe seven hundred warriors, and when it was done, maybe two hundred fled back through the forest."

Whispers began to eddy through the army, men and women relaying the story to those farther back who hadn't been able to hear. A low moan, composed of many voices, drifted on the wind. They had been forced to kill their relatives. There would be blood feuds and weeping for generations.

Zateri said, "We can hear the rest of the story after we've arrived at Canassatego Village. Let's move out."

As Thona tramped onto the trail and fell into a steady trot, warriors swarmed onto the trail behind him. The sound of thousands of feet striking the frozen earth resembled a deep-throated growl. The forest went still, the animals afraid to move.

Hiyawento said, "Give me a moment, matrons?"

Zateri, Kwahseti, and Gwinodje turned to him. Chief Canassatego waited, as well.

"Now that we know our villagers have made it safely to Canassatego Village, I request permission to join Sky Messenger. He should soon be in the Landing People villages. That's a single day's run for me."

Towa gripped his shoulder and a smile came to his exhausted face. "Will you let me join you? I know the Landing elders. I can make introductions."

"Towa, you're exhausted. I'll be moving as fast as I can."

"Even if I hold you back so that it takes two days to get there, I was in Shookas Village only one moon ago. They hate the Hills People so much that I assure you, without me, they will kill you on sight."

Hiyawento studied the man's fatigued eyes and trembling legs, but said, "Then I would welcome having you along, Towa."

Kwahseti tucked short gray hair behind one ear. "I have no objections to this."

Gwinodje turned to Canassatego. "What is your opinion, Chief?"

The man's deeply wrinkled face twisted. "One man will make no difference at our village."

Gwinodje nodded. "I agree."

Zateri's eyes tightened with worry. For a long time, she looked at him, as if memorizing his face should she never see it again. "I pray the Forest Spirits guide you. Be careful."

Hiyawento hugged her tightly, kissed her, and said, "Thank you. We'll return to Canassatego Village as quickly as we can."

Seventeen

Pewter moonlight penetrated the gaps between the Cloud People and shone upon the narrow trail that wound through the towering chestnuts and sycamores. Baji took another step, maintaining the tension on her bowstring.

The scent of snow and wet bark suffused the wind. As Grandmother Moon traveled across the night sky, the branch shadows that created a lattice on the forest floor shifted, striping the snow and the white bark of birches. Then it flashed upon faces. Sometimes, owl eyes reflected, other times wolf eyes. Neither held her attention for more than an instant. Instead, she focused on the two men and the dog in the forest ahead of her.

Dekanawida's knee-length cape, worn and soiled from the soot of many campfires, swayed around his tall body. Since she'd last seen him, he'd cut his black hair short in mourning for friends lost in the battle. It draped over his round face in irregular chopped-off locks. His brown eyes seemed focused on a small copse of pawpaws to his right, which meant he was paying no attention at all to his backtrail. Did he see another threat on the trail ahead? It was the only reason she could determine that he would be this careless. The unknown man sneaking through the forest twenty paces to Dekanawida's left had already nocked his bow. He was smiling, his rotted front teeth exposed in the moonlit gleam.

Gitchi had his white muzzle up, dutifully scenting the air for danger, but the breeze was blowing in his face, shoving the man's stink back over Baji. Gitchi's eyes, too, clung to the pawpaws.

With ghostly skill, Baji used the massive sycamore trunks—four times as wide as her body—as cover, slipping from one to another, slowly moving around behind the unknown man. He seemed oblivious to her presence.

She flared her nostrils. The odor of the man's sweat carried a particular pungency that she recognized. Despite his smile, he was afraid. Dekanawida was a formidable warrior. Even without weapons, if he got close enough, he would snap his assailant's spine in less than three heartbeats. Not only that, if this man had been involved in the battle at Bur Oak and Yellowtail villages, he'd seen the freak storm rise over the eastern hills, and crash down upon him like a ferocious monster. He was probably terrified that Dekanawida's Spirit Helpers were, even now, secreted in the forest shadows, waiting to attack anyone who attempted to harm the Dreamer.

Baji silently lifted her foot, tested the ground for snow-covered twigs that might snap beneath her weight, then eased her moccasin down. The hired killer paused suddenly, as though he'd heard something, and turned to look in her direction.

Baji shifted enough that she could just barely see him from the corner of her vision. Eyes drew eyes. Even in the darkness. It was an almost unnatural thing. A warrior may not see weapons, or capes, or distinctive human shapes, but his gaze would rivet upon other human eyes as though he sensed more than saw them. Once eyes caught his attention, everything else fell into place: arms, legs, weapons.

The man fidgeted, uneasy, as though he knew he was being tracked, but saw nothing behind him. He looked back at Dekanawida and Gitchi, who'd continued up the trail, and were now too far ahead of him for a sure bowshot. The unknown man's lips moved in what appeared to be a curse, and he foolishly hurried to catch up.

As he dodged behind trees and carelessly crunched twigs beneath his moccasins, Baji patiently stalked him.

The forest always knew what was about to happen long before humans did, and the land exuded an exotic fragrance. To Baji's right, thirty paces distant, a single lynx eye shone, half-hidden behind a boulder, focused on a snowshoe hare's glistening ears, almost invisible in the white blanket that littered the ground. There was an air of expectancy, as though the animals waited for the final moment so that they could thaw their muscles and continue on their nightly search for food.

When the killer was again in range of Dekanawida, he halted, leaned his shoulder against a tree to brace his shot, and drew back his bow.

An unearthly calm descended, as though the silence of eternity had smothered the pitiful sounds of the world's struggle. Peaceful eons seemed to pass as Baji spread her feet and aimed at his broad back. The white spirals on the fool's black cape provided excellent targets. She took a breath, held it, and let fly. The arrow glistened in the moonlight as it sailed between the tree trunks, hissing slightly as it lanced the darkness. *Shish-thump.* It was a soft sound, but the man stumbled and loosed his arrow. The shot went high, clattered in the branches over Dekanawida's head.

Gitchi barked, whirled, and lunged for the man.

Dekanawida breathlessly spun around.

Gitchi leaped upon the warrior, knocked him to the ground, and transformed from warm companion to a snarling whirlwind of muscled fur. When the dying man's scream erupted, it seemed to come from nowhere, directionless and terrifying.

As the lynx and snowshoe hare thrashed away into the forest, flurries of startled wings erupted from the branches. The night sky suddenly filled with birds.

Baji nocked another arrow and charged forward, leaping fallen branches, trying to get to the man before he could pick up his bow again.

Dekanawida must have seen her. He dashed for the dying man, too.

Just before she and Dekanawida converged, Gitchi ripped the murderer's throat out and danced back, barking and growling, leaving Baji and Dekanawida to finish the job. The man, who'd managed to get on his knees, toppled face-first into the snow.

Baji kept her bow aimed at him, but her first arrow had done the job. Taking him through the left side, it had pierced his lung. A dark stain spread across his back. The man briefly struggled, groaned. His fingers clenched nothing but snow.

When the killer sagged and his limbs stopped twitching, Baji looked up.

Dekanawida stood frozen, staring at her. His mouth was open, his brown eyes wide, as though stunned. "Baji. What . . . what are you doing here?"

She slung her bow over her shoulder and stalked forward to glare at him. "What's the matter with you? How could you let anyone get this close? If I hadn't been here, you'd be dead."

Sputtering with surprise, he said, "I—I thought I saw someone . . . ahead of me on the trail. I never even heard this warrior."

"Obviously," she chided. "Has your Dream killed your warrior's instincts?"

Gitchi, who'd waited as he'd been taught and now understood the danger was over, loped forward and leaped up to put his big paws in the middle of Baji's chest. She staggered beneath his weight, and ruffled the thick fur of his neck. "Gitchi, the warrior dog, good work!"

The love in his eyes was palpable. His tail swiped the air.

When Gitchi jumped down, Dekanawida embraced her hard enough to drive the air from her lungs. Tears filled Baji's eyes.

"I can't believe you're here. Blessed gods, how did you find me? I didn't myself know the trail I'd take, let alone—"

"Shh," she cautioned.

The feel of his muscular arms around her somewhat eased her panic, but her eyes continued to scan the forest over his shoulder, searching for the second killer she knew was out there somewhere.

"Where did you think you saw the other man?"

Dekanawida reluctantly released her and turned. He

dipped his head, indicating a dense copse of pawpaw saplings to the right of the trail. "Over there."

They stood side-by-side staring at it, their gazes sweeping the shadows, moving across the moonlit snow.

Gitchi noted their gazes and sniffed the wind, then trotted to stand at Dekanawida's side.

"I don't see anything now," Dekanawida whispered.

"Let's look for tracks, just to make certain."

"I'll go left. You go right."

"Not a good idea," she said bluntly. "I have weapons, you don't. I can't protect you if we're widely separated. Come with me."

Baji led the way, taking a few careful steps at a time, stopping to survey every moonlit shape, then taking a few more steps toward the saplings. As they neared the copse, she noticed the single gigantic pignut hickory that stood behind pawpaws. Twenty times her height, its leafless branches created a dark tracery against the moonlit Cloud People. The egg-shaped nuts had fallen all over the ground. They resembled a bumpy blanket beneath the snow. Dangerous to walk upon, they rolled beneath a warrior's feet.

"You're sure this is where you saw him?" she asked. "No warrior with sensibilities would walk here."

"I know," he whispered behind her shoulder. "But this is where I saw movement. It might have just been a deer . . . but it looked human-shaped."

Baji's eyes narrowed. She veered right around the copse, glanced down at the ground, then up to scan the forest for the man. As she tiptoed around behind the pawpaws, she saw the fresh tracks.

"Well, there they are," she murmured.

Gitchi bounded forward to sniff them.

"Just one man," Dekanawida said.

He slid around her and went to kneel beside Gitchi, examining the tracks, while Baji kept her eyes on the forest. Snow had collected in the crook of the hickory and resembled a white sparkling nest. Against the cobalt background of moon-silvered forest, it seemed unnaturally bright. Deeper in the shadows, white cedars dotted the landscape. Half the height of the hickory, slender, bell-shaped cones hung from their evergreen branches. If she concentrated, she could just smell their sweet scent. Nothing moved out there. Even Wind Woman had fled this part of the forest.

"Baji, come take a look."

When Dekanawida stood up and heaved a sigh, Gitchi trotted away, suddenly unconcerned, to sniff out a rabbit trail.

Baji worked her way over to Dekanawida, her bow still half-drawn, and glanced down at the clear tracks in the fresh snow. A big man, his feet had sunken deep, but there was something more interesting. As her gaze roved the area, she saw no tracks coming in or going out. It was as though he'd just appeared here, took a few steps, and disappeared into the moonlight.

Baji released the tension on her bow. "Sandal tracks. Herringbone pattern. Hills People."

Dekanawida's handsome face relaxed. "But if Shago-niyoh came to see me, why didn't he stay to speak—"

"He may have come to see me."

Dekanawida paused. "To see you?"

Baji listened to the night. The distant howling of wolves drifted through the moonlight. "Shago-niyoh visited me on the trail yesterday. Right after the battle."

Dekanawida didn't seem to be breathing. "What battle?"

"The day we left Bur Oak Village, we were ambushed by Atotarho's forces." A mixture of fear and hatred warmed her breast when she remembered the enemy flooding from the trees. *My fault. I am War Chief. I should have seen them long before we entered the valley. How many dead? How many friends . . .* "We lost hundreds in the first few moments. Father was wounded."

Dekanawida gripped her arm hard. "Is he all right?"

"I—I don't know." She rubbed behind her right ear. She'd combed out the caked blood, but the hair remained stiff. The swollen lump had given her an almost unbearable headache that dimmed her wits.

Dekanawida stepped around, pulled the long waves of her black hair aside, and sucked in a breath when he saw the club wound. "Blessed Ancestors, Baji! Why aren't you in bed somewhere? You should have stopped at the first village to see a Healer. You know better than to ignore a head wound—"

"There's another killer after you," she explained.

He backed away slightly. "How do you know?"

"Just before I received this club wound, the man yelled at me: 'Before I crush your skull, you should know that my brothers are hunting down your filthy lover right now.'"

"Sent by Atotarho?"

"Who else?"

Dekanawida eased her hair back into place over her wound, and reached down to tightly clasp her hand. "I was going to walk for most of the night, but I've changed my mind. We're making camp so I can tend that head wound."

Baji let him lead her out of the pawpaw copse and to a place beneath the arching branches of the pignut hickory, where an old log lay. After he'd brushed the snow from the wood, he ordered, "Sit down and rest while I get a fire going."

"Just for a moment." She sat on the log.

As Dekanawida went about cracking dead limbs from the tree trunk, Baji forced herself to concentrate. Her legs were shaking. When had that happened? She pulled her bow and quiver from her shoulder and propped them against the log beside her. Suddenly, she felt utterly exhausted. Her head now hurt so badly she knew it would explode at any instant. She leaned forward, braced her elbows on her knees, and massaged her temples. Fiery pokers stabbed behind her eyes.

Gitchi came around the log, apparently satisfied that the rabbit was nowhere to be found, and curled up at Baji's feet. She lowered one hand to pat his side, and went back to massaging her temple.

Dekanawida returned, dropped one armload of branches on the ground, smiled at her, and went back to gathering wood, cracking twigs from one of the nearby chestnuts.

Baji granted herself the luxury of closing her eyes. After all, Shago-niyoh was close. Surely, he and Gitchi would protect Dekanawida while she rested.

. . . A short while later, Baji sneaked through the forest, coming up behind the camp of the Hills warrior who'd shot Cord. The man sat with five friends before a campfire, tearing off big chunks of venison jerky with his rotted teeth, laughing too loudly. He liked to wave his hands as he talked. It made him appear a blustering fool. How strange. She thought she'd killed him. But here he was, surrounded by relatives, chortling like an imbecile, and obviously enjoying himself. One of the men had left a war ax lying at the edge of the trees. He'd probably been using it to hack off branches for the fire and forgotten it.

It lay half covered with snow five paces in front of her.

She might have let the man go if Dzadi hadn't appeared in the trees on the opposite side of the clearing and nodded his head to her, encouraging her to continue. Then her friend Ogwed appeared just to her right, and whispered, "We have them surrounded, War Chief."

"Good."

Ogwed led her forward, picked up the ax, brushed the snow off on his pants, then put it in her hand. "We all wish to kill him, but it is your right."

Baji's fingers went tight around the handle. Glimmering through the trees, she saw the firelit faces of many friends—men and women she had fought with. They would guard her back while she completed her task.

Baji stalked into the clearing and the men around the fire leaped to their feet. From the trees, arrows hissed and each fell silently to the ground, leaving only her quarry standing.

"Hello, fool."

Like the coward he was, the man rushed to put the fire between them. As he thrust out his empty hands, he said, "War Chief Baji! What are you doing here?"

Baji cautiously flanked him. She felt neither pity nor hatred, just the calculation of a warrior fulfilling her duty.

"Wait. Let's talk this over!" the man shouted, and tried to run.

Baji raced forward to cut off his escape. They circled each other.

The man said, "You bitch in heat! I'll club you like a fish." He kept glancing at a red-painted war club a few paces away, lying canted against a rolled blanket.

As Baji closed in, the man lunged for the club, grabbed it, and rolled away.

Baji dove for him. Her ax chopped into the spine at the base of his neck, and he went limp. Lying broken on the ground, his eyes were still upon hers, blinking feverishly. His fingers twitched and jerked. His lungs desperately sucked and expelled air. She tossed the ax aside and got her hands around his throat, grunting as she fought to strangle him.

Dzadi, Ogwed, and the others edged out of the trees to watch.

When she felt the enemy warriors's heart stop, when his frantic lungs no longer pulled at his throat, she staggered to her feet and stared down into his dead eyes. The fire had gone out. How quickly the night cooled! Darkness seeped close around her. She looked past Dzadi's blank face to a narrow starlit trail that weaved through the trees. In the distance, at the end of the trail, a bridge spanned a dark glistening river. Flint country lay on the other side. She knew it, could feel home in her bones, calling to her.

How would Cord take it when he heard that she had avenged him?

Baji walked out of the clearing, her friends following behind, and passed on into Wild River Village in search of a warm longhouse. The familar crowd filled the plaza. Women used mallets to pound corn in hollowed-out logs. Old men slept in the sunshine beneath the porches, with dogs curled at their sides. Children played stick-and-ball games along the palisade wall. None seemed to notice that Baji and a remnant of her war party had returned home. Not that it mattered. The day was warm and fragrant with the scent of dogwood blossoms. They would gather around the plaza bonfire with the other warriors who stood eating heaping bowls of freshly roasted grouse and talking of the latest news. And what was that in their hands? Cornmeal biscuits dripping with bumblebee honey! As she led her party closer, Baji saw twenty or more grouse, skewered on poles, being cooked over the flames, sizzling with fat.

"Baji?" Dzadi called happily. "How will we ever eat so much?"

She turned, smiling, but . . .

"Baji?"

Not Dzadi.

She suffered a moment of disorientation. Couldn't figure out . . .

"Baji, I need you to wake up."

Dekanawida's deep voice. A hand rested lightly on her shoulder.

She opened her eyes. "Gods, I'm sorry. I must have fallen to sleep."

She sat up and braced her hands on the log on either side of her hips. Her long black hair fell forward over her cape.

"I didn't want to wake you, but I need you to lie on your left side so I can get to your head wound. I must care for it tonight, before the Evil Spirits smell the blood and fly to nest in your flesh."

A wooden bowl clacked as he set it on the log, and she noticed in surprise that a small fire burned not two paces away. The bowl, filled with warm water and a piece of soaked hide, steamed.

She nodded tiredly. "Thank you. I'm just so tired."

Dekanawida's thick brows drew down over his slender nose. His jagged locks of short hair sleeked down around his wide mouth and blunt chin. In a tender voice, he instructed, "If you'll stretch out on your left side on the log, I'll try to work. I don't want any of the water to drip down and soak your cape. You need to stay dry and warm tonight. When I'm done, I'll wrap you in my blanket."

Baji's wounded arm shook as she braced it to ease down onto her left side, so that Dekanawida could clean the swollen lump behind her right ear.

In a stern voice, he said, "I'm heating willow bark tea for you. When I've finished cleaning, I want you to drink it. It will help with the headache."

"If I'm awake."

She thought he nodded. She wasn't sure.

Dekanawida squeezed out the soaked hide and started washing the lump. The warm water hurt. But his touch was a balm upon her soul. He had large hands, strong, and they worked with practiced skill. As a deputy war chief, he'd tended many wounds in his time. Tonight though, his face was aspen-bark white, his eyes blazing like polished brown chert.

"Close your eyes and try to rest," he ordered.

Hundreds of summers from now, while she slumbered in an old tree, the sound of his deep voice would fill her lonely dreams.

The firelight threw faint multiple shadows across his concerned face.

Gitchi's ears suddenly pricked, and he turned to stare out at the white cedars. Baji glimpsed something. The hem of a wind-blown black cape, flapping wildly, like a trick of moonlight in the saplings, for the forest around her was absolutely still.

A faint smile came to her lips.

He's standing guard. I don't have to.

Eighteen

For the moment, Yi ignored the dusty messenger who stood, breathing hard, on the opposite side of the fire. A shaft of afternoon sunlight streamed down through the smokehole, landing like a golden scarf across his dirty trail-weary face. Yi continued pacing the floor of the longhouse, thinking.

Yi's chamber in the Wolf Clan longhouse in Atotarho Village sat at the far end, eight hundred hands away from the former High Matron's chamber. Tila was gone, her chamber empty, but Yi still felt the weight of her presence, as if Tila's Spirit had refused to travel to the afterlife, and remained in the longhouse. Her afterlife soul had not been Requickened yet, and it was a terrible spiritual loss for the clan. It weakened all of them. Almost everyone had assumed that when Zateri returned from the battle, she would receive her grandmother's soul.

Yi looked down the length of the house, her gaze passing over the many chambers and people sitting around their fires. Women nearby weaved baskets from willow staves. Children played with cornhusk toys. Yi missed

Tila desperately. Especially now when the clan needed her guidance so desperately.

So much had happened in the past half-moon, she was having trouble making sense of things.

First, High Matron Tila had died, then had come the shocking news, delivered by one of Atotarho's messengers, that Tila had named Kelek, Matron of the Bear Clan, to replace her. One did not question the Chief without good cause, but they'd all known Tila for more than forty summers. It was simply impossible. Then, yesterday morning, news had come that Coldspring Village, their sister village, had been completely abandoned. The villagers had fled in a hurry, carrying only food and blankets with them. The rest of their possessions remained in place, as if awaiting their owners' return. Scouts had seen the Coldspring villagers running up the Canassatego Village trail. Later, Atotarho Village had been flooded with returning warriors, charging through the gates, proclaiming that they'd lost the battle against the Standing Stone nation after the prophet, Sky Messenger, had called a gigantic storm that swept their forces from the field of battle. There had also been wild rumors of betrayal and civil war. Finally, *finally,* this morning, more warriors had flooded in, fresh from burning Coldspring Village to the ground. Along with them, a messenger arrived from Atotarho verifying the rumor that Zateri, Kwahseti, and Gwinodje had betrayed the Hills nation and fought on the side of the Standing Stone People. Despite their treachery, Atotarho reported that he had won the battle, and devastated the Standing Stone nation. He'd said they were but a pitiful remnant of what they had once been, and informed the Ruling Council that he would remain in Standing Stone country for perhaps one more moon, by the end of which, he said, he would have completely destroyed the Standing Stone nation.

Atotarho's report had humiliated the Wolf Clan. Matrons from all three of its ohwachiras had betrayed the nation! Where just a few days ago, the Wolf Clan had been the most numerous and powerful clan among the People of the Hills, the news had thrown them down to the lowest level of society. People had actually spat upon Yi and Inawa when they'd gone to grovel before High Matron Kelek, begging forgiveness, and promising to do anything necessary to prove their clan's loyalty to the Hills nation.

And now this . . .

Yi stopped pacing and looked at the messenger. He'd run hard to get to her. His elkhide cape bore a thick coating of grime and dust, as did his black hair and round face. He looked to have seen perhaps seventeen summers.

"What is your name, warrior?"

"Skanawati, great Matron."

"Of Riverbank Village, I assume?"

"I am. Matron Kwahseti sent me to you."

Two little boys raced by, laughing, and ducked through the door curtain out into the cold afternoon air.

The messenger shifted, clearly wishing to be on his way. His gaze appeared fixed on the beautiful False Face masks that decorated the rear wall of Yi's chamber. They did not have bent noses, as other masks did, rather they had extremely long noses and fanged mouths. Her masks had been handed down from grandmother to grandmother for more than three centuries. The legends of her ohwachira said they came from the great cities of the ancient moundbuilders, from a distant ancestor named

Lichen. Sometimes late at night, she heard them whispering to one another.

"Well, Skanawati, your message has left me with many questions. Please, sit. Let us talk for a time."

The man nodded respectfully, and knelt on the mat on the opposite side of the fire. As he did so, a slave girl rushed to dunk a teacup, made from the skull of a Flint warrior, into the boiling bag that hung on the tripod near the fire, and brought it to him.

"You must be hungry and thirsty. I'll have food brought." Yi waved to the girl, who ran to fetch a basket of bread. She set it beside the warrior and dutifully backed away.

"Thank you for your kindness." Skanawati finished the tea in four gulps, looking like he cherished every swallow. Then he shoved two corncakes, filled with walnuts, into his mouth and seemed to swallow them whole. When he'd finished, he wiped his hands on his leggings, heaved a sigh, and looked up at Yi.

The afternoon gleam that streamed down from the smokehole lanced the thick blue wood smoke. As he lifted a hand to wipe his mouth, the sunlit smoke curled around it. He looked nervous, perhaps even afraid. As well, he should.

It had only been through her good graces that he had not been murdered when he'd appeared at the gates demanding to speak with her. After all, he came from a village that had just betrayed their nation.

Yi ran a hand through her graying black hair. She had seen forty-eight summers pass, but she'd never witnessed a winter like this. The wrinkles that cut around her mouth and across her forehead deepened when she glared at him.

"I need to know every detail of the battle."

"I'll be happy to answer any question you have, Matron."

Yi considered her words, before asking, "At some point matrons Zateri, Kwahseti, and Gwinodje decided to fight against Chief Atotarho. Was it after they'd received news of the former High Matron's journey to the afterlife?"

He nodded. "Yes. In the middle of the battle, Atotarho dispatched a messenger to Matron Zateri asking her to move her forces into position around Bur Oak and Yellowtail villages to prepare to attack. At the same time, he informed her that her grandmother was walking the Path of Souls, and told her the former High Matron had named Kelek to succeed her."

Zateri must have known it couldn't be true. Like every other matron in the Wolf Clan, she would have suspected foul play on Atotarho's part.

"Were matrons Kwahseti and Gwinodje present when the news came?"

"Yes, Matron." He nodded and respectfully bowed his head.

Yi resumed her pacing. Gods, how would she have felt if she'd just learned that her entire clan, thousands of people, had been stripped of their rightful place in the nation? A place their mothers, grandmothers, and great-great-great grandmothers had struggled for generations to achieve? The sacrifices their clan had made for the good of the People of the Hills were legendary. She would have been outraged. As, of course, she *had* been. But she'd been sitting here at home in her warm longhouse, not out on a battlefield watching her kin shed their blood for a nation that had betrayed them.

If it were true that the Wolf Clan's rightful place in the nation had been stolen through treachery while its warriors were dying on the field of battle . . . clan members would demand that the Law of Retribution be fulfilled.

"Have Zateri, Kwahseti, and Gwinodje set themselves on the path of retribution?"

"I have no knowledge of any official statement to that effect, Matron. However, our former High Matron told Matron Zateri's daughter, Kahn-Tineta, that she planned to appoint Zateri to succeed her. So . . ."

When he hesitated, she ordered, "So . . . what?"

"Well, there is talk that Atotarho knew this and had our former High Matron murdered before she could appoint Zateri. Rumors say that Kelek and the Bear Clan were accomplices. If it proves to be true, we have the right to retribution."

Yi's face slackened. Murder was the worst crime. It placed an absolute obligation on the relatives of the dead to avenge the murder. They could demand reparations, exotic trade goods, finely tanned beaver robes, food. They could also claim the life of the murderer, or the life of another member of his clan, including the new High Matron's life. Such a blood feud would devastate both clans and tear what was left of the Hills People apart.

"Tell me about the storm."

The messenger's head jerked up. "How do you know of it?"

"Hundreds of our warriors have been flooding in for days. It's all they can speak of. That and the fact that Zateri and her friends apparently managed to create an alliance between three nations, or portions of three nations."

Awe filled his sparkling eyes. "Then you already know—"

"I wish to hear every detail, Skanawati."

"Yes, Matron, forgive me." He took a breath and let it out haltingly. "Gods, Matron, the storm . . . it was . . . enormous. It came boiling over the eastern hills like the wrath of the ancestors. I—"

"What was happening in the battle before the storm?"

The warrior seemed to refocus his thoughts. "The Flint People had just joined the fight on Matron Zateri's side. The fighting was ferocious. When it started to look as though we had the upper hand, Chief Atotarho dragged Zateri's daughter from his war lodge—"

"*What?*" Her heart seemed to stop. "I've heard nothing of this! Atotarho had Zateri's last surviving daughter?"

Skanawati swallowed hard. "Yes. Actually, though, I said that incorrectly, Matron. The Bluebird Witch, Ohsinoh, dragged little Kahn-Tineta from the chief's lodge, where the chief had apparently been keeping her in case he needed—"

"To use her against Zateri and Hiyawento?" she said in shock. "Are you suggesting that Chief Atotarho was working with . . . with the most evil witch in the land?"

"He was, Matron. Clearly."

Yi stalked before the fire while blood rushed in her ears. "We wondered what happened to the girl. The day the former High Matron died, Kahn-Tineta and her cousin, Pedeza, vanished. We looked everywhere for them." She suddenly felt very weary. "All right. Finish telling me about the storm."

He nodded. "First, Matron, I should tell you that I was there. I was fighting not more than ten paces from Hiyawento when it happened. I saw these things with my own eyes."

"Go on."

"Chief Atotarho shouted at Hiyawento, 'You dare to defy me! I should kill your daughter before your eyes! I will kill her if your forces do not surrender and pledge themselves to me.'" Skanawati paused to take a breath. "Truly, Matron, Hiyawento looked like he was dying inside. He told Atotarho he didn't have the authority to order such a thing, that only the matrons could approve—"

"I know that. Continue."

"Atotarho told him to get the authority, and as Hiyawento trotted across the battlefield for the matrons' camp to the south, War Chief Sindak ordered your forces to disengage, to back away"—*Your forces, not our forces. How can I ever repair this?*—"then Ohsinoh hissed something to Sky Messenger, something I couldn't hear, but the words affected him like stilettos plunged into his heart. He staggered. Then Sindak said, 'Chief, end this battle. You're asking your warriors to murder their cousins!' He—"

"Sindak was right. It should have never happened."

"Yes, well, then Sky Messenger said, as you just did, 'Sindak's right. Chief, clear the battlefield so we can talk to one another. Please, just give me fifty heartbeats.' Atotarho laughed, Matron. He laughed out loud and told Sky Messenger that he'd always been a coward." Skanawati's eyes went huge, as though seeing it again. In a reverent voice, he continued, "That's when Sky Messenger stepped away and lifted his hands to Elder Brother Sun. He shouted across the battlefield, 'This war must end! We're killing Great Grandmother Earth!'"

Skanawati halted. He started breathing hard. "Matron, it was . . ."

He shook his head, as though he still couldn't believe what he'd seen.

She waited.

He blinked, and his eyes returned to her. "There was a strange far-off rushing sound. We all turned to the east, and people started asking so many questions, the battlefield hummed. Then, and I swear to you this is true, this is how it happened."

"Tell me."

"It—it was though the mist was suddenly sucked away. The sunlight was so bright and sparkling, it hurt. The rushing started growing louder, and louder, then a black wall boiled over the forest and swelled upward into the sky. It rose so high it blotted out Elder Brother Sun's face. As it flooded toward us, the roar shook the ground. It sounded like a monstrous growling creature straight out of the old stories. We all broke and ran, trying to find any shelter we could."

She clenched her fists at her sides. "I heard that Sky Messenger did not run."

"That's true, Matron. He—he grabbed Kahn-Tineta and held her in his arms as he turned to face the storm. It was madness. We all knew he'd be killed. Trees were exploding as the storm came on. Branches, leaves, and whole trunks blasted upward into the spinning darkness."

Skanawati seemed lost in memories again.

"And then what happened?"

He jerked at the sound of her voice. "Oh"—he licked his lips—"sorry. The storm . . . I swear. I swear to you . . . the storm parted and mist, like clouds, formed on Sky Messenger's cape. It looked like he was wearing a cape of white clouds and riding the winds of destruction. Just like the old stories about the human False Face who will come at the End time to save us."

He stopped.

Yi stared into his dazzled eyes, and even she felt awe-struck. She let out the breath she'd unwittingly been hold-ing. Could it be true? Stories had been running up and down the trails for over a moon, carrying bits and pieces of Sky Messenger's Dream. Supposedly he'd Dreamed the end of the world. Zateri had tried hard to get all the Hills matrons together to hear the story from Sky Mes-senger himself. They had refused. Yi had wanted to, but . . . so many others were against it. Now, much too late, she wished she had listened.

"Skanawati, I wish you to take a message back to Ma-tron Kwahseti."

He rose to his feet and his dusty cape swayed around him.

"Tell Kwahseti that I will do what I can, but she must promise me that while I am working on the clan's behalf, her warriors will not lift a hand against their relatives."

Skanawati spread his arms. "Matron Zateri has already given that instruction, Matron. If attacked by your forces, we will defend ourselves, but we will make no hostile moves toward our relatives unless provoked."

Respect for Zateri swelled in Yi's chest. *She must be con-sidering reunification.* "Tell your matrons I need time. I must find witnesses. There are always witnesses. I will send messengers as necessary to keep her informed of what's happening here." Yi stabbed a finger at him. "Now, go."

He bowed. "Yes, Matron."

Skanawati left in a hurry, ducking through the entry curtains. She heard his feet pound away.

Yi's thoughts raced, trying to figure out how in the world she could . . .

To her right, the leather curtain parted again. Light flashed, illuminating the thick smoke in the house. Matron Inawa stepped inside. Inawa had seen fifty summers pass, had plump cheeks and a red nose. Gray-streaked black hair hung limply over her shoulders. She fixed Yi with a look that stilled the blood in her veins.

"So," Inawa said, "you received a messenger, too. Mine came from Gwinodje. Yours?"

"From Kwahseti."

Inawa walked forward and stood beside Yi, warming her hands over the fire. Inawa's gaze moved up and down the longhouse, noting the positions of those standing close by, before she quietly said, "Tomorrow, with your agreement, I will send word to the other villages. We must call a council meeting of the Wolf Clan matrons to inform them of this news. There are only four of us now."

"Of course, I agree. You are next in line after Zateri." Yi stared at the finely woven mats around the fire. Light danced in the herringbone patterns.

Inawa leaned closer to her to whisper, "It is one little girl's voice against the Chief's voice, but if the former High Matron really did name Zateri as her successor—"

"One little girl's voice won't be enough, Inawa. Someone saw something, or overheard a conversation, or was part of a conversation. We must find the witness. After our meeting, the village matrons, Ganon and Edot, must return to Turtleback Village and Hilltop Village and start asking questions—and you and I must do the same here. There had to be someone nearby in the Wolf Clan longhouse when the High Matron died. Someone heard something that day."

Inawa's gaze locked with Yi's. "If Kelek catches wind of our questions, we may not survive long enough to bring the issue before the Ruling Council. If we're wrong, the Bear Clan will charge us with treason and declare a blood oath against us."

"As we will them if this is true."

Yi's gaze drifted down the length of the longhouse, meeting the eyes of those who watched them. Even though they'd kept their voices very low, people with good ears had at least caught words, maybe a phrase here or there. Just as people had that fateful day when Tila died and Kelek became the High Matron.

Softly, she said, "Who should we select as our messengers? They must be absolutely loyal to the Wolf Clan."

Nineteen

High above Gonda, pink Cloud People continued to glide slowly across the glacial blue sky. Their rich colors stood in stark contrast to those of Bur Oak Village, still cloaked in the iron-gray shadows before dawn. Snow outlined every undulation in the bark walls of the long-houses, and frost sheathed the palisade poles like a fine glitter of quartz crystals. Throughout the plaza, people moved as though their shoulders were weighted with lead. The feel of doom pervaded the morning.

Gonda folded his arms. He stood two paces away from where Jigonsaseh, Kittle, and Sindak engaged in a quiet debate outside the council house. The meeting of the Ruling Council had begun two hands of time ago, long before dawn, and just concluded. People were filtering back across the village, heading to the warmth of their own chambers. There had been no panicked shouting or fists shaken, no accusations that they'd made a mistake staying here rather than abandoning the village and moving on . . . though they would come. Instead, the last remnant of the once great Standing Stone nation had discussed their possible annihilation with a degree of dignity and logic that stunned Gonda.

Kittle tucked shoulder-length black hair behind one ear and gave Sindak a poignant look. "Tell me what Atotarho wants. You should know. You're his former war chief."

Sindak calmly replied, "Only he can see the tracks of his own souls, Matron, but I fear he is utterly mad. I think his soul was stolen by his witch sister many summers ago."

Gonda was an outsider from a destroyed village, a refugee who'd thrown himself upon the mercy of Bur Oak Village. He really had no right to comment unless asked a direct question by the matrons, but it was hard to keep his mouth closed. For many summers, he had served as a deputy war chief, then as the Speaker for the Warriors of White Dog Village. It didn't matter that his village no longer existed, the need to participate in decision-making persisted.

"But surely he plans to attack us this morning. Tell me—"

"I'm not sure of that," Sindak replied uncomfortably.

"What are you talking about?" Kittle gestured wildly to the world beyond the palisades. "His forces are on the move, getting into position around us."

Jigonsaseh's arm muscles bulged through her white cape. In the lavender gleam, the silver threads in her short black hair glinted. "I think Sindak is right, Kittle."

"About what?" Kittle demanded to know. "he's told us nothing!"

Sindak clamped his jaw. "High Matron, if I had to guess, I would say Chief Atotarho is not planning to attack today."

"How can you say that? He's—"

"Because, Kittle," Jigonsaseh interrupted, "he's not moving his warriors into attack positions. From what I can tell, they are moving into areas where there's better protection from the wind, off the hilltops, and down into the valley, closer to water, near the ponds and creeks."

Kittle ran a hand through her shoulder-length black hair. Her large dark eyes had a strained tightness. "Which means what?"

Sindak answered, "Maybe he's giving you time to truly panic."

"*Truly* panic? Truly? That's an interesting choice of words." She glanced at him like he was a fool.

Jigonsaseh shifted, and the black bear paws encircling the bottom of her white cape seemed to be bounding away. At twelve hands tall, she looked down upon everyone else in the circle. Blessed gods, she was still beautiful. Even at thirty-nine summers, with silver threads streaking her black hair, the sight of her oval face, jet black eyes, and full lips went straight to Gonda's soft spots—and he was married to another, a good woman named Pawen. But he'd been wed to Jigonsaseh for twelve summers. He couldn't help the way he felt. A part of him would always love her.

Gonda tugged his red-painted leather cape more tightly around him. The frosty wind pricked his bones. He tried to force his attention away from their debate and to the happenings in the plaza.

No one had really slept last night, but those who'd gone to bed at all had arisen many hands of time ago. As had the enemy. Out beyond the plaza, murmuring echoes of unknown forces moved across the hills and the brittle musty scent of old leaves, kicked by thousands of feet, wafted in on the wind.

Kittle was right. *Truly* panic was an odd choice of words, since Gonda doubted it was possible for them to be more panicked. Thousands of dead bodies lay rotting everywhere they looked. The stench was growing. This was a special kind of panic, however, not the frantic grouse-with-its-head-chopped-off kind. No, this was the sort of panic the end of the world was made from. A certainty felt in the bones. A knowledge that everything a person cherished was about to be taken from him, and there was little he could do about it.

It would be easier if Atotarho would just attack.

Gonda glanced away when two litters emerged from beneath the door curtain of the Deer Clan longhouse. Upon them lay the bodies of those who'd died during the night. Thirty or so mourners followed the litters. Their cries blended eerily with the cynical amusement of the warriors on the catwalks, men and women who could see the enemy surrounding the village, and were preparing for their own deaths the only way they knew how, with morbid jokes.

Gonda turned to the west. Just over the rim of the palisade, Grandmother Moon shone like an oblate silver pendant. Most of the noise came from that direction. Large war parties on the move resembled massive wolf packs. They yipped and growled. The effect was a combination of the clatter of weapons belts, arrows rattling in quivers, laughter, and feet puncturing crusted snow. It made the hair stand up on the back of Gonda's neck.

As well, the dawn smelled like resin. It was a subtle, but terrifying scent, known to every warrior. Bur Oak Village was virtually helpless, Atotarho's victory a near certainty. His army was eager for the kill, sweating in anticipation, and the vile stench of their emotions filled the air.

"Gonda," Kittle called. "Please assist us."

He lurched forward, covering the distance in two bounds. "Yes, High Matron? How may I help?"

Kittle shoved wind-blown hair away from her dark eyes. "What is your opinion of Atotarho's intentions? What does he want? What can we give him to convince him to leave in peace?"

Sindak vented a low close-mouthed laugh, and shook his head at the inane notion, which drew a lethal glare from Kittle.

"Would you rather answer first, Sindak?" she asked curtly.

"You already know my opinion, High Matron. I'd rather hear Gonda's ideas."

"Then endeavor to hold your tongue."

Sindak suppressed a grim smile. "Yes, High Matron. My apologies."

Gonda glanced around the circle. Expressions were hard and unyielding. Sweat beaded the curve of Sindak's hooked nose. Kittle's chest rose and fell in swift breaths. Only Jigonsaseh appeared to be in utter control of her senses.

He turned to her. "My former wife, I think there's only one thing Atotarho really wants. And I suspect you know it, too."

"Maybe, but tell me anyway."

"He wants our son."

Jigonsaseh held his gaze, then nodded. "You mean because of the Human False Face prophecies?"

"Yes. For most of Atotarho's life, his people believed him to be the prophesied Spirit-Man who would don the cape of clouds at the end of time and save the world. I remember, twelve summers ago, when he told us it had never been an easy title to bear."

"And now that Sky Messenger's vision is sweeping up and down the trails, and he sees his own people applying that title to Sky Messenger, he's desperate to—"

"I'd like to say something," Kittle broke in. Jigonsaseh gracefully yielded to the High Matron. "If Sky Messenger is the only thing Atotarho really wants, all he has to do is hunt him down and kill him. He doesn't have to destroy the entire Standing Stone nation. Yet, here he is, massed outside the last bastion of the Standing Stone People, a village filled largely with starving elders and children. Why?"

Sindak waited while Gonda, Jigonsaseh, and Kittle stared at each other, then he said, "Because Sky Messenger isn't all he wants." He dipped his head apologetically to Gonda. "I mean no disrespect, Gonda. You are right that Atotarho is obsessed with achieving Sky Messenger's death, but he wants a lot more than that. He wants to rule all five nations south of Skanodario Lake."

"Well, that's never going to happen," Kittle blustered. "He's an evil cannibal sorcerer. No one will agree to submit to his rule. He'll have to enslave us to do it."

As though to affirm her suggestion, the yips and growls of the huge army moving across the valley outside penetrated the palisades, and the warriors on the catwalk muttered darkly. Several nocked bows. Others reached uneasily to dip cups of water from the pots hanging from the palisade wall, getting one last drink while they had a chance.

Jigonsaseh's eyes suddenly cut to Sindak. "If that is his intention, we are no good to him dead. He needs us alive to work the fields, to build new longhouses, to repair his vast new territory and help to guard it."

Sindak nodded. "A few of you, at least."

"Does that mean he plans to negotiate? Is that why he didn't attack last night?"

"Well"—Sindak's head waffled—"you know as well as I do that night attacks are unwise. In the darkness, it's hard to tell your own warriors from the enemy's. Too many accidents happen. The only thing night is good for is sneaking warriors closer to their targets. As to whether he plans to negotiate your surrender . . ." He shrugged. "If so, why didn't he send a messenger to you yesterday?"

Gonda's souls sifted the information, trying to think like his enemy, and a feeling of impending disaster seeped through his veins. "Maybe he plans to wait until we're desperate enough to give him everything he wants. When our food and water run out, when our warriors have no more arrows to let fly . . ."

He let the conclusion hang.

"Anything he wants?" Kittle asked. "Including Sky Messenger's dead body?"

"Or live body. He probably thinks Sky Messenger is still in this village."

The litter bearers reached the inner palisade gate, and the warriors on duty obediently checked with the second palisade guards to confirm it was safe to exit, then swung the gates open. The guards had been instructed to allow the dead to be transported beyond the walls, for as long as it was safe to do so, to keep the plaza from becoming filled with rotting corpses.

Gonda watched the middle palisade gates swing open. As the litter bearers moved toward the exterior gates, he returned his attention to Sindak. "You realize, don't you, that in the end Atotarho will also demand that we turn over you and your warriors?"

Sindak gave him a level stare. "I do."

"Well," Kittle exhaled the word. "I give you my oath we won't do that."

Sindak smiled faintly, but it didn't reach his eyes. "That's nice to hear. However, High Matron, there will come a time in the struggle when the circumstances will require that you make a choice between my people, and your own villagers. I assure you, it won't be hard."

Kittle's eyes flashed in indignation. "If you were intelligent enough to allow us to adopt you into the Standing Stone nation, that choice would cease to exist. You would *be* my villagers." Her eyes blazed. "And in the future, do not presume to tell me what I will or will not do, or your next sight will be from high up on my longhouse wall." Meaning she'd keep his severed head for a trophy.

A breath of icy wind swept the plaza, swirling up snow, and sending it gusting about.

Jigonsaseh clutched her white cape beneath her chin. "With respect, Kittle, adopting Sindak and his people may change their status in our own nation, but it will also obliterate their status in the eyes of the Hills nation. Right now, though they have opted to fight on our side, the Hills nation may reunite and the new Ruling Council may forgive them. Especially if there are other Hills matrons and chiefs who think Atotarho is insane—"

"And there are," Sindak said.

"However, if Sindak and his people become sons and daughters of the Standing Stone nation, it's treason. A death penalty."

Kittle cocked her head slightly, as though seeing an opening to Sindak's vitals. In a soft deadly voice, she said, "I want to know the names of every matron and chief who thinks Atotarho is insane. If we can win them to our side—"

"I'll give them to you."

Sindak and Kittle stared at each other.

As the exterior palisade gates groaned open on damp leather hinges, the litter bearers trotted outside. Elder Brother Sun was still below the horizon, but a yellow halo arched into the eastern sky. The shadows of the hills scalloped the valley, and the dismantled ruin of Yellowtail Village glowed sadly, its palisade missing in too many places to count. The last two rings of palisades remained upright only because the gaps were held together by the catwalk. Through one of the gaps, Gonda spied movement, low to the ground, probably dogs hunting the ruins of the refugee shelters that had been built between the rings. Piles of debris cluttered the bent pole skeletons, which leaned precariously. Many of the ruins would collapse in the next strong wind.

Sindak turned to Kittle with an expression of guarded annoyance. "High Matron, if I may, I'd like to . . ."

A roar went up from the catwalk and warriors began running just as screams erupted outside.

Kittle said, "What . . ."

Litter bearers and mourners shoved one another as they scrambled to make it back inside the palisade gates ahead of a hail of falling arrows.

"I'm a fool!" Gonda cursed himself, and yelled, "Move! They're shooting from Yellowtail Village!"

As though part of a synchronized dance, Jigonsaseh, Gonda, and Sindak drew their war clubs simultaneously and ran to defend the gates.

Twenty

Before Baji opened her eyes, she was conscious of the slight steady rhythm of Sky Messenger's breathing and the feel of his ribs pressed against her back. His arms were around her, holding her.

A sensation of contentment possessed her.

When the morning breeze eddied, crackles sounded two paces away, and cedar smoke, rich and sweet, filled the air. Sky Messenger must have carried her to a bed beside the fire—though she didn't remember—and added branches throughout the night to keep her warm.

She inhaled a deep breath and let it out slowly.

The almost soundless shift of paws told her that Gitchi sat on his haunches nearby, his yellow eyes on the forest, guarding them, as he had always done.

When she opened her eyes and smiled at the old white-faced wolf, Gitchi's tail thumped the ground. He leaned down, licked her forehead, and vigilantly took up his duties again, glancing only briefly at the falcons that wheeled in the sky.

Sunlight streamed through the deep brown hickory

branches above her. Where it landed, the forest floor steamed. Already much of yesterday's snow had melted into shining pools. Had they slept so long? It must be at least two hands of time past dawn.

Gently, so as not to wake Sky Messenger, she tilted her head to look out across the vista. They slept upon a rocky high point overlooking a broad river valley. The largest boulders below appeared tiny and distant, like the dream of her own death that had tormented her for half the night . . . *falling, with him, bright light, can't get air* . . .

For a while, as the forest became luminescent, she lay there in Sky Messenger's warm arms, watching the bone-white winter light being born—light licked clean by the invisible Spirit predators that hunted the rolling land.

She eased one hand up to touch her head wound. The swelling had diminished by half, but pain continued to throb through her skull.

Sky Messenger must have felt her move. He tightened his arms around her, drawing her slender body more securely against his, and whispered, "How are you feeling?"

"Better today. I . . . for the past few days . . . I've been waking . . . with my heart thundering and I wonder if my heart is bursting . . . or if I'm just dying of loneliness."

She rolled to her back to look at him. Every line of his round face told her how much he cherished waking this way. His brown eyes shone. A small fragile smile turned his lips, as though he was afraid to be happy, for fear that she would vanish. Last summer, during the brief alliance between the Flint and Standing Stone nations, they'd awakened this way every morning.

"I'm here, Baji. You're not alone now."

He tenderly pressed his lips to hers, then pulled aside

the wealth of her long hair and studied the wound behind her right ear. "The wound looks better. Thank the Spirits you're a fighter. Last night, I was giving you poor odds."

"Fortunately, no one who knows me would ever count me out."

He smiled. "True. However, we must be careful. I don't think we should run the trail for a few days. Walking will be good enough until you're feeling stronger."

"I thought you were in a hurry to get to the country of the People of the Landing?"

"That was before I knew you were hurt."

The statement worried her. She did not wish, in any way, to detain or sway him from his mission. If coming here had . . .

He sat up and looked down, just staring into her eyes, as though what he saw there went straight to his heart. The blanket coiled around his waist. Like all warriors on the war trail, he'd slept in his cape. It hung crookedly about him.

Baji touched his short black hair. "Did you cut it for Tutelo's husband?"

It was dangerous to say the name of the dead too soon after they'd been lost, or it might draw their souls back to earth, and they'd never again be able to find their way to the afterlife.

"He was a good man."

"I'm sure he was. Tutelo wouldn't have loved him otherwise."

Sky Messenger petted the long waves of her hair that spread over the blanket. "I'll build up the fire and get breakfast made. Why don't you lie here and stay warm."

"For a little while."

He rose, pulled his soot-smudged cape straight, and tugged the blanket up to Baji's chin.

She rolled to her side to watch him.

Branches clacked as he pulled them from the wood-pile and tossed them onto the coals, then he knelt and blew upon them until flames leaped through the fresh tinder. The delicious tang of cedar smoke rose. Cedars were sacred trees. Their smoke healed and purified. She breathed it in, letting it work its magic on her wounded body.

Images from the dream she'd been having when she woke flitted behind her eyes.

She'd been with Cord, walking down the trail, looking for her own body among hundreds of dead Flint warriors. She'd rounded a bend and seen herself lying face-down, covered with a thin blanket of snow. She'd lived for a while. As her strength had waned, her feet and hands had dug troughs in the ground, kicking, clawing to get away. Afterward, the victorious Hills warriors had stolen her jewelry and weapons. Even her cape had been stripped off, probably to be carried home to a beloved wife back in Atotarho Village. In the process, her limbs had been left akimbo. Cord had let out a cry and rushed to her side. *"Gods, someone help me! I think she's alive!"* Cord had dragged her into his arms and clutched her tightly against him. What a curious sensation that had been. She'd understood that she no longer inhabited that body, but somehow, it was all right.

She'd had such dreams before. All warriors did. It was the afterlife soul's way of preparing for the inevitable, but the dreams had never before been so vivid, so lifelike. The tears in Cord's eyes still broke her heart.

Gitchi softly nosed her hand, as though to bring her back to this camp on the rocky hilltop.

"I'm here, Gitchi," she whispered. "Everything's all right."

Gitchi curled his bushy gray tail over his forefeet, and his yellow eyes studied her for a long moment, before returning to the valley below.

Save for the popping and snapping of the fire, a vast silence had imprisoned the morning. Down the hill in the trees, fifty paces away, she saw the corpse of the man she'd killed last night. Shadows darkened the spot, preserving the snow where he lay. His lips had shrunken back over his gums, revealing the rotted teeth in his gaping mouth. Where Gitchi had ripped out his throat, an ocean of frozen blood spread across the snow.

Looking at him gave her a strange otherworldly sensation.

It was as though a desolation lay upon the world, lifeless, its presence so cold and indifferent it possessed not even a hint of sadness. Rather, it seemed to be watching her with the infallible eyes of eternity . . . and waiting. Though she had no idea what the desolation waited for.

Baji propped herself up on one elbow, then gingerly shoved to a sitting position. Her headache pounded for ten heartbeats, making her nauseous, then it slacked off to a constant, but bearable, ache.

She staggered to her feet, and walked over to slump down beside the fire. When she extended her frozen hands to the warmth, it struck her as odd that they didn't immediately tingle, as they always did on cold winter mornings like this. She rubbed them together to get the blood going.

Sky Messenger frowned at her. When she'd risen, he'd

been in the process of twisting a pot of tea down into the hot coals. He finished, moved the tripod with the cook pot to the edge of the flames, and rose to his feet. "I don't want you to get cold."

He walked over, retrieved their blankets, and draped them snugly around her shoulders.

His breath frosted when he said, "You must stay warm, Baji. You know as well as I do that head wounds have curious effects. Do you recall what happened to young Janoh?"

"Janoh?" She had to search her memory. "Blessed Ancestors, I do."

"So do I. After he was clubbed in the head he seemed fine. He joked as never before. For two days he made everyone laugh out loud. His only complaint was that he couldn't feel his feet striking the earth."

"I remember. He told everyone that he'd learned to fly and grew angry when anyone insisted he was still running, but just didn't know it."

Sky Messenger gave her a grave nod. "Then on the third day he fell over dead right in the middle of the trail. It happened so fast, the warriors on the trail behind him had no idea what had happened."

"Until later, you mean, when we all understood that his soul *had* been flying. It had leaked from his cracked skull and been hovering close to his body."

Sky Messenger pointed a stern finger at her. "I'm taking no chances with your head wound."

"Don't want me to learn to fly, eh?"

"No."

He drew open the laces on his belt pouch and pulled out a bag of jerky. As he crumbled the dried meat into the cook pot hanging from the tripod, he said, "In fact, if you get light-headed, or lose feeling in your hands or feet, or have any other unusual symptoms, I expect you to tell me. Agreed?"

She pursed her lips in silent chastisement. "Of course. I'm not as dimwitted as you think."

"When you're thinking properly, no."

He reached out to stroke her throat, and a strange shimmer lit the air, as though the light itself had fluoresced, leaving all living things aglow, softening sight and sound. Sky Messenger's tanned face had a golden glitter.

Baji's heartbeat slowed, barely there. Time seemed to linger, stretching like a bobcat on a warm summer afternoon.

In a tone that was at once hurt and half-angry, he said, "I'm glad you're here. Don't ever leave me again, Baji. I couldn't bear it."

"I won't."

He stroked her throat again, then turned away, and drew two wooden cups and spoons from his pack. After he'd placed them beside the fire, he said, "Hiyawento is going to meet us."

"Really? Where?" The news gladdened her heart.

"On the trail to the east of Shookas Village, but it'll probably be a few days. First, he needs to lead his warriors to Canassatego Village. Coldspring Village, Riverbank Village, and Canassatego Village decided to combine into one village."

"To protect each other?"

"Yes."

Baji squinted at the mossy patterns on the rocks that thrust up here and there around camp. "I pray they make it. We didn't."

The words affected her like a knife, cutting a dark pathway inside her. She could see it—the tunnel twisted down toward an inner chamber where her soul awaited deliverance from the tormented sense of isolation. It persisted even with Sky Messenger so close she could reach out and touch him.

When he sat down and put an arm around her, the dark tunnel evaporated like fog in warm sunlight. "Tell me everything. Where did Atotarho ambush you?"

"On the main trail to Flint country. Do you recall the narrow defile that leads up over the crest of the hill and plunges down into that stubby second-growth country near the Seagull Shallows?"

"Near the Rocky Meadows?"

"Yes."

"Blessed gods, did they hit you as you came over the hill out of the defile?"

"No," she said solemnly, "on the far side of the valley. Just as our war party was climbing up the steep slope through the rocky ledges, I . . . I should have seen them. I don't know why I didn't."

"Probably because Atotarho's warriors were under penalty of death if they even breathed until you were in position. Sometimes, there's nothing you can do, Baji." He hugged her.

Guilt made her throat ache. "It was . . . bizarre. Father and I were talking about Shago-niyoh when the attack came. Did you know that Cord saw him the night the old woman died?"

Sky Messenger jerked around to stare at her. "He never told me that."

"Nor me." Baji fumbled with her fingers, squeezing

them in her lap as dread filtered through her. "Father had just asked me if I'd ever seen Shago-niyoh again, and I'd said no. Not even when I knew you were speaking with him. I used to try to see something, anything, moving around you, or hear his voice. I never did."

"Until a few days ago, you mean."

"Yes."

One memory from the battle repeated behind her eyes: Cord, bleeding badly, rising to his feet with his war club in his fist, suddenly right beside her.

"I wish I . . . maybe if I'd . . ."

Her voice trailed away, and Sky Messenger seemed to sense that scenes of the battle tormented her. *Hundreds of warriors stretched out like ants, climbing the steep incline . . . glitters in the sunlit air in front of the pines . . .*

"Stop blaming yourself," he ordered. "Cord didn't see them, either, and he was one of the greatest war chiefs your people have ever known. Did Dzadi see them and call a warning? What about your scouts?"

"No. No one saw them. But . . . hundreds died, Sky Messenger. Hundreds."

"How many warriors did Atotarho have?"

"Two thousand, maybe three. I didn't have time to get a good count. We were outnumbered at least four to one, and completely surrounded. Father was wounded, shot through the right side." Her hands clenched to fists. "Gods, I pray he's all right."

Sky Messenger's brow furrowed. He picked up one of the wooden spoons and used it to stir the cook pot. The scent of smoked venison jerky wafted up with the steam. "How did you escape?"

She shook her head. "I don't know. Truly. I heard your voice, and I—"

"My voice?" he said in surprise.

"Yes, you cried, 'Baji, get down!' and I leaped without thinking, just dove out of the way." She lightly massaged the wound behind her ear. "That's why I received a glancing blow rather than a crushed skull."

As Sky Messenger listened, the nostrils of his slender nose flared in and out, and the lines around his wide mouth went hard. He must be fighting the battle in his mind, trying to see what she had seen.

"And then?"

Baji struggled to remember. "I don't remember anything else."

"You were completely surrounded. You were hurt. Cord was injured. You must have fought back or run."

"Probably both . . . but I recall none of it."

Gitchi must have heard the tension in her voice. He trotted over and lay down at Baji's side. As he propped his big muzzle in her lap, he looked up at her with loving yellow eyes—as though he thought she needed comforting. She petted his soft back.

Sky Messenger said, "What's the next thing you remember after you escaped?"

Out in the trees, two deer slipped through the shadows, a buck and a doe. Their thick winter coats had a pearlescent ash-colored sheen. Quietly, she said, "There's dinner."

Sky Messenger turned. "I have plenty of food in my pack. Let them go. I'd rather hear your story."

The doe lifted her head at his voice and sniffed the air, startled that she hadn't scented them before, then she followed the buck onto the trail, and their hooves kicked up snow as they bounded away, heading down into the sunlit valley far below.

"Odd that they didn't scent us, or Gitchi, or the campfire."

"The wind must have been wrong."

Sky Messenger squinted down the trail for several long moments, before he repeated, "What's the next thing you remember?"

Her head had started to pound again, and with it nausea welled. She put a hand to her belly. "I don't remember a place as much as a feeling of pure panic. I knew I had to find you, to protect you. The need was overwhelming." She hesitated and watched the steam rising from the teapot. Behind her eyes she glimpsed trees passing, enormous chestnuts, hills in front of her that seemed to roll on forever. "Then I found myself running. That's the next thing I recall. Running as hard as I could . . . at the very edge of my endurance, my lungs bursting. I think I must have collapsed or fainted. I woke up in the middle of the night . . . on this trail." Nausea tickled the back of her throat. She squeezed her eyes closed, trying to force it away.

Softly, he said, "All right. That's enough for now."

"I think I need to eat something."

"I'll fill your bowl this instant."

As he went about filling their bowls and dipping cups of tea, Baji continued stroking Gitchi's thick fur. Why had she only told him about Shago-niyoh finding her on the trail, and not the details of their conversation?

Because I'm afraid to.

Twenty-one

As High Matron Kittle stalked in front of her fire in the Deer Clan longhouse, her many shell rings and bracelets clicked musically. Even through the walls and the three rings of palisades, she could hear the enemy calling taunts from the catwalks of Yellowtail Village. All day long both sides had been urinating off the palisades, yelling, shaking their penises at each other, and firing arrows smeared with feces. A combination of terror and indignation tormented her. She'd barely looked at the four women who sat around her fire, drinking cups of rosehip tea. Kittle had been an utter fool. She should have listened to Jigonsaseh. Because she hadn't, innocent people had died.

The Deer Clan longhouse was smaller than the longhouses in other nations, stretching only five hundred hands long. Twenty-five fires burned down the central aisle. People stood around each blaze, their faces firelit, engaged in barely audible conversations that mostly dealt with the probable extinction of the Standing Stone nation. The hum of voices carried the low dire quality of defeat.

Since the attack, people had begun looking longingly at

the corn, bean, squash, and sunflower plants that draped from the roof poles. Kittle wondered how long it would be before desperate parents started stealing them to feed their hungry children. She'd ordered all baskets of food and water pots kept in a single storehouse under heavy guard, but had not had time yet to pull down the whole plants from the roof poles. She must attend to that immediately.

Kittle swung around to glare at the other matrons. "Well? The enemy has just stuffed our kirtles down our throats. What are we going to do about it?"

She folded her arms over her knee-length dress, and waited for someone to answer. Instead, the matrons fell into a soft discussion, which Kittle found annoying. At least one of them should have shouted or raged. She wished they would. It would help relieve her tension.

Jigonsaseh of the Bear Clan sat across the fire, her smooth oval face impassive, the silver in her black hair shimmering in the firelight. To Jigonsaseh's left, Matron Dehot of the Wolf Clan hunched. She'd seen forty-five summers and had a gaunt face and black-streaked gray hair. White wolf tracks decorated her blue cape. Beside her, Matron Sihata of the Hawk Clan fiddled with her white hair, twisting it nervously. She'd seen sixty summers. Her deeply wrinkled face resembled a shriveled plum. To Jigonsaseh's right sat Matron Daga, formerly of White Dog Village, now a refugee. Her toothless mouth kept trembling, as though she couldn't keep it still.

Fear glittered in the eyes of each one, except Jigonsaseh's. Her large dark eyes were as calm as obsidian—hard and translucent. Warfare was something she understood better than any of them, and Kittle was heartily glad to have her on the Ruling Council.

Kittle irritably braced her legs. She hadn't eaten all day—as a symbol—and felt light-headed. Her hunger was exacerbated by the sweet scent of cornmeal mush that filled the air. She'd ordered rations cut by half. No one was happy about it. She looked down the length of the house, surveying haunted expressions.

Finally, Dehot leaned forward. "High Matron, I would speak." Her short black-streaked gray hair fell around her gaunt face.

"Please do."

Dehot respectfully dipped her head to Sihata, begging forbearance that she'd asked to speak first. If was generally accepted that Sihata's sixty summers gave her that right. Sihata gestured for Dehot to go on.

Dehot straightened her blue cape. "We all have different ideas, High Matron. Personally, I think we should send a messenger to Chief Atotarho telling him we agree to surrender if he will grant us the right to—"

"Surrender, Dehot?" Kittle's fists clenched. "Have you no confidence at all in our warriors?"

"You know I do, Kittle. But I am also a practical person. What good are three hundred trained warriors and a bunch of children with toy bows against perhaps two thousand? Even if we can trust War Chief Sindak, his group only adds another forty-one trained warriors. I do not see the utility in sacrificing our people in a futile cause."

Kittle started to respond, but Matron Daga said, "You're a coward, Dehot. You always have been. We should fight until our last breaths! When we surrender, Atotarho will murder our warriors anyway, and then he'll take the rest of us as slaves."

Dehot tartly replied, "He'll take the children and young

women. Atotarho makes a point of killing all the warriors and elders of any village he conquers. So—"

In a very quiet voice, Matron Sihata broke in, "May I speak, High Matron?" She was sweating; white hair stuck wetly to her wrinkled cheeks.

"Yes."

Sihata shifted to face Daga. Both snowy-haired and wrinkled, they would be twins were it not for Sihata's bulbous nose. "I agree with Kittle and Daga that we should fight for as long as we can before we are forced to surrender—though, like Daga, I have no illusions about our victory."

A particularly fierce gust of wind shivered the long-house's repaired walls, and ash swirled in the firelight.

"So," Kittle said in a hard-edged voice, "one of you wishes to surrender now, and two of you wish to surrender after we've been defeated. Is there anyone else here, besides me, who thinks we can win?"

The entire length of the longhouse went silent. Every person strained to hear. Her question must seem pure foolishness, yet she knew each wanted to believe, and belief was often the difference between survival and death.

Jigonsaseh's eyes narrowed.

Kittle stared at her. Jigonsaseh always waited until the elder matrons spoke before she addressed the matrons' council, but tonight she seemed to need time to process every other opinion before opening her mouth.

"Jigonsaseh?" Kittle prompted. "Have you anything to say?"

Jigonsaseh slowly lifted her gaze from the fire and her eyes locked with Kittle's. "I respectfully suggest that we cease focusing on the end, and start at the beginning."

"What do you mean?" Dehot asked.

Jigonsaseh extended her arm toward the longhouse entry where the curtain swayed in the night wind. "Let me tell you what's going on in the hearts of your warriors on the catwalks. They don't care how much food and water we have, or whether we will surrender or win. Each is concentrated on just one thing. Surviving for the next one hand of time. And that, matrons, is what should concern us."

"Are you saying we shouldn't plan in case we are defeated?" Dehot asked.

Jigonsaseh raised her voice. "Defeat is *impossible*, Dehot."

There was a stunned moment where people throughout the longhouse just blinked and shuffled their feet. Somewhere in the middle of the house a dog's tail thumped the floor.

Dehot, incredulous, said, "Why? Because you expect Sky Messenger to save us? I believe his vision, too, but—"

"No, Matron," Jigonsaseh slowly replied, "because we are going to kill our enemies."

The power and conviction in Jigonsaseh's voice rang through the longhouse. Jigonsaseh had been one of the great war chiefs of the Standing Stone nation. Though she had not been a war chief in many summers, people still trusted her.

Conversations eddied like waves up and down the length of the house, people repeating her words to elders who couldn't hear very well, questions washing back. A general cacophony rose, people murmuring, *"Jigonsaseh has a plan. . . . She's in charge of our warriors. . . . She's never lost a battle in her life!"*

Kittle lifted her chin and stared down her straight nose at Jigonsaseh. "Explain."

Dehot, Sihata, and Daga turned to Jigonsaseh, awaiting her next words. Jigonsaseh looked around the circle, meeting each elder's eyes, then scanned the listeners in the longhouse, and at last looked back at Kittle. When she wanted to, Jigonsaseh's gaze could pierce like an arrow to the heart—as it did now.

"War Chief Deru has informed me that there may be five hundred enemy warriors in Yellowtail Village. They've already started repairing the palisades and longhouses, which means they plan to stay."

"To use it as a stronghold from which to attack us?"

"Yes. They won't allow us to venture beyond our gates for food or water. While they repair Yellowtail Village, however, they'll probably conserve their arrows. They'll kill anyone who tries to go outside, and entertain themselves by firing a few random shots at our cat-calling warriors. Once they've secured their defenses, though, they'll start launching volleys of arrows into Bur Oak Village, probably flaming arrows into our longhouses. That will force us to use what little water we have to put out the fires. We must kill them before they can do that."

More murmurs echoed through the house, questioning voices. Speculations were running rampant.

"How?"

Jigonsaseh replied, "We're going to burn down Yellowtail Village with as many of them inside as we can. If we plan it correctly, we can kill all five hun—"

"Burn down Yellowtail Village?" Sihata asked in a frail elderly voice. "How will we accomplish that? They watch our gates like falcons. Any warriors we send out will be killed instantly."

"Not if we select the right warriors," Kittle said as her thoughts raced.

Dehot leaned toward Jigonsaseh and placed a clawlike hand upon her arm. "Who? If Sky Messenger were here, perhaps the Faces of the Forest might protect him long enough for him to—"

"Sindak and Gonda have volunteered for the task. They are the right people."

Kittle unfolded her arms. Like everyone else in the circle, she gaped at Jigonsaseh, who gazed back stoically. Kittle had to admit that she liked Sindak, but trust him? That was quite another thing.

Dehot said, "Gonda, of course, but War Chief Sindak? What makes you think he will fire the village instead of traipsing right over there and spilling every detail of our defenses?"

Kittle suddenly felt shaky. Everything might depend upon this, and Jigonsaseh wanted to send Sindak, rather than a group of their own loyal warriors? She went to the fire and sat down in her usual place, on a fire-warmed deerhide. As she dipped her cup into the teapot sunk into the coals at the edge of the flames, she said, "Let us all think about this for a time."

"Sindak is here because he was chosen by Power," Jigonsaseh said.

Dehot laughed. "Is that your opinion? Are you certain enough that you would risk everything—"

"I am," Jigonsaseh interrupted. She stared unblinking at Dehot, her eyes narrowed.

Kittle took a drink of tea to give herself time to

consider the ramifications of what would happen if Sindak betrayed them.

Daga said, "Only two days ago he *apparently* betrayed Atotarho. If he would betray his own people, why wouldn't he betray us even more easily—perhaps for a price?"

Dehot nodded vigorously. "I think he's unreliable. We need—"

"We need Sindak," Jigonsaseh countered. "He's not here by accident."

Kittle said, "Please explain why you think he's necessary for the assault."

The jeering and obscene calls coming from outside were growing louder. Something thumped the wall right behind Kittle. She spun around to see an arrow lodged in the bark wall just above her sleeping bench. The warriors had been exchanging shots all day, but this was the first one that had skewered her bedding hides. She hoped it wasn't one of the arrows smeared with feces.

She turned back and gave Jigonsaseh a "hurry, will you?" look. "Explain, please."

"First, Sindak knows the weaknesses of every warrior occupying Yellowtail Village. He knows if they tend to aim left or right, if they have vision problems, who their wives and husbands are, the names of their children, what frightens them. More important, Sindak was a greatly beloved war chief. I believe that if he's spotted, his warriors might hesitate for an instant before letting fly, and often that is enough time to kill an opponent."

Sihata twisted her clawlike hands in her lap. "That makes sense to me. There will certainly be no hesitation if they see one of our warriors."

"No," Kittle answered. "There won't. Dehot? Daga? What do you think of Matron Jigonsaseh's explanation?"

Dehot had her head down, thinking, staring at the glowing branches in the fire. "Well, I am not convinced. But perhaps it is an opportunity."

"An opportunity?"

"Yes. Why not give Atotarho's former war chief the chance to prove he's loyal to us? Frankly, if he does not survive, it will be an insignificant loss."

"But what if he reveals the details of our defenses?" Daga asked.

Kittle said, "Well, what could he tell them? That we only have three days of water left? They'll know that soon enough anyway."

"But they don't know we only have three hundred trained warriors. If he tells Ato—"

Jigonsaseh said, "Atotarho doesn't care. We could have one thousand left and it would make no difference. He knows he greatly outnumbers us. He thinks he's invincible. And that's why we're going to kill him."

Hadui flung aside the door curtain at the opposite end of the house and battered his way through the fires, shoving sparks and smoke in front of him. As it gushed over the matrons' council meeting, the women closed their eyes and turned away. Kittle waited until Hadui had whipped aside the curtain to her left, and sailed outside into the darkness before she drew up her knees and propped her teacup atop them. Steam curled into the warm air before her.

Kittle forced confidence into her voice, though she didn't feel it. "I am satisfied with Matron Jigonsaseh's suggested course of action. Are there any other questions?"

Dehot shook her head. Sihata stared at the hands in her lap, and Daga wiped her nose on her sleeve.

Kittle gave Jigonsaseh a firm nod. "Make your plan. I'll find a way to push it through the Ruling Council."

Jigonsaseh's mouth tightened. "I will speak with our warriors."

"Do it soon. If we don't get rain or snow, we have three days until our water is gone."

The people who'd been listening to the meeting began to filter back to their chambers. Without their bodies to block the light of twenty fires, it fluttered unhindered, coating the walls and roof, turning them liquid.

Kittle softly asked, "After the water's gone . . . how long?"

Without a shred of emotion, Jigonsaseh said, "Another three days. Probably."

Kittle swirled the tea in her cup, and took a long drink. "That's when the riots will start."

"Then we'd best start killing Atotarho's warriors."

Twenty-two

Matron Buckshen slowly ambled across the sunlit plaza of Wild River Village. Feeling her way with her black walnut walking stick, she placed her moccasins with care. She had seen sixty summers pass. Thin gray hair fell around her wrinkled face, framing her white-filmed eyes. Half-blind, she had to stare hard at things to make them out, but over the past five summers she'd discovered that if she just took her time she could do it.

She stopped and used her walking stick to poke at something on the ground.

Five heartbeats later, a little boy rushed up, panting. "I'm sorry, Matron. We're playing hoop-and-stick and the hoop got away from us."

Buckshen smiled and reached out to find his head, which she then patted. "Are you winning?"

"Not yet, Matron. Pibbig has a stronger arm than I do."

"Well, just keep practicing. Someday you'll be the best lance thrower in Wild River Village."

The boy laughed, picked up the hoop, and charged back to the game.

Bucksen concentrated and could see what looked like three boys racing across the plaza after the rolling hoop. It made her chuckle.

Propping her walking stick, she took another step and continued across the plaza. The day was cold, but the sunlight felt warm on her face. Many people filled the plaza, most working. The constant *thump-thump-thump* of women using mallets to pound corn in hollowed-out logs beat the air, and to her right she herd the *click-clack* of men knapping stone tools with an antler tine. Happy voices carried.

As she neared the Turtle Clan longhouse, she paused to look around. Four longhouses hemmed the plaza of Wild River Village, creating a rough square inside the palisade. Three hundred hands long, each longhouse had white birch bark walls. As the afternoon cooled, heading toward evening, Elder Brother Sun slipped lower in the sky and his light sheathed the longhouses with a rich gleam. Through her filmed eyes, they resembled enormous blurry creatures carved from pure amber.

She heaved a sigh. With the plague and attacks, they'd had a terrible summer. Many people she'd loved were gone. But for the first time in many summers, the Flint People had plenty of food to carry them through the long winter ahead. The corn bins were full to bursting. They'd buried beans, squash, goose and duck eggs, in large pits to keep them from freezing, and every house had hundreds of bags of dried raspberries, cherries, persimmons, and plums, not to mention the chestnuts, walnuts, and pecans they'd harvested last moon. If they didn't get raided, they'd have a joyous winter of storytelling and weaving baskets.

Just as she started walking again, surprised voices rose

from the palisade. Warriors hurried along the catwalk, staring down at something outside the village gates.

"Blessed gods!" a man shouted. "It's Kanika! He was with Chief Cord's war party. Open the gates!"

Buckshen carefully shuffled around to peer at the crowd gathering in front of the gates, waiting for the guards to remove the locking planks and shove them open. People sprinted past her.

She focused on the gates, saw them swing open. The crowd rushed out, and a din of concerned voices erupted.

More people raced by her. "What's happening? Someone, come tell me what's happening?"

"I'll be right back with the news, Matron!" a man yelled as he galloped by at full speed.

Buckshen fiddled with her walking stick, trying to be calm as cries rent the air, and she thought she saw a man being carried across the plaza. "What happened? Is he hurt?"

A tall man dashed toward her. Her hazy vision couldn't make out his face. He stopped, breathing hard. "Matron, it's Kanika. Chief Cord sent him ahead. He's been running flat out for two days and nights to get here. He's fevered and raving—"

"Where is Chief Cord and his war party?"

The man seemed to straighten up, and his fists clenched at his sides. "There were attacked by the Hills People, Matron, less than one day's run from Bur Oak Village."

She weakly reached out to clasp his arm, to keep her knees from buckling. "The war party contained over six hundred. How many did we lose?"

"I—I'm not sure, Matron. I think Kanika said four

hundred in the ambush. I don't know how many were lost in the battle the day before—"

"Four hundred? Dear gods. Where is Chief Cord?"

"He was wounded badly. The survivors of the attack are hauling him home on a litter, as well as many other wounded warriors. They can't travel very fast. They're probably two days away. You should also know that Kanika was spouting gibberish. Apparently, he and the other survivors hid in the forest near the Hills camp and heard the new war chief, Negano, telling his warriors that they were heading back to Bur Oak Village to destroy the Standing Stone nation once and for all."

"What else?"

"Something strange, garbled. About a miracle happening during the Bur Oak battle. Apparently, Sky Messenger's Dream is coming true. Kanika said the Prophet stretched out his hand and Elder Brother Sun brought a great storm that swept the Hills warriors from the battlefield. But he was raving, Matron. It may just be his fevered imaginings."

Buckshen's trembling fingers squeezed his arm. "Find the other matrons. Tell them to meet me in the council house. We will wish to question Kanika as soon as he's rested and eaten. Hurry."

Twenty-three

Hiyawento stopped on the crest of a hill to look down across the rolling hills. The smoky air clawed at the back of his throat. Afternoon sunlight enameled an endless vista of charred trees and scorched earth. As he pulled his water bag from his belt, and took a long drink, his gaze narrowed. The forest fire had been intense. It must have burned through almost one moon ago, for the ash had washed down every crevice and drainage, streaking the vista like deformed onyx roots. Agweron Village sat in the heart of the blackened chaos. From this distance, the longhouses resembled heaps of burnt splinters.

Towa finally caught up and stood beside him breathing hard, staring across the charred country. He'd seen thirty-two summers pass. Though his long hair had not yet surrendered to silver, lines carved the corners of his eyes and cut half-moons around his mouth. "Dear gods, this happened after I was last here."

Hiyawento handed him the water bag and waited while Towa gulped several swallows down his parched throat.

When Towa lowered the bag, Hiyawento said, "I heard the mysterious fever that ravaged the land last autumn hit the Landing villages especially hard."

"It did. When I was here the longhouses were half empty. There were so many orphans the clan mothers seemed overwhelmed. But surely they wouldn't have set fire to their own country to rid it of the evil Spirits that brought the fever? They must have been attacked by Mountain People, and the fires spread into the forest."

Hiyawento rested his hand on his belted war club. The quartzite cobble felt cold beneath his palm. "Why do you think it was Mountain People?"

Towa exhaled hard and looked at Hiyawento. "I passed through the Mountain People villages first, and they were much worse off than the Landing villages."

"In what way?"

"They were so sick they hadn't been able to harvest their fields. Most of their crops had withered and were eaten by animals. They were starving. They had nothing to Trade, not even a single kernel of corn. War Chief Yenda had just been named Chief of Wenisa Village. After he underwent the Requickening ritual, he flew into a tirade, blaming the Landing People for the fever and every other misfortune."

"I heard he'd been made chief. So he's Chief Wenisa now?"

"Yes. I left as soon as I could, praying I'd make it to the Landing villages while they were still standing."

"And you found them sick, too?"

Towa's mouth twisted. "Yes. Sick and desperate. Several people offered to Trade me their only blankets for what little food I carried in my pack. I refused the blankets and gave them everything I had, but it wasn't much. Blessed Ancestors, it was a terrible sight."

In the distance, Hiyawento could make out the vague form of the next Landing village, Shookas Village, the principal village of the Landing nation. The intact log palisade stood out in stark contrast to the blackened hills. He wondered what they would find there.

Wind Woman gusted over the hilltop, flapping Hiyawento's cape around his legs. "Sky Messenger would have headed straight to Shookas Village. If all went well, he should arrive tomorrow."

"Then we should hurry. If we get there before him, and there's any elder left to speak with, we can prepare the way for him."

Towa clapped Hiyawento on the shoulder, and broke into a shambling trot, heading down the hill through stark blackened trees that seemed to go on forever.

Twenty-four

"It will take just a few moments," Zateri said. "Kwahseti and Gwinodje are lodging in the Snipe Clan longhouse. It's all the way across the village."

"Matron Yi told me to wait, so it doesn't matter how long it takes, but I thank you for informing me."

Of average height, handsome, and somewhat boyish, Hikatoo had a reputation for being a fine singer. Zateri recalled the richness of his deep voice last summer at the green corn ceremony. He'd seen perhaps thirty summers, and spent the past three as one of her father's personal guards. She found it curious that Yi would choose this man as her messenger. He wasn't Wolf Clan, and though he was known as a reliable and courteous man, Zateri was certain to distrust him . . . which she did. He kept toying with his left arm, cradling it against his belly, then lowering it, only to pull it across his belly again.

"I heard you were wounded at the White Dog Village battle," Zateri said.

"It's nothing, Matron. The arrow skewered my upper arm. It's healing cleanly."

"I'm glad. We have lost far too many good warriors already."

He gave her a half-smile, perhaps wondering at her usage of the word "we."

Zateri looked away. The Wolf Clan longhouse in Canassatego Village had suffered during the recent attack. Charred holes gaped in the roof. Hastily covered with slabs of bark, none quite fit. Twilight seeped around the edges, creating a patchwork of luminous ovals. As many people as possible had been crowded into the forty chambers, so that the longhouse seemed to be bursting at the seams with humanity. Twenty fires glittered down the central aisle. People stood shoulder-to-shoulder in the warmth.

"May I dip you a cup of tea, Hikatoo?"

"That's kind of you. I would appreciate it, Matron. Thank you."

The sweet fragrance of dried cherries wafted around Zateri's flat face as she dipped a cup of tea from the soot-coated pot hanging on the tripod at the edge of the flames, and handed it to Hikatoo. She thought his buckskin cape had black snipes painted across the middle, but the soot of countless campfires obscured the designs. "You are Snipe Clan, aren't you?"

He bowed slightly. "I am, Matron."

"I know it must have been a dangerous trip, and you had no idea what sort of reception you would receive when you arrived here. Thank you for taking the risk."

"Since my injury, I am not of much use in the fighting, so I go where my elders send me, Matron." Hikatoo sipped the cherry tea and a smile came to his lips. "This is wonderful. We've eaten all the dried cherries at Atotarho Village. This is a special treat."

"On our way here, we passed a grove with a few cherries still clinging to the branches. We grabbed as many as we could before we had to . . ."

Conversations broke out as people cleared a path through the longhouse for Kwahseti and Gwinodje, who hurried past without a word to anyone, heading straight as arrows for Zateri's chamber in the center of the Wolf longhouse. Wind-blown gray hair spiked up around Kwahseti's face. Gwinodje looked very short and thin striding beside her. Her heart-shaped face had reddened in the cold air as she'd crossed the plaza. Both wore half-frightened expressions.

When they reached Zateri's fire, Kwahseti shoved gray locks away from her catlike nose, and eyed Hikatoo severely. "Who sent you?"

Hikatoo bowed to her. "Matrons Yi and Inawa."

Suspiciously Gwinodje asked, "You are not Wolf Clan. Why would they send you?"

Hikatoo's boyish face fell into stern lines. He spread his feet. "Matrons Yi and Inawa wish you to know that they have found witnesses." He took a deep breath and calmly met each of their gazes in turn, before continuing, "And I am one of them."

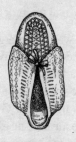

Twenty-five

Dusk came as a mournful solace to the long day. Tired, her headache pounding, Baji listened to the meltwater pouring from the roof of the rockshelter where they'd made camp. It drummed outside, sounding like the clattering hooves of panicked white-tailed deer.

Baji propped herself on her elbows in the warm nest of blankets, and her long hair scattered like black silk over Sky Messenger's chest and arm.

"I think Trade is the answer," Sky Messenger said. He had his fingers laced beneath his head. His eyes focused on the soot that blackened the roof above them. Many campfires had burned in this shelter, though they had not built one. In the heart of Hills country, they couldn't risk being seen. "Trade is peace."

"Trade?" Baji asked. "Why?"

The rockshelter stretched two body-lengths across and a single body-length wide, but rose five body-lengths over their heads. Like a dark gray eye-socket, it seemed to peer out into the densely forested hollow that surrounded them. Leafless cottonwoods and quaking aspens crowded near the mouth of the rockshelter. The location was, for the most part, windless. As a result, old autumn leaves clustered at the bases of the trees, contrasting sharply with the white bark of the aspens. The musty scent of moldering vegetation seemed concentrated in the rockshelter.

"The most important reason is that it's the answer to food shortages. If one village has a good summer and stockpiles lots of crops, it will be beneficial for them to be able to Trade that surplus for other goods they need—say Spirit plants, buffalohides from the west, salt, dried seafood, pots."

Baji paused as she thought about it. Where he lay at the foot of their blankets, Gitchi shifted to prop his white muzzle on his forepaws. His yellow eyes fixed intently on the world outside, concentrating on seeing through the waterfall of runoff and beyond the shining rivulets that poured down the hillside into the aspens.

"That sounds good, but the truth is no one will be willing to Trade food unless they are certain they're safe. It's the grouse and the egg. Which comes first? Peace or Trade? We all hoard food because we expect to be raided. If we keep our surpluses hidden in a variety of locations, we know we can still feed our peoples through the winter even if half is stolen."

As the brightest campfires of the dead appeared in the sky outside, their gleam played through the waterfalls and flickered over the rockshelter like cast handfuls of silver dust. Sky Messenger turned his head to look up at her, and his round face bleached to pale gray. The flicker danced in his short black hair.

"Baji, we can't go on like this. You know we can't. We're all starving."

"Not all of us. This winter, the Flint People have food."

"But only because you were ravaged by the plague that decimated your country. If half your population hadn't perished, you'd be just as desperate for food as everyone else."

"True."

"We are all weakening. Even the Hills People." His wide mouth tensed. She could see his teeth grinding beneath the thin veneer of his cheek. "Every time Atotarho wipes out a village and enslaves the women and children, it compounds his problems. Next year there will be one less village growing food he can steal, and more slaves mean more mouths to feed."

"That's not how he thinks of it. To him more women and children mean more people to cultivate, plant, and harvest the crops—and more warriors to guard the Hills nation."

Gray mist rolled in the low places outside, seeping down the hills toward the dark hollows below. She could just barely see the starlike points of enemy villages visible through the dense weave of trees.

Sky Messenger said, "More women also mean more babies, and while in the end that will mean more workers and warriors, in the short term infants drain their mothers' strength and the slave women must be fed more to keep the babies healthy."

Gitchi lifted his big head and his eyes narrowed, as though he'd seen something beyond the wall of water. Baji and Sky Messenger went still, listening, their glances moving from Gitchi to the darkening forest outside. Finally, two buck deer stepped out of the cottonwoods and stared at the rock shelter. The largest, his massive antlers shining in the glow, lifted his chin to sniff the air. He had one front hoof lifted. He took a tentative step toward the shelter, as though waiting for something. When his expectations did not materialize, both bucks trotted away into the striped forest shadows.

Gitchi slowly rested his muzzle on his forepaws again, and heaved a sigh.

Softly, Sky Messenger said, "No matter what it costs me, I have to convince the other nations to join our peace alliance."

Baji stiffened. "Even if it costs your life? If they kill you, it won't help any of us. And what of your vision?"

She felt his shoulder move beneath her hair, tugging it. "That's simple. If I'm killed, it means my vision was false. It will come as a shock to me, of course, but—"

Baji chuckled, unexpectedly amused. She leaned down and kissed his forehead. "I don't see how that's possible."

The reflected light flickered in his dark eyes. "I worry. Sometimes."

"Not often, I hope."

"No. Not often." He pulled a hand from behind his head and stroked her long hair where it draped his chest. "How are you feeling? How's your head?"

"Healing. Too slowly for my tastes, but better today. Tomorrow, I'll be able to run."

As his gaze moved across the undulations in the roof, he absently replied, "We'll see."

For a time, Baji let herself drown in the soothing feel of his hand stroking her hair. Contented, she contemplated his Dream. Cord had said: *Believing is the doorway to believing.*

Despite her best efforts, she could not escape the doubts

and fears of the skinny, tormented girl she'd been at twelve summers. Believing was a hard thing. Life had taught her that. She'd grown up, become a strong woman, discovered her talents and purpose in life—yet that little girl continued to cry inside her. At odd times, especially when she felt safe and warm, pitiful sobs seeped from the invisible internal world where the girl lived. For a long time, those sobs had startled her. She did not understand, and probably never would, why that little girl never grew up. Did her twelve-year-old soul live solely to remind her to stay vigilant, that life could go terribly wrong at any instant? And what was that soul? Obviously it wasn't her afterlife soul. Was it the soul that remained with the body forever? She found the notion odd and unsettling. It frightened her to think of that scared girl locked forever in her deteriorating bones.

When Sky Messenger spoke again, his voice was soft. "What are you thinking? Every muscle in your body has gone taut."

"Has it?" she asked in surprise and consciously willed her shoulders to relax. "I hadn't realized."

"You were thinking about the old woman, weren't you?"

She gave him a bitter smile. "Strange, isn't it? That each of us can tell when the other is remembering those awful moons?"

A particularly fierce gust of wind surged over the hill above them, and old leaves showered down through the hollow, piling against the bases of the cottonwoods and aspens. Gitchi's ears pricked as he surveyed them.

"Not so strange, perhaps," he said. "We had to protect ourselves. We watched each other so closely our senses are still tuned to the slightest shift in each other's posture.

There are times when I'll be watching Tutelo combing her daughter's hair, and she'll hesitate for a split instant, and I know she's back at Bog Willow Village."

"Do you ever ask her to make sure you're right?"

"I don't have to. I know. As I knew what you were thinking just now."

The old woman's shadow seemed to hover over Baji again, blotting the starlight as wrinkled hands reached down to drag her to her feet and shove her into the arms of waiting men. Men who had paid a lot for the privilege.

Baji's muscles clenched again. As her frosted breath rose toward the Sky World, she struggled to understand why she couldn't let go of those memories. The sickening throb of her heart choked her. She swallowed. Then swallowed again, forcing the memory away. A tremendous sadness came upon her.

Sky Messenger reached over to clasp her hand hard. "Stop thinking about it." A savage glitter lit his eyes. "She doesn't deserve your attention."

"No. She doesn't." But her veins felt as if glassy flakes of obsidian rushed through them. She couldn't move or breathe without pain.

His grip tightened, crushing her hand. "You're here with me. You're safe."

"Not if you break my thumb. How will I draw back my bow?"

The ghost of his smile warmed. He brought her hand to his mouth and pressed warm lips to her thumb. Changing the subject, he said, "Anyway, I need you to help me think about the People of the Landing."

"You mean how to approach them about peace?"

"Yes. Tomorrow, if we survive crossing through Hills

territory, we should reach the border of the People of the Landing. Soon after, we will reach their villages."

"Have you determined which village you will visit first?"

He stroked her palm while he contemplated the question. "Shookas Village. High Matron Weyra has a reputation for fairness and intelligence. At least among my People. What do the Flint People say about her?"

Baji shrugged. "Among my People, she's known as Slow Thinker."

"That doesn't sound very flattering."

"Well, she's called that because apparently she never makes rash decisions. She ponders matters for a long while, discussing every possible permutation with the clans, before bringing an issue before the Ruling Council. I've heard it can take weeks for any major decision to be agreed upon. Keep that in your heart, lest you hope to have a decision the same day you speak with her."

"I don't."

Baji watched him. "And what will you tell High Matron Weyra? You should begin with your Dream."

"I will. Then I'll explain that our alliance already includes three nations—"

"Be specific. Say it includes the Standing Stone nation, the Flint People, plus three Hills villages."

He frowned. "You're right. Yes. Then I will present the benefits of our alliance—"

"Explain them to me."

His mouth quirked, and he gave her a crooked smile. "I haven't really figured them all out yet."

"Don't you think you'd better?"

He heaved a breath. Moments later, he said, "Well . . .

mutual defense, for one thing. We will also redistribute food to needy villages . . . and expand our Trade networks, as we spoke about earlier."

Baji toyed with his hair. "May I question you as I believe High Matron Weyra will?"

He rolled to his side, braced his elbow, and propped his head on his hand. "I would welcome it." His breath frosted in the cold air.

As more of the campfires of the dead blazed to life outside, the prismatic reflections through the runoff streaming from the roof strengthened, swathing the rockshelter with what appeared to be a thousand silverfish swimming through a stardust ocean.

"Weyra will first note that you have no food to redistribute, and even after you tell her that the Flint nation will contribute to the cause, she'll say it won't be enough. How will you respond?"

He drew her hand to his heart and held it there. "I'll say she's right. This winter. However, next autumn the alliance will pool its harvests, so that we all have enough."

"Providing the crops are good."

"That is a given."

"And providing you can talk them into it, which won't be easy."

"I still have to promise her that we can."

"Yes, you do."

He frowned. "What else will she say?"

"Next, she'll tell you that the members of your pitiful alliance are too far away to help protect Landing villages from the Mountain People raiders. The Mountain People are their closest and most dangerous enemies."

His elbow shifted upon the folds of woven fox-hide

blankets. "If we create a war party and station it on the border between the Mountain and Landing peoples, they can block raids into Landing country."

"Who will compose such a war party?"

"Warriors from every nation."

"That's idealistic. How will you feed so many warriors?"

He gave Baji a lockjawed glare, as though he wished she hadn't asked that. After ten heartbeats, he answered, "I suppose every member of the alliance will have to provide for its own warriors."

"Which means they won't send warriors to serve in the war party."

"Maybe. Maybe not. What else?"

"That's all I can think of for now."

"Think they'll kill us on sight?"

Her grip tightened on his hand. "That's what I'd do."

"Well," he replied reasonably, "if they do, we won't have to solve all of these hard problems for High Matron Weyra."

Baji lay for a moment, not certain what to say. It was the first time he'd ever sounded so casual about his own life. She didn't like it. She released his hand and rearranged herself into a cross-legged position at his side, looking down at him. Her long hair fell forward in a black torrent. "Do not ever speak to me so offhandedly about your death again, or I'll—"

"Beat me to death to spite me?"

"Don't joke."

He laughed softly and forcefully took her hand again, though she tried to pull it away. "Let me hold it. Until your head wound is better it's one of the few things I can touch."

She smiled and yielded. As he stroked her fingers, she

said, "I think you need to remember the lessons Wakdanek taught you."

"Wakdanek? The Dawnland Healer? There isn't a day that goes by that I don't think about him." His deep voice turned soft, like cattail down against the skin. "He told me that everything in the world is related. People, animals, trees, stones, the Faces of the Forest, the Cloud People. We are all One. I remember Wakdanek telling Sindak that every time he placed his fingers upon a branch, the tree recognized him, and that if he listened he could hear the tree calling his name, trying to reach across the gulf that separated them to touch his heart."

"What did Sindak say?"

"He said that was usually when the first blow landed."

Baji chuckled. "That sounds like Sindak."

"Yes." Sky Messenger seemed to be lost in memories, smiling sadly. He caressed her hand. "Wakdanek also said that because all things are related, we must name our enemies carefully, because killing the enemy has only one outcome: We kill a part of our own soul. And by doing so, we cripple the world itself."

Baji laced her fingers with his and squeezed hard to get his full attention. When his gaze focused on her, she asked, "Do you believe him?"

"With all my heart."

"Then you must carry his words with you when you enter Shookas Village."

He stroked her hair. "I will. Thank you for helping me, Baji."

In a quiet voice, she answered, "That's why I'm here."

Twenty-six

The scent of hickory smoke filled the council house in Atotarho Village. A round structure forty paces across, it had been constructed of log saplings and roofed with elm bark. Six rings of wooden benches encircled the central fire. High Matron Kelek restlessly paced from one side of the house to the other, moving through the flickering firelight like a lone ghost.

Hadui buffeted the walls, rushing between the bark slabs and banging the sacred False Face masks that hung around the house. On occasion, he whistled or whimpered through their contorted mouths.

Kelek drew her long buckskin cape closed beneath her wrinkled chin and tried to keep her eyes off the large mask that hung to her left. The old stories said it had been created by Hadui himself. Called *He-of-Divided-Body,* the mask seemed to be trying to get her attention; its shell-inlaid eye sockets flashed, while a soft eerie hooting erupted from its mouth. *He-of-Divided-Body* was a Powerful Spirit. During the Creation, Hadui had traveled to a place where lay the body of a freshly dead human, and exclaimed, "Come, you who are my brother," then he'd bent down and divided the corpse in half. Taking up one half of the cold flesh, he'd conjoined it with half of his own Spirit body, and the two halves had become one. As a result, one half of the mask's head was covered with white human hair and the other half glistened with Hadui's coal black hair. *He-of-Divided-Body* was a creature of life and death, human and supernatural, of death and Requickening. One half of his face was red, the other black. He had chosen to live forever on the earth in the forests, so that he could help human beings in time of need.

Kelek refused to face him. Instead, she turned her attention to the door, watching for Little Matron Adusha. Adusha led the Bear Clan in Turtleback Village. Scouts had seen her hurrying up the southern trail with two guards. Kelek had ordered that she be escorted to the council house when she arrived, but that had been more than one-half hand of time ago. What was taking so long?

He-of-Divided-Body let out a long shrill wail that chilled Kelek's blood. As though to emphasize his words, he shuddered violently, battering the wall. She looked around. Every mask seemed to be rocking back and forth, as if ready to leap from the walls and pounce upon her elderly body in punishment for her crimes.

"I did what I had to," she hissed at them. "It was my duty to increase the Power of the Bear Clan! Any matron would have . . ."

The flapping door curtain was shoved aside and, as Adusha entered the council house, her plain moosehide cape whipped about her red leggings. Sweat plastered her short black hair to her round face, accentuating the width of her flat nose and thinness of her lips. A short woman, she had a husky voice. "I apologize for being late, High Matron."

She strode forward with her guards. The man to her left was tall and muscular. Kelek didn't know him, but he was Wolf Clan. Yi's lineage. Red paw prints encircled the bottom of his black cape. The man to Adusha's right was Hikatoo. Of average height, handsome in a boyish way, he had seen thirty summers. Kelek knew his grandmother well. Snipe Clan. For several summers, Hikatoo had been one of Atotarho's personal guards.

"Your messenger said to expect you at noon," Kelek called irritably.

"Yes, well, I've never seen Hadui this violent. He's ripping whole trees from the ground and casting them across the trails that lead into Atotarho Village. It's as though he's trying to block off the village to isolate you, High Matron. We were forced to veer around many such obstacles."

Kelek stiffened, frowning at the comment.

Adusha stopped less than a pace from Kelek. "I assume you know Hikatoo." She extended a hand to the guard on her left. "This is War Chief Tajan from Hilltop Village."

Kelek's gaze slowly examined the man. "Yi's lineage."

"I am, yes." The man's dark eyes had an eerie gleam.

This isn't right. Adusha is a Bear Clan matron from Turtleback Village. She should have Bear Clan guards.

"I hope things are well in Hilltop Village, War Chief. It is not usual for—"

"No, but nothing is 'usual' is it?" Adusha folded her arms tightly beneath her heavy moose-hide cape. "Things are not well in the world outside Atotarho Village, Kelek."

"I assume you're referring to the war."

"I'm referring to the fact that Hilltop and Turtleback villages are buzzing with the news that on her deathbed our former High Matron told Zateri's daughter she planned to name Zateri to replace her when she was gone."

Kelek lifted her chin to stare down her nose in disdain. "It's a rumor, nothing more."

Tajan's piercing gaze was like a hot lance thrust into Kelek's vitals.

Kelek waved a hand. "Come, come, you don't believe it, do you? Zateri probably told her daughter to say it in the hopes of ousting the Bear Clan."

Adusha shook her head gravely, and the War Chief shifted to prop his hand on his belted war club. At the strange threatening gesture, Kelek bristled and straightened.

"Your behavior is outrageous. What is the meaning of this?"

Adusha softly said, "Turtleback Village and Hilltop Village received messengers. Both villages called council meetings so everyone could hear the story from the messenger himself. The man who came to Turtleback Village repeated the girl's story perfectly and it was filled with so many small details that no child could have made them up. They could only have come from our former High Matron."

Kelek swallowed hard. No messenger had come to her, but she knew the story. Already four separate versions were circulating around Atotarho Village. "So . . . Turtleback Village believes it?"

"Every person outside of the Bear Clan believes it."

She glanced at the guards who nodded slightly. "And the Bear Clan? What's being said by our own relatives?"

Adusha's folded arms tightened, bulging beneath her cape. After Coldspring, Riverbank, and Canassatego villages split away, there were only three villages left in the true Hills nation: Turtleback Village, Hilltop Village, and Atotarho Village. No matter the cost, they had to remain united.

"I think most of our relatives believe it, too."

Kelek started pacing again to release some of her anxiety. "War Chief Tajan? What is the opinion of Hilltop Village?"

"Our village council believes Zateri is the rightful High Matron," he responded bluntly.

Kelek snorted. "And just how do they speculate that I became High Matron if not through the words of our former High Matron? Is the Bear Clan being accused of wrongdoing?"

Adusha unfolded her arms and lowered them to her sides where she clenched her fists. "Not the Bear Clan. Just you, Kelek. It is being whispered that you conspired with Chief Atotarho to deny Zateri her rightful place—"

"Other than a child's word, what evidence is there to support this claim?"

Hikatoo's eyes narrowed, as though he knew something.

Adusha said, "Some people—the kind ones who love you—say that Atotarho lied to you when he told you that our former High Matron had named you to succeed her, and you unwittingly accepted the position without further verification. After all, we were headed off to war with the Standing Stone villages. There was no time, and someone had to lead the nation."

Kelek hesitated. "And what is being said by those who do not love me?"

Adusha stared at her. "They say you so coveted the position that you were the one who approached Atotarho. That you offered him—"

"I most certainly did not!"

"No? Well, those who have ears find it odd that as soon as you ascended to the High Matronship you announced the marriage of your granddaughter to Atotarho." She cocked her head in a distasteful accusatory manner. "Is it true that you agreed to link Atotarho to the Bear Clan so he could remain as chief?"

"Stop looking at me like that," Kelek ordered. "It is impudent. I am the High Matron!"

Adusha's glare dimmed only slightly. "High Matron, these are perilous times. Our nation is split down the middle and Hills People are killing other Hills People. I am under orders to discover the truth. The other leaders of the Bear Clan are deeply worried that these rumors are true."

Kelek's knees felt slightly weak. In a dignified manner, she eased down to the bench beside the fire and straightened her buckskin cape around her. As she primly laced her hand in her lap, she said, "Go on. I need to hear every word."

"Our elders fear that you worked with Atotarho to kill the former High Matron—"

"How dare they! I did not!"

"Kelek, please listen. There is another reason I am here. I was in the Wolf Clan longhouse the day our former high matron died. I saw something."

"What?"

"I, along with five other people, saw Zateri's daughter, Kahn-Tineta, leave the former High Matron's chamber with her cousin Pedeza. Immediately afterward, we saw a

man come into the longhouse and enter the former High
Matron's chamber. His face was heavily painted with
black and white stripes. None of us recognized him, but
we heard later that many people had seen the evil witch,
Ohsinoh, speaking with Chief Atotarho that day, and he'd
had his face painted with black and white stripes. The
man left the High Matron's chamber in less than thirty
heartbeats. When we went to speak with her, to seek her
guidance, we found her dead. She still had the corner of
one of her bedding hides pressed over her nose and mouth.
No one can prove she was smothered, but we all suspected it."

"If so, I had nothing to do with it. I loved her! She had
served our nation well for more than thirty summers!"

"Right now the story is being whispered through the
entire nation. If it can be shown that you were involved in
her murder, the Wolf Clan will swear blood feuds against
every member of the Bear Clan. Isn't that right, War Chief
Tajan?"

He nodded once. "My clan elders have assured me that
we will."

Adusha continued, "If this happens, it will split the Hills
People yet again. The Wolf Clan greatly outnumbers us.
One by one, they will hunt the Bear Clan down, even if it
takes generations. The other Bear Clan elders fear that
our clan may not survive."

Legends spoke of many clans that had been wiped out by
blood feuds. The tragic stories were told around the winter
fires so that every child knew the possible outcome of a
blood feud initiated as a result of the Law of Retribution.

After thirty heartbeats, the blood surging in Kelek's
veins began to slow, and she could think again. Had she

been so desperate for her clan to rule the nation that she'd brought it to the brink of destruction? She'd thought her clan would be jubilant. And they had been . . . for a time. She felt Adusha watching her with eagle eyes, as though waiting for Kelek to lie so that she could give War Chief Tajan the order to strike a deadly blow.

Surely that's why he's here. He's Wolf Clan. Under the Law of Retribution it is his right, the right of his clan.

"The village councils of Hilltop and Turtleback respectfully ask to hear your version of how it happened, High Matron. I will carry the story back for their consideration."

Kelek swore the ground beneath her feet shifted, as though Great Grandmother Earth was preparing to suck her down into the depths of darkness.

Her mouth had gone bone dry. She licked her lips nervously. "It's a simple tale, Adusha. The night before our former High Matron died, Chief Atotarho came to me. It was the middle of the night. He was alone. He told me he'd just been with the High Matron, and that she'd named me to succeed her." *Does my face show the truth?* "However, since he had no ties to the Bear Clan, he knew we would probably choose to replace him as Chief. He made me an offer. He said that if I would grant permission for him to marry my granddaughter, and work on his behalf with our clan so that he could retain his position, he would assure that by next spring the People of the Hills would be the only nation left standing south of Skanodario Lake. He guaranteed that we would have conquered and adopted everyone else."

She paused to swallow and study their expressions. She couldn't tell whether they believed her or not.

Adusha's voice was low. "How did you think he could accomplish such a thing? Our Ruling Council would surely have refused—"

"Don't you see? *If* he could, the People of the Hills would become the most powerful nation in the world. Think of what we could do! We could send out armies to conquer the Algonquin and Cherokee to the south, and the Islander's Confederacy to the north. Our armies could sweep westward like locusts, taking whatever we wished. We would be wealthy beyond our wildest dreams! Our children would never be hungry or frightened again." *And I would become a legend. The greatest High Matron in the history of the People.* She extended a translucent parchment-like hand to Adusha. "Isn't that worth allowing him to retain his position? Of course, if he'd failed, we would have been forced to replace him with someone else, but I felt certain—"

"Certain*?*" Adusha's voice was terse. "Are you telling me that you betrayed us so our nation could make war on distant Peoples we don't even know?"

War Chief Tajan had his gaze on her. Curiosity filled his dark eyes. Hikatoo's mouth had tightened into a white bloodless line.

"Betrayed who? The Wolf Clan? I didn't betray them. Atotarho assured me that our former high matron had named me to replace her."

Adusha stared at Kelek for a long time. "Please tell your story, Hikatoo."

Kelek's panicked gaze jerked to the Snipe Clan warrior, and her heart thundered.

"I only heard a few words of the chief's conversation with Matron Kelek. As she says, he did go to her. One hand of time earlier, however, I was standing right outside the Wolf Clan longhouse, barely three paces from where the Chief spoke with the former High Matron in her chamber. Though the longhouse wall hid many of their words, all of his personal guards, me included, heard the former High Matron when she raised her voice to tell the Chief, *'You are unfit to rule this nation, but the council cannot afford to remove you on the eve of battle.'*" He paused to take a deep breath, and glared at Kelek. "One hand of time later, he ordered us to accompany him to the Bear Clan longhouse so he could speak with Matron Kelek. He stood under the porch until she appeared. The chief began their conversation by saying, *'I have a proposition I think you will appreciate.'* After that, I only caught certain words. But we were all worried by what had happened that day, so later that night we discussed what each of us had heard. Between the five of us, we filled in much of the conversation."

Kelek felt slightly faint. She gritted her teeth and lifted her chin, trying to glower. "You were standing twenty paces away. What could you have heard?"

Hikatoo's dark gaze did not waver. "You told the chief that in exchange for his saying the former high matron had named you to succeed her, you would marry him to your granddaughter, and you assured him that he would retain his position as Chief."

Adusha's head tilted in an unpleasant accusatory manner. After ten heartbeats of waiting for Kelek to deny it, she lifted her arm and pointed a finger at Kelek's chest. "When I said you had betrayed us, I didn't mean the Wolf Clan, Kelek. I meant the nation. Your own words make it clear that you conspired with Atotarho to circumvent the wisdom of the Ruling Council. That alone is treason, *High Matron*." She said the words with contempt. "And once the rest of the story has spread across the entire nation, the Bear Clan will be spat upon and hunted down like dogs. Our clan will be extinct."

Kelek rose to her feet, shaking with a combination of indignation and fear. "Tell your village councils that I demand they appear before me to discuss this issue in person. This 'pieced-together' conversation is pure fabrication! I refuse to stand here any longer being maligned by a cowardly warrior and an insignificant *Little Matron!*"

A cold smile came to Adusha's thin lips. "I will tell them. In the meantime, we have heard that Atotarho requested you to send two thousand warriors to join him in the destruction of the Standing Stone nation."

"Yes. I'd planned to bring the issue before the Ruling Council tomor—"

"Take no action until you've heard from our village councils."

Kelek stiffened. "But he needs those warriors."

Adusha didn't deign to respond. She turned on her heel and stalked toward the door with her guards behind her.

When they'd gone, Kelek stared at the wind-whipped curtain. The sacred False Faces on the walls rattled and hooted shrilly, crying out to each other. Her shaking knees finally gave way. She sank down to the bench and dropped her head in her hands.

Twenty-seven

Cloud People blanketed the night sky, turning it pitch black and ominous. The mist rising from Reed Marsh had a damp, caressing feel against Gonda's face. He adjusted his pack, checked his slung bow and quiver, and examined the shoulder-width hole they'd chopped from the frozen soil beneath the exterior palisade. The black oval was barely visible. Situated at the point farthest away from Yellowtail Village, the enemy warriors on the Yellowtail catwalks could not possibly observe their emergence from the ground. There could, however, be fifty men with bows sitting in the limbs of the nearby trees, watching for the slightest movements along the Bur Oak palisades.

Gonda turned to his volunteers. "Last chance. Anyone who wishes to back out should do so now."

Three warriors stood with him, their breaths frosting and mingling in the night air. Each carried a bow and over-stuffed quiver, and wore a knee-length black shirt and high-topped black moccasins. In addition, they'd covered every bit of exposed skin with soot. In the darkness he thought Sindak and Wampa had their arms folded, but couldn't be sure. Young Papon noisily swallowed. Eighteen summers old, he had buck teeth that made him tend to slur his words. He also had a reputation for exaggeration. But Jigonsaseh insisted he was a bold fighter—and that's what Gonda needed tonight.

He whispered, "All right. High Matron Kittle has ordered the fires extinguished to help cover our movements. Our opponents probably assume it is to conserve firewood. But they may also think we're up to something."

"They do," Sindak said from Gonda's right. "This isn't normal. They know we have wounded and children to keep warm. They'll be especially on guard."

Gonda nodded, though he knew they probably couldn't see it. "I just spoke with War Chief Deru. He's ready. He'll be watching for us to emerge from the marsh at the predetermined location. Once he either sees us, or the fires erupt, he will begin his diversion. When we're in the marsh, we must take our time. We don't want to startle any of the birds perched on the reeds and cattails. Any sudden squawking or chirping and we're all dead."

Sindak waited for Gonda to continue. When he didn't, Sindak added, "Also, if you must get out of the marsh, be vigilant about the patches of snow that still cling against the western palisade wall. Not only will they crunch if you step on them, your blackened body will show up clear as day."

Gonda looked for nodding heads, but the sable darkness cloaked their bodies so completely they were just faintly darker silhouettes cast against the cobalt background.

"One last thing," Gonda said. "As soon as we're through this hole, it will be covered up. The only way we're getting back into Bur Oak Village is through the front gates, and the guards have orders not to open them for us unless we're in the clear. Understand?"

Papon slurred, "So, if we're being closhely followed, they won't open the gates?"

"That's right."

Papon shifted uncomfortably. He had a wife and four children.

Gonda lowered his voice, and used a deadly tone. "And I don't want any misunderstandings. Each of us is expendable. Our only purpose is to buy the people in Bur Oak Village a chance. Anyone who is caught, wounded, or doesn't make the rendezvous *will be left behind.* Those are Matron Jigonsaseh's orders. Am I clear?"

He heard grunts of assent.

"Very well. Everyone ready?"

"Ready." Sindak's voice.

"Me, too." War Chief Wampa.

Barely audible, Papon hissed, "Yes."

Gonda got down on his knees, shrugged out of his pack and weapons, and pushed them through ahead of him as he slid into the hole on his belly. Coming up on the other side like a muskrat through an ice hole, he shouldered his load and crawled toward the marsh. The old autumn leaves that covered the ground were drenched with mist, quiet and slick. When he reached the marsh's edge, he eased aside the reeds, and glided into the water. He almost gasped at the bitter cold, but stopped himself. Sindak entered the water next, followed by Wampa and Papon.

Gonda looked around. Here, it was dark, but in forty paces the halo of firelight streaming from Yellowtail Village gave the calm water a supernatural sheen. The dark reflections of the trees stood out so clearly they might have been painted upon the marsh. Fortunately, the cattails grew thickly there, too. The stripes they cast upon the water would cloak their shapes . . . he hoped.

"You all know the plan," Gonda whispered.

Silence.

"Sindak comes with me. Wampa, you and Papon are the best shots in the village. You will remain in the marsh, paralleling our course, with your bows aimed at the palisade. You'll see warriors targeting us long before we do."

Wampa's head turned. Around two hundred enemy warriors stood on the catwalks, talking, joking, ripping off strips of jerky with their teeth. Their conversations drifted through the still night air. Wampa was probably wondering how the thirty arrows in her quiver, plus another thirty in Papon's, could possibly make a difference.

Gonda continued, "Wampa and Papon, don't leave the marsh unless you're forced to. Use the cattails, rushes, and trees as cover when you let fly. As soon as Sindak and I have finished our last duty—if we're able—we're going to come boiling back into the marsh, and we'll all make our way back to Bur Oak Village. Any questions?"

The only sound was the slight rustling of reeds.

"Then let's go."

Gonda bent low and began wading through the waist-deep water. Mist swirled by, scalloped here and there with the curls spun off their arm movements as they pushed aside a cattail, pointed to a floating branch, or sleeping bird, or adjusted quivers when they slipped sideways.

Cold, bitter and numbing, ate into Gonda's feet and legs. He moved around a thick stand of reeds, and waded into the copper-colored portion of the marsh that shone in the firelight streaming from Yellowtail Village. Reflections of tree branches combined with those of the reeds to form a dark filigree upon the water. The effect was stunningly beautiful—perhaps more so because Gonda suspected it might be his last such sight.

Gonda studied the treetops, then pointed out the two sentries high in the branches. Placed as they were, they'd be sure to spot anyone who tried to sneak between the marsh and Yellowtail Village. If it were Negano's work, it was smartly done.

Gonda hissed, "Wampa, shoot them first."

"Understood." She touched Papon's shoulder, pointed at herself, then the man on the right. Next, she pointed to Papon, and the man on the left. He jerked his head in understanding, and the two began to wade toward their targets.

Gonda's gaze returned to the Hills' warriors on the catwalks. One man was gesturing wildly as he told some story. The others around him smiled and nodded, then laughed out loud.

"All right, Sindak." Gonda gestured to chokecherries masking the shoreline. "I'll go first."

Gonda maneuvered through the cattails to the stand of chokecherries. Their smooth gray-brown bark shone with firelight. He ducked down behind them, waiting until Sindak caught up and crouched beside him.

Gonda looked at him. In the reflected light, patterned by cattails, Sindak's lean face might have been carved of stone, but the lines around his deeply sunken eyes had gone tight. The War Chief's gaze methodically studied the palisade, noting faces, probably saying names in his head. Was he remembering moments of laughter with these men and women? Perhaps times when he'd saved their lives? Or they, his?

Gonda asked, "The jokester and the three men beside him, who are they?"

"The jokester, on the far right, is War Chief Joondoh of Turtleback Village. He's short, so he makes up for it by being loud. The tall thin man beside him is Oswego, one of his deputy war chiefs. The other two warriors are from Atotarho Village." A barely audible tightness entered his voice: "Lonkol and Tadu."

Gonda was watching Sindak very closely. "Tell me about them."

Sindak shrugged as though there wasn't much to tell. "Both are good warriors."

"Married?"

"Yes."

"What are their wives names?"

Sindak shot Gonda a look that seemed to see straight through to Gonda's souls. "Osto and Tawisa." He hesitated. "Why?"

"I'm just wondering how you can kill them."

Sindak frowned. "Now is a fine time to ask."

"I thought I'd wait until you could see their faces."

"Their faces? You thought . . . What? That I'd crumble when I saw them?"

Gonda exhaled hard. "I suspect some of these warriors are lifelong friends, men and women who have guarded your back in a hundred battles. Some may have saved your life, and you are about to repay them by killing them." Gonda paused to study Sindak's stony features. "I'm not sure I could kill my friends and relatives."

Sindak didn't respond. He was staring at the people on

the catwalk. The longer he looked, the harder the set of his mouth became.

Wind Woman's gentle daughter, Gaha, swept the surface of the pond, turning it into a sea of golden glitter, broken here and there by swaying cattails. The scent of the oak fires kindled in Yellowtail Village wafted over them.

"Jigonsaseh says you were such a beloved war chief that your people will hesitate to kill you if they see you. I, on the other hand, think the reverse is probably more likely true."

Sindak took a deep breath and nodded his understanding. "You think I will be the one to hesitate?"

"Just tell me why you volunteered to do this."

Sindak looked back at the warriors on the palisade and his eyes glistened, as though he were straining against his better judgment. Standing silhouetted against the firelight, the warriors made perfect targets. Except for Joondoh's group, most were vigilantly watching Bur Oak Village, the marsh, and scanning the surrounding hills. "May I ask you a question, Gonda?"

"Of course."

"Do you think that you and I are here by chance?"

"Chance? What do you mean?"

"I mean that I think you and I are meant to be here. From that fateful instant twelve summers ago when Towa and I were ordered to help you and Koracoo find the missing children right up to this conversation, I don't think any of it has been chance. Do you believe in Sky Messenger's Dream?"

"If I didn't I wouldn't be out here with my testicles so frozen they've knotted up against the bottom of my throat."

Firelight reflecting from the marsh danced over Sindak's lean soot-coated face and seemed alive in his eyes. "Is there anything else you want to know?"

"No."

Gonda looked back at Papon and Wampa. They were almost invisible in the eddying mist. Both stood watching and waiting, undoubtedly wondering what was taking so long.

"When we get inside the palisade, I'll go right and you go left. The crumbling remains of refugee shelters fill the space between the palisades. It's a trash heap of charred bark, old cloth, torn baskets, and rush matting. Finding quiet footing is going to be the challenge."

"I understand."

Veering around the chokecherries, Gonda got down on his belly, and slid ashore. Sindak was right behind him. They slithered around the patches of snow that dotted the dark leafbed, and headed straight for the southwestern palisade wall of Yellowtail Village. Beneath where War Chief Joondoh and his friends stood, a black gaping hole had been burned through the palisade logs—a vulnerability in the defenses, which probably explained War Chief Joondoh's presence above it.

Heart pounding, Gonda moved with the stealth of a hunting serpent. He still half-expected Sindak to warn his friends and betray their mission.

Wampa and Papon must have managed their tasks in utter silence for the sentries in the marsh had called no alarm.

When they reached the blackened hole, Gonda flattened himself against the wall as he quietly slipped his pack from his shoulders and pushed it through the gap, before he crawled through. A few heartbeats later, Sindak pushed through, glanced at Gonda, then looked up. Through the slats in the catwalk above them, they could see the men moving, hear them talking.

"Ready?" Sindak asked, lips to Gonda's ears.

Gonda gave Sindak a firm nod and bent to his business. His fingers were shaking—from cold and fear—as he untied the laces. Carefully he removed the pots of walnut oil mixed with pitch, the bag of wood shavings, and pots of hot coals gathered from the fires of the Bur Oak longhouses.

He leaned close to Sindak, busy with his own pack, and whispered. "I think we have around six hundred heartbeats before Deru starts letting fly."

"Which means we have to hurry."

"I'll count to five hundred and meet you back here."

"Good luck!"

Gonda watched Sindak disappear among the shadows and pulled the wooden stopper from his own oil pot. Silently, he moved along beneath the catwalk, tiptoeing through ankle-deep ash, slabs of burned bark, and useless chunks of basketry.

Glancing up, he saw two men standing above him. He edged forward, moving ten paces farther down the wall to a twisted wad of half-burned reed matting.

Gonda dribbled oil on the mat, then shook out a small amount of hot coals in the middle. It would take a little while to catch, but not long. He had to move quickly. The warriors on the catwalks continued talking, laughing, completely unaware of his presence.

When he'd gone halfway around the curve in the wall, one of the warriors on the catwalk suddenly stopped talking in midsentence and leaned over. "Who's there?"

Motionless in the shadows, Gonda thought his heart was going to batter its way through his breastbone.

The man illuminated in the firelight above was a square-jawed man with long hair streaming over his shoulders.

In the midst of thick shadows, Gonda's black-clothed body should blend with the background, but mist glistened in the firelight. If it eddied around him, creating unusual swirls . . .

"What did you see?" the man's friend asked.

"I don't know. Something moved down there."

"Could be a wood rat. I just about jumped out of my skin last night when one knocked a pot over. They're after the moldy corn kernels scattered down there."

The warrior straightened up, sighed, and went back to his former conversation. "As I was saying, how did the Flint People expect Atotarho to act when he discovered they'd allied themselves with our enemies? They should have known he would ambush their trail home. I tell you, no one hides better than we do! No one is craftier than we are. This war is over. The world belongs to Atotarho."

His friend replied, "I'm sure the Flint People expected us to take revenge, just not so soon. That's one thing Negano did right. That ambush was perfect. You have to admit it."

"Any time you kill four hundred Flint warriors in a single attack, it's a great victory. But that's all Negano has done right. If you're as hungry as I am, you know he's an incompetent fool. Another quarter moon here, and we'll all be starving and desperate enough to slit Negano's throat and eat him to fill our bellies. I can't believe he's the new War Chief, he . . ."

Gonda stopped breathing. Atotarho ambushed and

killed four hundred Flint warriors? Blessed gods, not Cord's war party?

Worry about it later.

Gonda silently tiptoed forward, pouring more pitch and coals into the back of each of the crowded shelters, until he rounded the northern edge of the palisade and could see the Yellowtail gates. No guards stood outside, but around twenty warriors with slung bows overlooked the entry. He could just see the tops of their shoulders and heads over the palisade.

Gonda slipped up to a pile of charred timbers the enemy had scavenged for firewood. Charred wood caught fire quicker, burned hotter. He poured the last of his oil, shavings, and all of the remaining coals at the base of the woodpile. He could already smell smoke on the breeze.

A commotion started along on the southern palisade catwalk that overlooked Bur Oak Village. Questioning voices rose, then someone shouted, *"Fire!"* and a staccato of feet pounded the catwalk, shaking the palisade. *"There are fires all along the wall! Get water!"*

Several of the warriors stationed overlooking the northeastern gates ran back to help.

Gonda's heart kicked into a gallop as he raced back, using the noise on the catwalks as cover. Flames danced in at least half the shelters he'd fired. With the commotion, no one seemed to notice him as he thrashed back toward the gap where he was supposed to meet Sindak. He pressed his back against the wall and gritted his teeth, his gaze straining to see Sindak coming around the curve in the wall.

Wait. Wait . . .

Gonda's gaze shot upward when what appeared to be

falling stars began plunging from the darkness. War Chief Deru's diversion was right on time. Flaming arrows punctured the mist and rained down upon Yellowtail Village, lodging in the newly repaired roofs of longhouses, the piles of debris in the plaza, and piercing the bodies of anyone who stood in the plaza. Wave after wave of arrows arced through the night sky. Panicked cries erupted inside Yellowtail Village, accompanied by shouts and desperate running. Atotarho's warriors screamed orders.

Sindak, blessed gods, where are you?

War Chief Deru's voice boomed from the Bur Oak catwalks, "Fight you filthy worms!"

"We are attacked!" a man roared. "Get to the southern end of the village. Defend the walls!" Then, "Deru, you have the testicles of a gnat! Only a gutless coward attacks at night!"

The spitting hum of a thousand arrows launched and in flight combined with the rapid-fire *shish-thumps* of stone points impacting wood, frozen ground, and flesh. Ululating clan war cries split the darkness.

Sindak appeared like a ghost from the shadows, and Gonda said, "Come on. Hurry!" and shoved Sindak through the gap wall.

Gonda leaped out behind him to find Sindak staring to the north. Men were screaming. Two toppled over the palisade wall, landing hard not more than three paces from them. From the marsh, Wampa and Papon fired smoothly, one arrow after another, taking the warriors in the chests or heads. Several of the Hills warriors had rushed to the western wall to shoot into the marsh at their invisible assailants.

"I don't think we want to go running out there!" Sindak

pointed toward the marsh. "Did you notice the pile of timbers stacked outside the gate?"

"I set fire to a big stack of firewood on the inside. That's enough. Let's go!" Gonda grabbed his sleeve and tried to drag him away.

"No, wait!" Sindak jerked back so hard he almost toppled Gonda. "We can use the logs to block the gates. Look!"

Gonda turned and immediately saw what Sindak had noticed. Logs, evidently discarded during makeshift repairs, lay piled near the gate. Inside, a merry blaze was roaring through Gonda's woodpile.

"Blessed gods. You're a diabolical weasel, Sindak." He slapped him on the shoulder. "Just my kind." Then he glanced up at the archers overhead. "Think we can make it?"

"We're dead men anyway. Let's try."

The warriors above had all of their attention fixed on dodging the flaming arrows that continued to drop from the sky. Sindak led the charge to the timbers at a desperate run. Gonda followed right behind him.

"It'll take both of us!" Sindak shouted. They each took an end, lifted a log, and groaned as they hauled it toward the gates. The wood was wet and heavy.

The last remaining warrior over the gate ran to see what they were doing. *"Sindak. It's Sindak! Someone help me! It's War Chief Sindak!"*

To Gonda's amazement, the warrior hesitated long enough that they could brace their first log against the planks, and run back for another before arrows started slicing the air above and around them. Most of the arrows came from the marsh, where Wampa and Papon were covering them. They grabbed the second timber and charged for the gate again.

"Blessed gods!" the man on the catwalk yelled as he dove for the safety behind the palisade. Incoming arrows slammed the logs in front of him. *"I need help over here. Help!"*

Warriors rushed along the catwalks toward him, their bows drawn.

As Gonda and Sindak braced the timber, Sindak bellowed, "Run!" and they sprinted for the safety of the marsh.

We've done it! Exhilaration pumping in Gonda's veins, he leaped a rock and . . .

Crack!

A jolt ran through his bones. At the same time the muscles in his right calf ripped apart. He stumbled, went down hard, the wind knocked from his lungs. He slid face-first through the wet leaves at the edge of the marsh.

For a dazed instant he wondered what had gone wrong. He struggled to breathe, to get air into his now panicked lungs. The sounds of the battle had grown oddly distant, removed. Yellow sparks of light, like disembodied fireflies twinkled in his graying vision.

An arrow hissed past his right ear and thumped into the earth, quivering from the impact. A fierce agony burned in his leg. Gasping, he dug his fingers into the soggy leaves and tried to drag himself into the water.

"Gonda?" Sindak shouted.

Sindak charged back for him.

"No! No! Run!" Gonda ordered hoarsely.

Then Sindak was there, bending down.

"Leave me! Get of here, you fool!"

Grabbing a fistful of Gonda's shirt, Sindak dragged Gonda's wounded body up. The world spun crazily as Sindak muscled Gonda onto his shoulder and pounded back toward the marsh.

Gonda rasped, "My leg is broken! I can't run. You have to go on without me!"

Arrows cut the air around them as Sindak splashed into the reeds. Weaving, half-stumbling beneath Gonda's weight, he struggled deeper into the darkness, sloshing through the cattail stalks.

Gonda saw Wampa and Papon ahead, using the trees as cover to shoot at the archers on the catwalk, and he shouted, "Get back to Bur Oak Village! Now!"

Wampa and Papon immediately turned and splashed back through the marsh.

"Sindak, curse you, drop me! You have to get out of here!"

Instead of obeying, Sindak dragged Gonda's arm over his shoulder and hauled him out beyond the gaudy halo of firelight to where the black water was neck-deep.

"Put me down!" Gonda shouted. "Blast you! You have never been able to obey orders!"

Sindak heaved Gonda aside, and commanded, "Hold tight to my shirt or I'll knock you senseless and drag you!"

Gonda clamped on to the man's wet shirt and Sindak stroked hard for Bur Oak Village.

Gonda mostly managed to keep his head above water until they reached the cattail shallows. When he tried to stand, to follow Sindak out of the water to make a run for the gate, his leg went out from under him. He flipped to his side and, dragging his injured leg, pulled himself ashore, gasping in pain.

Sindak never hesitated. He grasped Gonda's arm, grunted, and lifted him, carrying Gonda behind the curve in the palisade wall, out of the shower of arrows. "Saponi! Disu! Where are you?"

Two of Sindak's warriors appeared out of the darkness where they'd been hiding, demanding, "Sindak? Is that you?"

"Yes, and Gonda's hurt!" Sindak managed through ragged breaths.

Through the pain, Gonda growled, "I swear you are the worst warrior in the world. One of these days, your problems with authority are going to get you killed."

Sindak spared only enough breath to reply, "This isn't my day to die . . . or yours apparently."

When Deru launched another wave of flaming arrows, the enemy warriors on the Yellowtail catwalks ducked down.

"We have to go now!" Saponi said.

Three heartbeats later, Saponi and Disu hoisted Gonda's arms over their shoulders and pelted for the gate.

Sindak covered the retreat, calling, "Deru, we're coming in! Don't shoot!"

Gonda's scrambled vision recorded images of the gate, as he was dragged through in the safety of the palisade, and unceremoniously dropped on the ground. The two guards on the gate swiftly swung it closed, but not before Gonda noticed that the mist had picked up the orange gleam from the fires. It had shimmered into a huge gauzy halo over Yellowtail Village.

Sindak, breathless, turned to Saponi and Disu. "Get back to the fight. Follow Deru's orders. I'll meet you soon."

"Yes, War Chief." The two men ran.

Sindak knelt beside Gonda. The marsh had washed most of the soot from his serious face, but his beaked nose still bore smears of black. "How's your leg?"

"It hurts!"

"Well, I know that . . ."

The timbre of screams rising from Yellowtail Village changed, going from pain to breathless shrieks, the screams of men on fire.

Sindak went still, listening, and his expression slackened.

Weakly, Gonda said, "Leave me. I'll be fine."

Sindak just nodded. He sprinted away, nocking an arrow as he ran.

Gonda barely had time to catch his breath before his stomach lurched and he threw up.

Twenty-eight

Negano jerked from a sound sleep when screams shredded the cold mist. In one fluid move, he rolled out of his blanket with his war club in his fist, and lunged to his feet. All around him, other sleeping warriors had grabbed weapons and leaped up. Panicked conversations erupted around hundreds of campfires.

It took only a few moments before Negano's sleep-numbed mind focused on Yellowtail Village where flames roared.

"Dear gods, what happened?"

From Negano's position on the hillside, he could gaze down, horror-struck, into the village where his warriors dodged toppling longhouse walls or sections of collapsing palisade, shrieking as they ran for their lives. Several men jumped from the palisade with their clothing flaming. A few managed to drag themselves out into the meadow, where showers of arrows, shot from the Bur Oak Village catwalks, lanced their bodies.

"Grab your weapons! We have to get down there to help

them!" Snatching up his bow and quiver, he shouted, "Follow me!"

Negano led the charge down the hillside, splashed across the small creek, and up the incline that led to the villages situated on the rise. He didn't know how many warriors had followed him, but could hear feet pounding behind him.

As he dashed for Yellowtail Village, he saw the logs propped against the gates, locking everyone inside. The burning palisades had effectively ringed the village with flames.

He swung around and saw perhaps three hundred warriors. When he spotted deputy war chief Nesi, he shouted, "Nesi! Form a team, knock those logs down, and get those gates open!"

Nesi and two men charged for the timbers. The gates in front of them flamed, singeing their hair. When they managed to shove aside the logs and throw the gates open, thick blinding smoke boiled out, swallowing them.

Negano threw up his sleeve to cover his nose and mouth and squinted, trying to make out . . .

Five men came hobbling out, supporting one another, coughing, their soot-coated faces streaked with tears. One man gasped, "They attacked . . . so quickly . . . there was nothing we . . ." He fell into an uncontrollable coughing fit. The warrior supporting him dragged him away from the extreme heat and smoke.

Negano stared through the entry into the plaza. As some of the smoke cleared, he could see a little better. There must have been debris piled everywhere. Stacks of bark, old chunks of catwalks, and useless palisade poles lay in flaming heaps right next to the longhouses. Gods! No wonder the place had gone up like a torch!

Negano shouted. "Nesi, anyone who can still walk can make it out now. Let's take care of the Bur Oak archers!"

He led his warriors around the eastern side of Yellowtail Village and straight into a volley of arrows. Men went down all around him, shrieking. Hoarse cries, groans, and coughing wavered like a haunted chorus. There had to be five hundred archers on the Bur Oak catwalks! Some were old gray-haired elders and children barely old enough to carry bows, but they shot straight.

Negano managed to let two arrows fly, before he called, *"Retreat! Go back!"*

As soon as they started to run, Jigonsaseh's deep voice rang out and the gates of Bur Oak Village were flung open. A flood of warriors sprinted out, chasing after Negano's forces with their bows singing.

He stumbled over his dead, dying, and wounded warriors as he dashed away from the shower of arrows. Something slammed into his quiver, the impact enough to send him staggering. In shock, his mind refused to believe the number of freshly killed men and women who lay sprawled across the frozen ground. Half? Maybe half the warriors who had followed him just moments ago? Gods, that couldn't be right.

When he veered around the blazing curve of the Yellowtail palisades, out of the line of fire, he turned to look back. Counting . . . counting warriors. Maybe forty. Forty out of three hundred. *No, no, there must be more.* The thick smoke boiling out of Yellowtail probably concealed . . .

"Don't stop! They're still after us!" Nesi shouted.

"Blessed gods, how many arrows did Bur Oak Village stockpile?"

Negano shouted back, "The only thing I care about is how many they still have!"

He spun to look through the wide-open gates of Yellowtail Village and into the inferno, and readied himself to lead his remaining warriors inside to get them out of the line of . . .

Nesi called, "Don't do it, Negano!"

"Why not?" He swung around to glare at Nesi. "It's safer inside than outside!"

"Look at it!" He flung out a muscular arm, pointing to the plaza roaring with flames. "You lead a team in there, and Deru will box the village up so that none of us gets out alive! We have to retreat and regroup!"

Negano didn't even think, he just shouted, "Grab as many of the wounded as you can. Support them back to our camp!"

As warriors scurried to obey, dragging arms over shoulders, hauling another twenty or so men and women to their feet, the Bur Oak archers rounded the curve in the wall and starting letting fly again.

"Run! Hurry!"

All across the battlefield cries erupted, the wounded he'd left behind pleading for him to save them. The screams became more panicked when he charged in the opposite direction.

Twenty terrible heartbeats later, Jigonsaseh yelled another command, and the Bur Oak archers ceased pursuing them, and turned to silencing the cries of the wounded. One by one the begging voices were cut short in mid-scream.

Negano slowed to a trot and stared at the twenty or so shocked warriors who ran behind him, breathing hard. They appeared as dazed as men who'd been struck in the heads with war clubs. Nostrils flared. The sickly sweet scent of burning human flesh and scorched hair filled the night. None of them hauled wounded. Those who had tried must have lagged behind and been cut down. *Gods, I should have never given that order. . . .*

Negano rubbed his numb face, struggling to gain a hold on his senses as he led the way through the firelit darkness toward the creek. From his own camp, hundreds of warriors flocked down the hillside, men and women who'd finally understood what was happening and grabbed their weapons to come help.

"Go back!" he ordered. "There's nothing more we can do tonight!"

Warriors stared wide-eyed as he tramped past. They gaped first at him, then at Yellowtail Village, then at the warriors who followed him as he splashed across the creek. Many called questions:

"What happened?"

"Night attack," he answered. "The enemy set their own village on fire with our warriors inside."

A man called, "Gods, who made it out alive? Where's my brother?"

Someone else yelled, "Where's my wife? She was assigned to guard the Yellowtail palisade!"

Negano felt physically ill. He should never have used Yellowtail . . .

"Stop it," Nesi said as he trotted up beside him.

Negano turned. The square-jawed giant wore a threatening expression. His facial scars twitched.

"Stop what?"

"Stop second-guessing yourself. You did the right thing sending those warriors into Yellowtail Village."

"But Nesi—"

"Listen to me!" He stabbed his war club at Negano's chest. "Joondoh was in charge of the Yellowtail Village defense. He missed something. I don't know what, but this would have never happened if he'd been paying attention. You know it as well as I."

"Maybe, but—"

"It was Joondoh's fault. Do you *understand*?" Nesi's eyes glanced suggestively up the slope toward the crest of the ridge where Atotarho's camp nestled.

The chief stood before his fire, propped on his walking stick. Silhouetted in front of the flames, his hunched form was black as coal. Because of the way the mist eddied and shifted, Atotarho appeared to be standing in the midst of the blaze with flames shooting up all around him. Even from here, Negano could sense the old man's rage: it shivered the air.

"I understand, Nesi."

Negano had to concentrate. He needed an explanation. It hadn't occurred to him that as soon as he set foot in camp, Chief Atotarho would be waiting for him.

"Good," Nesi said. "Now, before you have to face him, stop and let me pull this accursed arrow out of your quiver. A finger's width to the left or right, and you'd be back there dying with the rest."

Twenty-nine

Jigonsaseh slung her bow and turned to Deru where he stood beside her on the catwalk batting out the sparks that alighted on his hair and shoulders. The sweat had mixed with ash and filled in the hollow of his crushed cheek; it created a black oval that extended across his squashed nose. "War Chief? I'll return shortly. Keep a close eye out. They may return with reinforcements."

"Yes, Matron."

As she walked away, Deru began marching up and down, his red cape swinging, praising his warriors, clapping exhausted men and women on the shoulders.

The moans and cries of the wounded that had been carried to the council house drifted through the falling sparks and ash.

Jigonsaseh climbed down to the plaza where the three teams she'd organized waited for her just outside the inner gates. Her stride lengthened as she hurried toward Kittle.

"High Matron," Jigonsaseh said. "I don't like it that you are going out there. You should—"

"The scouts you dispatched will warn us if we are in grave danger. Any final instructions?" Kittle's beautiful face had a haunted expression. She used her sleeve to pound out the flickering sparks that landed on her hood. She must know, and fear, how enraged Atotarho would be when he discovered what they'd done to his army.

"Just work quickly. The enemy could be rallying to return. The mist and smoke make it impossible to know. We need to act now. Tell your party to collect as many usable arrows as you can find. Grab quivers, bows, and any other weapon you can carry."

Kittle nodded, lifted a hand, and ordered, "Open the gates. We're going out." She waved to the women in her group, gesturing for them to follow her.

Jigonsaseh shouldered through the crowd to reach Taya. Her fourteen-summers-old face had gone as pale as frost. She'd been vomiting every morning, and feeling queasy most of the day. Jigonsaseh had no doubts but that Taya carried her son's child.

"Taya, waste no time. Strip the corpses of belt pouches, packs, and water bags. If you have time, dispatch a small group with the water bags and meet Tutelo in the marsh to fill them. But hurry! Any questions?"

"No, Matron." Taya gave her a confident nod.

"Good. Be fast."

Taya called to the elders in her group, "We have to hurry! Our job is only food and water bags! Let's go." She led the elders through the gates.

Jigonsaseh turned to Tutelo, who stood ten paces away, talking with her group of fifty children. Each carried an empty pot.

"Tutelo? Are you ready to head to the marsh?"

"We are." Short black locks, irregularly layered, stuck to her cheeks.

"Go."

Tutelo and the children flooded for the gates.

When everyone was gone, the village seemed stunningly empty. Jigonsaseh looked around. The warriors on the catwalks had their bows nocked and aimed at the billowing smoke and firelit mist. The fires in Yellowtail Village had died down somewhat, but sudden roars and hisses still erupted at odd moments, and tornados of sparks spun continually into the night sky.

Like black snow cascading from charred heavens, ash fell. It coated everything. She absently brushed at her cape. Then she marched back for the ladder, climbed up to the catwalk, and returned to her position.

Outside, villagers worked in grisly silence, jerking quivers and packs from shoulders, racing across the meadow collecting arrows, rolling corpses over to find belt pouches and water bags. Tutelo's children in the marsh had already started streaming back through the gates with filled water jars. They lined them up neatly along the walls of the Deer Clan longhouse.

As Jigonsaseh unslung her bow and nocked an arrow, her gaze drifted out across the marsh to the hills in the distance where enemy campfires sparkled. They'd still be picking up the pieces, caring for their wounded, assessing what went wrong. But tomorrow morning . . .

"Matron?"

Sindak trotted down the catwalk. He carried his bow nocked. "We must talk."

"I want to know everything."

"First, did Papon and Wampa make it back?"

"Yes, unharmed."

He heaved a sigh of relief. "Next, Gonda is wounded. He—"

"Badly?"

"The small bone in his lower leg is broken."

She gripped his arm. "So he can't walk. Did he make it back?"

Sindak gave her a wry smile that barely cut the sadness in his eyes. "He's in the council house. It—it's a long story. When the shooting stopped, two of my warriors carried him there."

She loosened her grip and let her hand drop. She let out a relieved breath. "Then Bahna, our Healer, is already caring for him. I'll check on him later."

"We need to speak, Jigonsaseh. What is your plan for dawn?" His soaked cape conformed to his muscular shoulders.

Jigonsaseh surveyed the people flooding back through the gates with armloads of arrows, packs and belt pouches. Tutelo was also herding her flock of children with the last water pots toward the gates. Soon, everyone would be back inside, and she could at least get a deep breath into her lungs.

"You think he'll hit us just after dawn?" she asked, fixing him with tired eyes.

Sindak used his wet sleeve to wipe soot from his nose. "I think we'll be lucky to make it to dawn."

She leaned back against the palisade. Warriors stretched up and down the catwalks, talking, ruffling ash from their hair. Bone-weary, there would be little rest tonight. She had to think despite that. "How will he organize the attack?"

Sindak slung his bow and sank against the palisade beside her. "Right now, news is passing around every camp-fire. Rage and indignation are building . . . as well as fear. Few of Atotarho's warriors will be able to sleep, and they're already exhausted. Even more than we are."

"More than we are? How can you say—"

"Please let me finish. Negano is definitely War Chief. Gonda and I heard his warriors talking about him." He took a deep breath. "Even though we struck him hard to-night, Negano knows he still greatly outnumbers us. But he'll be cautious tomorrow. He won't commit all of his warriors to the assault on the palisades."

"Five hundred shooting at us will keep us plenty busy."

"My guess is he'll commit one thousand, Matron. With our losses today he'll be wagering that the terror alone will be enough to shock our meager forces—"

"Yes, and we will have our hands full dragging the dead and wounded off the catwalks." A familiar sinking sensation invaded her belly.

Sindak leaned closer to her. Softly, for her ears alone, he said, "That means Negano will be leaving two or three hundred in camp, as reserves. If he's smart, they'll all be grouped together, but if he's not . . ."

She fixed him with intense eyes. For a while, she didn't say anything. "Do you think Negano knows which Hills warriors switched sides?"

"No. Many fled the battle. He knows most probably went home. But I suspect Negano hopes a few just ran away briefly and plan to return."

She massaged her forehead as she forced her exhausted brain to think.

Sindak said, "It's a suicide mission. I don't know how many we can kill, but getting away again—"

"I don't want you to kill anyone." She lowered her hand, and considered him. "You've enough on your souls, old friend. We need another way. A smarter way. I want you to help me make them sick to death of Atotarho."

Sindak's bushy brows pulled together over his hooked nose. She could see him sorting through the possibilities of what else she might want him to do. "Are you thinking of kidnapping the old man, poisoning cook pots? Whatever it is, if we're going to do it, we have to hurry. My warriors need to get out of this village and into the forest before—"

"I agree. But I have another idea. Meet me under the porch of the Bear Clan longhouse. I'll be right there."

"I'll get them organized as quickly as I can." He spun around and jogged down the catwalk, tapping his warriors on the shoulders, speaking with them briefly, moving on.

Down in the plaza, Kittle's arms moved, pointing to people, assigning them duties. Already women searched the belt pouches and packs they'd looted from the battlefield, separating out anything edible. Elders stacked arrows and quivers along the palisade walls. Tutelo had groups of children carrying water jars, making sure they were equally distributed to each longhouse and the council house.

Jigonsaseh turned and walked down to where Deru stood speaking with Wampa. The woman warrior shivered in her wet dress.

"War Chief Wampa, you did excellent work tonight.

Now, I want you to return to your chamber. Warm up, eat, get some sleep. Deru will wake you in a few hands of time. Until this is over, I want one of you on the catwalks at all times. Switch off sleeping when you can."

"Understood," Deru said.

"Yes, Matron." Wampa nodded respectfully to her, and wearily walked toward the ladders.

Deru gave Jigonsaseh a quizzical look. "What about you? Are you planning on sleeping any time soon?"

They'd been friends for twenty summers. He knew how she thought. "We've seen some terrible battles together, haven't we?"

"Don't try to distract me. You have to sleep."

"I will. I give you my oath. There's just . . . much to be done. What kind of shifts are you planning for your warriors?"

Deru used his bow to scratch his chin. "I'll have blankets brought up to them. They can sleep on the catwalks. But I was thinking I'd keep one hundred on duty at all times."

"Good." She clapped him on the shoulder. "You were brilliant tonight, War Chief. The way you targeted the piles of debris in the plaza, then when Negano's forces arrived and you hit them squarely the instant they rounded the palisade wall . . ." A proud smile twisted her lips. "No one could have done it better."

He nodded briefly. He'd always been uncomfortable with praise. "Every warrior, even the children, performed exceptionally. They know the survival of our nation is at stake."

Deru seemed to be considering his next words. Finally, he said, "I was just wondering what you plan to do about

Sindak?" He gazed at her through slitted eyes, as though he expected to be reprimanded for asking.

"What do you mean?"

"He disobeyed your direct orders. You told Sindak and the others to leave the wounded behind and get back to the gates as soon as they could. Even though everything worked out, it sets a bad example."

"Worried that other warriors may now think they can disobey me, too?"

"Our warriors, no." He shook his head. "But his?"

If Sindak's warriors disobeyed her at a critical moment . . . ? If Sindak was close at hand, she'd no doubt they'd obey him. But what if Sindak wasn't at hand?

"You're right, Deru. I'll speak with Sindak about it."

"Thank you, Matron."

As she walked away, heading for the Bear Clan long-house, she pulled CorpseEye from her belt.

Thirty

Seething, Atotarho gripped his walking stick, longing to use it as a club. He glared at Negano and Nesi as they strode toward his camp on the hilltop. Both men kept coughing, their lungs struggling to get rid of the thick acrid smoke they'd inhaled at Yellowtail Village. The gaudy glare cast by the fires illuminated their tall, muscular bodies. Gray ash coated their shoulders and hair, and filled the lines in their faces, making both appear to be much older men.

Atotarho's jaw hurt from clenching his teeth. War Chief Negano hadn't looked at him yet. The man had seen thirty-two summers pass—many as the head of Atotarho's personal guards. He had little actual battlefield experience. Elevating him to his current position had, perhaps, been a grave error.

When the two men arrived at his fire, Nesi dipped his head respectfully to Atotarho, and split off from Negano, leaving the war chief to face Atotarho alone.

Negano stiffened his spine, and braced his feet. "My Chief, I—"

"How did it happen?" Atotarho asked in a chilling voice.

"No one knows yet. Tomorrow, we will question the survivors. All I can say is that Joondoh must have missed something."

Atotarho repositioned his walking stick and gripped the antler head with both hands. His knees and hips throbbed in agony. "Is he dead?"

"I haven't seen him, so I assume he is."

"Well, then, he's lucky, isn't he?"

Negano's eyes tightened. He did not look away, which demonstrated true bravery . . . or perhaps foolishness. He coughed again, then choked out the words, "Joondoh was a loud-mouthed fool. I should never have placed him in charge of the Yellowtail defense."

"It's a little late to realize that."

"Yes, my Chief." Negano sounded truly apologetic, almost obsequious.

"How many did we lose?"

Negano started to answer, but bent forward suddenly, hacking and wheezing for several moments before he gained control again. A shiver ran through him.

"Forgive me." He straightened to his full height, but his expression was that of a man fighting a sudden and consuming nausea. "The fires were so intense and the smoke so thick we couldn't count tonight. However, maybe around six hundred fifty. Perhaps a few more."

"Six hundred . . . !" Atotarho's veins seemed to be on fire. "*You* killed one-third of our forces?"

"My Chief, I hope you will take into account that I was not personally in charge of the Yellowtail defense. If I had been—"

"Do you think it makes me feel better that more than six hundred warriors would be alive if you'd had the good judgment to lead the defense yourself?"

Negano swallowed hard, but said nothing. Was he searching for a response?

"Answer me!"

Negano spread his arms in a gesture of helplessness. "In the future, I will not trust such situations to anyone else. I will assume the duty myself."

Atotarho gritted his teeth and looked out over the camp. No one slept. Every warrior who could stand was on his feet talking. The drone of their voices had a low angry timbre. Their discontent had been growing. Every day his warriors seemed a little more surly and rebellious. As the scent of their friends' and relatives' rotting bodies strengthened, more and more people clamored to go home. Their truculence would be worse after tonight. Much worse.

Atotarho's eyes slid back to Negano. "I saw the hunting parties return today. How much food did they shoot?"

"Not much, my Chief. Bur Oak Village has been here a long time. All of the nearby game was hunted out long ago. Tomorrow I'll dispatch more hunting parties to go further a field, hoping—"

"How much food did today's party shoot?" he repeated with lethal exactness.

Negano clenched his fists at his sides. "Enough to feed our army for two days."

Atotarho's grip tightened on his walking stick, as though strangling the life from it. "And what do you think High Matron Kittle is doing right now?"

He appeared mystified by the shift in subjects. "I—I can't say."

"Well, I can. She's a leader. She's out stripping the bodies of our dead for food and weapons. She's refilling every empty pot and bag with water." His voice went hoarse with restrained emotion. "Now she has another three or four days that she did not have this morning. The spirits of her villagers are running high. My hopes of starving her out in less than one-quarter moon are gone." He extended a finger that resembled a knobby twig and stabbed it at Negano's chest. "Because of you."

In an unnaturally high voice, Negano said, "Chief, as I said, I know I am at fault. If possible, I would like to discuss our attack plan for tomorrow. We need to take our revenge quickly. To hearten our warriors. If we do not, I fear—"

"Tell me your plan." Atotarho lowered his hand to grip his walking stick again. "It had better be good, War Chief."

Thirty-one

As the garish halo of firelight swelled over Bur Oak Village, the longhouses turned burnt orange and seemed to slip in and out of existence, light then dark, as though tugged at by the winds of nothingness.

In the shifting smoke, Jigonsaseh found Sindak standing to the left of the Bear Clan longhouse porch, speaking with his warriors. He'd lost four in the battle, and another five had been wounded. Thirty-one crowded around him, their expressions somber. Distinctive clan symbols decorated their painted capes. She could make out the wings of the Hawk Clan, bear claws for the Bear Clan, and interlocking green-and-blue rectangles for the Snipe Clan. All had mourning hair. Sindak had not yet changed out of the clothes he'd worn in the marsh. His black shirt clung wetly to his body; wet clothing made a warrior's movements awkward, sluggish.

Jigonsaseh walked up behind him, gripped CorpseEye, and in one powerful swing, struck Sindak in the backs of the knees. He landed with a grunt that knocked the breath out of him. She didn't give him time to respond, but leaped on top of him, straddling him, with CorpseEye jammed down across his throat.

Shocked cries of outrage erupted from his men. Several jerked stilettos and clubs from their belts.

Sindak's eyes widened when he looked up at her, then widened even more at something over her shoulder. He choked out, "No! Lower your weapons!"

She allowed Sindak to push the club away from his throat enough that he could speak, and he casually asked, "Have I done something to offend you, Matron?"

"I gave you a direct order that anyone who fell behind was to be left behind. No trying to rescue friends. I told you I didn't need dead heroes, I needed living fighters. Yet you went back for Gonda."

"I apologize. It was arrogant of me, not to mention dangerous and stupid. In this village, you give the orders."

She paused with her eyes narrowed. "You practiced that, didn't you?"

"Well, I knew I was going to have to use it at some point."

Jigonsaseh climbed off him and rose. Sindak's warriors' expressions were a combination of indignation, disbelief, and killing rage. She watched them from the corner of her eye. In a voice filled with deepest respect, the kind of respect she reserved only for her own war chiefs, she said, "Sindak, you are one of the finest warriors I've ever known, but if you ever disobey my orders again, it will be the last time." She tied CorpseEye to her belt, and extended a hand to him.

Sindak grabbed it and let her pull him to his feet. As he dusted away the old leaves and twigs that stuck to the wet leather, he said, "You're faster than I remember."

"A fact you'd be wise to ponder."

He rubbed his aching throat, and turned to his men. "Never disobey one of Matron Jigonsaseh's orders, or she will—without a shred of shame—publicly humiliate you before your friends."

Several of his men broke out in laughter, shook their heads, and slipped their war clubs and stilettos back into their belts.

Sindak gave her a sly look from the corner of his eye. Both of them smiled faintly, remembering times past when they'd had similar discussions. Men expelled breaths. Expressions relaxed.

Sindak spread his feet and turned back to face his warriors. "As I was saying before the arrival of the only war chief I respect more than myself"—more laughter—"Negano doesn't know which of our warriors pledged allegiance to our true high matron, Zateri. He doesn't know who has given up and gone home, or who has fled into the forest to fill his belly before he returns to duty. If we can get into position tonight, we can use that against him."

"Sindak," Saponi said abruptly. Burly, with a pockmarked face and a nose like a flattened beetle, he looked uneasily at the other warriors. He was Snipe Clan. Interlocking green-and-blue rectangles ran across the middle of his cape. He had a rocks-rubbing-together voice. "You can't go into that war camp. Negano may not know the identities of the men who joined you, but he does know for certain that you betrayed Atotarho. Every man saw you switch sides at the end of the battle and side with High Matron Zateri."

"That's right, Saponi. I'll remain in the forest, coordinating—"

"Respectfully, War Chief, you shouldn't go at all."

Whispers passed between his warriors.

Sindak's expression tightened. "Why do you say that?"

When Saponi propped his hands on his hips in defiance, it caused his cape to flare and sway. He appeared hesitant to speak.

Jigonsaseh filled the uncomfortable silence. "I agree with Saponi. I know you wish to lead your warriors, Sindak, but it's too risky."

"Too risky?" he objected. "You don't mind having me crawl around the base of Yellowtail Village while hundreds of Atotarho's warriors are staring over the edge of the palisade at me, but you—"

"War Chief?" Saponi softly said. "May I speak with you alone?"

Sindak nodded, and the two men walked a short distance away. Sindak let Saponi talk while he listened for twenty heartbeats. Jigonsaseh caught the phrases "death would be devastating," and "dishearten our men."

Jigonsaseh strained to hear more. Saponi was right: Sindak was the one thing that held his men together. They fought for him—not for her, not for the alliance.

When Saponi stopped, Sindak's mouth tightened into a line, and he grudgingly nodded. Loud enough for everyone to hear, he said, "I don't like it, but I yield to your judgment."

He started to walk back, but Saponi gripped his shoulder. "Now that we've settled that, I wish to volunteer for the duty. Allow me to lead our warriors. I'll make certain the task is accomplished."

Their gazes held. "I know you will."

As they walked back, Saponi added, "Once you tell us what the task is, of course."

Sindak stopped at Jigonsaseh's side. When he shoved wet hair behind his ear, a black smear striped his cheek. Ash falling from the night sky blended with mist so that where it alighted on skin and clothing it ran like watery charcoal paint.

"Matron Jigonsaseh," Sindak said, "tell us your goal tomorrow, and we will figure out how to accomplish it."

She scanned the faces of his warriors, meeting each man's gaze. From their expressions they undoubtedly thought she considered them as more expendable than Standing Stone warriors.

"First, let me make a few things clear. We're fighting for more than the survival of the Standing Stone People, or the Hills People. We're struggling for something greater. Sky Messenger's vision of a Peace Alliance. We're fighting for a better future for our families."

Saponi spread his hands. "Matron, don't worry. We'll attack with all of our hearts."

She gave him a smile filled with appreciation. "Saponi, you are a brave man. But I don't want you to attack anyone unless you're forced to defend yourselves. If everything goes well, no one—on either side—will die in this raid. If it goes wrong? Well, make your own decisions. Pretend you are Atotarho's loyal warriors, blend in with his army or head home and find your families. Do whatever is necessary to stay alive. Does everyone understand?"

Heads nodded, but warriors shared uncertain glances with one another.

Saponi looked confused. "What kind of a raid is this?"

"As soon as we're finished here, I will order every pack in the village emptied and delivered to you. All I expect you to do is find a way to fill them."

Saponi's brows drew together. The warriors looked around at each other.

Sindak laughed suddenly, and a slow admiring smile came to his lips. "Blessed Spirits, if you're thinking what I think you're thinking, the effect will be utterly demoralizing. I can't believe I didn't think of it myself."

Thirty-two

Gonda lay on the third row of benches in the council house, surrounded by around fifty men and women wounded far worse than he, many dying. Most of the victims were children and elders, not trained warriors. Their moans and tears tore his heart.

He squinted up at the ceiling poles and gritted his teeth, trying not to yell as the Healer, Old Bahna, set and splinted his broken leg with oak staves.

"The bone is aligned, now I'm going to tighten the cords to secure the staves," Bahna warned.

"I'm ready. I think."

Bahna had survived fifty-three summers. His deeply furrowed face cradled kind eyes. Gray hair draped like spiderwebs over his ears. He'd been working all night, Healing, and his brown cape bore the evidence of his efforts. Blood and gut juices spattered the buckskin. It had probably absorbed a river of tears as well.

Gonda concentrated on the roof poles. Like spokes, they radiated outward from the smokehole. Coal-black soot coated them. The mist outside must be thickening.

He could see it glistening through the smokehole, reflecting the fires outside.

Bahna grunted as he jerked the five cords tight, and Gonda gasped, "Blessed Ancestors!"

"All right, Gonda." Bahna placed a hand upon his forearm. "That's the best I can do for now. I want you to remain here for at least one hand of time, so I may see how you're doing, then you may return to the Hawk Clan longhouse. Tomorrow I will send poultices to your wife, Pawen. Ask her to place them on either side of the arrow wound. And be glad," he added pointedly, "that you were not shot with one of the feces-coated arrows, as so many others were. We found many such arrows lying in the plaza, arrows that missed their marks."

Gonda propped himself up on his elbows, grimacing as pain shot through him. The five cords around the oak staves had been woven together, creating a kind of net. His left leg was one gigantic aching throb. A minor concern compared to the wounds of everyone else.

"I can leave now, Bahna. I'm all right."

"No," Bahna said firmly. "Your leg is going to swell. I need to check on you later, to loosen the cords, if necessary. If Evil Spirits slip into the arrow wound and fester it, I'll be forced to cut off your leg to kill them. You don't want that, do you?"

Gonda scowled at him. "I'll stay. But only for one hand of time."

Bahna nodded and moved on to the next victim, a little boy of perhaps ten summers. He'd taken an arrow through the head. Gonda did not understand why he was still breathing—but he'd seen similar enigmas on the battlefield, things he'd rather not remember.

Firelight streamed around the entry curtain, and Gonda turned to see Jigonsaseh enter the council house. She stood for a few moments, allowing her eyes to adjust. A very tall woman, she towered over nearly everyone else in the village. Still slender and muscular, her beautiful face had just begun to crease—lines around her full lips, crow's-feet at the corners of her eyes. She spotted him as he sat up. She walked forward.

As it had for many summers, the sight of her was like the feel of a war club in his hands; it eased his fears. He could not count the number of times she had saved his life—and he hers. If truth be told, there was no one he trusted more.

Jigonsaseh's cape, covered with wet ash, moved pendulously as she came to a stop at his side, looking down at him with concerned eyes.

"Sindak told me you'd been wounded."

Gonda braced his hands on the bench to look up at her. "I swear he's the worst warrior I know. I ordered him to leave me in the marsh. Instead, he dragged me home. The fool could have been killed in the process, and we need him more than we need me. He's a powerful symbol of our alliance with Zateri's—"

"Yes. Yes. I've already attended to Sindak's errors in judgment." Jigonsaseh sat beside him. "Someday I hope to tell him how much I appreciate his gross disobedience. Assuming any of us live that long. How's your leg?"

Gonda stared down at it. "Bahna ordered me to stay here for one hand of time, or I'd already have hobbled back to the Hawk Clan longhouse. Tell me how the battle went. How many did we kill?"

Jigonsaseh's gaze scanned the other benches, taking

time to examine and identify faces, before she lowered her eyes and expelled a disheartened breath. "Hard to say. My guess is over six hundred."

A potent blend of relief and triumph surged through him. "Blessed Spirits, that's more than I'd hoped for."

She whispered, for his ears alone, "Yes, but it means they've no choice now but to hit us hard tomorrow. It's a matter of honor."

He jerked a nod. "Very true, but we'll be ready for them. Has Sindak lined out what he thinks may happen tomorrow?"

"He says Atotarho will throw one thousand warriors at us. At dawn, or just before."

Gonda squeezed his eyes closed for a few heartbeats, absorbing the news. The sobs that filled the council house seemed louder. Before he opened his eyes again, he said, "We have to get as many of these people back on their feet as we can. We're going to need every one of them on the catwalks with a bow."

"I'll speak with Bahna. Now, I should get back to . . ."

When she started to rise, he gripped her hand. "I have to tell you about the Flint massacre."

"What massacre?" She eased back down to the bench. "Which village?"

Gonda kept his voice low. "Not a village. As I was moving around the palisade wall, setting fires, I overheard two warriors talking. Apparently, Atotarho's warriors ambushed a Flint war party and killed four hundred warriors."

Her face slackened and her gaze darted over the council house while she thought about it. "Cord's war party?"

"Probably."

Jigonsaseh bowed her head and massaged her brow. "Blessed gods, they left here with around five hundred warriors, if Atotarho killed four hundred . . ."

Gonda gave her a few moments.

When she lifted her head, he said, "The survivors should be getting back to Flint country tomorrow. After they've told their story, the Flint Ruling Council will act."

"Yes, but what action will it take?"

"How many warriors do you suppose they have left?"

She waved a palm through the air. "If I know their chief"—Gonda winced when she did not say Cord's name; it meant she thought he was dead—"he talked the matrons into leaving a significant number at home to guard their three villages. I don't know . . . I suspect they have perhaps one thousand five hundred warriors remaining in the nation. Five hundred guarding each village. A pittance, compared to Atotarho's forces."

"Yes, even if they know we're in trouble, they will not wish to risk any of their remaining forces to help us."

Her lips tightened into a white bloodless line. "No."

They both exhaled at the same time, and their breaths frosted in the cold firelit air. When she looked back at him it was as though the summers had rolled back and he was still her deputy war chief. She depended upon him to give her good advice, advice that would save lives.

Gonda squeezed her hand and released it. "Tomorrow morning, we must get every person on the catwalks that we can. Even the members of the Ruling Council must take up bows."

Her head moved in a barely visible nod, but her eyes were focused elsewhere. He knew from long experience that her thoughts had turned to strategy and tactics, already envisioning what her enemy might do at dawn, and planning how to counter it. She had an unnatural ability to place her souls inside her enemy's body and see through his eyes.

He softly interrupted her thoughts, "Sky Messenger should have reached the villages of the People of the Landing yesterday or today."

"Only if he's been able to run the whole way. We can't count on that. We don't know how many war parties or other obstacles he might have faced. And even if he did, even if they joined the alliance, our son has no idea we're in a fight for our lives. There's no help coming, Gonda. Get used to it."

Gonda's head waffled in uncertainty. "Don't underestimate the Traders who've passed by here and seen what's happening. I suspect the news of our struggle is racing down the trails like wildfire. If we can just hold out—"

"We have to destroy our enemies by ourselves, Gonda."

Her beautiful exhausted face had set into determined lines. He nodded. "You're right. What do you need me to do?"

She glanced at his splinted leg. "When you are able—"

"I'll be able tomorrow. I may have to get around on a crutch, but at dawn, I'll be right there on the catwalk beside you."

Thirty-three

Opalescent gray light fell through the dark trees, weaving a gigantic spider's web of shadows across their camp on the densely forested hillside.

Baji sunk her water bag through the hole in the icy pond, filling it while she watched Gitchi. He lapped water from the other side of the pool, but his yellow eyes clung to the lone wolf out in the trees. The pack had moved on a little while ago, pouring in a silvery flood down the hillside and across the valley. From far away, their faint sharp yelps rose as they trotted up the trail that crested the tree-covered hill to the west. This wolf had remained behind. He stood motionless, as if carved of starlight. Long and lean, he seemed strangely curious about Gitchi. As well, he kept casting odd glances at Baji, tilting his head, as though not certain what she was.

Baji lifted her dripping bag from the hole, pulled the laces tight, and tied it to her belt. Then she lowered Dekanawida's water bag to fill it. He still slept rolled in their blankets five paces away, unaware that she and Gitchi had started the day without him. She'd been standing guard most of the night, adding branches to the fire to keep him warm. One hand of time ago, she'd started breakfast. The tripod with the suspended cook pot hung at the edge of the fire. Flames licked gently at the soot-coated bottom, keeping it at a slow boil. The mixture of *tic'ne*—powdered red corn—along with beechnuts, dried raspberries, and leftover chunks of last night's muskrat would make a hearty breakfast.

She pulled Dekanawida's filled water bag from the hole and snugged the laces. She would keep it on her weapons' belt until he rose. As she tied it beside her bag, the row of stilettos and knives rattled. It didn't seem to disturb the lone wolf. He kept his shining eyes on Gitchi.

Baji adjusted the bow and quiver slung over her left shoulder. Her headache was gone, and she felt so much better, she wondered if this sensation was akin to being Requickened in a strong healthy body after a long illness. The shapes of the waking forest appeared clearer, crisper. The Faces of the Forest might have carefully chosen the background shade to highlight the massive chestnut trunks and dark branches that laced over her head.

Gitchi finished drinking and turned to face the wolf. The stranger took a step forward, stopping with one paw lifted while he scented the air. Gitchi curled his lip in a snarl, just a warning, and his big paws crackled in the ice that skimmed the low spots. Every fallen leaf and twig sparkled with a white coating of ice.

The lone wolf whined softly, then backed away, yielding the dominance contest to Gitchi.

It occurred to Baji that it might be a female, perhaps out examining the packs for a future mate.

When she whined again, Gitchi must have tired of her

advances for the hair on his neck and shoulders stood straight up and he sprang forward with a ferocious growl, chasing the wolf out into the trees and down the hill. Branches cracked in their flight. Baji saw the wolves, stretched out full, shooting between the smoke-colored trunks like pewter lances.

Her gaze returned to the forest shadows, searching for odd shapes, textures, the slightest movement. Trees rocked in the breeze. Occasionally, an old leaf detached from a branch and fluttered through the air. The pungency of frozen bark wafted around her.

A short time later, Gitchi trotted back with his head held high, and dropped to his haunches beside her.

Baji stroked his soft back. "You protected the camp, Gitchi. Thank you."

He licked her face.

Above them, the shimmering Road of Light that the Standing Stone People called the Path of Souls had begun to fade. As night edged toward day, its cold crystal brilliance paled to a faint white swath, dotted here and there by the largest campfires of the dead.

She whispered, "What do you think the Road is like, Gitchi? Is it winter there? Or summer? From the number of campfires, it looks crowded. I'm not sure I'd like that. You wouldn't either, would you?" She scratched his neck and he half-closed his eyes in enjoyment. "Your ancestors are wilderness people, too. On cold nights they point their noses at Grandmother Moon and howl long and hard, complaining about the frozen forests and the dark, but you and I know they wouldn't trade it for anything."

Gitchi looked up, following her gaze, and seemed to be contemplating her soft words as he surveyed the sky, perhaps remembering litter mates and friends who had turned to dust long ago, A pained wistfulness filled his yellow eyes.

"Don't worry, old friend, you'll see them again. You'll romp with them in fields of wildflowers and be able to run for days without your paws hurting at all."

Baji reached down and gently petted his sore legs and feet.

Gitchi wagged his tail, and she slipped her arms around him and hugged him, resting her throat across his thickly furred neck. He vented a deep sigh and leaned into her embrace. They sat like that, loving each other, until Dekanawida's soft voice called, "When we get home, I'm going to paint that image on a rawhide shield."

At the sound of his voice, Gitchi slid from Baji's arms and trotted to where his best friend lay, propped on one elbow in the warm folds of blankets. Dekanawida scratched Gitchi's ears. "I saw you chase away the invader wolf. Well done, Gitchi."

Baji swore that Gitchi's yellow eyes gleamed brighter when he gazed at Dekanawida. Their love for each other was palpable. She could feel it warming the cold morning air—or perhaps it was just in her heart.

Dekanawida rose, straightened his cape, and knotted his belt around his waist. It disturbed her to see his belt strung with Power pouches instead of weapons. He adjusted the four different-colored pouches to their proper position, then spent a moment petting the red pouch that dangled like a cocoon on the far right. He touched the red one often, and she always wondered why? What did it contain? He knelt to roll up their blankets.

She just watched him. The familiarity of his movements

eased the peculiar loneliness that tormented her. Sometimes, when he was out of her sight, even for a few instants,
panic set in, as though she'd suddenly found herself abandoned, left alone in an alien forest utterly empty of other
human beings. The experience bore a striking similarity
to sitting a death vigil, which she'd done many times on
the war trail. As a person watched his friend's eyelids
flutter, and listened to lungs rattle, friendship seemed to
momentarily strengthen . . . then thin like the last beautiful note of a flute, dying into silence so complete its loss
stunned the soul. She wondered if all loneliness was a
death vigil.

"Breakfast smells wonderful," Dekanawida said as he
tied the blankets to the top of his pack.

She stood. "You need to eat well this morning. By afternoon, we'll reach Shookas Village, and then your troubles really begin."

"I'm ready. I've been thinking a lot about the things we
discussed."

"You are ready. I'm sure of it."

Baji untied his water bag from her belt, and walked
forward with it dangling from her fingers. Dekanawida
rose, said, "Thank you for filling it," and tied it to his belt.

They stood side-by-side in companionable silence, listening to the crackle and snap of the fire, and the rustle of
wind through the winter trees. Deep in the forest, deer
hooves rattled on stone.

Baji's gaze drifted over the predawn mosaic. Black
pools of shadow dappled the grayness, but quaking aspens glowed in the dark tangle of tree trunks, their ivory
bark shining. Her ears tracked the sounds, the low *shish* of
windblown dead ferns, branches sawing, mice feet whisper-

ing beneath the piles of old autumn leaves. Nothing unusual.

She leaned over to view the contents of the bubbling cook pot. The dried raspberries had combined with the red corn to turn the mush a deep purple color. "It will be ready soon."

"I love the fragrance of raspberries on a winter morning."

She smiled at him. "I know you do."

He put his arm around her shoulders, holding her close. "How's your headache today?"

"Gone, for the moment. Once we start running the trail we'll see how long that lasts."

"Is the swelling down?"

"Yes. Some."

He removed his arm and slipped his hands beneath her long hair to gently probe her head wound. His expression tensed.

"What's wrong?"

"It's better, but before we leave camp this morning, I want to wash it thoroughly again. You're sure you are feeling better?"

"I am. Truly."

He gave her a suspicious look, as though he sensed there was something she wasn't telling him. "I want the truth."

She sighed. "Nothing's wrong. Actually, I feel very good. I'm just afraid you might assume that means I'm about to fly away."

"Any numbness or odd pains in your body?"

"For the sake of the Spirits, I'd tell you if there were!"

"All right." He put his arm around her again and hugged her close. "It's just that I know you. If your leg had just been amputated, you'd tell me you felt fine."

What she didn't want to tell him was that something had happened to her last night. That's why she'd risen. Her senses had become remarkably intense. Even in deep sleep, the faintest sound had disturbed her, and she'd known instantly whether it announced danger or calm. When she'd opened her eyes, the forest had appeared translucent, shining as though every shred of bark and blade of grass were sculpted from quartz crystals. And the night scents! They'd struck her like blows. She didn't understand it, but she'd had the feeling that ancient instincts, long buried, had begun to stretch and move, awakening. She knew, *knew,* that somewhere inside her, her soul trotted through a primeval forest, running down food as her distant ancestors had done, hunting with fang and claw, rather than bow and knife, and it left her feeling more alive than she'd ever thought possible.

Dekanawida's stomach squealed, and she smiled. "It sounds like you're ready for purple cornmeal mush."

"Obviously."

Baji bent and retrieved their cups and spoons from where she'd stowed them beside the hearthstones. As she spooned their cups full, raspberry-scented steam encircled her face. Never before had the fragrance of raspberries been so overpowering. She might have been wandering through an endless field of ripe berries.

When she rose and handed him a cup with a spoon sticking in it, she asked, "I wonder where Hiyawento and Zateri are today? I'm worried about them. Do you think they've reached the safety of Canassatego Village yet?"

"I hope so. They should be close."

"Gods, I pray their villages made it to Canassatego unharmed and all is well."

"As I do."

He picked up his wooden spoon. After he'd tasted the mush, he smiled. "This is delicious. That was a fat muskrat we snared last night. The flavor of his meat goes well with the raspberries."

"I gave Gitchi one of the muskrat legs. I doubt he tasted it at all. He wolfed it down in four bites."

When he heard his name, Gitchi ambled over to sit on his haunches beside Dekanawida, looking up with soulful eyes, probably hoping for another leg.

As Dekanawida ate, his short black hair fell around his face, framing his slender nose and brown eyes. "Speaking of Hiyawento, I've been thinking about Shago-niyoh coming to you on the trail."

A thread of unease went through her. "What about it?"

She ate the rich cornmeal mush, and tried not to look at him. Her fear of discovery had not ebbed, but only increased as the days passed.

"Did Hiyawento ever tell you about Shago-niyoh coming to him?"

She lowered her spoon to her bowl where it clacked against the wood. Surprised, she said, "No. When did this happen?"

"Twelve summers ago. Soon after we all escaped from Bog Willow Village. At the time, you and I would have either been on the trail with Mother and Father, tracking the old woman, or maybe canoeing the river, I'm not sure about the timing."

A swallow went down his throat, as though memories filled the space behind his eyes, and they hurt.

"What happened?"

He tilted his head and frowned. "He said he was lying

in the old woman's canoe. He was very sick. You recall how badly they'd beaten him after he killed the warrior and made sure we got away."

"Yes." Love for Wrass filled her.

Dekanawida rubbed his eyes. "He thought he was dreaming when the man waded through the water to get to him. The man wore a black cape, and had a nose bent to the right. Wrass thought he might be one of the *hanehwa*."

Hanehwa were enchanted skin-beings. Witches—like the old woman—skinned their human victims alive, then cast spells upon the skins, forcing them to serve as guards. Hanehwa never slept. They warned the witch of danger by giving three shouts.

"How did he know it was Shago-niyoh and not one of the hanehwa?"

"The man spoke to him, which hanehwa never do."

"What did he say?"

Dekanawida seemed to pause to get the words right. "He said, *'We are all husks, Wrass, flayed from the soil of fire and blood. This won't be over for any of us until the Great Face shakes the World Tree. Then, when Elder Brother Sun blackens his face with the soot of the dying world, the judgment will take place.'*"

Baji frowned at Dekanawida. The Great Face was the chief of all False Faces. He guarded the sacred World Tree that stood at the center of the earth. Its flowers were made of pure light. The World Tree's branches pierced the Sky World where the Blessed Ancestors lived, and her roots twined deeply into the underworlds, planting themselves upon the back of the Great Tortoise that floated in the dark primeval ocean that spread forever around the land. Elder Brother Sun nested in the World Tree's highest branches.

"Why have you never told me this story?"

His shoulders lifted. "It's Hiyawento's story, not mine. The first time I heard it was twelve summers ago."

She studied his tormented face. "The first time? There was another?"

"Yes, just a few days ago. In Coldspring Village. I—I wanted Hiyawento to tell Taya about it."

There was a small awkward moment of silence, as though he feared she might view it as a betrayal; he'd wanted Taya to hear the story, but he'd never felt Baji needed to hear it.

Baji playfully bumped shoulders with him. "Good. That was the right thing to do." He gave her a small apologetic smile, and she said, "The images are different, though. From your Dream, I mean. In your Dream, Elder Brother Sun turns his back on the dying world and flies away into a dark hole in the sky. In Hiyawento's, Elder Brother Sun covers his face with the soot of the dying world. Are they the same event, or different?"

He took a bite of mush and chewed it. "I've wondered that same thing for many summers."

"Any conclusions?" She spooned mush into her mouth and ate it while she waited for him to answer. The sweet flavor of the red corn penetrated through the tang of the raspberries.

"A few. Despite the differences, there are also striking similarities. Elder Brother Sun vanishes into darkness. The flowers of the World Tree are shaken loose. The actions of humans are judged and condemned."

"What do you think it means?"

He frowned. "I'm not sure, but have you ever noticed that people on the same path see it a little differently? Some focus on the tracks in the trail. Others see only the campfires of the dead visible through the trees over their heads. Still others ignore the sky and ground completely and notice the birds and deer."

"So, you're saying it's possible they are the same event, just seen through different eyes?"

"Maybe." He shrugged.

Gitchi stood up and stretched. He was a beautiful old wolf. The white hair that had grown around his eyes gave him character, like the wrinkles of a wise old face.

Baji ate a few more bites of mush, then scooped the last chunks of muskrat out onto the frozen ground for Gitchi. He gulped them while he wagged his tail.

As Baji started to straighten up, sharp, birdlike chirping echoed nearby. Her head jerked around in time to see a flying squirrel leap from the tallest branches of a chestnut tree. Its enormous eyes shone. Using the fold of skin between its wrists and ankles to slow its descent, it glided down to land on the trunk of a maple, then quickly scampered up it and disappeared.

Baji set her bowl on the ground, quietly pulled her bow from her shoulder, and nocked an arrow. When she lifted her nose to scent the wind, the pungency of fear sweat wafted to her.

Dekanawida set his bowl down beside hers, and tried to follow her gaze out into the trees. He whispered, "Did you see something?"

"There's someone out there. Let's move out of the firelight."

Dekanawida glanced down at Gitchi happily licking their bowls clean. "Gitchi doesn't seem to smell anything."

"Trust me."

She led the way around the pond to stand half-hidden

behind a sycamore trunk as wide as three men standing shoulder-to-shoulder. Dekanawida took a position just behind her, peering over the top of her head.

The noise of Gitchi licking bowls suddenly stopped.

Baji glanced back at the wolf. He stood absolutely still, his tail straight out behind him, his muzzle pointed at something in the aspen grove on the other side of the pond.

Thirty-four

Sky Messenger

My heartbeat quickens as I follow Baji's gaze to a dense grove of aspens that shine faintly white in the dark forest weave. Gitchi growls, barely audible.

Baji hisses, "Keep Gitchi here until I've circled around behind the fool. Once my arrow is in flight, we'll both rush him."

"I don't see anything. Where is he?"

She half draws back her bow. "Standing right there in the aspens."

With the silence of Eagle hunting Rabbit, Baji eases into the trees and vanishes amid the warp and weft of branches and trunks. Her steps are completely silent.

I slide around the massive sycamore to get a different view of the forest, and softly call, "Gitchi, lie down. Don't move."

The wolf flattens out behind the hearth stones with his ears laid back. His yellow eyes dance with reflected firelight, still focused unblinking on the aspens.

I don't understand why Gitchi and Baji see the intruder and I do not. I cast a quick glance to my right at the thin, spiral-twisted pines where Baji disappeared. The morning air smells of hickory smoke and raspberries, almost obscuring the tangy forest fragrances.

I search for recognizable threats—human shapes like rounded heads, extended hands, legs amid the saplings. Often, strands of hair fluttering in the breeze or the swaying of a cape gives an opponent away. This murderer must be especially skilled, for I see absolutely nothing.

Then, far to the right of the aspens, a glint flashes and vanishes. It flashes again, moving through a thicket of chokecherries.

Jewelry? Cape decorations? Maybe a white arrow point being aimed at Baji or me?

I keep my gaze on the location, and slowly work my way through the frosty ferns that cover the forest floor. Each movement of my feet stirs a faint *shish*. Slipping from tree trunk to tree trunk, my gaze scans for movement. Where is Baji? She should be somewhere in the maples to my right. Can she see the light? Gitchi lies in the same place, at least partially sheltered behind the largest hearth stones. As the morning sky begins to shade deep purple, angled layers of snow-sheathed limestone appear and glisten amid the patchwork of shadows. Grass stems cluster at their bases. In the trees, fluffed out for warmth, birds hunch on the branches like small circular boles.

The light winks again and vanishes, heading into a grove of birch saplings.

I glance back at Gitchi. He hasn't moved. His coat shimmers in the newborn light as though strewn with crushed amethyst. From this position, I can't see where his eyes focus. He seems to still be looking at the aspens, some fifteen paces ahead of me and to my left. If so, he's not looking at the flashes, but at something else.

Maybe there are two men out there.

I squint at the dense stand of birch saplings that create a slatted white wall, interrupted here and there by black streaks of forest background. The only motion now is a tremble of old leaves clinging to branch tips. The flashes are gone. Which may mean the man has stopped moving because he's sighted his prey.

Me.

Wind Woman's breath carries the rich mineral scent of the forest floor at dawn, which tastes like iron on my tongue.

If I continue on this path, the space between my hiding place and next tree trunk is three paces. Without knowing where my opponent stands, that is a killing space. By the time I reach the next maple, I will have been in the clear for three heartbeats. He can easily aim and let fly.

I'd be smiling right now if I were him. I'd inhale through my nostrils, and hold my breath, anticipating the moment my enemy tried to step to the next tree.

I . . .

Brush thrashes, followed by a hoarse surprised cry, then a man shouts, *"Stay back!"*

He lunges from the aspens, releases two quick arrows at something behind him, then whirls and flees through the maples with his buckskin cape flying. He keeps glancing over his shoulder in terror. When he charges into the open, he sees me, gives me a wild look, and shouts, *"For the sake of the gods, don't you see it? What is it?"*

The faint whisper of an arrow lances the dawn, followed by a meaty splat.

The man grunts and careens forward, tumbling face-first to the ground, rolling several times before he can stop himself. The arrow has punched its way through his cape just above his heart. His voice turns into a high-pitched breathless wail. *"It—it's coming! Help me!"*

Sobbing, he manages to shove up on his hands and knees and struggles to crawl away.

I shout, "Gitchi!" and burst from cover, pounding for the man as I search the forest for whatever has so terrified him. There must be another warrior out there, or perhaps a bear, or one of the flying heads—fearsome Spirit creatures with long trailing hair and great paws like a bear's.

Gitchi leaps up and streaks out ahead of me, his lean, muscled body cutting a deadly swath through the pale lavender light. At the very edge of my vision, I catch sight of Baji leaping deadfall as she dashes for our enemy. She's slung her bow and grips her war club in her tight fist. Gleaming waist-length hair bounces across her back as she runs.

"Gitchi, don't kill him!" I shout. "Just guard!"

Gitchi leaps around the man in a snarling bristling blur. If the warrior even tries to grab for a weapon, Gitchi will tear his throat out.

I reach the man before Baji does. Hills People markings cover his cape. He lies on his back, his panicked eyes wide and unblinking. Blood already bubbles at his lips, rising from his wounded lung. He has a severe triangular face with a nose so thin the bones appear to have been removed. When Baji arrives holding her bow nocked and aimed down at his head, the man lets out a shrill cry and tries in vain to slide away from her.

I kneel beside him. "Who sent you? Chief Atotarho?"

Only his eyes move, sliding to me in dazed confusion. He chokes out the words, *"What . . . is . . . it?"*

Thinking that he means he didn't hear me, I repeat, "Did Chief Atotarho send you to murder me?"

His gaze returns to Baji and his eyes go so wide they resemble those of the flying squirrel, too huge for his face, bulging slightly from their sockets. He tries to speak again, but falls into a coughing fit that spatters gouts of blood across his chest and face. As the life drains from his eyes, a red pool spreads around him, looking faintly blue in the murky gleam.

Baji slowly releases the tension on her bowstring and her aim moves aside. "He was less than one heartbeat from killing you," she says, "when he suddenly went crazy and started shrieking. What do you make of that?"

I rise to my feet and frown down at him. "I think his soul was loose, Baji. That explains the strange light I saw."

"You saw a light?"

"Yes, winking in the trees. When a person's afterlife soul is loose, it tries to stay as close to the body as it can, hoping to be allowed back inside. The flashes must have been his soul chasing after him."

Gitchi growls and edges forward to sniff the man's eyes. Bits of wind-blown forest duff stick the wide orbs. After Gitchi has convinced himself that the enemy is dead, he backs away and drops to his haunches, patiently awaiting whatever comes next.

Baji and I stare at each other. The white knife scar that cuts across her pointed chin has picked up the bluish tint of coming dawn. Black wavy hair frames her beautiful oval face and flutters over her buckskin cape. Her knee-high black leggings are speckled with old pine needles, collected in her mad dash through the forest. Seeing her standing there over the body of the man who was about to kill me is ethereal. Her hair blows softly in the breeze, feathering over her shoulders.

"You are so beautiful."

She tilts her head reprovingly and her mouth quirks. "We were talking about insanity and murder."

"Well, I'm past that now. I'd rather talk about you, about how you look in the blue morning light, your long legs spread and your bow half-drawn. The image is heartrending."

She tucks her arrow back in her quiver, slings her bow over her left shoulder, and walks around the dead man to step into my arms. As she embraces me, a warm sensation tingles through my muscles. I rest my chin against her temple, and drown for a time in the silken texture of her hair. The glossy strands smell of campfires and leather, things that comfort me.

"I'm glad you're here with me," I whisper. "Being with you is all I've ever wanted."

She hugs me harder, her strong muscular arms like granite bands, but says, "I think you want peace more than me."

The soft words remind me of my duty to our Peoples. I heave a sigh. "I take it that you do not wish to stay here in my embrace any longer than necessary."

She laughs and looks up at me with shining eyes. "If I could wish for anything that would be it. But we do not have the luxury of wishing, Dekanawida. We still have to pack up our camp. As it is, we won't make it to Shookas Village until late afternoon. And I have the feeling, somewhere deep inside me, that we *need* to get there. I don't know why, but I want to hurry."

She pushes away from me, and clasps my hand. We walk back toward our fire with Gitchi at our heels.

As the day brightens, the scent of pine suffuses the cold air.

Out of curiosity, I ask, "Baji, where were you when the man burst from his hiding place in the aspens?"

Black waves dance around her face as she looks up, and gives me a hesitant smile. "In the birch grove, why?"

"No reason. I just didn't see you out there. I . . ."

She smiles again and looks away. She's avoiding my eyes. Why?

My heart starts to pound harder as a strange weightless sensation comes over me. The light. *No, no, it's not possible, but . . .* Images cascade. *Baji appearing on a trail I didn't even know I would take . . . running all the way to find me with a head wound that would have killed most men. No . . . I—I would know.*

I look down at her, my gaze searching for some sign . . .

As though my unspoken words are bludgeoning her, she stops and a shiver goes through her. "What's wrong?"

"Nothing, I . . . I was just wondering . . ."

She looks up and the lines around her eyes tighten as though she senses my thoughts. Her gaze shifts, scanning the forest as she sighs, "Dekanawida, before we leave, there's something I need to tell you." She clutches my hand tighter.

"About what?"

Her black eyes glisten like jewels. "About what Shago-niyoh said to me on the trail."

Thirty-five

A short while later, Baji crouched across the ashes of the campfire, staring at Dekanawida in the resplendent pre-dawn glow. Gitchi lay between them, his gray muzzle propped on his forepaws, watching in utter silence. Occasionally, when their voices grew strained, his tail lightly tapped the ground trying to ease the tension by showing them he loved them.

Baji pulled a branch from the woodpile and toyed with it to keep her hands busy. Dekanawida's handsome face showed barely endurable pain. She could feel every shifting thought that moved behind his eyes. Like obsidian-sharp lances, they stabbed and jerked, cutting and carving her souls. Is this what strong emotions felt like in the afterworld? Is that why the Land of the Dead was beautiful and peaceful, and people only made war for sport? They couldn't bear anything else?

She gripped the branch harder. Generations of civilization, of corn and squash, had fallen away from her, leaving the sublime purity of the wild behind—and like an ancient wolf she could smell the storm coming. The air tasted of snow and cold sweat. If it had been nightfall, she'd be digging her den in a snowbank, on the leeward side, where later she would be sheltered from the freezing darkness that engulfed the world outside.

"Baji, listen to me," Dekanawida insisted. "It means nothing. I tell you it doesn't. Shago-niyoh frequently asks cryptic questions. He does it to teach—"

"I know. You've told me. But this is different. You and I both know it. I don't think he was trying to be cryptic. I think he came to help me find my way."

Dekanawida clamped his jaw to keep it still, and gazed at her like a man who refused to believe in the Faces of the Forest though he saw one hovering right before his eyes. He balled his fists. Stubborn, he enunciated, "I—would—know."

She smiled. All the love in her heart must have shone on her face, for his tight jaw hardened. "All right. I just needed to tell you. I was tired of carrying the weight of it by myself."

She rose to her feet and adjusted her bow and quiver where they draped her left shoulder. Her weapons belt clacked. "I'm ready to go if you are."

He drew a shallow breath and stood up. Short black hair blew over his face, and jet strands glued themselves to his high cheekbones. She hadn't realized he'd been crying.

Baji walked around the fire and embraced him hard enough to drive the air from his lungs. "Promise me that if you're wrong, you'll always take the time to stop and speak gently to old trees."

He crushed her against him. In her ear, he hoarsely whispered, "I'm not wrong."

Thirty-six

As Sonon watched them trot away, moving up the snowy trail that led to Shookas Village, he placed a hand on the ancient oak beneath which he stood and caressed the cold bark. It had a rough, ridged texture. He could feel the brave soul of the warrior who slept inside, breathing deeply. All around him, massive sycamores and giant chestnuts dotted the forest, each filled with an old, old warrior. They towered above the rest of the canopy, their winter twigs like dark trembling fingers grasping for wisps of drifting Cloud People.

Though Baji and Sky Messenger had vanished into the indigo shadows, the faint drumlike rhythm of their moccasins carried.

He closed his eyes to listen.

It was, perhaps, a strange truth that for most of their journey, human beings lived as impostors, wearing fear masks to ward off true intimacy. When their disguises at last failed, and they became truly present with one another, everything sensed it. Animals and trees turned to look.

Great Grandmother Earth heaved a sigh. The universe itself tilted, balancing on each precious moment.

He didn't wish to disturb it. Better than most, he knew that great beauty and tears were inseparable, bound together in a crystalline shimmer of longing that tore the heart. Even at the end, love was the only thing that turned suffering into a beauty too great to be borne. Perhaps especially at the end.

A low bark split the morning.

Sonon opened his eyes to see Gitchi loping back down the trail. The old wolf stopped and cocked his head at Sonon, waiting, as though to say, *"What's taking you so long?"*

As Sonon lifted his hand to the wolf, signaling that he was coming, his black hood waffled around his face. Gitchi's bushy tail wagged, then he turned and trotted back the way he'd come, returning to Sky Messenger's side.

Sonon expelled a deep breath and stepped onto the trail.

Carefully, so as not to smudge them, he placed his sandals in the tracks they'd left in the snow, hoping to touch their luminous paths, knowing that the dying world lay just ahead.

Thirty-seven

Atotarho stood before his campfire gripping the head of his walking stick with crooked aching fingers. The icy morning air had turned pink with the coming dawn. The heads of war clubs and arrow points glimmered as his warriors marched up the rise in the distance, weaving drunkenly across the old battlefield, avoiding the frozen corpses that covered the ground.

A smile turned his lips. Right now, High Matron Kittle must be shuddering, her knees quaking at the sight of over one thousand warriors surrounding Bur Oak Village. If he . . .

"My Chief?"

He turned to see Qonde and two wounded warriors climbing the slope to reach his camp. Atotarho had sent Nesi off to fight, which left Qonde in charge of his personal guards for the day. A short, stocky man, Qonde's hawkish face bore streaks of soot. The tall man behind Qonde had his left arm in a sling, and the other man wore a bloody head bandage. Several other wounded warriors stood waiting thirty hands away. From the looks of them, they'd probably been injured in last night's fiery debacle at Yellowtail Village. As Qonde got closer, Atotarho called, "What is it?"

Qonde spoke to the men, and came forward alone. "Forgive me, my Chief. War Chief Negano ordered the wounded to rest today, but these men would like to be of some use."

"So put them to use."

Qonde spread his arms. "I realize this is an intrusion, my Chief." He respectfully bowed again. "But I cannot countermand Negano's orders without your approval."

Annoyed, Atotarho waved the tall wounded warrior forward. "What is your name, warrior?"

"Saponi, my Chief." The man bowed.

"Tell me what you wish to do? The battle is about to begin. I have more important duties than assigning menial tasks."

Saponi shifted his slung arm as though it hurt, and his narrowed gaze went over the camps. His face was so blackened with ash and soot the whites of his eyes seemed to glow. Only about two hundred warriors remained scattered around dozens of fires. Most were wounded, useless. Several slept, curled as close to the fires as they could safely get. Somewhere, he heard corn popping.

Saponi said, "My Chief, it's hard staying out of the battle. There are many small duties we could accomplish to stay busy, carrying water, gathering branches for firewood, organizing the food stores."

Saponi gestured, and Atotarho's gaze slid to the stockpiled food guarded by two exhausted warriors who appeared to be asleep on their feet. Haunches of venison lay on the ground before them as though dropped by men too tired to stack them. All around, pots of nuts and seeds canted at angles, about to topple over if someone didn't right them. The baskets of high cranberries that had been collected yesterday had been left uncovered. In the night, raccoons and other animals had strewn many across through the frosty grass. *Negano is so incompetent!*

A shout went up. Atotarho turned.

Shrill calls carried across the hills as the first wave of his army began to move, at a slow march, closing in around Bur Oak Village. Far off, in the trees to the east and south, he saw the second and third waves slithering like long serpents, silently walking forward, their nocked arrows gleaming, readying themselves to lay siege. Clan flags of many colors hung slack in the morning stillness as men marched into position. Atotarho's blood began to surge in his ears.

"My Chief?" Saponi said softly.

Atotarho flicked a hand. "Yes, I place you in charge of such things. Now go away and let me concentrate."

"Yes, my Chief. Thank you." Saponi bowed deeply then nodded gratefully to Qonde for allowing him to approach Atotarho.

Qonde sighed and went back to his position with Atotarho's other guards. He could hear them joking, but couldn't make out the words. Nervous laughter erupted.

Saponi rejoined the group of wounded warriors, where he seemed to be assigning duties. Heads nodded, and warriors plodded off to obey whatever orders he'd given.

As Elder Brother Sun lifted from the World Tree, his shining face crested the eastern horizon and sunlight swathed the tallest branches with gold. Moments later, his light flooded across the valley, sparkling through the frost, turning it the palest of yellows.

Negano's voice rang out, giving the call to advance.

Atotarho searched for his War Chief, but saw only his warriors charging forward. Atotarho had ordered Negano to hit hard immediately, hoping it would shock the enemy into submission. As the first line, men carrying ladders, raced to the exterior palisade, and attempted to climb up and over into the village, the second line, all archers, let fly. Up and down the Bur Oak catwalks enemy warriors fell, but it didn't stop the Standing Stone warriors. They concentrated their fire upon his warriors scaling the ladders, cleanly picking them off, leaving them lying in bristly heaps at the base of the palisade. From every direction, cries wavered in a singsong of agony. The Bur Oak defenders shoved away the ladders. Where they fell upon the frosty ground, they resembled crisscrossing sticks. The second line moved up and a third line of archers took its place, preparing to let fly. The fourth line, still in the trees, appeared to have frozen solid. They resembled human-shaped ice sculptures, white and still, watching.

"F-forgive me, my Chief," Qonde said from behind Atotarho.

He swung around in rage. *"What?"*

Qonde's shoulders hunched defensively. He extended a hand to point at a white-haired man with a battered face, scarred around the mouth like an old fighter. He wore a grim expression.

"Who is that?"

"Chief Wenisa of the Mountain People sent him to speak with you."

"Tell him to come forward. Quickly."

Qonde waved and the man came forward in a half-crouch, as though he couldn't straighten up.

"What is your name?"

The old man bowed. "I am Wasa, Beaver Clan of the People of the Mountain, and messenger for the great Chief Wenisa."

"Yes, what is it?"

The square-headed elder took a breath, as though about to deliver a lengthy message. "Our Ruling Council wishes you to know that it received your message asking if we wished to participate in the final destruction of the Standing Stone nation—"

"Is it sending forces?"

"Yes. They should arrive in two days, if the weather—"

"How many?"

The elder shifted, as though not accustomed to being interrupted. "Two thousand will be at your disposal, providing we can come to an agreement. Our Ruling Council assigned me to negotiate with you."

"Negotiate?" Atortarho glared. "I offered to split Standing Stone territory equally between our peoples. There's nothing else to negotiate. Either your Ruling Council wishes to accept, or it doesn't." But a vague unease went through Atotarho. If two thousand Mountain warriors were on their way here, the situation could rapidly deteriorate. After today's battle, he estimated that he would have perhaps nine hundred warriors left. If Wenisa wanted, when he arrived, he could turn his forces on Atotarho's.

"With respect, Chief," Wasa said. "Your offer of half the territory was enough to get us to send warriors, but not enough to guarantee our full support."

From the corner of his vision, Atotarho saw his warriors launch a shimmering wave of arrows into the morning sunlight. He gritted his teeth, longing to watch, but kept his attention on the messenger.

"I see. What would be enough?"

Wasa took a moment to watch the volley strike Bur Oak Village. Screams, shouts, and cheers rose.

"Should we decide to give you our full support, the Mountain People's Ruling Council will wish to have your full support in return."

"My full support to do what?" Atotarho gripped his walking stick, ready to strike the old hunchback if he didn't get to the point.

Wasa straightened slightly, as though sensing Atotarho's patience was at an end. "Just as you wish to completely destroy the Standing Stone nation, we wish to obliterate the Landing People. After we're finished helping you here, we ask that you lead your army back to the Landing villages and help us wipe them from the face of Great Grandmother Earth. In exchange, we will give you half of their territory."

He needed time to consider the ramifications of such an arrangement. "When do you require an answer to this request? My Ruling Council—"

"Perhaps we are mistaken." Wasa tilted his head as though he knew he was being toyed with. "We have heard you have supreme control of the Hills nation. The Ruling Council merely advises you. Is that wrong?"

Atotarho's livid expression must have worried the elder, for the old man's eyes narrowed to slits. With deadly softness, he said, "I have control."

"Then, since you do not have to send a message to your Ruling Council seeking permission for this agreement, we require an answer immediately."

Atotarho took a new grip on the head of his walking stick. The impudence was stunning! Not only that, it would outrage the Ruling Council if the Hills army destroyed the Standing Stone nation today, and no longer needed the Mountain People's help. Chief Wenisa would arrive expecting to be awarded half the Standing Stone territory for coming as he'd asked, and Atotarho would be forced to give it to him, lest Wenisa turn his army on Atotarho's decimated forces.

Which the greedy fool might do anyway once he sees that his forces greatly outnumber mine.

Cheers echoed from across the valley, high-pitched, pounding the air. Atotarho kept his gaze on Wasa's.

"Tell your Ruling Council its offer is acceptable."

Wasa bowed deeply and smiled. "Then our army will be at your service."

Wasa backed away and hobbled toward four men Atotarho had not seen before. They stood just on the other side of his personal guards, carrying the litter that must have borne Wasa here.

Atotarho watched the old man climb onto the litter, then his bearers carried the old man off toward the trail to the west.

He turned back to the battle. The Bur Oak palisade was on fire in several places. Warriors scurried along the catwalks dumping water onto the flames. Every drop brought them closer to destruction.

A low laugh shook Atotarho.

No matter how many warriors he lost today, with the two thousand that he'd instructed Kelek to send back to him, and the two thousand Mountain warriors already on their way . . . the Standing Stone nation would soon be nothing but a despicable memory.

Thirty-eight

Clusters of black willows and yellow birches whiskered the slope in front of Hiyawento and Towa, running like a rumpled blanket down to Shookas Village. In the late afternoon light, the windblown branches created a vista of constant movement where shadows leaped and danced across the hills. Fortunately, the forest fire had not reached here. This was the first time since dawn that Hiyawento had been able to get a breath of fresh air into his ash-choked lungs.

Hiyawento gripped his war club and studied the hastily constructed camps that completely encircled the village palisades. Most were composed of scavenged branches that had been tied together at the tops and covered with hides; they resembled small rounded huts. From this perspective, he couldn't see inside Shookas Village, but warriors crowded the catwalks of the double palisade. He tried to estimate their numbers. Maybe eight hundred on the walls?

They're expecting an attack.

To the west of Shookas Village, Sapling River cut an arc that paralleled the curve of the oval palisades. The dark green water glinted with sunlight as it wound its way across the countryside.

"Blessed Ancestors," Towa said in a dire voice. "The entire nation must have fled to Shookas Village."

"My guess is that there are two or three thousand people outside the walls, living in the huts. How many usually live inside?"

Towa shrugged and his long black braid, which hung like a frizzy rope over his left shoulder, bobbed up and down. "After the fever that devastated them last moon? Maybe two thousand. There are six longhouses, each is six hundred to seven hundred hands long. Before the fever around three thousand people occupied the village. If there are three thousand outside, plus two thousand living here, and even more refugees from other villages in the plaza . . . there are probably another three or four thousand people inside the walls."

"Then six or seven thousand people total? Of those, around two thousand are trained warriors. What do you think is going on?"

Towa shook his head. "I don't know. Perhaps, like our own faction of the Hills nation, they've abandoned all their other villages and joined forces to protect each other."

"Or every other Landing village has been destroyed, like Agweron Village."

"Yes, that's possible." Towa's brown eyes narrowed as he surveyed the thousands of people roaming between the huts. Children darted around, playing games, as though nothing was wrong. Occasionally dogs barked. "Where are we supposed to meet Sky Messenger?"

"About where we're standing, on the eastern trail into Shookas Village."

Towa rubbed his jaw with his sleeve. "I don't like the looks of this. There are too many warriors on the cat-walks. I think they're expecting a raid."

"I agree. Which means they're going to be especially vigilant. Are you sure you can get us through that crowd and into the village to see High Matron Weyra?"

"Well"—Towa gestured uncertainly—"no one has ever tried to stop me before."

"No, but have you ever entered their village with a Hills War Chief at your side?"

"I'm still alive, aren't I? Of course not. And I won't to-day, either. As of this instant you are not a war chief. You're my new assistant, a young Trader from the Stand-ing Stone People on his first visit to the Landing villages."

Hiyawento shifted uncomfortably. "Why the Standing Stone nation, and not—"

"Because they hate the Hills People almost as much as they hate the Mountain People, though not quite. They're attacked far more frequently by Mountain raiders. And your Standing Stone accent may help us. Matron Jigon-saseh and Matron Kittle routinely feed Landing war par-ties as they pass through Standing Stone country. As a result, a small amount of goodwill exists between the Landing and Standing Stone nations."

Hiyawento thought about that. Not so long ago High Matron Kittle had made a point of telling him that he had no name among their people. He was Outcast. Forgotten. When he'd allowed himself to be adopted into the Hills nation so that he could marry Zateri, he'd committed treason. It had been a moment of generosity on Kittle's part that she had not carried out his death sentence on the spot. Of course, that was before he'd switched sides and fought shoulder-to-shoulder with Sky Messenger against Atotarho. But he still felt uncomfortable about pretending to be a Standing Stone Trader. However, if such a deception would help Sky Messenger? Well, his feelings were of no consequence. "Very well. What's my name?"

Towa gazed at him thoughtfully. "I'd go by my boyhood name: Wrass. It's easier to remember. You're Bear Clan of Yellowtail Village, just as you were before you wed Zateri. And when Sky Messenger arrives, he will be Odion."

"What if someone recognizes us? Most war chiefs know each other."

"True, but many of their war chiefs died when the fever swept their villages. Still, I think we should paint our faces before we approach the camps."

Towa shrugged out of his Trader's pack and knelt on the trail before it. As he pulled out his paints box, Hiyawento glimpsed the black pointed shapes of buffalo horn sheaths. Since they were worth a fortune, Hiyawento was surprised that Towa hadn't hidden them somewhere, waiting for a more opportune time to Trade them.

"Are you hoping to Trade here?"

"Absolutely. That's why we're here. And you'd better remember it." As he opened his paints box, the cold leather hinges squealed. "As we Trade, we will talk about the great miracle that occurred during the Bur Oak battle, but we'll just be gossiping, passing along the news of other nations, as Traders do."

"What about Sky Messenger's vision? Shouldn't we—"

"Really, Hiyawento." Towa looked up and his mouth quirked. "How poor a Trader do you think I am? Since I first heard of his vision, I've been carrying the story everywhere I go. The last time I was here, the Ruling Council called in every storyteller. They asked me to re-tell the story over and over, to make sure they had the details right, so they could go home and repeat it."

"Do they believe his vision?"

Towa rose with his paints box in hand, studied Hiyawento's eaglelike face and dipped a fingertip into the white paint. A mixture of clay, crushed shell, and bear fat, it had a pleasing sparkle. As he began painting Hiyawento's face, he answered, "I happen to be a very good storyteller. When I was finished with the fifth telling, no one with a soul could have doubted its truth. Every jaw in the council house hung slack with awe. Even the children had hushed and stared at me with huge eyes."

Hiyawento smiled. "Sky Messenger will appreciate that, old friend."

"He'd better. Retelling the story forced me to remain in the midst of the sickness far longer than I'd intended. I had to stay away from Riverbank Village for another five days to make sure I hadn't been infested with the Evil Spirits. The last thing I wished to do was carry them home to Riverbank Village." In a sad voice he added, "Though when I arrived I discovered sickness had already entered the village, carried in the bodies of Flint captives taken during the latest raid on Monster Rock Village."

Concerned, Hiyawento asked, "How are your wife and son?"

"Both were sickened, but got well. I was fortunate. Many others perished."

The expressions on Towa's handsome face shifted as he scrutinized his painting, then decided to add black circles around Hiyawento's eyes and mouth. "There, not even Sky Messenger would recognize you."

While Towa painted his own face, red on top and gray on the bottom, Hiyawento's gaze returned to the village. As Elder Brother Sun descended in the west, the colors of the late afternoon began to shade toward dusk. The yellow sunlight that had illuminated hundreds of huts only moments ago had turned deep amber, and the lengthening forest shadows pointed eastward like black lightning bolts zigzagging across the hills.

When the breeze shifted, the scent of hundreds of campfires blew around him.

Towa tucked his paints box back into his pack, tugged the laces tight and slipped it over his shoulders again. As he rose, he exhaled the words, "I think we should get a little closer. Their scouts will already have spotted us. If we just keep standing here they will become suspicious that we are Mountain People spies. Are you ready?"

"Yes."

"Then let's go, Wrass."

Towa led the way down the hill at a slow trot.

Thirty-nine

Matron Jigonsaseh stopped long enough to tuck grimy black hair behind her ears. As the hush of evening settled over Bur Oak Village, small fires continued to burn, mostly in the longhouse roofs, sending ash floating across the plaza in waves. The cool air was pungent with the odor of charred slippery elm bark, and redolent with the cries of the wounded and grieving. Their losses had been devastating. When they were attacked again, *not if,* they'd be overrun. She suspected it would take Negano less than four hands of time to completely destroy the last survivors of the Standing Stone nation.

She propped a hand on CorpseEye where he rested in her belt, and continued toward the wounded where they were laid out in rows. The few remaining pots of water had been stashed close to them. From this point on, only the wounded that were certain to live would receive water. Her long-empty stomach—empty of both food and water, for she would not eat or drink if her warriors couldn't—had been playing tricks on her souls. Sometimes the screams and sobs seemed far away and tiny, like the incoherent dreams born of a fever. Later, they bombarded her like huge fists, beating her heart to dust. She was tired, so tired, but she could not lie down until this was finished.

A curious numbness had begun to filter through her body at noon, and totally possessed her by sundown, killing her emotions. She should feel glad that they had survived another day, but the only thought that came to her was that she had to figure out a way to make it just one more. *One more day, my ancestors, just let me fight for one more day.*

The only good news was that the major fires had been doused . . . but it had required almost all of their precious water to keep the village from becoming one gigantic fireball.

"Matron?" a wounded warrior called from where he lay on the ground. "Matron, a moment?"

Jigonsaseh knelt at his side. She'd seen Bahna working on his wound earlier. He was one of Sindak's men. Barely seventeen summers old, with long filthy hair draped around his narrow face in stringy locks, the youth had kind brown eyes. She suspected he had a family back home in Atotarho village. He must be worried about them. "What is it, warrior?"

"I know we have . . . very little water, but . . . one sip?" He tipped his head to the pot that rested just out of his reach with a cup over the top, and gazed up at her with a pained expression.

She reached for the pot, poured a small amount into the cup and gently lifted his head to tip the cup to his lips. He drank the three swallows greedily, then sighed, "Thank you, Matron."

She gently eased his head back to the blanket and reached to return the cup to its place over the water pot.

"Matron?" the warrior asked in an exhausted voice. "I can't feel my legs. Tell me why?"

She did not hesitate. "The arrow struck close to your lower spine." His face visibly paled, and she added, "It didn't sever your spine. Our Healers say you will heal and walk again, perhaps in one moon. Be grateful. You will live to see your family again. Many others lying in the plaza will not."

His gaze scanned the bodies, arranged in rows, and lingered for a long time on the wounded children and elders who'd stood on the palisade firing their bows until the very last. "I appreciate hearing the truth, Matron."

She gave him a confident nod. "You fought bravely today. Your service to the alliance will never—"

"Will there be an alliance after tomorrow, Matron? Or will it die with us?"

Jigonsaseh stared into his eyes. Given the severity of his wound, it surprised her that he realized the truth of their situation. She reached down to take his hand in a powerful grip. "No one will forget what we did here today, warrior. What *you* did here. Our sacrifices will be the glue that will bind the alliance and keep it together for generations."

He smiled at the absolute certainty in her deep voice. "Thank you, Matron." When he released her hand, he sank into his blankets to close his eyes as though he couldn't stay awake for another instant.

Jigonsaseh rose to her feet. The warriors on the catwalks had begun to walk around briskly as their voices rose in pitch. To the east, she saw High Matron Kittle standing between Sindak and Gonda. Gonda leaned heavily on his crutch, trying to relieve the pain in his splinted leg, but he was pointing at something.

She put her head down, and marched to the closest ladder to climb up to the catwalk. As she made her way toward them, warriors buzzed with excited conversation. Out across the old battlefield hundreds of campfire had glimmered to life. Negano was taking no chances. He'd moved his entire army into a ring around Bur Oak Village, bottling them up tight, making certain no one could reach the marsh again. Just out of bowshot, hundreds of Hills warriors paraded around, some shouting. Others waved their arms furiously.

As she walked up, Gonda turned. His round face had a pain-stricken expression. He maneuvered his crutch so he could hobble around to face her. "Something's going on out there."

She squinted out across the battlefield. The commotion was spreading through the ranks, men and women stalking around like stiff-legged dogs while they cursed.

Kittle said, "What do you think is happening? It looks like a riot."

A grim smile turned Sindak's lips. He laughed softly and looked at Jigonsaseh. Ash coated his lean face. "Saponi did it." Pride filled his voice. "He did it."

What do you mean all the food is gone! Our warriors are starving!" War Chief Negano shook both fists in face of the warrior hunching before him. Qonde's hawkish face had a tortured expression, as though he expected Negano to strike him. "What happened to it? When I left before dawn, we had plenty—"

"Negano, it's not my fault!" Short and stocky, Qonde bravely straightened to his full height and clenched his fists at his sides. Sweat matted his black hair to his cheeks. "After you left, a group of wounded warriors came to me asking to speak with the chief! They said they wished to be useful, and Atotarho told them to reorganize the food stores. They said they were hauling the deer haunches into the forest shadows to keep them cold. It made sense, and the battle had just started, I was watching—"

"When did you discover all the food was gone?"

"Not until late afternoon! I sent warriors to search the ground, even the tree branches, thinking they might have—"

"Dear gods." Negano rubbed a hand over his stunned face.

His warriors had fought hard all day long. Exhausted and with empty bellies, most had just miserably walked away when the news had come. But around two hundred had encircled Negano. Shouting curses, they shook war clubs and fists in the air, ready to kill whoever was responsible for denying them a well-deserved supper.

Fear twisted deep in Negano's belly. "Where is the chief?"

Qonde's shoulders hunched again. He swung around to point to the northern end of the camp. "I warn you. He's not happy, Negano."

Negano squeezed his eyes closed and massaged his forehead. "It's too late to send out hunting parties, which means there will be no food for breakfast tomorrow, either. Tell the chief that I expect many warriors will desert tonight, and more will vanish tomorrow. Even if we—"

"You want *me* to tell him? I'm not War Chief, you are! You tell him!"

His nerves humming, Negano grabbed Qonde by the front of his cape, shook him violently, and shouted in his face, "Do it! *I gave you an order!*"

Forty

Baji and Dekanawida had avoided the main trail that led to Shookas Village, choosing instead a narrow trail that wound through the eastern hills. Though they ran through forest, the acrid scent of forest fires clung in the air.

She felt a new stirring in the land. Oddly, the knowledge came to her not by sight and sound, but something deeper. As though she could extend her soul beyond her body and out into the forest, every part of her, muscle and sinew, felt the land awakening. The animals felt it, too. Bounding deer chirped the news, squirrels leaping between branches chittered about it, Great Grandmother Earth tried to beat the awareness into Baji each time her moccasins struck the ground.

When she broke into a run, passing Dekanawida on a downward slope, he gave her a curious glance and pounded after her.

He must sense it, too. We are almost there. The last meadow in the belly of the clouds awaits us.

As they careened down the slope and headed up the next rise, Shookas Village appeared. Dekanawida let out a low confused sound and staggered to a stop, staring at the fire-devastated landscape. His round face streamed sweat. Breathing hard, Baji halted beside him to assess what they saw. Hundreds of camps dotted the flats around the village, and thousands of people milled around them.

"Why are so many people here?" he asked.

"It looks like the end of the world to me. And I feel it, don't you?"

Sky Messenger sucked in a breath and exhaled the words, "All I feel is scared, Baji."

Gitchi growled as he paced back and forth in front of them with his neck fur bristling and rippling. The old wolf had lived a long, strong life, filled with battle, and bitter cold, and hunger that stalked the souls. He knew without being told that war was in the air he breathed.

"I fear," Baji said, "that they are preparing a giant war party." Her gaze scanned the crowded palisades and lightly skimmed across the hide huts. "Weapons are everywhere."

Dekanawida said, "I don't see Hiyawento."

The dread in his voice made her smile. She reached out and clasped his hand. "Has he ever let any of us down? No. Not even when we were children. He's here. I'm looking forward to seeing—"

"Baji, I want you to stay here," he said suddenly. He turned to stare down at her, and his cape flapped around his tall body, whipping into snapping folds when the wind gusted just right. His broad chest expanded and shrank with his panting lungs.

Calmly, she asked, "Why?"

"When this is over, if I survive, I'll meet you on this very spot."

She tilted her head. "Why do you want me to stay behind?"

"Because"—he reached out to still the long black hair that blew around her face—"if things go wrong in there, I'll be so worried about you that I will forget everything else I must do."

"Is that it, really?" she asked mildly. "Or are you afraid that no one else will be able to see—"

"That's not it. I swear it." He shook his head as though denying something he knew in his heart. "Please do this? Just stay here and wait for me."

She searched his taut expression. "I'll do whatever you need me to. You know that."

He heaved a relieved breath, as if she'd removed a great weight from his shoulders, and bent down to kiss her. His lips were warm and soft, caressing. When he drew back, he said, "I'll return as soon as I can. No matter what happens, never forget how much I love you."

Baji smiled and gestured to the trail. "Stop stalling. I'll be waiting right over there in the trees, watching for you."

Dekanawida backed away and his eyes narrowed. "Gitchi, stay. Guard Baji."

The wolf trotted over to Baji's side and stood looking up at her. She scratched his head.

As Dekanawida trotted away, Gitchi's big front paws nervously kneaded the ground, as though eager to run after his best friend.

Baji looked down at him. As he leaned against her leg, she said, "He's afraid to lose you, too, you know?"

Gitchi's ears pricked, listening attentively. She petted the wolf's neck for a long time, letting his soft warmth seep into her, before she walked off the trail through the frozen brown leaves to stand beneath the arching branches of a beech tree.

She braced her shoulder against the smooth gray bark and gazed upward at the crows sailing through the sky with their ebony wings flashing in the sunlight. Gitchi stood beside her, his nose up, sniffing for danger.

Baji tingled. She didn't understand it, but every time she got off the trail and stole cat-footed into the forest shadows, a supernatural vitality filled her. Life seemed to rear up and charge through her veins with such exquisite freedom she felt she would burst with the sheer ecstasy of it.

I feel so alive.

Her entire life, in one form or another, she had existed in perpetual fear of things seen or unseen. Now all that was gone. Like white water rushing away down a river, it had receded into the far country.

Gitchi whimpered.

She lowered her fingers to absently stroke his head. As though the wolf understood more than she did, he whimpered again.

Baji looked down. His yellow eyes had a tight look, as though he sensed her leaving him, and didn't want her to go.

"I'm still here, fool," she teased.

Gitchi gently licked her hand.

Forty-one

When they reached the eastern-most periphery of the camps, Towa slowed to a walk and lifted his hand to every person he saw. Almost everyone recognized him and smiled in return. Hiyawento carefully examined them. These people's capes hung about them in shreds, and their moccasins and leggings were a patchwork of sewn-up holes. No jewelry clicked or glinted.

Towa whispered, "Let's just walk along the edge of the camps. That will look perfectly normal to the warriors on the palisades."

"I understand."

As they passed each fire, Hiyawento tried to identify the thin soups that filled the supper pots: dried milkweed and ferns were the main ingredients, but occasionally he caught sight of mushrooms or chunks of desiccated grasshoppers.

Hiyawento said, "They have no meat? No corn, beans, or squash? No sunflowers?"

Towa shook his head as he weaved between two huts. Four women sat outside, talking, using bone awls threaded with cordage to sew up the holes in badly worn hides—hides anyone else would have thrown away.

"A pleasant afternoon to you," Towa said warmly.

One of the women lifted a hand, and they fell back into their conversation, barely glancing up at Towa and Hiyawento as they casually walked by.

"A little rude," Hiyawento murmured.

"Don't blame them. They have nothing to Trade. My presence just reminds them of how poor they are."

The remnants of last autumn's cornfields stood along the river bank. The stalks—hacked off at the ground—had barely grown to the size of Hiyawento's little finger. They'd obviously gotten no corn from these fields. They'd cut the stalks to weave into mats, baskets, dolls, ropes, or sandals, maybe even boiled them to extract what little nutrients they contained, but they hadn't fed many people, if any.

A group of five boys walked by, and Hiyawento stared at their bulging eyes. Their heads appeared huge, wobbling on bony necks. When Towa noticed Hiyawento's undue attention, he whispered, "Take a good look. The next time you think your people are hungry, remember these children."

Hiyawento swallowed hard. "No wonder the Mountain People have been hitting them so hard."

Every nation was struggling to survive, so they viewed the troubles of others as opportunities. Any village that was sick or starving became a target. Their neighbors waited until they were too weak to fight back, then they attacked, ransacked the food stores, and killed their enemies.

A memory slipped from the locked door where

Hiyawento kept it buried . . . *last spring . . . boiling maple sap with my three daughters . . . pouring the syrup into wooden molds . . . waiting until it hardened and turned to sugar . . . sweet treats and laughter . . . so much love in their eyes . . .*

His steps faltered as he forced their smiling faces away. Jimer and Catta had been so beautiful.

"Are you all right?" Towa asked. He gazed at Hiyawento in concern. "You just made an agonized sound."

"Sorry. I . . ." He took a breath and held it for a few heartbeats. "I was thinking about last spring. We made maple sugar candy in Coldspring Village."

"Yes, we did in Riverbank Village, as well. I know for a fact that the Landing People didn't have a chance to. Mountain raiders tapped all their trees long before they could get to them."

To Hiyawento's right, he glimpsed a tall man striding between huts, heading straight for them, his short black hair flapping over his high cheekbones.

As he trotted up, Sky Messenger said, "I almost didn't recognize you."

He embraced Hiyawento and for the first time in days, Hiyawento smiled in true happiness. He pounded his friend's back. "It's good to see you. I've been worried. We've spent half our time dodging war parties."

"Me, too."

When they separated, Hiyawento said, "We should probably paint your face, before we try to—"

"No, not me." Sky Messenger turned abruptly to embrace Towa. "Gods, it's good to see you."

"And you, my friend."

Then Sky Messenger looked from Towa to Hiyawento

and his smile faded. "Tell me everyone made it safely to Canassatego Village."

"Yes," Hiyawento answered, "though Canassatego was attacked shortly after they arrived. But that's a long story for another time. It will be dark soon."

Sky Messenger's eyes shifted to the village gates. "We have more important duties."

Towa sternly said, "All right, listen to me, both of you. Let me do the talking. Sky Messenger, until you reveal yourself, I will introduce you as my new assistant, Odion. Do you understand?"

"Perfectly." He nodded.

"All right. Follow me and act obsequious, like you worship me."

Towa walked up to the gates and cupped a hand to his mouth. "Towa, the greatest Trader in the land, requests entry to Shookas Village!"

Laughter ran down the catwalks, and a man with a shaved scalp leaned over to look down at them. Tattoos covered his face, including a spiral on the tip of his long nose. "Towa! You're back sooner than we thought. Who are these men with you?"

"My new assistants, Wrass and Odion, both are from the Standing Stone nation. I am training them in the great and noble art of Trading."

"And what worthless trinkets have you brought this time?"

"Many worthless trinkets, Nokweh! You will be amazed and delighted by the price I ask, I assure you!"

"Oh, yes," the man said doubtfully. "I'm sure I will." He signaled to someone Hiyawento couldn't see, and said, "The gates will be open shortly."

Towa grinned up. "I'm glad to see you alive, Deputy War Chief. I feared you'd fallen to the—"

"I'm War Chief now, Towa. Our former War Chief is traveling the Path of Souls." Grief twisted the man's bony face.

"Ah," Towa said sadly. "I will miss him. Did the fever take him?"

"No. The Mountain People have been ravaging our country, killing anyone they can. Our women and children are afraid to go out to fill pots at the river for fear that they'll be ambushed by the vile beasts. Our former War Chief fought to his last breath to protect his people; he fell to one of their arrows."

Towa glanced back at the huts that extended for as far as they could see. "Is that why so many people are camped around Shookas? Are these all refugees from destroyed villages?"

"A few survivors ran here from Agweron Village. The others are not refugees. Three days ago our scouts reported a huge Mountain army on the move. We assumed they would be coming here to finish us for good. Decanasora Village and Elehana Village chose to abandon their homes and move here to consolidate our forces. It makes strategy easier."

"Strategy?"

"Yes, my friend. Haven't you heard? It's the news of the camps. We are organizing the largest army in the history of our People. Apparently the Mountain army was not on its way here, but headed elsewhere. That means their villages are poorly defended. We are going to attack and annihilate every Mountain village in the land."

Towa gave Nokweh a pained nod. "I'm sure you will, too. Landing warriors are the best in the world."

Nokweh glanced to his left, and said, "Get ready. The guards are opening the gates."

"We thank you!" Towa lifted a hand again.

The gates swung open and Towa, Hiyawento, and Sky Messenger passed by the guards with respectful nods, and walked out into the crowded plaza.

Sky Messenger softly said, "If they destroy the Mountain villages it will provoke a war of annihilation. You know that, don't you?"

"Yes, of course," Towa whispered. "But look around you. No parent can peer into the eyes of a starving child without picking up weapons and doing whatever is necessary to keep that child alive."

"Attacking the Mountain villages will not accomplish that. They are as bad off, or worse, than—"

"I know that, Sky Messenger. I've been there."

Five longhouses encircled the broad plaza, each stretching six or seven hundred hands long, and forty wide. Chunks of the elm bark walls had been ripped out, others were charred. Firelight gleamed through the holes like the campfires of the dead.

Forty paces ahead of them, in the middle of the plaza, people packed shoulder-to-shoulder around a large bonfire, apparently listening to an ugly little man. The fellow shouted from where he stood on a massive hickory stump overlooking the assembly. He wore his hair in a traditional Flint roach, shaved on the sides with a black bristly strip in the middle. Few teeth remained in his mouth and they were yellowed and half-rotted. To the speaker's left, the Ruling Council of the Landing People, composed of twelve elders, sat on log benches, listening. They each wore a white cape, decorated with the symbols of their clans.

"Who's the orator?" Sky Messenger asked softly. "I can't tell from here."

"That's Tagohsah," Towa said. "I wonder what he's doing here? His rounds usually bring him to Shookas Village in the middle of the moon. I try to arrive several days before just to avoid him."

Hiyawento whispered, "Let's move closer so we can hear what he's saying."

The crowd's attention, riveted on Tagohsah, didn't shift as Hiyawento, Sky Messenger, and Towa weaved through the tightly packed bodies, stepping into any gap that opened. Tagohsah must have begun talking only a short while ago, because fragments of the story had just begun filtering back through the listeners, relayed in awed whispers.

A young woman in front of Hiyawento said, "Atotarho attacked Bur Oak and Yellowtail villages with eight thousand warriors . . ." Then she turned back to hear the next few words being repeated, and said, "The Standing Stone army was cut down like blades of dry grass. . . ." She turned to listen again.

Sky Messenger and Hiyawento exchanged a look, and slipped closer, shouldering between two men. Towa followed along behind them.

A toothless old man whispered, "Atotarho's forces killed over two thousand five hundred Standing Stone warriors . . . that's when the Hills nation crumbled to dust . . . Coldspring Village, along with Riverbank and

Canassatego villages, turned against Atotarho and fought on the side of the Standing Stone nation."

Hiyawento murmured, "They're talking about the battle five days ago."

"Yes," Towa replied, and stepped into a slim space that allowed him to move two steps closer.

Hiyawento and Sky Messenger followed. A young warrior carrying a war club propped on his shoulder said, "Then a Flint war party appeared, lined out on the hills to the east . . . the Flint warriors, too, fought on the side of the Standing Stone nation . . . the battle was so great and terrible it shook the ground . . . just when it looked like the Standing Stone alliance was about to be overrun, killed to the last person . . . the Prophet stepped out . . ."

Sky Messenger's expression changed, as though the sense of wonder in the youth's voice had made his heart thunder.

Hiyawento clung to his friend's side, his hands invisible beneath his long cape, holding tight to his belted war club. A low hum of awed voices spread across the plaza, coming in waves, each portion of the tale repeated from one person to the next, but there was always someone who didn't believe. Someone who longed to earn a reputation by killing legends. Well, he'd have to kill Hiyawento first.

The youth swung around again, his starved face alight. "The Prophet, the human False Face known to the Standing Stone nation as Sky Messenger, lifted his hands, ordering the armies to stop fighting . . . Elder Brother Sun saw him . . . he sent a great monstrous storm crashing down upon the battlefield, scattering Atotarho's army like old leaves in a hurricane! Atotarho's forces ran. *They ran!*"

Hiyawento slid into a new gap in the milling crowd and managed to get four steps closer. Sky Messenger and Towa were right behind him.

"Blessed gods!" a woman half-shouted, "the Prophet alone remained to face the storm! Just before the spinning darkness swallowed him, his cape transformed into billows of white clouds, and he rode the winds of destruction like one of the Cloud People. When the storm had passed over the battlefield, the Prophet appeared again, hovering over the battlefield like one of the Sky People. Not a single hair upon his head had been disturbed!"

Towa leaned sideways to murmur to Sky Messenger, "I heard it a bit differently."

A tight smile tensed Sky Messenger's face. "Someone should tell them the truth."

Towa shook his head. "Bad idea. Look at them."

Reverence lined every face and filled every voice.

Hiyawento looked around, trying to hear words through the general noise of thousands of voices.

"... the human False Face has come ... he is among us right now ... the Faces of the Forest walk with him ..."

There was a momentary hush, then an old man with a deeply wrinkled face turned and repeated, "Atotarho attacked them again ... just a few days ago. He's there now trying to starve the last survivors to death!"

Towa jerked around to look at Hiyawento and Sky Messenger. "Dear gods. Did you know this?"

"No." Sky Messenger's voice had gone deep with shock.

Hiyawento clutched his war club tighter. He had to get word to Zateri. She'd probably already sent back as many warriors as she could afford, as she'd promised Kittle she would, but—

"I wish to speak." High Matron Weyra stood and lifted a hand to the crowd. Thin white hair fluttered around her wrinkled face. She'd seen perhaps fifty-five summers, and had a fleshy nose that rippled when she scratched it. After the voices died down, she called, "It seems the Hills People have the same designs on Standing Stone territory as the Mountain People do on ours, and neither nation will stop at anything to achieve its goals. We must—"

Sky Messenger shouted, *"That's because we have an amnesia of the heart. We've forgotten that we were once one People!"*

Towa hissed, "It's unhealthy to interrupt the most powerful woman in the nation."

Sky Messenger boldly shouldered through the crowd. As he passed, eyes went wide, men and women shuffled backward, and a stunned chorus began to whisper across the plaza, *"It's him . . . Blessed Gods, it's the Prophet . . . it's Sky Messenger! . . . No, it's not, you fool . . . I tell you, it is! Look how tall he is. He fits the descriptions . . ."*

"Let him through!" High Matron Weyra called. "Who are you?"

Sky Messenger stopped long enough to meet and hold her gaze. His brown eyes blazed so brilliantly that people gaped at him, their faces immobile, as though afraid to move in his presence.

In a strong, powerful voice, he said, "I am Sky Messenger, called Dekanawida by the Flint People. I've come to offer you something better than battle, better than death! Reason and righteousness must prevail, elders, or none of us will survive the coming darkness!"

As he strode forward, the crowd fell back before him,

shoving one another to get out of his way, and opening a narrow pathway that led straight to the Ruling Council.

Hiyawento and Towa had to hurry to stay close.

"It's him! I fought against him once . . . look at the cut of his cape . . . definitely Standing Stone . . ."

Hiyawento's fingers went tight around his war club as he scanned every face they passed, noting those who scowled and sneered, paying special attention to hands that rested upon belted weapons.

Sky Messenger bowed deeply before the elders. In a deep respectful voice, he said, "Council Members, I ask your forgiveness for disturbing this meeting."

Most of the elders stared at him slack-jawed, almost certain they sat in the presence of a living legend, but not quite. One or two gave Sky Messenger wary looks.

High Matron Weyra said, "You really are Sky Messenger, the son of Matron Jigonsaseh and Speaker Gonda?"

"Yes, High Matron. I am Bear Clan, from Yellowtail Village. If you will allow it, I would request an audience with your Ruling Council."

Ghostly silence possessed the inside of the council house. The warm air was still. Only the firelight wavered as elders' hands clenched, or feet shuffled.

Hiyawento and Towa stood to the left and right of Sky Messenger, ready for anything, their gazes scanning the small gathering. High Matron Weyra had wisely limited the audience to just the Ruling Council, but thumps sounded around the walls outside as people shifted, pressing close, ears to the walls in an attempt to hear anything. Sky

Messenger had just finished relating his Dream, and a low awed drone penetrated the elm bark walls.

Where he sat on the log bench on the opposite side of the fire, Sky Messenger leaned forward. He propped his elbows on his knees and laced his fingers before him. As he gazed across the flames at the twelve most influential people in the Landing nation, worry cut lines across his forehead and around his wide mouth. He appeared much older than his twenty-three summers. A stranger entering the house just now, seeing him for the first time, would guess Sky Messenger's age at perhaps forty summers. Each layer of Sky Messenger's hair caught the glow and created short jagged lines around his head. His long black cape had fallen into folds on the floor.

"There is one point I do not understand," High Matron Weyra said. Her white hair, thinning on top, hung limp over her ears, but it was her wrinkled face that held a man's attention. Shadows darkened the cavernous hollows of her cheeks, and filled in her skeletal eye sockets. Wiry gray eyebrows created bushy tufts above her kind, thoughtful eyes. "You said that just before Elder Brother Sun turns his back on the world, there will be gray shades drifting through the air around you, their voices hushed like those of lost souls. But are they lost souls? Do you know?"

"I was wondering the same thing," an old man said with a tottering nod. "It sounds to me as though all lost souls will be found. That they are the last congregation."

Sky Messenger's eyes tightened. "The shades are the dead who still walk and breathe, elders. More than that, I don't know."

The old man said, "But the dead do not walk and breathe, Prophet. They are dead."

Sky Messenger bowed his head to stare briefly at the flames dancing around the logs in the fire hearth. A thick bed of red coals glowed around the edges. "Are they? I'm not sure, elder. I can't explain these things."

When Sky Messenger paused, the council members, six men and six women, shifted silently, waiting for him to continue.

"But I know that the darkness will swallow Great Grandmother Earth." Sky Messenger looked up to meet their gazes. "I can't stop it without your help, elders."

More shifting as soft voices discussed what they'd heard.

"How may we help?" Weyra asked softly.

Sky Messenger seemed to be listening to the voices outside, perhaps to the barking dogs. "I have come to believe that compassion is the highest form of politics, elders. Many of you are much older and wiser than I am. I'm sure you've known this truth since long before I was born, but it is new to me. As many of you have heard, I spent most of my life as a warrior. Killing my enemies was the only form of politics I knew. Elders, we must replace blood revenge as a means of justice. It has to end."

"Replace it with what?" the old man snapped, as though appalled by the notion. His lips puckered over toothless gums. Bear claws decorated the throat of his cape. *Bear Clan.* "The Law of Retribution gives us the right to—"

"Yes, it does." Sky Messenger respectfully dipped his head, silently apologizing for interrupting. He hesitated as though preparing himself, then in a deep resonant voice, he said, "When I look across this fire, I see that there have been deaths in many of your families. I grieve with you, elders. If I could, I would wipe away your falling tears and take the sorrow from your hearts, so that you might open your minds and look around peacefully, without hatred. I know this is not an easy thing. The spirits of our bereaved nations are tired. We all starve. We all lash out in fear. There *is* a better way. A peace alliance between all of our peoples."

One of the younger elders, a very thin man with black-streaked gray hair and close-set eyes, laughed. "And how many nations have you convinced to join this alliance?" Wolf tracks scattered his white cape. *Wolf Clan.*

"The alliance is currently composed of the Standing Stone nation, the Flint nation, and three villages of the Hills nation."

"The same three villages that broke away from Atotarho to fight on your side in the recent battle?" Weyra asked.

Sky Messenger nodded. "Yes, High Matron. Coldspring Village, Riverbank and Canassatego Village have joined us."

"I suppose at some point you plan to tell us the benefits of this alliance?" the Wolf Clan elder pressed. "Why don't you get to it? If Tagohsah can be believed, your own people are under attack, and likely to be destroyed in the next few days. Which means the Standing Stone nation will be of no use to us in our current situation."

Sky Messenger unlaced his fingers and opened his hands to them. "I'm not sure I believe his words, but even if my People are not under attack right now, they will be soon. Just as yours will. It is inevitable. This winter is going to be desperate for every nation. If we don't join forces to help each other survive, I fear that by springtime we will all be dead."

Hiyawento watched the expressions. Two elders clearly opposed the alliance. From their cape decorations, Heron Clan and Beaver Clan. Their eyes had turned dark and brooding, and they sat rigid on the benches. The other ten council members, however, watched Sky Messenger with such hope in their eyes, it hurt to look at. They wanted peace more than anything on earth.

"Will you ask the filthy Mountain People to join the alliance?" the frail old woman from the Beaver Clan demanded to know.

"I will."

"Well, I do not wish to be part of any alliance that allows the Mountain People to live," she said. "They *must* be destroyed! My clan will accept nothing less."

Sky Messenger spread his arms in a quieting gesture. "Let me explain the alliance. First, each nation that joins must pledge to give its life, and lives of its people, for every other member. Second, any alliance member that violates this oath will be punished by the combined might of the alliance. If the Landing People join, the alliance will help to protect your borders. We will also send more Traders to you, so that you may exchange the magnificent bowls you make for our corn, or our blankets. When necessary the members of the alliance will pool a portion of their harvests and redistribute the food to needy villages, no matter their nation. We—"

"How quickly could you send food?" Weyra asked almost breathlessly.

Ravenous looks entered the eyes of every council member.

"Once you join us, we will begin pooling what little we have so that we may take care of hungry villages like yours. I won't lie to you. No one has much this winter. But we will do the best we can."

Weyra blinked around the house, as though judging the mood of the other council members. "I have doubts about the alliance's ability to keep its promises. Does anyone else?"

Nods went round.

Sky Messenger said, "Please explain these doubts."

Weyra looked back at him. "Prophet, we are far away from the countries of the current alliance members. What if the Mountain People refuse to join you? They are our closest neighbors, and they wish to destroy us. How will the alliance get here in time if we ask for help to defend ourselves?"

Sky Messenger sat back and squared his broad shoulders. "Details will have to be worked out, of course, but I think the wisest course may be to have each nation assign warriors to your borders to block raids into Landing country."

Elders whispered behind their hands.

The Beaver Clan elder said, "And how will you feed such huge numbers of warriors? You don't expect us to provide for them, do you?"

"No, that would be too great a burden. I think each nation should be required to contribute equal amounts of food to sustain the army."

Council members cast glances at one another, unwilling to openly state their opinions at this time.

Sky Messenger lifted his hands. "Allow me to say one final thing, and then I will go and leave you to your deliberations. Elders, I truly believe that no nation can create an empire by conquering its enemies. Empires arise when enemies forget their own interests and become of one mind, one heart, and one body."

The Bear Clan elder sneered. "And how can such a thing be accomplished? We have too many different clans—"

"We must remember the truth of our origins. We are all relatives. Clans of alliance members shall recognize each other as such. Every member of the Bear Clan, no matter his or her nation, will be my relative, and I will treat him as such. Wolf Clan will be Wolf Clan. Turtle Clan will be Turtle Clan. We will return to the ways of our Blessed Ancestors." He laced his fingers and squeezed them together in one hard fist. "One mind, one heart, one body. We will become one *Haudenosaunee,* one People of the Longhouse."

High Matron Weyra's elderly face slackened, as though she was beginning to understand the kind of alliance he proposed. "So, the clans will be the binding that holds the alliance together?"

"As they are in individual nations, clan mothers will be the heart of all decisions. In my vision, I see clan mothers from every nation sitting around the same fire, guiding the course of the alliance, assisted by a Ruling Council of chiefs."

The elders began a spirited discussion.

Sky Messenger rose to his feet and slowly took the time to meet each gaze. "I must return to my home. I am needed there. If you wish to join us, please send word to me as soon as possible, and I will begin organizing the alliance to help you. Or better yet, send emissaries from your Ruling Council to Bur Oak Village so that you can meet with alliance representatives personally. We hope to welcome you soon."

He bowed deeply and walked around the fire. Hiyawento and Towa followed him down the central aisle, through the leather door hanging, and stepped outside into the crowd. Six guards, including War Chief Nokweh, stood just outside the council house door with worried expressions on their young faces.

Hiyawento swore another thousand people had squeezed into the plaza. He stepped in front of Sky Messenger, shielding his friend with his body. "Stay close behind me," Hiyawento ordered.

"Blessed Spirits, I can't believe—"

"You'd better start believing, my friend. As things become more desperate, this is going to get much worse. The only thing they have is hope."

Towa called, "Hiyawento! I'll cover Sky Messenger's back. Go!"

They started walking through a writhing sea of reaching hands.

"Stop! Let me touch him. I must touch him!"

"Move! Please, I have to get close . . ."

"I just need to speak with the human False Face for a moment . . . get out of my way!"

"Let me through! I must tell him something. He must hear this! Stop pushing me!"

"Gods!" Hiyawento shoved a man away. The panicked insanity of the crowd would smother them if they didn't get out of the village.

Towa yelled, "Hiyawento! Use your war club if you have to!"

He pulled his club from beneath his belt, and waved it over his head. "Move, or I'll start crushing skulls! The Prophet must leave!"

"No, don't take him . . . belongs to all of us, doesn't he . . . Let him go! He's tired, he needs to stay here for the . . . We'll kill you if you try to take him!"

People, many of them weeping, stumbled over each other trying to move as Hiyawento bulled through the mass of humanity, clearing a path to the gates. When he neared the plaza bonfire and saw Tagohsah still standing there, Hiyawento shouted, "Tagohsah! Meet us outside!"

"Why? What do you want?" The man's voice was shrill, frightened. He kept looking around at the eddying crowd as though he knew he'd be crushed long before he made it to the gates.

"If you're not out there in one-quarter hand of time, I'm coming back in to find you!" Hiyawento glared at the ugly little Flint Trader, then turned back to forcing his way through the grasping sea of hands.

Forty-two

"Gitchi?" Baji whispered and cocked her ear to the forest. "What's that sound? Do you hear it?"

The wolf, who lay curled in the grass at her side, blinked up at her, as though he sensed nothing wrong, or perhaps he didn't hear the strange wistful cry that had begun to seep across the land the instant Elder Brother Sun passed below the horizon. Riding the wind like a falcon, it rose and fell, sometimes seeming very close, other times vastly far away.

The cold quiet forest stood perfectly still. She listened. A fox over the next ridge? No, she didn't think so. Tremulous, descending in pitch like an eerie wail of longing, it seemed not to be of this earth.

Baji hesitated, listening for a time longer, then she tiptoed into the forest. Nightfall had drained the colors from the land, leaving it slate gray. Downy woodpeckers peeked at her from holes in the trees, their feathers fluffed out for warmth.

She stopped. The woods had gone peaceful. A screech owl sailed through the trees barely six hands over her head, so silent it might have been a shadow rather than a living creature hunting the pine-scented evening.

Baji watched it alight in a red pine twenty paces away. Small, no longer than her hand, he lacked the usual rusty ear tufts. Probably a young owl. When he turned to study her, his eyes glowed with a silvered brilliance.

The call came again, stronger, trying to pull her deeper into the growing darkness.

Baji placed her hand on her belted war club and took another step. The arrows in her quiver uttered a faint rattle, like a rattlesnake's warning.

Gitchi's paws crunched behind her. He whimpered, urging her to go back to the trail, to return to a place where Dekanawida could find her, but the call was too powerful. It continued to pull her into the falling darkness where towering trees turned black, and frost grew like quartz crystals on rocks and deadfall. The astonishing fragrance of wet bark melted into her body. Her nostrils quivered. Just the movement of breath in her lungs filled her with such gladness she might have become one of the sailing Cloud People.

"Wolves?" she whispered. "Maybe that cry is a pack of wolves in the distance?"

The cry turned into long drawn-out wailing. The chorus seemed to resonate in Baji's chest, wild and free, and she strained so hard to hear it that her throat ached. As though untold generations of ancestors Sang to her of a primeval time before fire and roof, of a time before Elder Brother Sun existed, her souls thrilled to the melody. In her heart, she was running with them, hunting the cold and dark in the frost dance of constant winter.

Barely audible, she murmured, "I don't think it's wolves, Gitchi."

He nosed her hand.

"Don't worry," she said softly. "I'm fine. Everything is fine."

But it wasn't, and she knew it. Something was happening to her.

As evening blanketed the forest, dove-colored and iridescent, patches of snow became radiant, turning the air liquid and faintly blue, and shivering light upon the delicate ferns that hid between the rocks. The ache in her heart had become too much to bear.

Baji had to squeeze her eyes closed against it. *What is that unearthly crying?*

Against her leg, Gitchi's tail wagged.

She opened her eyes. In the small clearing surrounded by fire cherries and pawpaws, she caught movement. She kept her eyes on it. When she could make out darkness rippling around a black cape, she quickly called, "I don't need you! Leave."

No sound. No response.

The quiet of evening seemed to intensify. The call faded, leaving behind a huge maw of silence.

As he started to turn, to leave, she swallowed hard. "No, wait. Just tell me one thing."

He turned back to stare at her. Obviously trying not to frighten her, he slowly walked closer. Dark sad eyes glinted in the frame of his hood. He stopped three paces away, folded his arms beneath his cape, and gently asked, "What do you need to know?"

"Tell me why I feel so alive?"

He blinked, and his gaze shifted. He seemed to be staring over her shoulder, seeing something far away. "It's
part of preparing."

"Preparing?"

He nodded. "Yes. You're at a place where every step
you take is illuminated by the Road of Light." He glanced
up at the twilight sky where the brightest campfires of the
dead had just begun to shine. The contours of the Road
were dimly visible. "It wakes a person up, and that's necessary, because to live your dying fully you must wake up."

To live my dying fully . . .

She braced her feet. "So I'm dying?"

A faint smile turned his lips. "That's all any of us ever
do, Baji. When the deer come for you, if you let them, you
will understand that the Road is all there is. We set foot
upon it long before we're born."

Gitchi slid around her leg and went to stand in front of
Shago-niyoh, looking up with loving eyes. When Shago-
niyoh smiled down at him, the wolf stretched and wagged
his tail again.

"All right," Baji said as though dismissing a war council. "You can go now."

He hesitated. "Don't you want to ask me about the
strange many-voiced cry?"

Her heart stuttered. She took a quick step toward him,
breathlessly asking, "What is it? Do you hear it? Is it human?"

He cocked his head in a curious birdlike manner, examining her with only one shining eye. "They stand at
the foot of the bridge. They start calling very early, when
we are children. Their Song changes over the summers,
as more and more come and lie down, to wait. They're

trying to guide you to them so you won't get lost on the way. If you find them, they will protect you as you cross to the other side."

The animals who wait at the bridge that spans the dark abyss . . .

Her eyes burned. She wiped them on her sleeve. "So, I'm still alive?"

He stood for a long time, gazing up at the evening sky. Wind waffled his black hood around his face and sent icy fingers probing beneath her cape. When she shivered, he looked back at her.

Baji said, "I'm not sure anymore. I was when I started, but . . . I'm not sure now. Tell me."

Shago-niyoh waited for a time, staring at her with kind eyes, then he turned and walked away into the deepening shadows with his cape swaying about his long legs.

She watched until he disappeared. "He knows, Gitchi. Why won't he tell me? I'd still be doing exactly what I am. It wouldn't change a thing."

The wolf stayed very close to her side as they walked through the old leaves, listening to the wavering moans and sobs that seemed to flutter in the air around them. The cry grew fainter with each step, until it thinned to nothingness across the distances, and the forest felt suddenly hollow beyond words.

Forty-three

Sky Messenger

As twilight settles over the forest, I hike up the steep trail behind Hiyawento, heading toward the crest of the hill where I know Baji and Gitchi wait. My friend's broad back sways with his long stride. He has his war club clenched in his fist. Each time he glances over his shoulder at the rumbling crowd that trails behind us like a great thunderstorm, worry and near-panic fill his face. We move rapidly, trying to lose them. The camps surrounding Shookas Village emptied out as we wound our way between the fires, coalescing into a ragged horde of six or seven hundred people. They follow like walking skeletons. Enormous sunken eyes ringed with black circles peer at me from inside ragged hoods.

Hiyawento's nerves are fraying. He keeps looking back, his jaw grinding. His beaked nose glistens with sweat. He doesn't like this any more than I do. Crowds are unpredictable, and none of us is certain why they follow us.

Towa calls, "Hiyawento, let's stop. It's getting dark. We need to speak with Tagohsah."

"All right, but let's get the information we need quickly,

so we can move on. It's impossible to know how many people in that crowd wish to kill Sky Messenger."

Dusk has coaxed the fragrances of night from the trees and earth and set them loose on the breeze.

Towa's gaze fixes on the ugly little Flint Trader. He waits until Hiyawento strides back to tower over Tagohsah like an avenging Earth Spirit, then the three of us close ranks around him, pinning Tagohsah inside our small circle.

Tagohsah hunches like a trapped packrat pushed into a corner by predators. His roached black hair has picked up a coating of dust that gives it a gray tint. The red porcupine quill chevrons across the front of his cape flash with his uneasy fidgeting.

Tagohsah blurts, "What do you want? If you don't hurry we'll all be trampled to death!" He runs a pink tongue over his rotted teeth and stares in horror at the crowd moving up the slope.

Hiyawento's voice is iron: "You told the Landing People that Bur Oak Village was being attacked. How do you know that? Did you hear it from another Trader? Is the story running the trails?"

"I saw it with my own eyes," Tagohsah insists. "Towa, you know my rounds take me to Bur Oak and Yellowtail villages around the first of the moon. As I came down the hill, heading toward the valley, two of Atotarho's warriors stepped out and blocked the trail. They told me to go home, that there was nothing left of the Standing Stone nation."

Towa grimaces. "Then you saw nothing except two warriors."

"Don't be ridiculous! Do you think I actually turned around and left? I'm a Trader. I need good stories. I sneaked through the trees until I could see down into the valley."

He shakes his head grimly. "Your People are in trouble, Prophet."

"Describe what you saw," Hiyawento orders.

Fear has begun to beat a stark refrain inside me. Since I first heard Tagohsah speaking, my souls have been conjuring images too terrible to believe. *Bur Oak Village burned, littered with dead bodies, all my family, my friends . . .*

"I saw around two thousand Hills warriors surrounding the last smoldering villages of the Standing Stone nation."

Towa glances back at the crowd. The leading edge has arrived and begun forming up into a murmuring multitude, crowding closer and closer. "How do you know they were Atotarho's warriors?"

"I saw the evil chief himself! He stood like a hunchback, wearing the black cape covered with circlets cut from human skulls. It was him. I'm sure of it."

I'm breathing hard when I turn to meet Hiyawento's tight eyes. "After the battle, he must have split his forces, sending some warriors to punish the rogue Hills villages, while the rest of his army circled back to finish the job at Bur Oak."

Hiyawento nods, and glances uneasily at the crowd pushing in around us, listening to our every word. Wide eyes stare up at me, as though I'm no longer human, but some strange otherworld phantom. Their hushed voices tremble with awe and fear.

Hiyawento pulls his war club up and menacingly props it on his shoulder for all to see. "If he returned the day after we left, the villages have been under siege for five days. Do you think they could have held out so long?"

Fire seems to rush in my veins, burning a path through my body. "I don't know." *But I don't think so.*

Towa hisses, "Don't forget that Matron Jigonsaseh is there. Sindak, too. He knows how Atotarho's army thinks."

"If they've made it this long, they need help badly," Hiyawento replies. "Their water and food must be gone."

I say, "Do you think Zateri sent the warriors that High Matron Kittle requested?"

"Even if she did, there's no way to know how many she could spare. But it won't be enough to make a real difference. Not if what Tagohsah says is true." He glowered at the ugly Trader.

"It is! I swear it."

Towa turns to me. "What of the Flint nation?"

"I doubt they even know the Standing Stone nation is in trouble. Chief Cord's army was attacked by Atotarho right outside—"

"What?" Towa and Hiyawento shout at once.

They crowd closer to me and Hiyawento says, "When? How do you know that?"

"Baji escaped the massacre. She came after me."

"She's here? With you?" Hope strains Hiyawento's voice as his eyes scan the trail and the trees. "Where is she?"

I gesture vaguely over my shoulder and am surprised when the entire crowd goes still and turns to look up the hill. "Hiding in the trees up there. She has no idea if any other survivor of the massacre made it home to the Flint nation."

"Massacre?" Towa's eyes went hard. "How many were killed?"

As the crowd pushes closer, hemming us in, I whisper, "Hundreds."

"Dear gods." Hiyawento rubs his forehead. "Then Cord may be unable to—"

"If he lived," I say. "Baji says he was badly wounded."

Tagohsah's gaze darts over the hungry faces surrounding us. "Whether he's alive or dead won't matter. The Mountain People will reach Bur Oak Village long before Chief Cord could pull together a war party and get there to help them."

We all turn to stare at him.

"What are you talking about?"

He gestures to the east. "On my way here, I passed a huge Mountain army. They said they were on their way to join Atotarho's forces. They told me they were going to annihilate the Standing Stone nation and split up the country between them."

Rage fires my veins. "How many warriors did you see?"

"They were scattered through the trees, I don't know. Thousands."

Towa and Hiyawento whisper to each other. My gaze shifts to the tree line, searching for Baji and Gitchi. Where are they? My eyes are trained to identify Gitchi's coat even in a tight weave of grass. I don't see him.

Hands touch the back of my cape, subtle, almost not there. Then people grow more bold, pushing one another to get closer to me. Whispers pass from mouth to mouth: "...the Mountain People have joined Atotarho... great darkness is almost upon us... Elder Brother Sun is ready to turn his back... that's where they were headed... Hills People going to destroy the Prophet's nation... we should help... starving... not enough warriors to..."

I ignore the grasping hands, reach out, twine my fingers in Tagohsah's cape, and drag him close. When our faces are less than one hand's breadth apart, I hiss, "I want you to deliver a message for me."

"What message?"

In a voice loud enough for everyone around me to hear, I call, "Run to every village in the land. Tell them I have foreseen the destruction of Chief Atotarho. Tell them it happens just outside Bur Oak Village!"

I shove him away and the crowd rumbles, a mixture of gasps and voices relaying the message through the ranks.

Tagohsah stumbles and looks at me with half-panicked eyes. "Is it true? Have you?"

I straighten and let my eyes roam the masses. Hundreds of gazes are riveted to my face, as though waiting for me to continue.

I lift my hands, and shout, *"I have foreseen the destruction of the evil Atotarho, the man who murdered so many of your loved ones, and it happens right outside Bur Oak Village! Landing warriors are there standing shoulder-to-shoulder with the rest of the alliance! I have seen it! We stand as One. Together, we will do this!"*

An awed hush falls, then several people shove through the crowd and run back to Shookas Village, carrying my words, hopefully, to the Ruling Council.

"Sky Messenger," Towa says as he steps around behind me and begins shoving people back, "we have to get out of here. Now."

"Wait." Hiyawento steps in front of me, and shouts, "I need thirty of the greatest warriors of the Landing People to serve as personal guards for the Prophet! Come forward! Who will help me protect him from his enemies?"

Men and women murmur and blink. Feet shuffle, creating an ominous rumble. There seems to be a discussion going on, people talking between themselves about what they should do. I see several heads shake violently and men and women back away.

"He is the greatest Dreamer our Peoples have ever known! Help him!" Hiyawento lifts his war club and waves it over his head so people can see him. *"I need thirty warriors!"*

Hiyawento has placed them in a difficult position. In essence, he has asked them to swear loyalty to me without the approval of their Ruling Council. It could be construed as treason. Not only that, each knows that Shookas Village needs every warrior in the nation now. The Landing People are more vulnerable than they have ever been, and despite what Tagohsah says, no one can be sure that the huge Mountain army won't return here to destroy Shookas Village.

"Hiyawento, you know they can't—"

"These people chose to follow you up the hill without the approval of their elders," he answers. "I have to know now how much faith lives in their hearts. Enough to willingly follow you all the way back to Bur Oak Village? Let them make the decision, my friend."

Towa's back presses against mine, and I wonder if he's been crowded against me, or just chosen to stand so close. When he stumbles, shoving me into Hiyawento, I know the answer. The crowd is growing too brave.

Hiyawento cups a hand to his mouth. "I'm only asking for thirty warriors. Just thirty! The rest of you must return home to help protect your nation."

Slowly, as though accepting their fate, a handful of warriors come forward. Then more. One by one, they shoulder to the front of the crowd, circling me. Most are big burly men with quivers and bows slung over their shoulders. A few are strong women with hard eyes. I count only sixteen, but their eyes glow when they look at me.

Hiyawento studies them, deciding their worthiness. He

pounds fists into arm muscles judging strength, scrutinizes bows and arrows to see how well they've been cared for, and looks into each person's eyes assessing something far more subtle, character. He is a renowned War Chief, greatly feared by the Landing People. These warriors clearly respect him, but several glare into his eyes. Have they fought against him? Will they obey him when the time comes?

A tidal wave of questions rolls through the crowd. People shift, arms extend to point.

I turn.

At the top of the hill, Baji stands with her long hair blowing around her broad shoulders in the soft winds of evening. She has her bow nocked and aimed at the ground, but her chin is held high as she scans the crowd. Gitchi lopes nervous circles around her, hair bristling, guarding her. I know without a doubt that he will fight to protect her until he cannot fight any longer. The sight of them standing together is like a Spirit plant rushing in my veins.

Everyone sees her! Look at them. They're all looking at her. She's here . . . Blessed Spirits . . . she's here.

Hiyawento lifts a hand to Baji, and she lifts a hand back and gives him a firm nod.

Hiyawento yells, "Guards, we have to move up the trail to that hilltop in the distance where we can protect the Prophet. Do whatever you have to to keep the crowd back as we walk!"

Forty-four

As High Matron Kelek made her way across the dark plaza of Atotarho Village with her guard, her old heart thumped. She felt weary beyond exhaustion. White hair hung about her wrinkled face like a cloud of spiderwebs. The meeting with the village councils from Turtleback and Hilltop had not gone well. All day long Atotarho Village had been in an uproar. Accusations had flown about like diving falcons. No one had been left unscathed, especially Kelek. She felt as though she'd been pecked to pieces by a flock of rabid turkeys.

The sight of the Bear Clan longhouse made her utter a deep sigh. She longed to sleep. As she parted the entry curtain, she shivered in the sudden warmth, and headed toward her chamber at the far end of the house. Her guard dutifully stuck close behind her, his war club in hand.

At just past midnight, the six-hundred-hand-long house appeared still and quiet. Less than a dozen people sat around the thirty fires that sparkled down the center aisle. A few of the curtains had been drawn closed across chambers, but most remained opened to the warmth from the hearths. People slept beneath piles of hides with dogs curled up beside them.

When she reached her chamber near the south entry, Kelek turned to her guard. Thirty summers old, with short black hair, he wore a greasy cape streaked with soot. He'd just returned from the Standing Stone battle, like so many other warriors, and looked as though he hadn't even changed clothes. It was disgraceful.

"Be vigilant, Hakowane."

"I will, High Matron."

His voice was utterly devoid of emotion, which she found peculiar after the day's emotional turmoil.

Kelek scrutinized him. He was slender now, but as a child, he'd been known as a glutton. He'd seemed to spend every waking moment shoving food into his mouth, which is why she'd never really liked him. Not only that, he had a pointed face that resembled a long-tailed weasel's, the eyes dark and beady, the nose pink, and ears too big for his small head. When he smiled, his pointed teeth resembled fangs.

"You're from the Eti'gowane's lineage, aren't you?"

"Yes, Matron."

"*High* Matron," she corrected.

"Forgive me, High Matron." He bowed in apology.

"The Eti'gowane has been a good Matron of the Cornfields."

"It's kind of you to say so, High Matron."

The man seemed distracted, his eyes shifting around as though he expected monsters to emerge from the night shadows. She reached over to unhook her curtain from its peg. As it fell closed across her chamber, he vanished, but as the curtain swung, she glimpsed him slip his war club into his belt and draw a chert knife. An odd choice. Any warrior worth his reputation would have stood guard with his war club. It was more threatening.

At this moment, however, she didn't have the strength to care.

Kelek walked over and sank down on the deerhide-covered bench that lined the rear wall. Her chamber was large, four paces long by three wide. Pots and baskets nestled on the floor beneath the bench, and sacred masks hung upon the divider walls.

As she tiredly leaned her head back, a soft groan escaped her lips. The Wolf and Snipe clans had been especially vindictive today, going so far as to threaten to Outcast the entire Bear Clan, but she'd paid them little attention. It was the Bear Clan elders who had stunned her. For the first time in her life, her relatives had accused her of shaming them. It had been a difficult fight, almost unbearable.

"The old fools have no vision. If they'd leave me alone, I would make our clan legendary!"

She blinked up at the dried plants that hung from the roof poles. The corn husks had been peeled back from the ears and braided together into long ropes, allowing the kernels to dry faster. Each time someone walked by outside, his or her shadow danced over the corn braids, sunflower heads, and bean vines. Occasionally she heard soft voices, people briefly speaking with Hakowane.

Cold and desperate for sleep, Kelek didn't bother to undress. She stretched out on her sleeping bench and pulled the hides up over her cape.

Some time later—she couldn't say how long—Kelek was jerked from deep sleep by what sounded like someone entering her chamber. Her eyelids felt like granite weights as she fought to open them. The fires must have burned down to ashes. The only light in the longhouse came from the campfires of the dead. Streaming down through the smokeholes, their gleam coated Kelek's chamber like a faint wash of gray paint.

She blinked at the dimness, saw nothing, and closed her eyes again. The door curtain had probably just been carelessly brushed by Hakowane.

She was almost back to sleep when she heard someone breathing close by. Barely audible, the rhythmic puffs fluttered her hair across her cheeks. Like slow poison, terror crept through her veins. Her eyes jerked open.

Less than two hands away, wide feral eyes blinked down at her. She tried to scream, but a heavy hand clamped over her nose and mouth.

He whispered in her ear, "I have been instructed to tell you that I am not Wolf Clan. I am Bear Clan, sent by our clan elders."

He struck like lightning, the sharp knife slicing her throat in one clean stroke. When he removed his hand from her mouth, she tried to scream, but her lungs didn't seem to have air. For twenty heartbeats she flailed on her bench, while warm blood spurted over her shoulders and chest.

Her murderer stood by watching, apparently ordered to remain until it was over.

Anger filtered through her panic. *The Bear Clan bargained with the Wolf Clan. To prevent a war of retribution, they must have offered to eliminate the problem themselves . . .*

As her vision started to go gray and sparkling, her muscles relaxed and her body went featherlight, floating.

She faintly heard her door curtain whisper when her murderer left.

Forty-five

The Path of Souls glittered brilliantly across the dark night sky, sparkled through the forest, and reflected from the branches with a liquid-silver intensity. Voices and laughter rose from around the hundreds of campfires that scattered the valley below. The air felt warmer tonight, cold, but not bone-cold, which probably meant they had a few warm days coming. Winter solstice was still about two moons away. If they were lucky, they'd have more than a handful of unseasonably pleasant days before winter's frigid presence arrived in earnest.

Saponi lay on his belly in a dogwood thicket, staring down at Bur Oak Village. The palisades had been devastated. Glowing orange gaps flared as the breeze shifted. A short distance away, Yellowtail Village stood like a black burned-out husk.

"Gods, the battle was terrible. I really felt for them today." Disu, who lay stretched out beside him, shook his head. "I wonder how many they lost?"

Saponi didn't answer for a time. "More than Matron Jigonsaseh could afford to lose."

"That's for certain. If she lost only one-third of her trained warriors, that means she has less than two hundred left."

"Two hundred against perhaps one thousand Hills warriors . . . and there are another two thousand Mountain warriors on the way."

When they'd heard the story racing through Atotarho's camp, it had stunned them. Mountain warriors joining forces with their old enemy, the Hills People? One moon ago no one would have believed it possible. Not just because they'd spent half of last summer killing each other, but the Mountain People were in a bad way. The plague had hit them hardest of all. Many Traders had carried the tale far and wide. The Mountain People had been so sick they hadn't even been able to harvest their crops. Their corn had moldered in the fields, and their sunflowers been plucked clean by birds and squirrels. Any other crops that had survived had been taken in raids by their neighbors.

"I hate to say it, Saponi, but it's hard to imagine how the Standing Stone nation can survive another assault."

Saponi turned to look at his old friend. Disu had seen twenty-four summers. A thin, lanky man, he stood two heads taller than Saponi, but what Saponi lost in height, he made up for in muscles. His burly shoulders spread twice as wide as Disu's.

This was the first either of them had spoken since they'd made it to the southern hilltop at midnight, less than a hand of time ago. The future was just too terrible to think about.

"I believe in Sky Messenger's Dream, old friend," Saponi said with a sudden fervency. "I *believe* he can stop this war. Whether he can do it before his own people are gone . . . I do not know. Perhaps the destruction of his nation is what triggers the unfolding of his Dream. If it is, he'll pay a terrible price."

Disu hesitated. His hood, which lay upon his back, waffled in the wind, creating a soft thumping sound. "We're never going to make it back into Bur Oak Village with this food. You know that, don't you?"

He squinted at the campfires. "I know."

War Chief Negano had apparently decided to take no chances. He'd lost many warriors today. Though Saponi couldn't guess how many, at least two hundred bodies were visible in the flickering firelight. That meant many more lay freezing in the darkness beyond. Rather than moving his forces back to their camps across the valley, Negano must have known that he had to keep the noose tight, or Matron Jigonsaseh would manage to restock the village with food and water. The noose was tight indeed. Camped approximately one hundred paces from the walls, Negano's warriors completely encircled the village and the marsh. No one could get in or out.

Saponi shifted to brace himself on one elbow so he could look back over his shoulder at the twenty-eight warriors gathered in the shadows. Sixty packs of food made a dark hump behind them, piled in a small clearing surrounded by leafless maples. Soft voices eddied, his men talking over supper, finally able to eat after a long day of tireless effort. They couldn't build a fire, but they'd filled their fire pots with coals before they'd left Atotarho's camp. The scent of roasting crickets, being tossed with hot coals, wafted on the cold breeze. That had been the real find today. Ten pots of crickets! Negano must have had warriors out in the forest kicking over every pile of leaves to find them. When parched in ceramic bowls, the crickets had a crunchy exterior and creamy interior that tasted just like crab legs. His mouth watered. They were all starving. They'd spent most of the day hauling food into the forest, supposedly to transfer it to shadowed area beneath the trees where it would stay frozen. Instead, they'd filled as many packs as they could carry back, two each, and buried the rest beneath piles of leaves and branches: bags of nuts and acorns, venison haunches, and rabbits that had yet to be skinned.

Their mission today had been a great success. He hadn't lost a single warrior, nor had they been forced to kill any of their relatives in Atotarho's camp.

Disu propped his cheek on a fist, and stared at Saponi with tight eyes. "From what I could see today, they poured a lot of water on the palisade."

He left the question of *how much* to Saponi's reckoning. The glowing holes in the exterior palisade of Bur Oak Village stood as a mute testament; they'd probably been forced to use every drop they had to quench the flames. "Yes, and since we can't get back with our packs, they have very little food left, too."

As Wind Woman's daughter Gaha softly moved around the village, fanning the smoldering logs, reddish light wavered over the bodies piled against the base of the palisade. Including the dead from the battle six days ago—corpses they hadn't had time to bury—there had to be six or seven hundred bodies total. Even from his position on the hilltop, he could see the contorted arms and legs, bent-back heads, and gaping mouths. White teeth glistened. Over the next few days, as the temperature warmed up, the stench of rotting corpses would become unbearable.

If they have a few days, which I doubt.

Disu said, "How many do you think deserted tonight?"

"I counted a group of around one hundred trotting away up the trail before it got too dark to see. More probably left under the cover of night."

"I was surprised that Negano didn't try to stop them."

"He didn't want to split his army in half. People would have been forced to take sides. If he'd tried to stop them, another two or three hundred warriors would have sided with them and left, too."

"You're probably right. I always liked Negano. To tell you the truth, I feel sorry for him."

Saponi toyed with the grass beneath his fingers, absently stroking it while he thought. "Don't feel too sorry. His army still outnumbers the Standing Stone nation by at least three to one, and he has reinforcements coming."

Disu heaved a taut breath and sat up. "Well, there's nothing more we can do about it tonight. Let's go grab a bowl of roasted crickets before they're gone."

Forty-six

Sky Messenger

In the middle of the night, Gitchi growls softly, and I hear Hiyawento call, "Sky Messenger?"

I roll over and sleepily blink up at the three people standing over me. Hiyawento, Baji, and an unknown Landing warrior, a tall square-jawed man wearing a ragged buckskin cape, stare down at me. Hiyawento has his jaw clenched.

I sit up in my blankets and rub my eyes with the back of my hand. Gitchi lays on the foot of the blanket, his yellow eyes fixed on the Landing warrior. While he knows and trusts Hiyawento and Baji, this man poses a threat, and he knows it. "What's wrong? Where's Towa?"

Hiyawento squats beside me and props his war club across his knees. Exhaustion lines his tight eyes. "He's in charge of the guards tonight."

Below Hiyawento, I see men and women standing in a ring around the small hilltop with war clubs clutched in their hands. Their attention is focused on the people bedded down on the slopes below. It's dark. No campfires glow. Snores and coughs ride the wind that sweeps up the hillside.

Hiyawento extends a hand to the Landing warrior. "This is Deputy War Chief Tiyosh, formerly of Agweron Village." The man bows respectfully. I nod back. "We've been talking. We think you and Baji need to get away from here as soon as possible. If you run most of the night, you should be far ahead of the crowd by morning."

Baji kneels beside Hiyawento and gives me one of those distinctive, *don't argue* looks. Wind flutters long hair around her beautiful stern face. "Tiyosh says most of the people who followed you when you left Shookas Village are desperate. Their villages were just destroyed. They're sure the Mountain People are coming to kill them. You are their only hope."

Desperation can drive even the best of people to madness. "I understand, but how do you propose that we get out of here? We're surrounded."

"Yes, Prophet," Tiyosh says with soft reverence, "but most people are asleep. You and I are about the same height. I think if you exchange capes with me, and keep your hood pulled up to shield your face, you and War Chief Baji may be able to make it out without being recognized."

My limbs feel like dead weights as I throw back my blankets and rise to my feet. Hiyawento and Baji stand up and move to either side of me, protecting me. I hate being treated like a fragile pot . . . but I know they're right. I saw the glazed, almost stunned, looks in my followers' eyes, and felt them shoving each other just to get close enough to touch my clothing. I pull my cape over my head and hand it to Hiyawento to hold, while Tiyosh removes his own cape and gives it to me. As I slip it on, I ask, "How long will Tiyosh be forced to feign being me? I'm not comfortable with this. I'm putting him in danger."

Hiyawento looks at Tiyosh, who shrugs. "Before dawn, we will hit the trail and run hard. The new guards will keep Tiyosh surrounded so that no one can get a good look at him. Hopefully we will lose most of the crowd on the way."

"Before we do this, I want you to consider what the crowd will do when they discover Tiyosh is not me. They will feel betrayed."

Hiyawento's mouth curves into a half-smile, a determined expression I know well. He will do whatever it takes to keep me safe. He always has. "I have considered it. As has Tiyosh. All of your new guards discussed the matter thoroughly. We will tell them something. Now, you and Baji need to go. By the time you reach Bur Oak Village, we should be no more than a few hands of time behind you. I'll send a messenger ahead to tell you when we'll arrive."

"How will I know the message is from you, and not someone claiming to—"

"I'll send you this." Hiyawento's hand slowly drops to his shell-bead belt and he caresses it, his fingers slowly moving over the small human figures that decorate the front near the ties. Deep purple, they have childlike shapes. "I'll send my belt with the messenger so you know he speaks the truth."

Gitchi rises and stretches, preparing his aching joints for the run ahead. His yellow eyes and thick fur glow silver in the light cast by the campfires of the dead.

Through a heavy sigh, I say, "All right. I'll be expecting the Truth Belt. We'll see you there day after tomorrow."

Hiyawento's head dips in a firm nod. "Yes, you will."

As he hands my cape to Tiyosh, the man's expression slackens. He puts it on and smoothes it down as though it is a sacrament, a rare ritual object with a soul of its own that must be handled with great care.

Baji flips up her hood and gestures for me to do the same. I hesitantly comply. All of this . . . this ruse . . . makes me feel dishonest, as though I'm pretending to be something I am not.

Baji grabs Hiyawento in a bear hug, and says, "I'll take care of him."

Hiyawento hugs her back. "I know you will. I'll see you soon."

Baji scratches Gitchi's ears and gestures to the winding deer trail that leads down the steepest side of the hill, where only a few people are camped because of the slope. "Gitchi, you go first. I'll guard his back."

Gitchi looks at her with adoring eyes, then trots out into the starlight.

Forty-seven

Two hands of time before dawn, Baji lay snuggled beneath the blankets with Dekanawida's muscular arms around her. His soft breathing warmed her ear. They'd run until they'd started stumbling. As soon as they'd made camp at the base of a gray rock wall and crawled between the blankets, he'd fallen into a dead sleep.

Baji, on the other hand, had been staring out at the glistening forest, listening. The intoxicating far-off cry lilted through the darkness. It was especially powerful tonight, calling to her like a lover's summons, begging her to come. It had grown constant, echoing across the distances, sometimes barely audible, others times so loud it rang inside her as though the callers had their muzzles pressed to her ears.

At such times, Gitchi's gaze never left her.

The wolf lay close beside Baji, watching her as the campfires of the dead wheeled through the sky high above them. His yellow eyes were alert, attentive to the slightest change in her expression, looking up into her face with keen unfathomable interest. He seemed to be concentrating on her breathing, as though he greatly feared it might cease. Even when she tried to sleep, the strength of the old wolf's gaze woke her. Each time she blinked and yawned, his tail wagged, and his whole heart shone in his eyes.

Trying not to wake Sky Messenger, she eased her arm from beneath the blanket to scratch Gitchi's chest, and he sighed in that way that only a contented dog can. As she petted him, images fleeted across her souls. He'd been so small and scared when they'd found him tied up in that bag on the shore of the river outside of Bog Willow Village. She remembered it as though it had happened moments ago.

She, Odion, and Tutelo had heard Gitchi crying, and had followed the sound down to the riverbank. The shore had been strewn with refuse. Victorious warriors with packs of new plunder had cast their shabby old belongings on the ground just before they'd shoved off in their canoes. Threadbare packs and capes, blankets with too many stitched holes, and hide bags filled with who-knows-what, had littered the shore.

As they'd walked, a soft muffled "woof" erupted.

A short distance ahead, a sack wriggled. They'd all charged up the bank and encircled it. At the time, she'd seen twelve summers, Odion eleven, and Tutelo eight summers.

"Hurry, open it and let him out," Tutelo had urged. "There's no telling how long he's been in there. He may be dying of thirst."

Odion had hesitated, taking a few moments to gently pet the warm body inside. Barks had erupted as the sack had flopped around like a big dying fish.

Baji had taken Tutelo's hand, preparing to drag her away if the puppy emerged in a flying snarling bundle of fur.

As soon as Odion loosened the laces, a soft gray nose poked up through the opening. The little wolf had wriggled the top half of his lean body out onto Odion's lap and looked around with bright yellow eyes. He'd seen perhaps four or five moons.

"I'll bet the puppy was supposed to be dinner." Tutelo had said as she'd edged forward to pet the puppy's silken back. "He's the color of a ghost. Maybe his name was Ghost."

"Or *oki*," Baji had suggested.

Odion and Tutelo had turned to stare at her.

Oki were Spirits that inhabited powerful beings, including the seven Thunderers, rivers, certain rocks, valiant warriors, even lunatics. Oki could bring either good luck or bad. People who possessed supernatural powers—shamans, witches—were believed to have a companion spirit, an oki, whose power they could call upon to help them.

"He definitely has some special power," Odion had said, "or we'd never have found him. He called us to him. Oki sounds like a good name."

Tutelo had shaken her head vehemently. "I don't like that. What if somebody thinks he's an evil Spirit? If somebody's having a bad day, that name could cost him his life."

"Well . . . then think of something else," Odion had said.

Baji smiled at the memories.

Gitchi.

Yes, Gitchi. Baji had named him those many summers ago. *Gitchi Manitou* were words she'd heard from a Trader who'd come from north of Skanodario Lake. She had no idea what it meant, but she'd always liked it.

She lowered her hand to stroke his sore foreleg and Gitchi licked her fingers with his eyes half-closed in gratitude.

Gitchi had grown up on the war trail, and his white face testified that he was far older than the number of breaths he had drawn, or the long winter nights he'd slept curled beside Dekanawida. When Baji looked at him an old, old soul looked back, one that had witnessed far too much, and loved too deeply to ever be quite ordinary again.

Odion had been right. Gitchi did have a special power. She thought that maybe her souls, and his, were intertwined. Baji had been born Wolf Clan. Though Cord had adopted her into the Turtle Clan when she'd seen twelve summers, some part of her still heard the wolf songs that seeped up from the primeval darkness between her souls. Often, she wondered if Gitchi could hear them, too. It was a strange thing. There had been many nights last summer when she'd been lying in Dekanawida's arms, blinking dreamily into Gitchi's eyes, and she swore they had both drifted out of this world to somewhere beyond. Perhaps they'd sat together beside one of the campfires of the dead? She knew only that he was there with her, standing guard, keeping her safe. They'd scented the wind together, shared blankets, and listened to that far-off cry that Baji swore was the same cry she heard tonight. His devotion, in this life and the life beyond, was both wonderful and wrenching.

Last summer, she'd seen the effects firsthand when two

Flint warriors, Ogwed and Yondwi, had gotten into a fight on the war trail. Baji had been a deputy war chief. She'd stepped between them to shove them apart and started shouting at them to stop. Gitchi, as usual, was curled up on the ground at Dekanawida's feet ten paces away, but he'd been watching. Ignoring Baji, Ogwed had swung a fist into his opponent's temple, and Yondwi responded by grabbing Baji's shoulders and hurling her aside like a cornhusk doll so he could get to Ogwed. She'd hit the ground so hard it had knocked the wind from her lungs.

The other warriors standing around watching the fight heard neither snarl nor growl, but a sound that more closely resembled a soul-chilling bellow, and they'd seen Gitchi's gray body streak across the ten paces and become airborne, launched straight at Yondwi. Yondwi had been in the process of drawing back his arm to throw another punch, when Gitchi slammed into the chest, toppled him backward to the ground, and grabbed him by the throat. Yondwi lived only because Dekanawida had shouted, *"Gitchi, no!"*

While friends rushed to Yondwi's side to examine his bleeding neck, Gitchi had run circles around them, his fangs slathering foam, snarling ferociously. Every hair on his body had stood straight up. The threat had been clear: *Don't you ever touch Baji again.*

The story had traveled through every camp, up and down the war trails even into enemy villages where Gitchi's name was whispered in the same breath as *Oki* and *Witch Dog.* Gitchi had become legend. No man or woman dared lay a hand on Baji if Gitchi was in sight.

"Maybe I should have named you Oki after all," she murmured to him.

Gitchi wagged his tail and propped his muzzle on her

blanket so that his black nose almost touched Baji's. For a long time, they breathed each other's souls. In his yellow eyes she saw stars reflecting, one in particular, bright and faintly reddish.

When the mournful many-voiced cry blared again, Gitchi pricked his ears to listen, but his gaze remained fixed upon her. She felt strangely certain that he was convinced she could not possibly leave him as long as he could see her with his own eyes.

Baji gently slid forward to hug him. His thick fur smelled of old leaves and campfires. "You're a good friend," she whispered.

Gitchi licked her shoulder and vented a deep sigh.

In a sleepy voice, Dekanawida whispered, "Are you awake?"

"Yes, but you should sleep."

As she lay down again, he shifted to cup his body against her, bringing his knees up behind hers, and encircling her with his muscular arms.

"Why are you awake?" he murmured. "What are you thinking about?"

Baji's gaze drifted upward to the Road of Light glittering across the belly of Brother Sky. "I was looking at the fork in the trail."

Confused, he said, "Hmm?"

"The fork in what your people call the Path of Souls, and mine call the Road of Light."

He nuzzled his chin against her long hair. "What about it?"

"Do you believe there's a bridge at the fork? A bridge where all the animals you've ever known wait for you? The animals who loved you protect you and help you across, while the animals you've hurt chase you, trying to force you to fall off the bridge in the eternal darkness below."

She felt him smile. "I believe."

Baji's gaze returned to Gitchi. He was still staring at her with that worried expression, something akin to grief, in his yellow eyes. She reached out to stroke the white hair beside his left eye.

"Do you think the animals call to you?"

Dekanawida's arms tightened around her. "You mean just before you die?"

"Or after."

Where his wrist rested just below her heart, she felt his pulse speed up, thumping against her ribs. After ten heartbeats, he firmly said, "First, I've never heard any of our storytellers say that. Second, everyone saw you today. *Everyone*. Third, why did you ask? Do you hear something?"

Baji grasped his arm and pulled it more tightly around her. "No, but a holy man told me that once. I was just wondering if you'd ever heard of such a thing?"

"No, and I really wish you'd stop thinking about death."

"Me?" she said in a teasing voice. "You're the one who keeps Dreaming the end of the world. How can you expect me to think of anything else?"

Offhandedly, he replied, "Well, there is that," and tenderly kissed her hair. Then his lips moved down to her throat, warm and inviting.

Baji rolled to her back to look up into his eyes and found so much love shining in those brown depths that her heart ached. She smoothed her fingers down his side and slipped them beneath his cape and shirt to touch his bare skin. "My head is much better, you know."

He reached around to feel her head wound, frowned a moment, then said, "Yes. It is."

They laughed together.

As Grandmother Moon rose above the dark hills, the ghostly pewter landscape took on an opalescent sheen that painted every swell and hollow with an edge of silver fire.

Baji looked up into his face, haloed by short black hair, and her gaze slipped across his slender nose and blunt chin, coming to rest at the lines that cut deeply around his eyes. He had seen only twenty-three summers, but so many had been difficult. Her hand lifted to massage his left shoulder, broken by a war club when he'd seen eleven summers. It still hurt him on cold winter nights.

He whispered, "Baji, don't think about those days," and rolled over to kiss her.

As his lips grew more passionate, she yielded completely to him, letting herself drown in the tingling warmth of his hands gliding over her breasts, trailing down her waist to her thighs, lifting her war shirt and whispering like ermine fur across her bare skin. *One moment of perfect happiness . . .*

As if a fever had been lifted from her, she wept.

His whisper sounded loud in the buried stillness of the moonlit night. "Are you all right?"

"Happy." She wrapped her arms around his back and pulled him hard against her, holding him desperately. "I want this to last forever."

He kissed her and said against her lips, "I'll do my best."

Their touching drifted with the silence of river mist into love. As Grandmother Moon rose higher in the sky, her light brightened and streamed through the forest. Baji never closed her eyes. She watched his leisurely movements repeat in vast amorphous shadows on the rock wall to her right. Gitchi kept wagging his bushy tail, and Baji kept smiling at him. All the way to the enchanted lavender dawn, she ached with joy.

Forty-eight

Kwahseti stood beside Gwinodje on the catwalk of Canassatego Village, overlooking the main trail below. Six hundred men and women with bows aimed, manned the catwalk around them. Another four hundred lined the trail that led to the village, standing in neat rows. Their nocked bows glimmered in the newborn sunlight that filtered across the valley. In the distance, two clan matrons, one from the Wolf Clan and one from the Bear Clan, walked at the head of a procession of approximately two hundred warriors—enough to protect the matrons, but not enough to threaten Canassatego Village. *No show of force. Interesting.*

A messenger had arrived late last night informing them that the Hills nation would be sending a delegation to negotiate with the New Hills nation. They'd spent most of the night discussing what they would say. Gwinodje wore a plain doeskin cape with no decorations, as did Kwahseti. If they were forced to become a separate nation, they would immediately change their cape designs, and wanted to foster no wrong ideas about their loyalty in the minds of the delegation from Atotarho Village.

Gwinodje gripped the palisade. "Is that Yi? Her white cape has red paw prints."

Short gray hair blew around Kwahseti's eyes when she turned to look at Gwinodje. Her friend's heart-shaped face had flushed with excitement. "Yes, that's Yi."

Leafless maples and a few towering chestnuts swayed along the path, casting windblown shadows over the delegation's distinctive capes.

Kwahseti scrutinized the face she saw in the white hood. Yi had seen forty-eight summers. Silver strands glittered in her short black hair. She walked with her back straight, her bearing stately, demanding respect. Deep wrinkles cut around her mouth and across her forehead. Yi had her gaze focused on the catwalk where Kwahseti and Gwinodje stood, already taking command. In clan meetings, Yi traditionally said little, but each careful word had a knifelike quality, cutting to the heart of the matter.

Kwahseti was of Yi's lineage, but she lifted her chin and stared back at the leader of her ohwachira with defiance. Kwahseti had been instructed by the Ruling Council of the New People of the Hills to give no ground until she knew where the Old Hills nation stood on two issues: the position of the High Matron, and the Peace Alliance.

Kwahseti leaned over the palisade and called, "War Chief Thona, allow only the matrons inside the gates. Their warriors remain outside. No exceptions."

He craned his neck to look up at her. The web of scars on his face had a white sheen. "But what if they wish to have guards, Matron?"

"As a sign of good faith, we agreed to speak with them, but we owe them nothing. No guards, Thona."

Thona bowed obediently. "Yes, Matron."

As Yi approached, her eyes narrowed, and fixed upon Kwahseti. Kwahseti did not bow in respect, as was customary. She kept her back stiff and straight. A slight smile touched Yi's lips.

Yi called, "Matron Kwahseti, we wish you a pleasant morning." She extended a hand to the Bear Clan matron standing beside her. "This is Little Matron Adusha."

Without further delay, Kwahseti said, "A pleasant morning to both of you. Order your warriors to lay down their weapons."

Yi stared at her with her mouth open. When she finally found her voice, she cried, "That is an *outrageous* demand. Surely you don't expect us to leave our war party completely vulner—"

"We do, Matron Yi. Your forces attacked us only a few days ago." Kwahseti's hand swept across the vista. "As you can see from our charred palisade and the freshly dug graves to the east of the village, you killed many of our people."

Yi's mouth pressed into a hard white line. Indignant, Yi's face turned ugly. She looked like she might turn around and leave. But after five heartbeats, she called, "War Chief, order your warriors to lay down their weapons."

A commotion rose across the field, disgruntled warriors crying out in opposition . . . but they did it. Clattering sounded as bows, quivers, war clubs, and other weapons were all placed on the ground.

Kwahseti said, "War Chief Thona, allow the matrons inside our gates, but only the matrons."

"What?" Yi cried. "I will not enter this village without guards!"

"You will, Yi, if you wish to address the Ruling Council

of the New People of the Hills. Our wounds are still bleeding. We will allow no enemy warriors inside these gates."

After a staring match where Yi's eyes blazed like freshly flaked mahogany chert, she said, "Very well. Open the gates."

Kwahseti nodded to Thona who pulled the gates open just wide enough for them to enter one at a time. After Yi and Adusha slid through, he closed them tight, and the warriors dropped the locking plank into place with a loud thump.

Gwinodje started to hurry down to meet them, but Kwahseti subtly gripped her arm to stop her. "Make them wait for us. They are not our leaders. We are not part of their nation."

Gwinodje wet her lips nervously. "You're right."

Kwahseti and Gwinodje continued to stand on the catwalk, watching as their four hundred warriors completely encircled Yi's two-hundred-strong escort. As expected, the Old Hills warriors called and glared threateningly. The New Hills warriors had been ordered to say nothing to their enemies. They stood in perfect silence with arrows nocked and ready to be loosed at their enemies' hearts. It was a magnificent sight.

"All right, Gwinodje. You lead the way to the council house—slowly. We are in no hurry. They requested this meeting, we agreed with reluctance. I'll walk at Yi's side. Since she has always been the leader of my ohwachira, I owe her that much."

"I understand."

They climbed down the ladder to the plaza and walked shoulder-to-shoulder toward the two enemy matrons. Yi, her eyes half-slitted, watched Kwahseti's every move.

Little Matron Adusha had a thin face and sharply pointed nose. Her expression was subdued, even apologetic. Kwahseti didn't know her well, but she'd always liked her.

When Kwahseti and Gwinodje stopped before them, Adusha bowed and remained down for a long time before she straightened to face them. In a soft voice, she said, "I offer my deepest condolence for your recent losses, matrons. Let me tell you that the Bear Clan requested this meeting. We beg that you hear what we have to say."

"We will hear you, Adusha. Please follow Matron Gwinodje to the council house." She extended a hand toward the round log structure squatting to the left of the plaza along the eastern wall.

Adusha looked at the hundreds of people crowding the plaza, and swallowed hard at the hatred that contorted her relatives' faces. Canassatego Village had just finished burying its dead. Their hearts were raw. They had no love for these women who, as members of the Ruling Council of the Old People of the Hills, had undoubtedly given the orders for the attack that killed their loved ones.

Kwahseti walked to Yi's side and gestured for her to follow Adusha and Gwinodje. Yi complied.

As they walked, Yi spoke in a quiet voice, for Kwahseti's ears alone, "Where is Matron Zateri?"

"*High* Matron Zateri is not available today."

Yi gave her a look that would have frozen lava. "Are you telling me that she refuses to meet with us? That is unaccept—"

"You have no rights here, Yi. None at all. If our High Matron deems it unnecessary to—"

"The former Bear Clan High Matron is dead."

Kwahseti stopped dead in her tracks to stare wide-eyed at Yi. *"Dead?"*

Yi glanced around, studying the inquisitive faces of the people crowding in around them. "Let's keep walking. There may be Bear Clan members standing close. They need to hear this from their own clan. I just wanted you to know that I, too, keep my promises. I gave you my oath that I would do what I could to help you."

Kwahseti stared dumbly at Yi, not certain what to say. *Kelek is dead?* She felt herself deflating like a water bag being emptied.

In a friendly gesture, Yi slipped her arm through Kwahseti's, and they continued toward the council house as though close companions of many trials—which they had been until recently.

Blood pounded in Kwahseti's ears. "How did it happen?"

Yi murmured, "The Bear Clan has honor. We brought forward the witnesses. When they grasped the problem, they took care of it."

"Because they wished to avoid a blood feud with the Wolf Clan?"

Kwahseti stood one head taller than Yi. When Yi tilted her head to look up at Kwahseti, the bruised crescents beneath her dark eyes shown purple. She'd endured many sleepless nights of late. "No one wanted it to come to that, least of all our clan."

As they rounded the curve of the council house and the leather door curtain came into view, Kwahseti asked, "So, she's dead. What now?"

Yi's head waffled. "That remains to be seen. Are you

of my lineage, or have you founded your own lineage, as well as your own nation?"

Kwahseti's chest moved with a low disbelieving laugh. She walked ahead, leaving Yi to catch up with her. Four guards stood outside the entry, including War Chief Waswanosh. She dipped her head to him, drew the entry curtain aside, and held it back while Yi entered the council house. Yi exchanged a potent glance with her before she stepped inside.

Kwahseti turned to Waswanosh. "For the moment, this is a closed council meeting. Let no one enter without permission from a member of the Ruling Council."

"Of course, Matron."

Kwahseti let the curtain fall closed behind her. As it swayed, dawn light flashed through the council house, illuminating the three circles of benches around the central fire, and the fifty council members seated upon them. Yi had not waited for her. She'd resolutely marched down the central aisle alone and gone to stand beside Gwinodje and Adusha in the orange gleam of the flames. They made an interesting trio. Gwinodje's slender frame looked childlike standing stiffly between the two taller women. Gwinodje and Adusha both had coal black hair that almost disappeared in the darkness, while the silver threads in Yi's hair glittered like sunlit webs.

Kwahseti silently walked forward to take her place on the first ring of benches with the other elders from Riverbank Village. Chief Riverbank sat to her right. He had seen fifty-four summers. Wispy white hair clung to his freckled scalp. He was a large man, larger than life, black-eyed, ominous, and slow-talking, he'd lost his entire family in last moon's plague, then he'd been forced to abandon his village, leaving it to be burned to the ground. Yet he looked at her with clear calm eyes, ready for anything. Over the past five summers, since Kwahseti had become the Village Matron, she had come to appreciate him greatly. He would speak his heart. Always his heart. He engaged in neither guile nor fits of temper.

Riverbank gave her a questioning look, as though he sensed she had news.

Kwahseti beckoned him to lean down, and whispered in his ear, *"The Bear Clan High Matron is dead at the hands of her own clan."*

Riverbank drew back suddenly. He gazed at her as if for confirmation. Kwahseti nodded, and he squeezed his eyes closed and bowed his head. She couldn't tell if it was in mourning or overwhelming relief.

Kwahseti had both galloping through her veins, so perhaps he did, as well.

Gwinodje raised her hands to the assembly, and called, "We come together at the request of the Bear Clan of the Old People of the Hills. Matron Yi from Atotarho Village and Little Matron Adusha of Turtleback Village have been empowered to speak on behalf of the old Ruling Council."

Every time Gwinodje had used the word "old," Yi had flinched. She squared her shoulders and stared boldly out at the congregation of elders seated on the benches around her.

Gwinodje turned to Yi. "Matron Yi? As the eldest great-grandmother here, would you address this council first?"

Yi extended a hand to Adusha. "I yield the privilege to Little Matron Adusha of the Bear Clan."

Gwinodje nodded for Adusha to proceed.

Adusha wet her lips and stepped forward. As she clasped

her hands before her, she called out, "I believe, regardless of the terrible injustices that have been committed by a handful of traitors, that this is one nation, and I will address you, with all the love in my heart, as my relatives."

Whispers passed around the benches. Many heads shook violently. A general din of competing voices arose.

Gwinodje lifted her hands again. "Please, Little Matron Adusha entered our village unarmed and without guards. She deserves our utmost courtesy. I ask that you listen carefully to her words before you make any judgments."

The assembly reluctantly hushed, anxiously awaiting the next volley from the other side.

Adusha seemed to have prepared herself for the hostility. She mildly looked around, meeting and holding gazes as she scanned the fifty people seated upon the benches around the fire. In a deeply apologetic voice, she continued, "You were betrayed. We know that now."

Another flurry of voices rose and dwindled.

Adusha continued, "I am not your enemy. I give you my oath. I was one of the witnesses who testified on *your* behalf before our Ruling Council. You see, I was there in the Wolf Longhouse when Matron Zateri's grandmother was murdered." She patiently waited until the voices died down. "Though I didn't know who he was at the time, I saw the terrible witch, Ohsinoh, enter her chamber. He left very quickly, and when we went to check on the High Matron we found her dead."

The council house hummed with conversation. Rumors that High Matron Tila had been murdered had been flying about like summer bats, but no one in the New Hills nation knew their truth until this moment. Kwahseti was as stunned as everyone else.

Adusha called, "Let me tell you what conclusions our Ruling Council has come to after listening to many witnesses brought forward by the Wolf Clan elders."

Yi inhaled a deep breath and slowly let it out. Her wrinkled face had rearranged into somber lines.

"First, Atotarho's personal guards testified that they had accompanied the Chief to the Bear Clan longhouse in Atotarho Village the night before the High Matron's murder. The Chief told the Bear Clan matron that he had 'a proposition' he thought she would appreciate. It seems clear that in exchange for retaining his position as chief, and being given free rein to make war on distant nations, he offered to claim that the murdered High Matron had named the Bear Clan matron as her successor." Only the crackle of the fire filled her pause. All eyes focused unblinking on Adusha. "Matron Zateri of Coldspring Village is clearly the rightful High Matron of *our* nation."

While the Ruling Council retained its dignity, the people who'd had their ears pressed to the council house walls, listening to the proceedings, burst into cheers. A riot of hoots and cries erupted, along with the sound of pounding feet, as the news swept Canassatego Village.

Kwahseti felt slightly weak in the knees. Chief Riverbank leaned to whisper to her, "I hope they know that the Bear Clan High Matron was only part of the problem."

"We will make sure they know."

Yi looked pointedly at Adusha. The Little Matron bowed deferentially and stepped back, yielding the floor to Matron Yi.

Yi walked to the edge of the benches. "The former matron of the Bear Clan, who stole the position of High Matron, is dead."

Cries of joy exploded in the plaza, while the council house was filled with gasps and murmuring.

Yi raised her voice. "There is—as you all know—another matter to be considered. Chief Atotarho. While our Ruling Council refused to send him the two thousand warriors he requested, he remains in Standing Stone country with a large war party intent upon crushing the Standing Stone People once and for all. What is your opinion of this?"

"She asks our opinion?" Riverbank noted with a frown. "As though we have already agreed to reunification and are part of her nation?"

Little Matron Tarha of the Beaver Clan rose to her feet. Hunched and gray-haired, she used her walking stick to prop up her thin body. "Before we discuss Chief Atotarho, I wish to address another matter. Riverbank Village and Coldspring are both gone, destroyed by *your warriors,* Matron Yi, and Canassatego Village barely survived. Did the Old Hills council order the destruction of our villages?"

Hateful voices rumbled around the circumference of the house.

Yi answered, "Blessed Spirits, no, Little Matron. Our council knew *nothing* of these attacks until warriors came streaming into Atotarho Village carrying their wounded. From what the warriors told us, Atotarho ordered the attacks to punish your villages for turning against him during the Bur Oak battle. It was completely Atotarho's decision."

Kwahseti thought about it for a time before she rose to her feet. "If it pleases the council, I would speak on the issue of Atotarho and his war party."

Matron Tarha sat down, and Gwinodje said, "Please do so, Matron Kwahseti."

Kwahseti didn't look at Yi. Instead, she turned around to face the other council members. "Atotarho is utterly mad. I don't know when he lost his soul, but it's been wandering aimlessly in the forest for at least thirty summers that I can recall. He must be stopped. As you all know, High Matron Zateri sent one hundred warriors back to Bur Oak Village to help protect them, as she promised she would do, but if Matron Yi is telling us the whole truth, it will not be enough to stop Atotarho from wiping the Standing Stone nation from the face of the world."

Kwahseti turned back around and stared directly at Yi. Yi's face had gone rigid. "So, we ask you, Matron Yi, will the *old* Ruling Council join the new alliance and send warriors to reinforce ours . . . or does it prefer to wait and see how many of its enemies Atotarho can kill?"

Yi lifted her chin and gazed down her nose at Kwahseti, but a tiny grudging smile of respect tugged at her lips. "The Ruling Council has already carefully considered this matter. We will *tentatively* agree to join the Peace Alliance, and order our forces to support yours, but only, *only,* if you agree to reunify our nation."

From the rear of the house, a flash of dawn light filled the chamber as someone entered. Kwahseti turned to see Zateri gracefully marching forward. Her long white cape gleamed in the firelight. The blue paw prints around the bottom swayed with her steps. The High Matron stopped in front of Yi with her feet spread and her fists clenched. In a powerful voice, raised for all to hear, Zateri asked, "If we agree, will the Ruling Council send word to Atotarho that his people have declared him Outcast, and he is a member of the walking dead? He must become a man with no name!"

A cacophony of shouts and supporting voices exploded

inside the council house, and more outside. The entire village roared.

One of Yi's delicate black brows lifted. She gave Zateri a challenging look. In an equally strong voice, she called, "Only the full council of matrons has the right to take back his name and depose him from his position. If you rejoin the nation, and undergo the Requickening Ceremony to accept your grandmother's Spirit, I give you my oath that I will support that motion in council. But first, *High Matron*"—the assembly hissed in response to her calling Zateri the High Matron of the nation, which forced Yi to hold up a hand to get their attention—"let's make this nation whole again."

Every nerve in Kwahseti's body tingled with shock. Zateri stood like a small statue. Her cape was so still it appeared to be carved of white marble. Her face showed no give.

Gwinodje edged forward to whisper, "Blessed gods, Zateri, this is what we've been praying for."

When Yi heard Gwinodje's words, some of the fire went out of her eyes. She reached out to place a gentle hand upon Zateri's shoulder, and softly said, "You are not my enemy. You never have been. If your people agree to reunification, we can immediately send a runner to War Chief Negano telling him to use our army to support the alliance. But it will take almost two days, running day and night, for him to get there. We must do this quickly, Zateri. Or we will be too late."

Forty-nine

Sky Messenger

Weary. We've run almost straight through. . . .

As the slanting rays of sundown filter through the trees, amber-tinted mist seeps up from the piles of old leaves that cover the forest floor and twines around the bases of the maples like gossamer vines. It is so quiet. Baji and I run side-by-side down the trail that leads to Bur Oak Village, listening to the sound of our moccasins striking earth. Gitchi trots behind Baji, staying right at her heels, as though he senses she's in danger. We have no idea what lurks in the forest ahead. Three more rises to go, and we will know for certain if Tagohsah told the truth and Atotarho's army surrounds Bur Oak Village. Smoke fills the air, but this far away it is faint. It may come from the fire hearths in the longhouses, not from enemy campfires. My heart thunders in anticipation.

Sweat mats my black hair to my temples and soaks the hide of my shirt, trickling down my sides. Warmth like this two moons before winter solstice is very odd, almost supernatural. By early morning we'd removed our capes and tied them around our waists. Tiny damp curls fringe Baji's forehead, but the rest of her long hair flies around her shoulders in sinuous glistening locks. Her bow and quiver sway with her motions. She has tied her arrows together to keep them from rattling, and carries her war club in both hands, clutched across her chest for balance. Her candid black eyes scan the trees incessantly.

As I watch her, my heart aches. It seems impossible that we are separated by six hands distance. I feel her presence like a physical thing, a warm sea swirling around me, penetrating my body, washing against my souls in languid waves. We are both exhausted. I have no ability for long complex thoughts. The trail has turned into a series of precious moments . . . light dancing on the curve of her cheek . . . snatches of birdsong falling around us, spiraling down from the branches like wing seeds . . . the heart-numbing scent of her hair . . . my body sulking, longing . . . memories of silken textures . . . of skin sliding, inflaming the darkness.

The sunset-varnished air grows cool as evening comes, stroking the fevered flesh beneath my shirt. The odor of hot earth slaked with mist is strong. I breathe it in as though my lungs can't get enough and try not to let my worries overwhelm me.

Blessed gods, I love her. Since she's been at my side, I haven't had the Dream. What does that mean? Is her presence enough to stop the horror from unfolding? Or . . . is her presence something else?

In the hundreds of times the Dream has come to me, I have never seen her there with me at the end. The soot of the dying world does not darken her face as it does Hiyawento's. I never hear her voice or feel her touch. The possibility that she dies before the final events begin is too much to bear. It haunts me, gnawing at my vitals like a wild beast. I will do whatever I must to protect her . . . no matter the cost.

Nor have I seen Shago-niyoh there, or heard The Voice seeping from the air around me. Have I done something wrong? Is he gone forever?

We crest the swell in the trail and plunge down the other side into a hollow filled with oaks and dry ferns that *shish* when Gaha softly breathes across the land.

Baji glances at me. I feel it like a huge hand squeezing my heart. "You have to stop worrying about me."

"How did you know I was—"

"Dekanawida, I know every expression you're capable of."

"Well, that's unnerving."

"Get used to it. Even if I die I'm going to haunt you forever."

"Promise?"

"Absolutely," she says with such dire certainty it makes me laugh.

Tension drains from my exhausted muscles, leaving me feeling slightly light-headed. The world takes on a shimmer.

"Can you feel it?" she asks.

"Yes, we're headed into it."

"What does it feel like to you?" Her head tilts in curiosity.

I think about how to describe it. The dark tingling sensation of Power swells and eddies through the trees. "It's a . . . fire . . . searing my veins. I . . ."

Baji suddenly cocks her head and her eyes go wide as she stares to the west with such longing that it tears my heart. It's as though she sees the Blessed Ancestors marching over the hills, coming right at us in a vast spectral army.

"What's wrong, Baji?"

Her smile is heartrending. "Nothing's wrong. I just thought I heard something."

Gitchi suddenly goes stone still in the trail, and the hair on the back of his neck rises into stiff bristles. Baji and I both stumble to a stop. His yellow eyes are focused unblinking on something. . . .

As though they emerge from the Land of the Dead, the warriors seem to step from nothingness into this world of rich amber light. While I only see twenty or so, more move out in the trees. I hear their legs threshing ferns, coming. It sounds like thousands. These men and women have been on the trail for many hard days. Each dusty face has sleepless bloodshot eyes, and a greasy mop of mourning hair. Walking skeletons in windblown rags. Ghastly eyes that seem too huge for bony faces. As they draw back their nocked bows, emaciated muscles tremble in arms that once bulged through war shirts.

"Mountain warriors," I whisper.

Gitchi lets out a vicious growl and starts barking, preparing to defend us with his life.

Baji shouts, "Gitchi down! Stop it!"

The old wolf obeys instantly, sitting close at her side, but he can't suppress the barely audible deep-throated growls that vibrate his throat.

A big man pushes through the crowd of warriors. A dark cold man with ghastly scars, his right eye is missing, plucked out by an enemy long ago. The socket has been sewn closed and creates a shriveled pucker in his face.

"Blessed gods, that's Yenda," I murmur to Baji.

"Let's show them our empty hands."

We both slowly lift our arms.

From out of a locked chamber deep inside me, the sound

of shrieks rise . . . *Father drags us out of our beds and orders us to run . . . burning longhouses . . . screaming people racing through the firelit darkness . . . dead bodies. Then standing in the forest, clutching my eight-summers-old sister's hand, stunned, as enemy warriors round us up and march us away . . .*

At the command of the man who now stands before me.

Yenda, now called Chief Wenisa, led the war party that destroyed Yellowtail Village when I'd seen eleven summers. He is the reason Wrass, Tutelo, and I were captured and sold to Gannajero.

For a time, Yenda just stares at us, as though trying to confirm a suspicion.

I've fought against him many times. Bitter and angry, he is a brilliant strategist, careful to a fault, but slippery as an eel, a man who prefers to achieve his goals through torture rather than negotiation. He has no patience for words. He's built his reputation by destroying opponents.

He cocks his head in a birdlike manner, and stares at me with one blazing eye. "I know you."

More warriors emerge from the trees. It's forty to two, and increasing. Now or never . . .

I shout, "Baji, take Gitchi and run!" as I launch myself directly at the horde in front of me, roaring like a madman, hopefully distracting them long enough for Baji to escape.

"Shoot the dog!" a man shouts. "Quickly! It's getting away!"

Arrows hiss, loosed from too many bows to count. I don't make it ten strides before Mountain warriors fall upon me like starving panthers, dragging me to the ground. Fists knock the wind out of me. Feet slam my sides and face. I'm rolling, fighting.

Yenda calls, "Don't kill him!" and strides up to glare at me. "Yes, I know you, Deputy War Chief *Sky Messenger.*"

My name flits through the war party in gasps and blurts.

Yenda lifts a hand to his warriors. "Hear me! We have just captured the infamous Standing Stone Prophet! The one known as the human False Face!"

Like a flock of frightened grouses, warriors scuttle backward to get away from me, and a cacophony of hisses and disbelieving voices erupt, filling the air.

Yenda stalks around me, smiling in diabolical glee. "You have all been afraid of this"—he thrusts a hand at me—"*this* man! Look at him. He's pathetic! He can't even defend himself."

His warriors apparently do not believe him. There is a rush of men and women retreating through the forest. Twigs and branches crack in their wakes as they flee.

Yenda roars, "You weak fools! Come back here!"

When they do not, he turns upon me like a ravening wolf. "Look at him! All of you. He has no Power. He's just a man!"

At the edge of my vision, I glimpse Yenda's war club slicing the air. He brings it down on my skull with a crack that every warrior nearby seems to feel in his teeth. Men and women flinch. Then I am hauled to my feet again, half-conscious and disoriented, still struggling. A futile bellow rises from my lungs and echoes down the trail.

With a low chilling laugh, Yenda orders, "Let's drag him to Matron Jigonsaseh. She may wish to gaze one last time upon her dying son."

Fifty

The sound of distant voices woke Negano from a dead sleep. As he blinked up at the glittering Path of Souls, he moved his stiff limbs. His exhausted body longed to return to slumber. If he just closed his eyes, he'd be asleep again in less than five heartbeats. He felt himself sinking back and down, his muscles relaxing. . . .

Then Chief Atotarho's voice carried: "I don't believe it! I sent two of my best warriors to kill him. Are you sure it's him? How would you . . ."

A man may have answered, but Negano didn't hear the response.

He exhaled tiredly and rolled to his side to look out across the dark vista where warriors slept wrapped in blankets and capes. Tree-filtered moonlight fell across their bodies in glowing streaks. When the siege had ended, his surviving warriors had fallen into their blankets like lumps of clay. Only a handful of campfires burned. The night had been so warm that fires had been allowed to die and hadn't been restoked. These were probably breakfast fires, which meant the warriors had been out hunting the darkness for owls and flying squirrels, and the mice that scampered through the piles of old leaves, anything to fill their bellies.

Thirty paces down the slope, in the very center of the camp, a ring of warriors surrounded Atotarho. He could make out Nesi, because he towered over everyone else, and Atotarho was unmistakable. The elderly Chief stood propped on his walking stick with his black cape flapping around him. The rattlesnake skins braided into his gray hair winked eerily in the moonlight.

Atotarho continued, ". . . and if your army arrived last night, where is it? These games are foolishness. Tell Chief Wenisa . . . speak with him . . . no more messengers."

A short gaunt man, barely visible in the moonlight, bowed deeply and trotted away.

Negano forced himself to sit up. Gods, he longed to go back to sleep, but the mention of Wenisa's name meant the Mountain People had arrived. He didn't see them out there, but they must be close, perhaps bedded down in the valley of corpses to the west of Bur Oak Village. He shifted to look in that direction.

Two hundred paces away, down the hill, Bur Oak Village wavered in and out of sight, cloaked by the downy mist that rose from Reed Marsh and rolled across the valley bottom like moonlit clouds. The village was completely dark. Matron Jigonsaseh probably didn't want to fire-blind her warriors, just in case Negano decided to launch a night attack, or perhaps she was saving wood. Though that seemed unlikely. She must know that today would be the last day of the Standing Stone nation. Her people weren't going to need wood. By midmorning at the latest, they would be dead or slaves. It was a miracle, a testament to her skill, that they had managed to survive as long as they had. He was fairly certain he could lay the blame for the destruction of his food supplies at her feet. He shook his head as grudging respect filled him.

Nesi said, "I don't like this. Wenisa is a weasel, he can't be trust . . ."

Negano strained to hear more. When he couldn't, he dragged himself to his feet and straightened his cape. The unbelievable warmth of the night had made him sweat. His war shirt stuck to his chest in clammy folds. In a rumpled line on the eastern horizon, the faintest hint of blue gleamed. Soon, dawn would overwhelm the black pools of moon shadow that splotched the valley.

He reached down to pick up his weapons. While he'd slept in his weapons belt, he'd removed and placed his quiver and bow beside him, within reach. It took all of his strength to bend down, grab them, and sling them over his shoulder.

As he started down the slope for Atotarho's circle, he saw two warriors off to his right, moving through the camp, apparently kicking men and women awake. Even in the dim moonlight, he could see blankets flying when feet connected—probably warriors scrambling up and throwing off their blankets. It annoyed him. Everyone except the sentries should be allowed to sleep for as long as they could. Who had given the order to wake the army?

His gaze returned to Atotarho, and his brows drew together. Negano had lost another three-hundred-forty-two warriors yesterday. He wouldn't know for certain until dawn how many more had died from wounds during the night . . . but he suspected he had perhaps six hundred fighters left, and though severely damaged, the Bur Oak palisades still stood. Even with two thousand Mountain warriors as reinforcements, many more of his warriors would lose their lives today.

"War Chief?" a man called from his right.

Negano turned to see a young warrior, sixteen summers, trotting through the moonlight. The youth had a lean hungry face with shoulder-length black hair. His dark eyes looked huge. "What is it, Yekonis?"

The man slowed to a halt two paces away, as though he wanted some distance between them. "War Chief, I don't know how to tell you this. Tarha and I were walking across the camp when we noticed that many of the bundles of blankets on the ground were too small to be sleeping people. We started kicking them over." The man spread his arms in a helpless gesture. "They're gone, War Chief."

Negano tried to focus his foggy thoughts. "Who's gone?"

"The warriors. Our warriors. Some time in the night they formed their blankets into human-shaped bundles, probably hoping to fool us long enough that they could get far away before we discovered their ruse. They—"

Negano lurched forward to grip his shoulder hard. "How many fled?"

Yekonis nervously licked his lips. "I don't know. We've only just begun searching. We've discovered about seventy so far. I thought I should come and tell you before we continued."

Negano's fingers dug into Yekonis' shoulder. Did they have enough of an army left to defend itself? The ramifications could be deadly. "Does anyone else know about this?"

"I don't think so, but I can't be cer—"

"*Tell no one.* Do you understand? No one! When you've finished your count, report to me."

"Yes, War Chief."

Negano released him and Yekonis trotted back to join Tarha. Their faint upset voices carried through the moonlight. A short while later they returned to kicking over empty blankets.

Dear gods, I should have known. After I put down the food riot yesterday, the disgruntled warriors gathered into a knot and talked long into the night. They planned this well. . . .

Negano lifted his eyes heavenward for several stunned moments. As the blue of dawn seeped across the sky, the campfires of the dead began to fade to soft twinkles, and the Path of Souls dimmed.

Gods, this was too terrible to think about. He felt lightheaded as he turned and plodded down the hill.

Before he entered Atotarho's circle, he heard Nesi say, "Blessed Ancestors, is that the Mountain army?"

Negano swung around. As he squinted, trying to make out the movements he saw along the tree line, a premonition of calamity filled him. From three sides, Mountain warriors with nocked bows slid from the trees and slowly started forward, hemming in Atotarho's camp. The only side left open was the eastern edge of their camp which stretched along a wavy line just out of bow range of the warriors on the Bur Oak catwalks.

Blood surged in Negano's veins as the Mountain warriors closed in. He shouted, "Rise and grab your weapons! We are surrounded! Get up! But loose no arrows!"

All across the meadow a flurry of shouts, groans, and breathless grunts erupted as men and women lunged for weapons and struggled to their feet to face the enemy. Negano repeated, "Loose no arrows! We don't know their intentions yet!"

They're supposed to be our new friends . . . but why would Wenisa surround us if he planned to honor our agreement?

A group of ten or so warriors detached from the line to the east and marched down the slope. Two men dragged an unconscious warrior between them. They had his arms stretched over their shoulders. His head flopped while his feet dragged behind him, generating a scraping sound.

"Negano?" Chief Atotarho called. "Join us."

Negano broke into a trot, hurrying to stand in Atotarho's circle. The mad chief glanced at him, then his gaze slid back to the man walking out front of the ten Mountain warriors. He might have been dressed in thin rags, but he wore a magnificent wolfhide headdress with the ears pricked. Negano had heard that Wenisa's long-dead evil brother, Manidos, had favored similar wear during battle. For much of Negano's childhood the two men had terrorized the world. Stories of their merciless cruelty had plagued his nightmares until he'd finally become a man and somewhat outgrown them.

"Chief Wenisa," Atotarho greeted when the man arrived.

Negano studied him. Grisly scars sliced Wenisa's face and his right eye was missing. Whoever had sewn it up had done a poor job. The big irregular stitches had created a shrunken pucker in his repulsive face.

"Chief Atotarho. My messenger says you doubted my word." Wenisa flicked his hand, gesturing to the warriors hauling the unconscious man between them. "Bring him here and drop him."

The warriors dragged the man forward and let his limp body fall on the ground at Atotarho's feet. "Take a good look. This is the dreaded Standing Stone Prophet."

Atotarho scoffed. "It can't be. I sent two warriors to kill him in case one failed." The Chief squinted down at the limp form. The man was unusually tall, broad-shouldered, but his face was so battered it was impossible in the moonlight to identify him. One of his eyes had swollen closed. His jaw bulged, as though several teeth had been knocked out. Atotarho used his walking stick to prod the man, trying to wake him. "What makes you think this is Sky Messenger?"

Wenisa's mouth twisted into a smile that could at best be described as a ghastly grimace. "I saw him before my warriors got to him. It's definitely Sky Messenger."

"Well, I can't verify that claim in this light."

As though to taunt Atotarho, Wenisa lifted both fists into the air and shouted to his warriors, "The great and powerful Standing Stone Prophet who terrifies every warrior on this field lies at my feet with barely the strength to keep breathing. He has *not* called a storm from the sky! None of the Faces of the Forest have slipped from the trees to free him! Elder Brother Sun has not come to his aid! He is a pathetic fool. I could swat him like a fly because my Power is greater than his!" To emphasize his point, Wenisa leveled a bone-breaking kick at Sky Messenger's ribs. The man didn't even groan.

Is he alive?

Whispers of awe and fear ran through both armies. These warriors were clearly terrified of what the Prophet might do to them . . . as Negano was. Just a few days ago, Negano had seen Sky Messenger lift his hands and call the monstrous whirling blackness that had swept down over the battlefield.

But . . . as he stared down at the Prophet lying helpless and alone, completely surrounded by his enemies, it seemed somehow unreal, like a made-up dream from another time.

Atotarho's wrinkled face hardened as he watched Wenisa's theatrics. "Why did you bring him to me? As a gift?"

"A *gift*?" Wenisa laughed. "Of course not. He is mine to do with as I please. At dawn, I'm going to drag him—"

A soft voice sounded behind Negano, "War Chief? Forgive me?"

Negano turned to see Yekonis standing with his fists clenched. Negano bowed, said, "Forgive me, I mean no disrespect," and stepped away from Atotarho's circle to grip Yekonis' sleeve and escort him a few paces away where they could speak privately. "What did you find?"

Yekonis' gaze darted around the meadow, as though to reassure himself that they were indeed surrounded. "War Chief, one-hundred-ninety-six blankets are empty."

Negano hissed, "Are you telling me we have only four hundred warriors left?"

Yekonis nodded. "Less. I went to the place of the wounded. Around thirty died in the night."

The hand Negano used to grip the young man's sleeve shook. The ramifications were just beginning to sink into his exhausted souls. "Wenisa will not know the truth until dawn when he can see our forces with his own eyes. I want you to quietly move through our ranks. Inform everyone of this. They'll know soon enough anyway. Tell them to be prepared for the worst."

"But . . . what does that mean? They're on our side, aren't they?"

Negano hesitated. He didn't want to panic his warriors. The first chance they got, they'd run off. He squinted out at his camp and the Mountain army that stood so still around it. From the moment Sindak had betrayed them, this entire effort had been a gigantic failure. He'd already lost more than three-quarters of his forces, and would lose more today, maybe even all of them. Negano would go down in the history of his People as the War Chief who had gutted the nation by destroying his entire army. Stories of his missteps would be told for generations, as warnings to others.

His fatigued eyes returned to Atotarho. *I let a madman ruin my name, my family's name, and taint the legacy of my clan for generations. By obeying his orders, I did this. I killed my friends, my relatives.*

"War Chief?" Yekonis was staring at the man lying curled on his side at Atotarho's feet, and said, "Is that really Sky Messenger? Is the great Prophet dead?"

Negano shook his head. "No, but don't expect him to conjure a miracle to save you from the Mountain army. I don't think he has long to live."

Yekonis swallowed hard. "So . . . you don't think they're on our side?"

Negano's jaw clenched. He stared at Yekonis, then his gaze shifted to Bur Oak Village. As the darkness brightened, he could start to make out warriors standing on the palisade. He scanned each one until he thought he saw Sindak. He appeared to be speaking with another man, probably trying to decipher the events happening in the meadow.

Strange and treasonous notions slipped around Negano's skull.

It took him a few moments to work up enough courage to face them. He released his grip on Yekonis, and said, "There's something I need you to do."

"Yes, War Chief?"

"As though nothing's wrong, I want you to organize a party of three men, including yourself, to go down to the marsh to fill water bags. Take your time. Three water-bearers shouldn't be a threat to anyone. While you're there, I want you to deliver a message for me."

Yekonis gave him a confused look. "To whom? The only people down by the marsh . . ." His voice trailed away. As though the devastating truth of their situation was really settling into his souls and he, too, was trying to fathom a way out of the calamity that might well descend upon them shortly after dawn, his eyes scanned the Mountain army that surrounded them on three sides. "What message? To whom?"

Negano began, "After you deliver it, do not return to this army. I'm releasing you. Do you understand?"

Yekonis' eyes had a glazed look, a combination of terror and relief. "No, but . . . I'm listening."

Fifty-one

"Who are they?" Sindak asked.

The bottom seemed to have fallen out of Gonda's stomach. He shifted on his oak crutch, wobbling around to survey the positions of the warriors who had just oozed from the trees like dark specters. Breathlessly, he suggested, "Reinforcements from the Hills nation?"

Sindak propped his fist on top of the palisade wall as he scrutinized the scene with narrowed eyes. His lean face and hooked nose shone in the pale blue gleam. "I don't think so."

"Who else could they be?"

Sindak didn't answer for a time while he continued his evaluation. Moans and cries filled the plaza below and seeped from every smoldering longhouse. While they still had two hundred real fighters perched on the catwalks and another three hundred elders and children with bows, their losses yesterday had been staggering: approximately four hundred dead, and five hundred wounded. Jigonsaseh had developed a system. Minor wounds were tended by family and friends in the longhouses. Major wounds that Old Bahna thought would Heal went to the council house. Those who had no chance of getting well were laid in rows at the south end of the plaza . . . near the growing pile of dead. The worst cries, mostly screams for water, came from the south end of the plaza.

Sindak pointed. "Can you see the headdress worn by the big man in front of Atotarho?"

Gonda peered out into the muted gleam, trying to make out what the man wore. As the image congealed, and he saw the pricked wolf ears, blood seemed to drain from his head. "Blessed gods, that's Chief Wenisa." His heart slammed his ribs so hard he felt sick to his stomach. "They're Mountain People."

"That's what I thought."

Speculations ran up and down the catwalks, creating a low ominous hum.

Gonda's gaze darted over the valley, trying to verify their suspicions. Dawn was coming fast, but not fast enough. He still couldn't see very well. Only the most brilliant campfires of the dead, the big council fires, continued to burn. Flaming points of red and azure, and one lonely fire beaming gold lit the sky.

Wenisa began pacing in front of Atotarho, striding back and forth with his arms waving. From this distance, he was as shadowy and quiet as the wind. Yenda had always been an arrogant fool. Having Chief Wenisa's soul Requickened in his body probably hadn't helped. Wenisa had been known far and wide as the most brutal chief in the land.

In an unnaturally calm voice, Gonda asked, "There must be . . . what? . . . two thousand Mountain warriors out there?"

"Two thousand that we can see."

"Then the Mountain People and the Hills nation have created some sort of alliance?"

Sindak examined the irregular line of warriors that surrounded Atotarho's army on three sides, probably wondering what he would do if he were in Negano's place. He frowned. "Do you want the truth, or should I lie to make you feel better?"

Gonda ran his tongue over his chapped lips. They were all desperately thirsty, but there was no water, not even for the wounded children. His souls briefly spun thoughts of hot tea steaming in a cup, warming his hands. Tangy and sweet, it ran warm into his body, easing his rigid joints, and the agony in his broken leg. It was amazing how even dreaming of hot tea helped, especially when a man was staring death in the face. "When have you ever lied to make me feel better?"

"Never, but I thought you might want me to make an exception on this last morning."

Bizarrely, Gonda felt like laughing. "No exceptions, thanks."

Sindak straightened. "Then I suspect they've allied for just this one battle. They're here to take part in the destruction of the Standing Stone nation."

Gonda's voice had an annoyingly desperate ring to it. "What do you think Atotarho promised them in exchange for their help?" *As though it matters ...* .

Sindak shrugged. "Enough to get them here."

Gonda massaged his brow. It occurred to him that by the end of the day, he would be his old enemy's personal slave ... or his body would be lying on top of the pile of corpses. Hopefully, the second.

Sindak said, "There's a man on the ground at Atotar-ho's feet. I didn't notice him before, but as the light gets better, I'm starting to see more. Who do you think he is?"

"A prisoner delivered to Atotarho? A Hills deserter?"

Softly, he answered, "Possibly." He must be worried that it was one of his own warriors, Saponi, or another trusted friend.

As Elder Brother Sun lifted from the celestial tree and neared the eastern horizon, the sky took on a pinkish hue. The breeze picked up, sawing through the leafless branches, and sending the musty fragrances of smoke and old leaves sweeping down over them.

"I don't recognize the prisoner's cape, do you?" Gonda asked.

"No, but I can't really make out the designs—just white figures around the bottom."

With an odd fatalistic composure, Gonda said, "Well, I hate to—she's had so little rest—but we should wake Ma-tron Jigonsaseh."

Sindak turned to look at where Matron Jigonsaseh slept on her side on the catwalk. She had no blanket. All blankets had gone to warm the wounded. She had her knees pulled up beneath her woven foxhide cape. Of course, the night had been so warm no one had really needed a blan-ket. CorpseEye rested limply in her hand. Short, gray-streaked black hair rimmed the furry edges of her hood. She hadn't left the palisade all night. She knew the end was close. Gonda hated to be the one to tell her it was even closer than she'd thought.

"Do you want me to do it?" Sindak said.

Gonda shook his head. "No, I'll do it. I suspect she'd rather hear it from me."

"And why is that?"

"Over the long summers, I've brought her the news that we're doomed so many times she doesn't really believe me."

"Ah. I see."

As Gonda put his weight on his crutch, his broken left leg shrieked in pain. He clumped down the catwalk, one step at a time, smiling at the warriors he passed, trying to exude a confidence he in no way felt. Each regarded him soberly.

"Who are they, Gonda?" War Chief Wampa hissed as he passed. Red-rimmed eyes and cracked lips dominated her pretty face as she turned to look at him. Her gray cape with brown spirals looked charcoal in the dimness.

"We're not sure yet, but don't worry about it until it gets light. Then we'll know for sure."

"But there are thousands!" She glanced at the warriors nearby, trying to keep her worried voice low. "Are they Hills People?"

"We've been fighting 'thousands' for days, Wampa, and managed to hold out. Matron Jigonsaseh isn't going to let you down. She'll figure out something to keep you alive. She *always* does."

Those simple words seemed to affect Wampa like a cool salve on a fevered wound. Her shoulder muscles relaxed. "Yes, I know she will. Thank you, Gonda." She turned back to the wall, taking up her duties again.

As he continued down the catwalk, the warriors who'd heard their conversation stared at him, their gazes flicking back and forth between Gonda and the strange army that had just appeared. Dire whispers eddied.

Despite the noise on the catwalks and the groans and cries in the plaza, when he stood over Jigonsaseh, she still hadn't awakened. Softly, he said, "Jigonsaseh? I'm sorry to wake you." No response. Not even a wiggle. "My former wife, forgive me, but I know you will wish to hear that Chief Wenisa is here with a Mountain—"

She jerked awake as though the name had punctured her dreams like a war lance. "Wenisa? Are you sure?"

"Fairly sure. The man is wearing a wolfhide head-dress, which you know Wenisa favors."

As she sat up, she exhaled hard, then leaned back against the palisade and rubbed her eyes on her sleeve. "What does Sindak say about this?"

"He suspects Wenisa joined forces with Atotarho just to destroy the Standing Stone nation."

She inhaled a deep breath and let it out slowly before she dragged herself to her feet. "Then Wenisa is going to be disappointed." Bluish half-moons darkened the skin beneath her eyes. Her narrow nose and full lips bore a fine layer of ash—which had fallen all night from the smoldering village.

"My former wife, it's as bad as can be."

Jigonsaseh tucked CorpseEye into her belt and reached down to grasp her bow and quiver where they stood canted at an angle against the palisade. She slung them over her shoulder and blinked at the warriors on the cat-walk. Every eye had turned to her, and she knew it. She squared her shoulders and called, in a voice loud enough for everyone to hear: "Show me where they are."

As she marched toward Sindak, her black eyes blazed, inspiring every warrior with the confidence that once she understood the situation, she'd get them out of this.

Despite the fact that Gonda had known her for more

than thirty summers, the sight of her striding down the catwalk even buoyed his spirits.

The whispers along the palisade changed, going from ominous to something more like guarded determination. She was a living prayer, their last prayer, and if it took every breath in their bodies, they would not let her down. They would fight for her until they simply could not lift their hands.

Gonda clumped along behind her, not trying to keep up, just watching the worshipful expressions of the warriors as she passed without a word, gripping shoulders here and there.

When she reached Sindak's side, her gaze carefully scanned the meadow. As Gaha sailed over the catwalk, Jigonsaseh's foxhide hood waffled around her exhausted face.

Sindak didn't say anything for a time, letting her take it in before he softly commented, "With these new forces, I suspect we have a couple hands of time after dawn before the walls are breached."

Jigonsaseh propped her elbows on the palisade beside Sindak, blinking awake, fighting to gain her desperately needed senses. "How many?"

"Maybe two thousand Mountain warriors, but he could have more in reserve in the trees."

"I doubt it. From what I've heard, two thousand is about all they have left in the nation. Which means he's wagering everything on this battle."

Sindak stared at her for a moment. "I hadn't thought of that, but you're right, and it means they're going to fight even harder."

"What's Negano doing?"

"I can't tell, but something is not right out there."

She shifted to face him. "How do you know?"

"It's more of a feeling than anything else." Sindak stared at her and you would have thought they were the only two at the Dance. "Negano's warriors should be on their feet, each one facing the Mountain army. I only count perhaps three hundred fifty to four hundred."

"Yes, but it looks like many are still sleeping. Perhaps he wants to give them—"

Sindak shook his head. "Doubtful. I suspect those rolled blankets are empty."

Jigonsaseh's black eyes moved over the blankets. As the wind picked up and the light brightened, many could be seen flapping. "What makes you think so?"

"Earlier, I saw two men kicking over bundles. Blankets flew, but no one stood up."

Gonda lurched forward, his heart thundering, to hiss, "Blessed gods! You mean hundreds deserted during the night?"

"I think it's a strong possibility."

Jigonsaseh stood perfectly still. Only her eyes moved. Studying. "If you're right, and Negano has only around four hundred warriors left, he must know that Wenisa's archers could skewer his forces in a few hundred heart-beats."

Sindak gave her a sober look. "As soon as it's light, Wenisa is going to come to that same conclusion."

Jigonsaseh closed her eyes and rubbed them on her sleeve again. Gonda knew that gesture. She was tired, but she was also thinking, working out what she would do if that turned out to be the case. When she opened her eyes, she said, "Then, within a single hand of time, we may only be fighting a desperate Mountain army. And one greatly diminished. I suspect Negano's warriors will manage to get eight hundred arrows into the air before they fall, and they'll be letting fly from close range. Sindak, how many will Wenisa lose?"

Sindak's brows plunged down over his hooked nose. He blinked out at the warrior-filled meadow as he tried to calculate. "I say . . . six hundred. Probably three hundred killed outright and another three hundred down with wounds that take them out of the fight."

"Gonda?" she turned to him.

He leaned heavily on his crutch. "I think Sindak doesn't want to get your hopes up, so he's guessing low. I'm going to guess high. If Negano forms his warriors up properly, he'll lose the front line of archers immediately, but it will give his remaining warriors time to loose four or five arrows each. "I say one thousand out of the battle."

She nodded, mulling the information. "So . . . if they turn on each other first, instead of facing two thousand four hundred, we'll be facing somewhere between one thousand and one thousand two hundred."

Sindak and Gonda nodded simultaneously. A frail tendril of hope twined through Gonda's chest.

"But I don't think that will happen," Sindak said. "Wenisa is an overconfident fool, but not that much a fool. He'll want us to kill as many of Atotarho's warriors as possible to save him the trouble. Which means they won't turn on each other until the middle of the battle, maybe not even until the end."

As she listened, Jigonsaseh continued her examination of the brightening meadow, noting the positions of warriors, trying to see the coming attack before it happened. When she abruptly gripped the palisade, both Gonda and Sindak went rigid. For a time she seemed to be holding her breath, then almost too soft to hear, she said, "The man on the ground in front of Atotarho—"

"We don't know who he is. Wenisa—"

"That's Sky Messenger."

"What?" Gonda stumbled forward to grab the palisade and stare at the distant figure. He was stirring. He weakly rolled to his back. "That's not Sky Messenger's cape. And if so, where's Gitchi? Gitchi wouldn't leave—"

"They would have killed Gitchi first," Sindak replied.

The man on the ground rolled to his knees and started wretching violently. He sounded like he was bringing up his insides. After five heartbeats, he collapsed again as though unconscious.

Gonda whispered to Jigonsaseh, "Don't jump to conclusions. You can't possibly know for certain in this light."

She seemed to realize she'd slumped against the palisade, and her warriors were watching her. She straightened to her full height again, braced her feet and propped her hand on her belted war club. "That's Sky Messenger. Believe me."

Sindak's teeth ground beneath his cheek. He studied her for a long time, before he said, "If you're right, Wenisa is going to use him against us. That's why he's still alive."

None of them said anything for another twenty heartbeats, then Jigonsaseh responded, "Sky Messenger is more valuable to him alive. If Wenisa takes him home and parades him around as proof that he has greater Spirit Power than the renowned Standing Stone Prophet, Wenisa's reputation will soar."

Sindak's head waffled. "Maybe."

As the possibility that it really was Sky Messenger out there began to solidify, Gonda's chest seemed to hollow out and refill with panicked desolation. He blurted, "Then he won't kill Sky Messenger unless we force him to. Is there a way we can get to our son? If there's a break in the battle and we can send out a party to . . ."

Sindak and Jigonsaseh both stared at him as though his souls had flown away and his body was a senseless piece of useless flesh. *I'm a selfish fool. Any party sent out to rescue Sky Messenger will be slaughtered like dogs at a ritual sacrifice.* Jigonsaseh would never kill twenty in a vain attempt to save one. Not even her son. The suggestion had been ludicrous. He whispered, "I—I wasn't thinking."

A small commotion erupted along the eastern wall overlooking the marsh.

Jigonsaseh ignored it and reached out to put a hand on Gonda's shoulder. "If I could, Gonda, you know that I . . ."

"War Chief Sindak?" Wampa called as she trotted down the catwalk.

Sindak stepped away from the palisade, and walked out to meet her.

Wampa glanced at the warriors nearby and very quietly said, "There's a man in the marsh asking to speak with you. He says War Chief Negano sent him."

"Negano?" Sindak strode down the catwalk briskly, heading for the group of warriors who'd gathered to peer down into the marsh.

Gonda squinted after him. As did Jigonsaseh.

Less than two hundred heartbeats later, Sindak straightened and turned to Wampa. "Get every water pot and canteen you can find and lower them down to Yekonis. Do it now, before it gets light enough that he becomes a perfect target."

Wampa didn't bother responding. She charged down the catwalk, tapping men and women on the shoulders. Her rushed words sent them scurrying down the ladders and toward the longhouses.

As Sindak's stride lengthened on the way back toward Jigonsaseh and Gonda, the news was already spreading around the catwalk like wildfire.

"*. . . Sindak working with Negano . . . not possible . . . Atotarho must have thought he could talk Sindak into betraying us . . . I don't believe . . .*"

Sindak didn't bother to respond. He just clenched his jaw and kept his eye on Jigonsaseh.

Gonda saw her turn. By the time Sindak arrived, she stood facing him, her feet braced, a beautiful muscular woman with obsidian-hard eyes that could cut out a man's heart. She'd removed her foxhide cape and slung it over the palisade where the wind softly ruffled the fine red hair. She still had CorpseEye tucked into her belt, but her fingers had tightened around the smooth wooden shaft. She stared at Sindak: a silent question.

"His name is Yekonis, Hawk Clan, from Atotarho Village. He's going to fill as many pots and canteens as he can before full dawn. He's vowed to serve me as a loyal warrior."

Her face showed nothing. "Why?"

"I made no promises. I wouldn't do that without your app—"

"What does Atotarho want?"

Sindak propped his hands on his hips and bowed his head slightly. Gonda watched him. He appeared to be hesitating because he didn't know what to make of the message himself. "It isn't Atotarho who's asking. It's Negano. He suspects Wenisa is going to betray them, and he wants to save as many of his warriors as he can."

The breeze tousled Jigonsaseh's gray-streaked black hair around her still face. "Do you believe this?"

Sindak kept his head bowed, and Gonda suspected he was considering the fact that she hadn't yet asked him "how?" He'd known her a long time. Perhaps Sindak understood that how mattered less to her than his opinion of Negano's trustworthiness.

Sindak looked up. Their gazes held. Finally, he replied, "I don't think we have a choice."

Fifty-two

As Hiyawento and Towa trotted eastward along the trail to Bur Oak Village, Hiyawento's body entered that timeless void of running where thoughts ceased to exist and there was nothing except motion and raw heightened sensation. He reveled in the brilliant streamers of orange that spiked up from the eastern horizon. They shot through the hearts of the drifting Cloud People, turning them a sulphurous shade of yellow he had never seen before. Across the forest, balmy air hissed through the trees, setting warm pungent scents loose to wander with the breeze.

When they crested a high point along the rolling trail, he saw smoke rising from Bur Oak Village. Towa momentarily hesitated, as though he wanted to stop, but Hiyawento didn't slow down. He plunged down the rise, heading for the small creek that crossed the trail ahead.

One hand of time ago, he'd sent a runner ahead with the Truth Belt to let Sky Messenger know they were very close. He'd instructed the runner to come back with information on what was happening there, so they'd have some warning of what they'd be facing. The man had not returned.

Hiyawento feared he'd been killed. Which probably meant a battle raged just head, and they'd arrive in the roaring chaos with a crowd of half-starved women and children at their heels.

Hiyawento wiped his sweating face on his sleeve. It felt like the Moon of Newborn Fawns. All along the periphery of the forest, huge columns of insects spiraled, their membranous wings creating glimmering torrents that spun like tornadoes above the tallest trees.

He and Towa had been moving fast, trying to outrun the weakest followers. They'd lost maybe two hundred of the elders, women, and children, but the heartiest clung to them like boiled pine pitch. They were dedicated, he'd say that for them. Hiyawento cast a glance over his shoulder to see how close they were.

Twenty paces back, Tiyosh ran encircled by fifteen guards, still wearing Sky Messenger's cape with the hood pulled up, despite the heat. He must be roasting alive. Another four hundred paces behind him, the ocean of humanity washed up and spilled over the rolling trail. How many? Three hundred? Four? Laughter drifted through the sea of waving arms as people whirled and clapped their hands in joy, singing their hearts out. They'd been dancing since long before dawn.

To see what Hiyawento was looking at, Towa jerked around, and his straight nose slung sweat. His handsome face ran with it. "I don't know how they have the strength to dance. Most have barely enough flesh left on their bones to walk. It's the most bizarre thing I've ever seen."

"Especially since we're headed into the midst of a

battle with Atotarho's army or the Mountain People, or both."

"Exactly! What's there to be happy about? I swear they're demented."

"They're true believers. Their faith is like a Spirit Plant in their veins."

As they plummeted down the slope and through the low spot, Elder Brother Sun slid over the horizon and threw the onyx shadows of the trees across their path. The cool air felt wonderful. The scent of water swelled from the tiny stream that meandered across the trail. Barely one body length across, Hiyawento leaped it easily, and continued on.

Towa leaped, splashed, and cursed before he ran to catch up. "Yes, but Hiyawento, I also believe in Sky Messenger's Dream. The difference is that it scares the heart out of my body." He cast another glance back at the celebration that followed them. "This jubilance is—well, it's unnatural."

"Isn't everything these days?"

"True enough, but do you think they're happy because anything, even death, is better than the life they've been forced to live these past few summers?"

Hiyawento glanced at Towa before he turned his gaze back to the smoke rising into the sky in the distance. "Maybe. I have to admit that I feel a bit of it myself. Anyone who tells me he can end the constant warfare and suffering, which has tormented our Peoples for generations, must be a supernatural Spirit hero. In fact, Towa, I am absolutely certain that Sky Messenger is the human False Face promised in the old stories."

Towa shifted the pack on his back, rebalancing it upon

his shoulders. "I am, too, but I still do not understand this raucous euphoria." He paused a moment, then a broad smile came to his face. "I mean within a few days, we'll probably all be in the Land of the Dead, and it doesn't have a single decent Trader. I'm not ready for that."

"How do you know it doesn't have any decent Traders?"

"Oh, come, come, do you know *anyone* who's seen a Spirit wearing an exceptional buffalo wool shirt, or carrying arrows made from extra hard chokecherry from the far west?"

Hiyawento thought about it. "No."

"See? Someone would have noticed. People always notice such things."

"You're trying to take my mind off what's ahead, aren't you?"

Towa chuckled. "Just making conversation."

"Yes, I see." Hiyawento smiled.

In the distance, a man's head appeared, bobbing along the trail. Hiyawento couldn't see his body yet. He ran just below the swell of the trail.

"Runner coming."

"Hmm?" Towa followed Hiyawento's gaze, but apparently didn't see anything. "How far away?"

"I forgot you can't see well at distances. If we maintain our pace, our paths will collide in five hundred heartbeats."

Towa squinted hard at the place he thought the runner must be. "If the runner has any sense, he'll take one look at the crowd behind us and veer off the trail into the forest until we pass."

"Unless he's coming to find us. The Bur Oak scouts should have spotted us one-half hand of time ago. I'd hoped they would give my runner information about what was happening and send him back as I'd asked."

Towa's handsome face tensed. "Maybe the scouts saw the horde following us, and they're still trying to figure out what to do—providing they're not already under attack and too busy to care about us."

"Towa, can you stay here? Slow Tiyosh down while I run ahead to see who he is?"

"Yes, go on."

Hiyawento forced his legs to work harder, trying to get far enough ahead that he'd have at least thirty heartbeats before the masses arrived.

As he pounded down the trail, he saw the man crest the hill. Different cape. Not his messenger. Hiyawento pulled an arrow from his quiver, nocked his bow, and held it aimed at the ground—just in case.

The man shouted, "Hiyawento!" and pounded to meet him, his short black hair flopping over his ears.

"Disu?"

Sindak's man, from Atotarho Village.

Disu's broad face looked like sculpted walnut—tanned and shiny—running sweat. As he trotted up, Hiyawento opened his mouth to speak, and Disu said, "Don't talk, just listen. First, your messenger is safe. He was just exhausted. That's why I came. Second, Tagohsah did not lie to you. Bur Oak is about to be attacked by both Atotarho and Wenisa. And"—he took a deep halting breath—"Sky Messenger is Wenisa's prisoner. I don't know how it happened, but he—"

"Are you sure?" he asked in panic.

"Yes, absolutely."

"Is he alive?" Hiyawento's mouth had gone dust dry.

"For now, but his head wound looks bad."

"Where's Baji?" He didn't ask about Gitchi because if Sky Messenger had been captured the dog had certainly been killed while trying to protect him.

"Baji? The Flint War Chief? I have no knowledge of her whereabouts. Are you expecting a Flint war party?"

"No. I—"

"Then please listen. We have no time. When your messenger told us you and the crowd would arrive around dawn, we gathered our warriors to discuss—"

"You have warriors?" He gripped Disu's arm. "How many?"

Disu sliced a hand through the air to cut off the discussion. "It's a long story. There are thirty-one of us hiding in the forest to the south of Bur Oak Village. In the spirit of the new alliance, Saponi wishes me to tell you that while he can lead them into battle, he is not a War Chief, and you have led warriors against Wenisa many times. If you will accept command of these warriors, they have each sworn loyalty to you. Including me."

Hiyawento's grip tightened. "Tell me quickly about the battlefield. How many warriors will we be facing?"

"Around two thousand from the Mountain People and another three to four hundred of Atotarho's warriors."

The numbers stunned Hiyawento. "Atotarho only has three or four hundred? What hap—"

"Will you command or not?" Disu asked impatiently.

"Yes, I accept. I don't know how much we can do, but thirty good warriors can do something, and we will. Where exactly is Saponi holding his warriors?"

"In the hills just south of where Matron Zateri's forces were camped a few days ago."

Hiyawento swung around to look behind him. Towa and Tiyosh were still twenty paces away. He said, "Wait here," and ran back to them.

Towa's face had gone pale. "Is that Disu?"

"Yes. Bur Oak is surrounded and Sky Messenger has been captured. I must accompany Disu back to evaluate what's going on. Can you lead the crowd to the hills just beyond the old sunflower fields south of Bur Oak Village? Keep them hidden. Even if they will not fight on our side, when the time comes the sight of so many people suddenly appearing will disrupt the battle and give Jigonsaseh a little more time. One last thing." He put a hand on Towa's shoulder. "Before you arrive, make Tiyosh remove that cape. If you and Tiyosh can arrive a few hundred heartbeats before the crowd, it will look like Sky Messenger was just captured by the Mountain People moments ago. There's a slim chance it might rally the Landing warriors to join the Peace Alliance. If it does, we need to get the warriors separated from the rest of the crowd, and ready to fight. Can you do that?"

"Of course I can, I'm a Trader. I can talk people into anything." He slapped Hiyawento's shoulder. "I'll meet you there."

Hiyawento sprinted back to Disu.

If the Faces of the Forest were on Sky Messenger's side, how could everything have gone so wrong?

Fifty-three

When sunlight finally crept across the meadow, Negano was standing beside Atotarho and Nesi, but his eyes had fixed upon Chief Wenisa, waiting to see the big man's reaction when he finally noticed how few warriors Atotarho possessed. Wenisa's army remained in the same position, surrounding the camp on three sides, but many warriors had squatted down or gathered into small groups to talk. Their strange Mountain People accents lilted through the warm smoky air.

Chief Wenisa's voice trailed away suddenly and his jaw slackened as his gaze swept the meadow. After a time, he bent down to whisper something to his War Chief, Powink. Powink subtly nodded. A tall, skinny man, Powink had a long sallow face that gave him a perpetually sad expression. Like Wenisa, his clothing was little more than a thin leather sieve. So many tears and rips shredded his knee-length war shirt that from a distance a man might mistake them for black paintings.

Nesi whispered, "They know."

"Apparently," Negano softly replied.

For the first time, Negano could see that Wenisa had one extraordinary eye. It was dark as coal and filled with a strange wolflike clarity. The cruelty of a predator that feels neither regret nor shame in the act of killing, for it is simply life. His shaggy eyebrows tilted upward and had wild gray hairs curling from their midst.

Negano shifted his weight, trying not to appear uneasy. He'd ordered his three hundred seventy-six warriors to align on the western edge of camp, just out of bowshot of Bur Oak Village, and out of bowshot of most of Wenisa's army. In the open space between the armies, rotting corpses sprawled. Bones, kicked and scattered about in yesterday's attack, lay in tangles, held together by fragments of shirts and pants. Barely fleshed skulls studded the battlefield like half-sunken rocks. Each wore a shrunken rictus that resembled a gleeful smile, as though the souls that remained with the bodies knew they would have company by nightfall. All day yesterday, as his warriors had run back and forth across the meadow, the skulls had rolled and tumbled. At one point, there'd been so many bouncing in the air that the battlefield had resembled a macabre ball game.

Atotarho's gaze slid to Wenisa and his wrinkled mouth tightened. Gray hair hung over his sunken leathery face, flipping in the light breeze. The rattlesnakes braided into the locks flashed when he repositioned his walking stick to support his crooked body. "There's nothing we can do about it."

Atotarho turned and gave Negano a hateful look, as though it were his fault that so many had deserted in the night.

Negano took the hint. "If you don't mind, Chief, I think I'll walk among our warriors to judge their moods."

"Do so."

Atotarho returned to discussing the strategic situation with Nesi, his former war chief of many summers ago. As Negano started to walk away, Nesi gave him an apologetic look.

Negano needed to speak with Nesi alone . . . but the opportunity had not yet arisen, and he had to face the fact that it may not.

Negano weaved silently between the tangled corpses, his empty hands clasped behind his back, threatening no one. He wandered, nodded to warriors, and soaked in the fragments of conversations he heard. These were tired men and women, disheartened more than ever. As he'd ordered, they stood with their backs to the Standing Stone nation, and their lowered bows aimed vaguely in the direction of the huge Mountain army facing them across the meadow. Each studied Negano as he passed, ready even now, even after everything he'd done to them, to follow him into the Land of the Dead if that's where he led them. Loyalty lasted too long. It cost too much. Though he thanked the Spirits that warriors had that failing.

Negano slowly made his way to the southern end of the line, and stopped beside a muscular woman warrior named Ohonsta. She had a reputation for humor, but this morning her smooth triangular face showed nothing; it was empty, inscrutable. Her red-rimmed eyes stared at him as though gazing out across some vast unfamiliar country, which he knew came from utter exhaustion. "It won't be long now. Pass the word down the line that my first order

is going to sound like madness, but they must not hesitate
to follow it."

Ohonsta blinked. She seemed to be trying to imagine
what that order might be. She said, "You're going to order
us to slice our own throats? Everybody is ready to do that
anyway. It will make perfect sense."

He smiled briefly. "We aren't certain the Mountain
People will betray our agreement, but if they do, we've
made other arrangements. Be ready."

"I'll pass the word."

Negano continued walking. To his left the charred palisade of Bur Oak Village rose like a hulking forty-hand tall
monster. Widely spaced warriors with bows stood upon the
exterior catwalk. The two interior catwalks, however,
looked vacant, which meant High Matron Kittle no longer
had the warriors to guard them. In addition, many of the
guards he could see were white-haired elders or children
barely tall enough to peer over the top of the palisade. Yesterday, every time a child had fired, he or she had first
climbed up, probably onto a wooden block, to aim and let
fly. His warriors had, of course, seen the same thing and
begun targeting the children before they fully got into position to aim. Negano had no notion how many they'd killed,
but the number had surely left parents reeling with grief.

Today they would fight to their last breaths to justify
the sacrifice of their childrens' lives.

When Negano reached the place in the middle of the
line that stood fifty paces from the gates of Bur Oak Village, he stopped and took a long moment to stare up at
Sindak who was staring squarely back. The slant of sunlight cast shadows over Sindak's deeply sunken eyes, but
his hooked nose and lean face were clearly identifiable.

As Ohonsta's message traveled down the line of warriors, it moved from mouth to mouth past Negano, and his warriors stared questioningly at him . . . then they turned and followed his gaze to Sindak. Barely a handful of days ago, Sindak had been their War Chief. He had led them to victory after victory, and they'd loved him for it. Ominous chatter started. Negano made no attempt to still it.

He was walking a tightrope over the abyss. He had to watch his step. He'd positioned his forces here in the hopes that his words would not get back to Atotarho. If they did, the old chief would suspect treachery and immediately issue an order of his own designed to supercede anything Negano ordered. Would his warriors still obey him if he countermanded their Chief? He didn't know.

He came to the last man in line and stood silently, his hands clasped behind his back, staring not at his warrior, but up at Sindak. The man had been watching Negano, his gaze following him down the line of warriors. Negano knew the kinds of questions Sindak must be asking himself. He also knew that Sindak must have a nest of vipers slithering around in his belly—just as Negano did.

In the end, everything, *everything,* came down to a matter of trust.

Fifty-four

Sky Messenger

I'm not sure where I am. Smoke fills the warm air. My left eye won't open, and all I see through my right eye is a cloudy shifting haze filled with golden twinkles that shoot across my vision like meteors falling to earth. My fingers spastically clench, unclench.

I squint, trying to focus, to make out faces in the haze. All I see are ghostly gray figures spinning like wind-touched mist, without substance or form. Distant voices rush close, then fade to nothingness; I'm not sure they're real.

I faintly remember being struck with a war club. Many times when warriors are struck in the head one of their eyes goes milky. I think that's what happened to me.

Somewhere high above me, crows caw, and I hear birds singing. Insects hum in the grass.

Baji? Gitchi? Where are they? Are they right here beside me, guarding me?

Maybe they didn't escape. . . .

Pain too terrible to endure suddenly wrenches me, turning me inside out. I think my arms and legs are flopping, but

I'm not sure. When the seizure ends, tears leak from my eyes and trail hotly down my cheeks.

I have the vague sensation that my condition is placing everyone around me in danger, and I have the overwhelming urge to run . . . but I can't feel my legs.

Fifty-five

Hiyawento followed Disu, sliding through the dry grass on his belly, heading for Saponi, who wore Hiyawento's Truth Belt around his waist. When the runner had realized Sky Messenger was not here, he'd obviously delivered it to the man in charge. Saponi had wedged himself between two rocks overlooking the battlefield and Bur Oak Village. Even from ten paces away, Hiyawento could see that Saponi's pockmarked face was cold and gray. The scent of fear sweat filled the air. The rest of Saponi's warriors crouched behind the boulders that scattered the hilltop.

Disu shifted to whisper, "Let me tell him you're here."

Hiyawento nodded and wiped his brow while he waited.

A short while ago, Hadui had begun tormenting the hills, thrashing through the forest and hurling old leaves and gravel like weapons. To the north, a black wall of Cloud People was pushing south, and Hiyawento had the feeling the unseasonably warm weather was about to end.

Brittle leaves had blown into every hollow, making the hill look smooth and rounded, though Hiyawento knew from experience, it was not. Dips and rocky holes stippled the ground, making it treacherous footing, especially if a man were running for his life. He'd move these warriors immediately, as soon as he'd talked it over with Saponi.

Disu made it to Saponi and touched his friend's foot, announcing his presence before he crawled up beside Saponi and started talking.

Saponi shoved up on one elbow to search for Hiyawento, then he lifted a hand, waving Hiyawento to join them.

As he crawled forward, the smell of death, of rotting muscles and intestines, drifted through the trees like an invisible miasma, blowing up from the corpses piled against the Bur Oak palisades and the surrounding meadows. It would get worse as the day wore on.

Hiyawento slid forward and Disu moved to the side, yielding his position next to Saponi. Saponi was a burly man with brown eyes and a nose like a flattened beetle. His cape bore the interlocking green and blue rectangles of the Snipe Clan. Hiyawento wedged himself, shoulder-to-shoulder, between Saponi and Disu. Boulders rose twenty hands tall on either side of them.

"We're very glad to see you, War Chief Hiyawento," Saponi said.

"And I to see you. After I heard about the Mountain army, I feared all I would find here was a smoldering pile of rubble."

"Not yet, but we just received word from one of our scouts that there's a Flint war party heading this way."

"They're part of the alliance, Saponi. They—"

"If I knew Chief Cord was still alive, I wouldn't be worried, but he may be dead and the new Chief no friend of ours."

Hiyawento took a breath and through a long exhalation said, "How long until the Flint war party arrives?"

"Nightfall. Even if they're on our side, they won't make it in time to help us."

Hiyawento thought the ramifications through. He didn't have the luxury of worrying about the Flint People right now. He'd consider them later, if he was still alive. "All right. Here's the situation: Towa will arrive shortly, dragging hundreds of Landing People with him. Some are warriors. By the time he reports, he'll have the warriors who wish to fight for us separated out. There may be one hundred. Two if we're very fortunate. The rest are starving women, children, and elders." He vented a breath. "Now, tell me what's happening here?"

Through the narrow crack in the rocks, Hiyawento could see almost the entire battlefield below. He scanned it quickly . . . Bur Oak Village on the left, along with the useless burned-out husk of Yellowtail Village. Just in front of Bur Oak, in a wavy line, stood around four hundred warriors. Then, out at a distance of perhaps seventy paces, the Mountain army created an enormous crescent. It cupped the meadow on three sides, and was perfectly positioned to close in with crushing force.

"Those are Negano's warriors." Saponi pointed to the four hundred.

Hiyawento grimaced. "Why on earth does Negano have his people sandwiched between the Standing Stone archers and the Mountain warriors? Is he trying to get them killed?"

"We've been wondering the same thing. It is . . . incomprehensible."

"When the battle starts, the Mountain army will push

the Hills warriors right into the range of the Standing Stone archers. They'll be butchered."

Disu added, "Unless they are shot from behind first—as many will be. I don't care what agreement has been made, this is the chance of a lifetime for Mountain warriors to fulfill blood oaths against the Hills People."

A ghostly wail, high and thin, wavered in the distance and Hiyawento thought for a moment it was mingled cries of unbearable pain, then he saw the Mountain army shaking fists with their heads thrown back. Clan war cries. The army began to move. Like a many-legged beast, it lurched forward with ragged clan flags jerking about in blurs of blue, red, and black.

A wayward arrow thunked into the boulder to Hiyawento's left and splintered into a thousand flying pieces. Disu covered his head and flattened out on the ground. Saponi and Hiyawento just flinched and continued watching the advancing army.

The warriors on the Bur Oak catwalks had their bows fully drawn back, patiently waiting for the enemy to get into range.

Hiyawento shook his head. "Why haven't Negano's warriors already started picking off the people in the open on the catwalk? They're just standing there."

"I don't know how he thinks, but . . ." Saponi extended a finger toward the far right where the curve of the meadow butted against the rocky eastern hills. Twenty or so people stood in a knot. "You should know that the man lying on the ground before Atotarho is the Prophet, Sky Messenger." Reverence touched Saponi's voice. He was a believer. He had witnessed the monstrous storm.

Hiyawento examined the body. Sky Messenger appeared

to be unconscious. *Blessed Ancestors, please don't let him be dead.* "I can identify Atotarho and Nesi, and Chief Wenisa must be the big man, correct?"

"Yes. The others are the chief's personal guards. They . . ."

A din of gasps and soft cries erupted from the warriors surrounding them, and Disu said, *"I don't believe it! What are they doing?"*

Hiyawento looked just in time to see the Hills warriors pivot on their heels, swinging full around to face the oncoming Mountain army. They loosed a devastating volley of arrows into the onslaught. Hundreds of Mountain warriors fell, forcing the rushing people behind them to stumble and leap over their fallen friends before they could continue their charge. Enraged roars rumbled across the valley. In the stunned moments after the volley, Negano shouted something Hiyawento couldn't hear, but he watched in fascination as Negano's forces turned tail and ran as hard as they could for the Bur Oak Village gates. Screaming Mountain warriors chased after them, loosing arrows on the run. Many of Negano's warriors went down. Just before the survivors hit the gates, they swung open, and his warriors flooded inside to a deafening bellow of outrage from the Mountain People. The gates immediately swung closed, and Wenisa's army hit the walls like a hurricane, shrieking and shouting curses, while Standing Stone arrows rained down upon them.

"Gods," Saponi said. "What just happened?"

Hiyawento shook his head. "I'm not sure."

Disu let out a bizarre cackle, then he threw his head back and laughed. "Don't you see? Negano and his people just joined the Peace Alliance!"

* * *

Negano brought up the rear, shoving his warriors through the gates in front of him, shouting, "Move! Get inside! Hurry!"

As he pushed his warriors into the plaza, he heard the guards slam the locking planks on the gates into position behind him, and found himself surrounded by Standing Stone warriors with drawn bows. He shouted to his warriors, "Lay down your weapons! Lift your hands!"

With shocked expressions, his warriors did it. White-faced, they lifted their empty hands, and stared at the circle of bows that had closed like a bristly noose around them.

Negano desperately searched for Sindak but didn't see him anywhere. He was probably still on the catwalk handling the murderous onslaught outside. Instead, a tall woman, half a head taller than Negano, strode across the plaza. They knew her. Every last one of them. An odd hush came over his warriors. They shoved each other aside to create a path for her to reach Negano, and she walked through the press alone, her stony black eyes fixed on Negano's.

He held his hands higher in the air. She had just allowed around three hundred enemy warriors into her village, into the midst of vulnerable women, children, and elders—warriors who had been murdering her people yesterday. He didn't know what to expect, and nothing on her expressionless face told him.

Blessed Spirits, she had a presence. She looked completely unafraid, or maybe she'd just given herself up for dead days ago. When she stood before him, her black eyes glistened with deadly intent.

Negano said, "Matron Jigonsaseh, thank you for helping us, we—"

"Get your people up on the catwalk immediately. We're going to be short on arrows. I want one dead Mountain warrior for every arrow loosed. Move!"

"Y-Yes, Matron," he stammered. He half-bowed, hesitated for only a heartbeat, then marched into the middle of his warriors to shout, "Pick up your bows and get to the catwalk now! Careful shots. One arrow for one kill. Go!"

She watched him with stone-cold eyes as Negano led his people to the closest ladders, and they charged up to join the battle.

Fifty-six

Nesi stood gaping, momentarily frozen at the sight of Hills warriors flooding across the Bur Oak catwalks. Heartbeats later, they fired a coordinated, decimating volley of arrows into the Mountain warriors at the base of the palisades, warriors who'd been scrambling on top of the corpses, shooting straight up into the faces of anyone who leaned over to aim at them. Hundreds went down. Then more, as Negano's archers launched arrows into the fleeing horde whose senseless rage had led them way too close to the village.

Yesterday, most of the people standing on the catwalk had been elders and children with poor aims. As of this moment, the Standing Stone nation had three hundred of the finest warriors in the land.

Nesi's fists ached as he clenched them tight, and turned to face Chief Wenisa. Nesi was a big man, but Wenisa was bigger, his shoulders wider, his upper arms more massive. Though a cacophony of threats and curses had erupted from Wenisa's personal guards as they stalked about in fury . . . Wenisa stood eerily quiet. Just calmly watching the battle with his bulging muscles about to burst through his shirt.

Nesi's gaze slid to Chief Atotarho. The old man hunched over his walking stick, gripping the head with knobby parchment-like hands. His crooked body quaked with repressed violence. Muscle spasms twitched across his wrinkled face with such ferocity that Nesi thought he might be about to collapse in convulsions. Negano's move had left the Chief with five personal guards in the midst of a swarm of deadly Mountain warriors.

Nesi met the gazes of Atotarho's other guards. Terrified and stunned, they looked like they didn't know what to do. Each one who silently glanced down at his weapons belt, or shifted his shoulder to indicate his slung bow, received a subtle shake of Nesi's head. Gods, that was the last thing . . .

A wild-eyed youth came careening across the battlefield, leaping corpses in a heedless charge to reach Chief Wenisa. Shoulder-length black hair flew around his face. "Chief! Chief! I saw her first!"

Nesi studied the youth of perhaps fifteen summers. He had misshapen eyes, and spoke like a simpleton. Tears streamed down his bucktoothed face to stain the front of his ragged deerhide shirt. His eyes glistened as though he'd seen Sky Woman herself descending from the clouds.

Wenisa sneered, as though the youth was a well-known imbecile. "Get him away from me."

As two of Wenisa's personal guards grabbed the young warrior, he shouted, "She's coming! *She's coming!* Listen to me. I saw her in the forest. I was the first one!"

"Shut the fool up!" Wenisa shouted.

One of the guards clamped a hand over the warrior's mouth and dragged him off.

Someone must have called retreat. Mountain warriors fell back from the village, out of bowshot, and a curious sound—like eels coiling in mud—moved across the battlefield. It started slowly. As a mass, warriors turned to the north, then came bursts of low questions.

Nesi followed their gazes.

Where trees disturbed the path of Hadui, a lilting symphony of whistles and shrieks answered back: the music of the windswept forest.

Only slowly did he become aware of her. She appeared standing in the deepest forest shadows. A tall figure, broad-shouldered for a woman, wearing a simple doehide war shirt. Long black hair whipped around her beautiful face. Strangely eerie, the locks resembled black serpents striking at the air.

"Blessed Faces of the Forest," someone whispered.

As she started walking down the slope and across the meadow, her skin had an alabaster radiance. A huge wolf strode close at her side. Where they stepped butterflies flitted from the warm grass and danced around them. The woman carried no bow or quiver, but her weapons belt glistened with light, the bone stilettos casting slender iridescent flashes.

Nesi shook his head, jimmied the images, the odd shadows. Her movements were so graceful she seemed to be floating, not tethered to the ground. It had to be a trick of light, that or he was dead and didn't know it. Perhaps he'd stepped out of his body into the world of the corpses that surrounded him.

Wenisa shifted to stare at her through his one good eye. "Who is that?"

One of his guards replied, "I . . . I think that's War Chief Baji from the People of the Flint. We fought against her two moons ago. She led the defense of Wild River Village."

No one loosed an arrow at her or the wolf. Her sudden appearance—or perhaps her beauty—had stilled every fighter on the field of battle.

She walked straight to the unconscious Standing Stone Prophet and spread her feet as though ready to fight the world to defend him. Her expression was granite hard, her dark eyes brilliant with challenge. When the wolf lay down on the ground and began licking the Prophet's swollen cheek, murmurs passed through the guards. The animal whimpered softly.

As though the woman could have cared less that she was surrounded by enemies, she knelt beside the Prophet.

"It's me," she softly said, then she sat down in the dry grass and gently drew his wounded head into her lap.

Fifty-seven

Baji smoothed the tear-soaked black hair from Dekanawida's cheeks. His purpled misshapen face was almost
unrecognizable. His left eye had swollen closed, and his
right eye was filled with milky fluid. Dried blood covered
his shirt.

"Dekanawida?"

No answer.

Thunder rumbled in the distance, bringing the storm
closer. Trees battered one another, and everything loose
on the battlefield tumbled across the ground as though
hurled by gigantic fists. Broken arrows and torn quivers
cartwheeled by her.

"Dekanawida? Can you hear me?"

He roused slightly, then seemed to sink back into the
oblivion that had swallowed him.

She stroked his short black hair. "I'm here. I'm right
here beside you."

Barely audible, he said, "Baji?"

"Yes. I'm here. I'm not leaving you."

His lips twitched in what might have been an attempt at a smile.

Baji bent down to examine Dekanawida's milky eye. "Can you see anything? Can you see me?"

He whispered, "Clouds . . . just clouds."

She lightly pressed her lips to his. As she lifted her head, the whirling columns of insects that had, moments before, glistened at the edge of the trees, evaporated, and the bird-song faded away until it lay stone dead upon the forest.

The Thunderers rumbled again, and a brilliant flash of lightning lashed outward from the leading Cloud People to crackle white fire across the sky. The afterimage burned into her eyes was of a gigantic tree of light.

"Wr-wrass?" Dekanawida asked.

"He'll be here. You know he will."

". . . yes."

As the storm approached the air cooled, and the light shifted, flickering across the meadow in curious stripes. At first she thought it was just the leading edge of the clouds blotting Elder Brother Sun, then she noticed the butter-flies settling into the grass, hiding themselves as though afraid.

Her heart started to pound. She murmured, "Dekana-wida?"

As though Great Grandmother Earth had exhaled her last breath, the wind stopped. Just stopped. Conversations hummed as warriors turned to each other in confusion.

Baji's gaze darted around. *"Dekanawida? I think . . ."*

His fingers flexed, and he shifted in her lap as though feeling was coming back to his limbs. Upon his swollen face, she saw the sunlight turn from amber to an un-earthly blue, and she lifted her eyes to the sky.

In the strange shadow-bands of light, Elder Brother Sun seemed to tremble, then a midnight abyss opened beside him, and slid forward, cutting a black hole in the universe.

Gasps and cries swept the meadow.

"It's the Dream!"

"Dear gods, it's happening . . . I told you it was true. I knew it!"

Every warrior lifted his face to the sky, and a low moan quavered on the air.

A sliver of Elder Brother Sun's face disappeared, then more, his light and warmth being sucked away into eternal darkness.

Gasps rose, followed by shrieks.

"Run . . . Run before it's too late!"

Mountain warriors started to throw down their weapons. The clatter of a thousand quivers hitting the ground at once sounded like the sky splitting.

"I'm leaving!" One of Wenisa's guards pounded away.

Wenisa took a step backward, then another. Finally, he whirled and ran as hard as he could for the cover of the trees.

Atotarho and his guards stood gaping, as though too shocked to move as Elder Brother Sun fled the world.

Finally Nesi shouted, "Come on!" He grabbed Chief Atotarho, threw him over his shoulder, and sprinted away with his men behind him.

As soon as they entered the forest, a surprised roar went up, and Baji saw hundreds of warriors surrounding them. Their clan symbols were from both the Hills and Landing nations. Wenisa roared in outrage, and she saw him fighting the strong hands that held him.

Hiyawento appeared at the crest of the hill. Tall, his eyes blazing, he briefly studied the situation, then charged toward her, his long legs pumping.

With a stunningly brilliant flash, Elder Brother Sun vanished and white fire, *white feathers,* sprouted from his shoulders. His newborn wings fluttered wildly. He was flying away into the darkness. . . .

"Baji?" Dekanawida weakly rolled to his knees. "Help me up."

As she carefully pulled his arm over her shoulder, she said, "Hiyawento's coming."

Dekanawida heaved a deep sigh, as though all was now as it should be.

Hiyawento tossed his bow to the ground, and said, "Let me help you."

Together, Baji and Hiyawento lifted Dekanawida onto his feet. "I can stand."

"No. No, you need me—"

"Back away, Baji," Hiyawento said. "He has to stand alone."

Reluctantly, she stepped back, leaving Dekanawida wobbling in the bizarre fluttering light. Gitchi leaped in front of Dekanawida with his fangs bared, daring anyone to try to hurt him.

On the verge of collapsing, Dekanawida stumbled and righted himself. When he'd managed to stiffen his knees, he sucked in a breath, and slowly lifted his arms as though to embrace the vanishing heavens themselves.

Fifty-eight

Sky Messenger

I fight to clear my vision. Images are jumbled. Like thin sheets of ice struck with a rock, everything appears shattered. Warriors are splintered shards of colors. Hiyawento could be made of fire-cracked quartz. Each angle of his face reflects the unnatural gleam differently. At my feet, Gitchi stands like a melting ice-sculpture dog, his shoulder blades sharp as knives.

The only thing whole in the entire world is Baji. To my right, she stands as a coherent woman-shaped shadow, a living shadow, moving, breathing. I long to reach out and touch her, but dare not move. My legs are shaking too badly. I don't know how long I can stand.

I let my head drop forward long enough to get a full breath into my lungs. Sounds and scents seem exaggerated. The cries on the battlefield surround me like soaring birds, flying about, puncturing the air. And the tears! The scent of tears claws at the back of my throat like a stone hand trying to find a way into my heart—a way to die a meaningful death.

I exhale hard before I tilt my face up to the sky.

In the center of the eerie blue background, a single black eye wavers, watching me. Huge and velvet.

"Please, Elder Brother, I beg you . . ."

My knees are about to buckle. I fight to keep them rigid as I stretch out my hands, and in a deep agonized voice, cry, *"No more! No more war!"*

In the distance, a defeaning roar booms and rolls across the sky. The ground beneath my feet trembles. Then the blast comes. Blinding flashes sear my eyes as gigantic white roots split the Skyworld and crackle outward to the four directions.

Hundreds of warriors throw down their weapons and flee, abandoning the field of battle. The sound of frantic feet tripping over corpses strikes like fists.

. . . And I wait.

I wait for a voice. For a child to cry out. I have heard that suffocating little boy's voice so many times in my nightmares.

Hoarse breath tears my lungs.

It's growing darker as Elder Brother Sun flies farther and farther away, but I can't hold my arms up any longer. As I lower them to my sides, tears trickle from my wounded eyes and flow down my face.

Hiyawento suddenly shouts, *"Look!"*

My heart seems to stop when a blinding crescent of Elder Brother Sun's face reappears. As he steps from the abyss, white veils flutter, pouring down from the heavens. A man yells, *"Elder Brother Sun is turning his face back to the world!"*

I see it. The light in the darkness shines.

Something cold strikes my face.

Snow. Snow drifting down. Spinning flakes flash and dance around me like tumbling petals of pure light.

"Odion?" Hiyawento points.

The gates of Bur Oak Village are thrown open. People rush out carrying clan flags. As the carriers weave across the meadow, cheering at the tops of their lungs, their lines furl and unfurl like dark tines raking through a sea of white.

Hiyawento reverently whispers, "I finally understand. Gods, Odion, I understand."

From the southern hills beyond the old sunflower fields, women, children, and elders flood down the slopes and onto the battlefield. Sobs of joy and cheers shred the cold air. I know that accent. They are Landing People.

As my knees shudder, and give way, my vision sparkles.

Both Baji and Hiyawento lunge to grab me, but I fall . . . and fall . . . landing without a word in the glistening blanket of newfallen snow.

Fifty-nine

That night, Baji sat around a campfire to the east of Bur Oak Village, listening to the stunningly beautiful cries echoing across the moonlit hills. It was as though the very fabric of the air was woven of long drawn-out howls, melodic hooting, and the shrill calls of plummeting eagles. For the first time since Atotarho's ambush on her war party, the cries were unbearable. They created an ache of longing in her soul like nothing she had ever known, and she knew at last that such beauty could not possibly exist in this world.

She looked around the fire. The most important people in her life were here—except for Cord, Jigonsaseh, and Zateri. As they talked, her heart thumped painfully. To her right, next to the warm flames, Dekanawida lay on a litter beneath a pile of hides. Jigonsaseh had ordered that he be taken to one of the warm longhouses, but he had refused, saying he had to be out among the people where they could see him and know that he had not been killed.

For many hands of time, the line of awestruck people

had passed by him, reverently looking down, whispering gratefully to him, then moving on to allow others to see.

Finally, at dusk, they'd gathered in the meadow below, where they danced around dozens of great fires, singing and laughing with joy. Scents of roasting venison and acorn bread wafted on the cold breeze. It was as though not a single person doubted the war was over, and with the burden gone, their happiness overflowed. Most of their songs were about the Creator and Sky Woman. Rumors had already begun to filter across the camps that Dekanawida was the returned soul of Sapling, and Jigonsaseh was Sky Woman herself. Within a moon, Baji suspected everyone south of Skanodario Lake would believe it . . . and even unknown peoples far beyond.

She looked down at Dekanawida's swollen face. In the firelight, the purple bruises had a bluish-orange tint. It comforted her to see him. He was still here. Still alive . . . after all the horrors they had lived through together. If only she could lie at his side with her arms around him, watching his breath rise and fall, absorbing every small movement of his body, while the long summers etched the lines deeper into his face, her life would be perfect. During the long periods when they had not seen each other—she had lived in fear that he would vanish as her parents and sisters had vanished. The terror had tormented her dreams.

And now . . . now . . .

She reached beneath his hides to squeeze his warm hand, and sighed.

Across the fire, Towa and Sindak carried on a quiet conversation with Gonda and Hiyawento. To Gonda's left, Tutelo listened. Occasionally, Tutelo's young daughters asked her some question. Baji barely noticed when a messenger arrived from the darkness requesting to speak with Sindak, and he rose and walked away.

She concentrated on stroking Dekanawida's hand. He'd been drifting from consciousness to unconsciousness throughout the night. Each time he opened his milky eye, he gave her a faint smile, and glanced down to make certain that Gitchi still slept on the soft blanket at the bottom of his litter. The old wolf always wagged his tail when Dekanawida woke and looked at him. As Dekanawida sank into sleep again, Gitchi's luminous gaze returned to Baji, and his heart shone out of his eyes, as hers did when she looked at him.

Sindak returned to the fire, and said, "That messenger was from the Ruling Council of the reunited Hills nation. They ordered Negano to use his forces to help us. He was so thankful I thought he was going to faint. His warriors now consider him a great hero."

Gonda replied, "I'm sure he thought he was going to be executed as a traitor . . . along with you."

"He wasn't the only one who thought that," Sindak replied. "Gods, I hope the Landing People join us."

Towa's long braid sawed across his cape as he turned to stare at Sindak in disbelief. "Are you joking? Of course, they will join us. Look at the Landing People below! Once Sky Messenger's followers return to Shookas Village and tell their stories of what happened today, how can they refuse?"

Sindak paused as though wondering. "Do you think the same will be true of the Mountain People?"

There was a moment of rustling shirts and shifting feet as they all turned to look northward to where Chief

Atotarho and Chief Wenisa were being held in a heavily guarded camp. A small spruce-bough structure had been thrown up beside a campfire. Guards passed back and forth in front of the flames.

Gonda said, "I know Sky Messenger ordered that we release both chiefs, but I plan to spend some time talking to them before we do that."

Towa added, "I'm no longer worried about Atotarho. High Matron Zateri and the Ruling Council will tend to him. But Wenisa is another question, I—"

"He won't be a problem," Hiyawento said. His eyes still glistened. A strange peace had come over him. "It will be the same thing as with the Landing People. By the time he gets back to his village, his warriors will have been there for a full day telling their stories. The Mountain People's Ruling Council will have already made up its mind."

They all went silent, staring at the fire. Tutelo's youngest daughter, perhaps five summers, whispered something to her, and Tutelo kissed the little girl's head and hugged her.

"Baji?" Dekanawida breathed her name, and exhaled a shallow breath.

"I'm right here. I've been here all along." Baji laced her fingers with his, and a sensation of contentment filtered through her. He weakly squeezed her hand back.

". . . I know."

Hiyawento saw them speaking, and said, "Baji, ask Sky Messenger if he's hungry or thirsty. We have plenty . . ."

A commotion suddenly rose from below. People ran across the meadow, and the singing stopped. Curious voices rose to replace it. Someone shouted. From the east, a large party, perhaps five hundred warriors, trotted into the firelight. Near the front, four warriors carried a man on a litter.

"Is that Chief Cord?" Hiyawento asked.

Baji's gaze longingly clung to her father as he was carried toward Bur Oak Village.

Gonda said, "Yes, it's the Flint war party. Let's go greet them. The Ruling Council is going to ask Cord to address the entire village."

He'll tell the story of the ambush at Rocky Meadows.

Baji's hands trembled.

Out in the trees the lonesome howls and the drumming of partridge wings were growing stronger, getting closer. Somewhere very near, just beyond the circle of firelight, deer hooves crackled through piles of old leaves, kneading the ground as though anxious to be on their way.

Dekanawida seemed to sense her tension. He opened his right eye, and peered up at her through the milky haze. As she leaned over him, making sure he could see her, her long black hair tumbled around his face. In the firelight, his eyes had a sheen like tears. "Not yet . . . please . . . stay?"

She blinked down through suddenly blurry eyes. "Do you hear them?"

"I've heard them . . . off and on . . . all day."

Baji's throat ached as she bent down to press her lips to his.

Across the fire, Sindak and Towa rose to their feet. Through her hazy vision, they seemed to swim in the firelight. Gonda, Tutelo, and her daughters rose as well. Their gazes remained on the Flint war party, studying it as it wound through the camps. Cord's litter-bearers carried him through the Bur Oak gates, where he disappeared.

"We'll meet you there," Gonda said. He and Tutelo, with children trailing behind them, started down the hill toward the village.

Sindak said, "Towa, why don't you take the bottom of Sky Messenger's litter. I'll grab the top."

They walked forward, and Baji backed away. They carefully lifted the litter and started to carry it down to the village.

"Wait . . . wait!" Dekanawida's hand extended from beneath the hides, blindly reaching for Baji.

Hiyawento came around the fire, frowning. "What's wrong?"

Sindak and Towa had confused looks on their faces, but they stopped. Baji walked forward, grasped his hand between both of her palms, and squeezed hard. "I'm still here."

He forced his left eye open a slit to look at her with both eyes. She'd seen that same look the night they'd been rescued outside of Bog Willow Village. Koracoo had told Odion that Wrass would not be meeting them at Fire Cherry Camp, as he'd promised, because he'd been recaptured by Gannajero. Odion's high-pitched little boy scream of *"No!"* still rang in Baji's ears.

He whispered, "I'm sorry . . . I'm sorry."

"You have nothing to be sorry for. You saved me so many times."

". . . kept you . . . too long."

"No, no, you didn't."

Hiyawento walked around the litter to stand beside Baji and gaze into her eyes. "What's he talking about?"

"He's delirious. That's all. His fever is very high."

Sindak shifted the weight of the litter, indicating they were ready to head back to the village.

Baji squeezed Dekanawida's hand one last time and bent to whisper in his ear, "I'll see you soon," then she kissed him and forced herself to back away from the litter.

Hiyawento gave her a strange look. "Coming, Baji?"

"I'll be along shortly. Tell my father not to worry about me. Tell him I'm all right."

Hiyawento nodded and followed several paces behind Sindak and Towa as they started down the slope.

In ten heartbeats, Baji was alone. She watched Dekanawida's litter travel through the middle of the celebration. As he passed, people gently ran their hands down the side-rails, or reverently touched his blankets. Several fell into line behind the litter and followed it through the Bur Oak gates into the village.

She didn't realize until he nosed her hand that Gitchi had remained at her side. Baji looked down and found the old wolf gazing up at her with hurt yellow eyes. As she scratched his ears, Gitchi sat on his haunches and leaned heavily against her leg, as though he would never leave her.

"Want to run with me for a little way?"

Gitchi stood up, hesitantly turned to look at the village, at the place where Dekanawida had been taken, then whined.

They started out at a slow pace, trotting through the camps until they hit the trail that led westward. In swift silence they wound through the snowy woods, their footsteps barely audible. Shining owl eyes watched them, and wolves yipped when they glimpsed them passing through the striped moon-shadows.

Every step increased the mysterious euphoria that possessed her.

On the opposite side of the valley, the forest grew thicker, the trees taller, and frozen acorns scattered the trail like small rocks. She was wildly happy, running with Gitchi faithfully loping at her side.

When she crested the hill, a herd of four deer, all bucks, came into view idly grazing in the silvered gleam. Their antlers shone when they lifted their heads to look up at Baji and Gitchi.

She studied them, only mildly afraid, then knelt beside Gitchi to stare into his beautiful old face. Rings of white hair encircled his worried eyes. She hugged his big body against her chest, and held him for a long time, stroking his back. "I suspect I'll see you first. I'll be waiting for you at the bridge, old friend."

When she released him and rose, she pointed to Bur Oak Village. "Now. Go find Dekanawida."

Gitchi cocked his head, as though trying to understand why she didn't want him.

"You have to guard him for me, Gitchi. He needs you."

Gitchi whimpered and backed up, but refused to leave her.

"Go on now," she said gently. "You have to go home. Please, go home."

Finally, he loped down the hillside, but he kept glancing back at her. Several times he looked like he might disobey her and charge back to her side.

She waited until he disappeared over the crest of the hill, then she slowly turned back to the deer.

They'd started frolicking, kicking up their heels, playfully tossing their antlers.

She clenched her fists and walked toward them.

From somewhere behind her, Gitchi let out a soul-rending howl that echoed through the stillness . . . but his agonized voice grew fainter and fainter, until it blended with the many-voiced cry that serenaded the brilliant darkness.

Sixty

So many people had crowded in front of Hiyawento that he'd fallen far behind Sindak and Towa. But he was in no hurry. It seemed that everyone wished to hear Chief Cord. The gathering in the plaza had spilled outside the gates and flowed around the palisade. Cord was being bombarded with questions. In another one or two hands of time, things would settle down, and Hiyawento would get his chance to speak with Cord personally.

Hiyawento turned and walked out away from the camps into the moonlight that streamed across the forest. He could faintly hear Cord's voice rising over the Bur Oak palisade, and warmth spread through him. Every man had heroes in his life, and so many of his were here tonight, Cord among them.

He tilted his head back to look up at the night sky. The Path of Souls had dimmed with Grandmother Moon's rising, but he could make out its outline. His gaze unconsciously fixed on the fork in the Path where it was said that all the animals a man had ever known in his life waited at the bridge that led from this life to the next. He wondered . . .

A hushed roar went up in the village. What had Cord said? He was probably telling the story of how he and Baji were ambushed after they left Bur Oak Village. It must have been exciting. The roar grew louder before it faded, and Cord's voice rang out again.

Hiyawento bowed his head, just standing in the darkness, trying not to think or feel. The day had drained him of both abilities.

From the corner of his eye, he saw Gitchi come out of the trees to the west. The old wolf walked through the moonlight with his head down, his muzzle hanging so low it almost touched the snow-covered ground. His shoulders rolled as though every step hurt.

Hiyawento walked out across the field to meet the wolf. When Gitchi spied Hiyawento, he looked up at him with sad eyes.

"Gitchi? Are you all right? Where's Baji?"

Gitchi's ears pricked at her name, then he walked forward and slumped down at Hiyawento's feet with a deep sigh.

Hiyawento frowned. "What's wrong?" He sat down beside Gitchi and ruffled the thick fur on the wolf's neck. "Everything's all right."

Gitchi lifted his gray muzzle, whimpered, and stretched his neck across Hiyawento's lap. The wolf's luminous eyes seemed to be staring mournfully up at the night sky where the Path of Souls shimmered.

As he petted Gitchi's side, Hiyawento thought about Zateri and Kahn-Tineta. He missed them desperately. In a few days, once they'd collected their dead and helped the

Standing Stone nation Sing their relatives to the Land of the Dead, he would accompany the war party that carried Atotarho home to face the Ruling Council. Before they entered the village, Hiyawento would comb the snakes from the old chief's hair. Symbols of war were no longer . . .

"I don't believe it," Taya shouted as she exited the village with Sindak. "Everyone saw her. People touched her!"

Hiyawento frowned. She sounded distraught.

Sindak touched Taya's arm, then swiftly strode out across the meadow, vaguely heading toward Hiyawento.

When he got closer, he called, "Hiyawento? Is that you?"

"Yes, I'm over here."

Sindak stopped two paces away, and shifted uncomfortably. "I don't know how to . . . how to tell you . . . I . . . please, you have to come. Cord needs to speak with you."

"I thought he was busy telling stories. I was going to wait—"

"He wants to speak with you *now*. We've all told him our stories, but he wishes to hear it from you."

Gitchi heaved a sigh, and shoved to his feet with a groan. He knew the word "come."

Hiyawento rose and dusted the snow from his pants. "Wishes to hear what from me?" Gitchi took a few moments to lovingly lick his hand and lean against his leg. Hiyawento petted his head.

Sindak said, "Just . . . come with me."

"Lead the way. We'll need to go slow, though. Gitchi's bones really hurt tonight."

Sixty-one

Sky Messenger

MOON OF NEW FAWNS

Dogwood blossoms tumble through the fragrant late afternoon air, whirling around Wrass where he stands beside me on the hilltop to the south of Bur Oak Village. Brilliant green maples surround us, filtering the sunlight that falls through the canopy. Wavering yellow diamonds flutter across the forest floor at our feet. I wonder if he has the same aching hollow inside him that I do. It's been a long day, one that has been long in coming.

Thousands fill the meadow below, commemorating the last great battle in a war that almost destroyed our Peoples. Far to my right, just at the crest of the hills, Shago-niyoh stands with one hand braced upon a boulder. He hasn't spoken to me, and I fear that he thinks, as of today, I no longer need him.

A shout goes up from below.

As the clans parade across the lush wildflower-strewn meadow toward the deep hole we've dug beneath the old pine tree, Hiyawento says, "I can't believe that all five nations joined the Peace Alliance. I swear it's the greatest miracle in the history of our Peoples."

My eyes tighten. I do not answer, because I can't find any words that have meaning. For thirteen summers, he has stood behind me like a stone wall in the bitter campaign for survival—always there, always fighting for me with blind loyalty. But . . . after today, there will be no more fighting. I suspect part of my emptiness comes from the fact that I don't know how to face a world without war. I have never seen one. Nor has anyone in the meadow below.

I squint at the gathering.

The last representatives come forward. They wear their best clothing, heavily painted with bright clan symbols. When it is his or her turn, the chosen one reverently places weapons in the hole, submerging them in the river of Great Grandmother Earth's blood that rushes beneath the ground, cleansing them of the taint of death.

I heave a sigh, and unconsciously reach down to pat Gitchi's head. The old wolf stands beside me with his ears pricked, listening attentively.

Mother is the final representative. She stands at the head of the Bear Clan, beside her new husband, Cord, wearing a white ritual cape painted with black bear tracks. When she walks forward and places CorpseEye on top of the cache of weapons, I wonder what she must be thinking. CorpseEye has saved her life many times . . . he is an old and dear friend. The war club has been a part of her family, handed down from warrior to warrior, for generations. But she understands the symbolism.

No more war . . .

As he straightens, Shago-niyoh's black cape catches my attention. I turn in time to see him stride away into the trees where he melts with the shadows.

Have I done something? Has he forsaken me? Perhaps

it's just that others need him more now. I pray that someday he will show me where his bones lie so that I can collect them and Sing his soul to the next world. He deserves to be released from this earth. His loved ones in the Land of the Dead have been waiting for him too long.

When the ceremony below is over, Gitchi rises to his feet and silently trots away up the trail that leads westward, and I realize it's time. Elder Brother Sun sits just above the western horizon.

"Where's Gitchi going?" Hiyawento asks.

"To his special place. I usually run with him. Do you want to come along?"

"I do."

We trot side by side, following Gitchi, who lopes in front with his tongue hanging out. The forest scents strike me like blows today, moss and deadfall warmed in the dappled sunlight, dogwood and wildflower blossoms. Ferns sway as Gaha silently creeps beneath the trees.

"Today is a day of great joy, yet you look sad, my friend."

I smile faintly and study the ground passing beneath my feet. When I turn to look at him, he's frowning at me in concern. His shoulder-length black hair jerks with the beat of his feet, and sweat shines on his eagle face. I have not seen Hiyawento without a weapons belt, bow or quiver, since we were eleven summers. It must feel odd not to have the weight around his waist. My gaze drops to his hands, and lingers on the missing tip of his finger—sawn off by Gannajero long ago.

"Not sad, Wrass. I think it's just . . . loneliness."

We wind through the growing shadows, our moccasins quiet on the trail. Ahead, Gitchi enters a grove of ancient oaks that cast gigantic wavering shadows. The old wolf slows to a walk, as though the cool air feels good on his gray coat, and he wants to absorb it before he enters the small clearing where sunlight sheaves every blade of grass and nodding wildflower.

"He comes here every day," I explain.

Hiyawento frowns. "Why?"

We follow Gitchi out into the center of the meadow where he lies down and braces his white muzzle on his forepaws, watching. Just watching the meadow.

"I first noticed he was doing this right after my head wound began to heal. Every afternoon, he was gone. Finally, I followed him. He came here, stretched out, and watched the meadow until darkness fell. Then he came home."

"What's he doing?"

"I'm not sure. I think . . . I think this is the last place he saw her. I think he's waiting for her to come back to him."

As I am.

Hiyawento puts a companionable hand on my shoulder. Only Hiyawento, who knew her and loved her, can understand that this one single act of an old grieving wolf rends my heart like nothing else.

"I believe there is a bridge, Odion. I believe Gitchi will be waiting for you on this side, to help you across, and she will run to meet you on the other side."

As evening slowly descends around us, the trees drip dampness. A soft pattering fills the forest.

I listen to it and watch Gitchi. He hasn't moved. His shining yellow eyes monitor the meadow.

"I'm going to sit with him until he's ready to go," I say. "You don't have to stay. I know Zateri and Kahn-Tineta are waiting for you back in the village. Everyone will be feasting. The Songs and storytelling have probably already begun."

Hiyawento grips my shoulder hard. "I want to sit with him, too."

Together, we walk out across the meadow, and sit down on either side of the old wolf who waits so patiently, his eyes filled with unbearable longing.

Authors' Note

Some of the Peacemaker stories say that in the end Atotarho submitted to Hiyawento and let him comb the snakes from his hair. When Hiyawento had finished, the evil cannibal-sorcerer transformed before his eyes. The Chief's lost soul returned, his crooked body straightened out, and his heart turned toward reason and compassion. For the rest of his life, Atotarho was a good and just leader who dedicated himself to implementing Dekanawida's message of peace. The Great Council Fire of the League of the Haudenosaunce is still safely kept in the land of the On-ondaga.

Glossary

Flying Heads—Just heads with no bodies that thrash wildly through the forests. These fearsome creatures have long trailing hair and great paws like a bear's.

Gaha—The soft wind. She is spoken of as Elder Sister Gaha.

Gahai—Spectral lights that guide sorcerers as they fly through the air on their evil journeys. Sometimes gahai lead their masters to victims, other times to places where they can find charms.

Hadui—A violent wind.

Hanehwa—Skin-beings. Witches sometimes skin their victims, enchant their skins, and force them to do their bidding. Hanehwa warn witches of danger by giving three shouts.

Hatho—The Frost Spirit.

Haudenosaunee—The People of the Longhouse, called "Iroquois" by the French.

Ohwachira—The basic family unit. An ohwachira is a kinship group that traces its descent from a common female ancestor. The ohwachira bestows chieftainship titles, and holds the names of the great people of the past. It bestows those names by raising up the souls of the dead and requickening them in the bodies of newly elected chiefs, adoptees, or other people. In the same way, if a new chief disappoints the ohwachira, after consultation with the clan, it can take back the name, remove the soul, and depose the chief. It is also the sisterhood of ohwachiras that decides when to go to war and when to make peace.

Otkon—One of the two halves of Spirit Power that inhabit the world. The other is Uki. Don't think of these as good and evil, however. Both powers share equally in light and dark. Otkon and Uki form a unified spiritual universe that must be kept in balance. Otkon has a trickster-like character. It's unpredictable and can be either beneficial or harmful to human beings. Its half of the day lasts from noon to midnight. Otkon is often associated with the Evil-Minded One, the hero twin also known as Flint.

People of the Flint—The Mohawk nation. However, the word *Mohawk* is an Algonquian term meaning "flesh eaters." They call themselves the Kanienkahaka, or Ganienkeh, meaning "People of the Flint."

People of the Hills—The Onondaga nation. The word *Onondaga* is an anglicized version of their name for themselves, *Onundagaono,* which means "People of the Hills."

People of the Landing—The Cayuga nation. Including People of the Landing, several other possible derivations have been offered for the word *Cayuga,* including "People of the Place Where Locusts Were Taken Out," "People of the Mucky Land," and "People of the Place Where Boats Are Taken Out."

People of the Mountain—The Seneca nation. They call themselves the *Onondowahgah.* Their name can also be translated as "People of the Great Hill."

People of the Standing Stone—The Oneida nation. The word *Oneida* may be a rather poor Anglicization of their name for themselves, *Onayotekaono,* meaning "Granite People," or "People of the Standing Stone."

Requickening Ceremony—The raising up of souls for the purpose of placing them in other bodies, such as those of adoptees. This concept does not exactly correspond to the eastern religions' concept of reincarnation. For example, there's no idea of karma to be accounted for. Being reborn is neither punishment, nor reward. Instead, there is strong concept of duty to the People. Only strong souls were requickened, usually within the same maternal lineage. The ceremony was performed in the hopes of easing grief and restoring the spiritual strength of the clans, but a returning soul also had an obligation to help the People in times of crises. Many "Keepings" of the Peacemaker story say that Dekanawida was the returned soul of Tarenyawagon (also Tarachiawagon), the culture hero also known as Sapling, the Good-Minded One, who served as the Creator. Those same traditions identify Atotarho as Sapling's troublesome younger brother, Flint (Tawiscaro/Tawiscaron), who was called the Evil-Minded One. Jigonsaseh, similarly, was sometimes identified as the returned soul of Sky Woman's daughter, the Lynx.

Uki—One of the two halves of Spirit Power that inhabit the world (see *Otkon*). Uki is never harmful to human beings. Its half of the day lasts from midnight to noon. Uki is often associated with the Good-Minded One, the hero twin also known as Sapling, or Tarenyawagon.

Selected Bibliography

Bruchac, Joseph.
  Iroquois Stories: Heroes and Heroines, Monsters and Magic. Freedom, CA: The Crossing Press, 1985.
Calloway, Colin G.
  The Western Abenakis of Vermont, 1600–1800. Norman: University of Oklahoma Press, 1990.
Converse, Harriet Maxwell.
  "Origin of the Wampum Belt" and "The Legendary Origin of Wampum." In *Myths and Legends of New York State Iroquois,* New York State Museum Bulletin 125, edited by Arthur Caswell Parker, 138–145 and 187–190. Albany: University of the State of New York, 1908.
Custer, Jay F.
  Delaware Prehistoric Archaeology: An Ecological Approach. Cranberry, NJ: Associated University Presses, 1984.
Dye, David H.
  War Paths, Peace Paths: An Archaeology of Cooperation and Conflict in Native Eastern North America. Lanham, MD: Altamira Press, 2009.
Ellis, Chris J., and Neal Ferris, eds.
  The Archaeology of Southern Ontario to A.D. 1650. London, Ontario, Canada: Occasional Papers of the London Chapter, OAS Number 5, 1990.

Elm, Demus, and Harvey Antone.
  The Oneida Creation Story. Lincoln: University of
  Nebraska, 2000.

Engelbrecht, William E.
  Iroquoia: The Development of a Native World. Syracuse University Press, 2003.

Fagan, Brian M.
  *Ancient North America: The Archaeology of a Con-
  tinent*. 4th ed. London: Thames and Hudson Press,
  2005.

Fenton, William N.
  The False Faces of the Iroquois. Norman: University
  of Oklahoma Press, 1987.

———.

  *The Iroquois Eagle Dance: An Offshoot of the Calu-
  met Dance*. Syracuse: Syracuse University Press, 1991.

———.

  *The Roll Call of the Iroquois Chiefs. A Study of a Pne-
  monic Cane from the Six Nations Reserve*. Cranbook
  Institute of Science, Bulletin No. 30, 1950.

Foster, Steven, and James A. Duke.
  Eastern/Central Medicinal Plants. The Peterson
  Guides Series. Boston: Houghton Mifflin Company,
  1990.

Hart, John P., and Christina B. Rieth, eds.
  *Northeast Subsistence-Settlement Change: A.D. 700–
  1300*, New York State Museum Bulletin 496. Albany:
  University of the State of New York, 2002.

Heckewelder, John.
  *History, Manners, and Customs of the Indian Nations
  Who Once Inhabited Pennsylvania and the Neighbor-
  ing States*. New York: Arno Press, 1971.

Herrick, James W.
Iroquois Medical Botany. Syracuse: Syracuse University Press, 1995.

Hewitt, J. N. B.
"The Iroquoian Concept of the Soul." *Journal of American Folklore,* 8 (1895): 107–116.

―――.
"Orenda and a Definition of Religion." *American Anthropologist,* N.S., 4 (1902): 33–46.

―――.
"Status of Woman in Iroquois Polity before 1784." In *Annual Report of the Board of Regents,* 475–488. Washington, D.C.: Smithsonian Institution, 1933.

―――.
"Wampum." In *Handbook of North American Indians North of Mexico,* 904–909. New York: Rowman and Littlefield, 1965.

Jemison, Pete.
"Mother of Nations: The Peace Queen, a Neglected Tradition." *Akwe:kon* 5 (1988): 68–70.

Jennings, Francis.
The Ambiguous Iroquois Empire. New York: W. W. Norton, 1984.

Jennings, Francis, ed.
The History and Culture of Iroquois Diplomacy. Syracuse University Press, 1995.

Johansen, Bruce Elliot, and Barbara Alice Mann.
Encyclopedia of the Haudenosaunee (Iroquois Confederacy). Westport, CT: Greenwood Press, 2000.

Kapches, Mima.
"Intra-Longhouse Spatial Analysis." *Pennsylvania Archaeologist,* 49, No. 4 (December 1979): 24–29.

Kurath, Gertrude P.

   Iroquois Music and Dance: Ceremonial Arts of Two Seneca Longhouses. Smithsonian Institution, Bureau of American Ethnology, Bulletin 187. Washington, D.C.: U.S. Government Printing Office, 1964.

Levine, Mary Ann, Kenneth E. Sassaman, and Michael S. Nassaney, eds.

   The Archaeological Northeast. Westport, CT: Bergin and Garvey, 1999.

Mann, Barbara A., and Jerry L. Fields.

   "The Fire at Onondaga: Wampum as Proto-writing." *Akwesasne Notes* (1995): 40–48.

———.

   Iroquoian Women: Gantowisas of the Haudenosaunee League. New York: Peter Lang, 2000.

———.

   "A Sign in the Sky: Dating the League of the Haudenosaunee." The Wampum Chronicles, www.wampumchronicles.com/signinthesky.html.

Martin, Calvin.

   Keepers of the Game: Indian-Animal Relationships and the Fur Trade. Berkeley: University of California Press, 1978.

Mensforth, Robert P.

   "Human Trophy Taking in Eastern North America During the Archaic Period: The Relationship to Warfare and Social Complexity." Chap. 9 in *The Taking and Displaying of Human Body Parts as Trophies by Amerindians,* edited by Richard J. Chacon and David Dye. New York: Springer, 2007.

Miroff, Laurie E., and Timothy D. Knapp.
  Iroquoian Archaeology and Analytic Scale. Knoxville:
  University of Tennessee Press, 2009.
Morgan, Lewis Henry.
  League of the Iroquois. New York: Corinth Books, 1962.
Mullen, Grant J., and Robert D. Hoppa.
  "Rogers Ossuary (AgHb-131): An Early Ontario Iro-
  quois Burial Feature from Brantford Township." *The
  Canadian Journal of Archaeology/Journal Canadien
  d'Archeologie* 16, (1992).
Murray, David.
  *Forked Tongues: Speech, Writing, and Representation
  in North American Indian Texts*. Bloomington: Indiana
  University Press, 1991.
O'Callaghan, E. B., ed.
  The Documentary History of the State of New York. 4
  vols. Albany: Weed, Parsons and Co., 1849–1851.
Parker, Arthur C.
  Iroquois Uses of Maize and Other Food Plants, New
  York State Museum Bulletin 144. Albany: University
  of the State of New York, 1910.
  ———.
  Seneca Myths and Folk Tales. Lincoln: University of
  Nebraska Press, 1989.
  ———,
  writing as Gawasco Wanneh. *An Analytical History of
  the Seneca Indians,* 1926. Researches and Transactions
  of the New York State Archeological Association, Lewis
  H. Morgan Chapter. New York: Kraus Reprint Co., 1970.
Parker, Arthur C. ed.
  Myths and Legends of the New York State Iroquois,

New York State Museum Bulletin 125, 138–145 and 187–190. Albany: University of the State of New York, 1908.

Richter, Daniel.
The Ordeal of the Longhouse: The People of the Iroquois League in the Era of European Colonization. Chapel Hill: University of North Carolina Press, 1992.

Scheiber, Laura L., and Mark D. Mitchell, eds.
Across a Great Divide: Continuity and Change in Native North American Societies, 1400–1900. Tucson: University of Arizona Press, 2010.

Slotkin, J. S., and Karl Schmitt.
"Studies of Wampum." *American Anthropologist* 51 (1949): 223–236.

Snow, Dean.
The Archaeology of New England. New York: Academic Press, 1980.

———.
The Iroquois. Oxford: Blackwell, 1996.

Snyderman, George S.
"The Function of Wampum in Iroquois Religion." *Proceedings of the American Philosophical Society* (1961): 571–608.

Spittal, W. G.
Iroquois Women: An Anthology. Ohsweken, ON: Iroqrafts, Ltd., 1990.

Talbot, Francis Xavier.
Saint Among the Hurons: The Life of Jean De Brebeuf. New York: Harper and Brothers, 1949.

Tehanetorens.
Wampum Belts of the Iroquois. Summertown, TN: Book Publishing Company, 1999.

Tooker, Elizabeth, ed.

Iroquois Culture, History, and Prehistory. Albany: University of the State of New York, 1967.

Trigger, Bruce.

The Children of Aataentsic: A History of the Huron People to 1660. Montreal: McGill-Queen's University Press, 1987.

Trigger, Bruce, ed.

Handbook of North American Indians, Vol. 15: Northeast. Washington, D.C.: Smithsonian Institution Press, 1978.

Tuck, James A.

Onondaga Iroquois Prehistory: A Study in Settlement Archaeology. Syracuse: Syracuse University Press, 1971.

Wallace, Anthony F. C.

The Death and Rebirth of the Seneca. New York: Vintage Books, 1972.

Walthall, John A., and Thomas E. Emerson, eds.

Calumet and Fleur-de-Lys: Archaeology of the Indian and French Contact in the Midcontinent. Washington, D.C.: Smithsonian Institution Press, 1992.

Weer, Paul.

Preliminary Notes on the Iroquoian Family. Prehistory Research Series. Indianapolis: Indiana Historical Society, 1937.

Whitehead, Ruth Holmes.

Stories from the Six Worlds: Micmac Legends. Halifax: Nimbus Publishing, 1988.

Williamson, Ronald F., and Susan Pfeiffer.

Bones of the Ancestors: The Archaeology and Osteobiography of the Moatfield Ossuary. Gatineau, Quebec: Canadian Museum of Civilization, 2003.

TOR

Award-winning authors
Compelling stories

Please join us at the website
below for more information
about this author and other great
Tor selections, and to sign up for
our monthly newsletter!

www.tor-forge.com